SLOTH

A Sinful Secrets Novel

ELLA JAMES

Mariana, XO!

This book is a work of fiction. Any resemblance to actual events or persons, living or dead, is entirely coincidental.

"Sloth: A Sinful Secrets Story," by Ella James.

Interior Formatting by Kassi Cooper of Kassi's Kandids Formatting

Dear A. —

I am writing to express my gratitude for your gift. There are no sufficient words, but please accept my sincerest thank you.

Yours,

R.

She writes me back.

I didn't expect that.

She tells me she's a lover of chicken pizza and video games, a hot sorority girl with the nickname Sloth. She wants to know something about me in return. She says I owe her.

This is how she saves my life. She doesn't even know it. We've never even seen each other. But I need a reason. Just one reason to continue. She becomes mine.

The anonymity is good. She doesn't need to know me, but I need her kindness. We both live our lives: a letter here, a post card there. For three years, I escape my demons. And then one day I'm pulled back in.

I've resigned myself to what I know is coming. Until the girl I'm spanking gives her safe word: Sloth.

And then the lie I'm living starts to unravel.

To Jamie Davis—
For Much Slothing

PART I

"I was never insane except upon occasions when my heart was touched."

-Edgar Allen Poe

October 2, 2011

Dear A.—

I am writing to express my gratitude for your gift. There are no sufficient words, but please accept my sincerest thank you.

Yours,

R.

October 17, 2011

Dear. R.~

I hope you don't mind me writing back. I don't mean to be an asshole, but I guess I was a little... disappointed by your letter. I have accepted your sincere thank you and have folded it into an origami sparrow that I wear around my neck. Just kidding. I don't wear anything around my neck except my trusty sloth necklace. Why a sloth? It's my nickname. It suits me because I'm slow-moving, and I like to sleep. Also, sloths are fucking adorable and weird. What better combination? I promise I am not a stalker, at least not in my real life, but the truth is, I would love to hear a little bit about you.

~Sloth

October 31, 2011

Sloth -

Please don't waste your time writing to me. I am not interested in befriending you. We are close enough already, don't you think? In any event, have a wonderful life.

R.

November 11, 2011

R.,

Yeah, I guess so.

For what it's worth, I'm a Georgia peach with a Final Fantasy obsession and a never-ending appetite for chicken pizza. (That's pizza with chicken on it. FABULOUS.) I hope my Sloth-ly traits haven't rubbed off on you too much. Have a wonderful life yourself.

-S.

P.S. Are you male or female?

November 23, 2011

Sloth,

I am male. And surprised you had to ask.

-R.

December 1, 2011

R.-

I can't believe you paid the postage on that. You must be a very interesting person. Interesting = weird. Remember, though, I like weird. Are you near my age? I'm 18. I turned 18 this past April, but I'm only a senior in high school. Weird, right? See... I have secrets too. I think I'll hoard them until you cough up some of yours. You might say you owe me?

Too much?

Too soon?

Please don't report me.

I swear, I'm not as weird as I seem on paper. I'm just bored and curious. And sealing this into an envelope now, so I don't get tempted to throw it into the fire.

-Slothfully Yours

December 19, 2011

Sloth-

You have a fire in Georgia? Hmm. Are you anemic?

-R.

December 26, 2011

R.—

Are you inquiring about the quality of my blood? Believe me, if blood was money, I'd be king.

The fire was a bon fire. The night I wrote that letter, my friend Bentley and I went to a field party. It was cold, for here. I think like 43 degrees. Have you ever been to a field party? A kegger? A rave? I'd like to think so. Somehow I imagine you behind a desk, in a suit or something. Might I ask your age, sir?

-Sloth

P.S. Merry Christmas or Happy Hanukkah—or both!

January 8, 2012

Sloth-

Why not a queen? You think a King is superior? How very un-feminist of you.

You might ask my age. If you did, I might or might not tell you.

Forty-five degrees is not cold. Where I am, it's 9 today. I went outside and got icicles in my nose.

I don't do suits. Try jeans, a ratty old jacket, and boots.

Age is just a number. My number isn't far from yours.

I've been to a few house parties. Vaped a little. I don't drink much but like vodka—top shelf.

Is that enough to pay my debt?

-R.

January 20, 2012

R.~

Vape, you say? What is it to vape? Is it vaping? Vape-ing?

You owe me no debt. That was a rude thing for me to say. I'm sorry.

How not far from my number is yours? Are they side by side? Or a few seats away from each other? What do you do every day? Are you a wood-chopper? I am now picturing you in flannel and work boots. I think I kind of like that look.

Are you in New York? Somewhere else? Are you living with family?

I've got stalker tendencies, okay? So sue me.

I'm getting really tired of school. I can't wait for college!

-Sloth

February 2, 2012

Sloth-

I am in New York state. How did you know?

This seems like the right time to reiterate my thanks. I'm sorry it was so... stiff originally. Yeah, I said stiff.

Vaping is something one does with marijuana. It's like... smoking from a bong, but the impurities are removed via... some process. It involves a lot of heat. That's all I know. It's been a while.

I hope you had a good Christmas or Hanukkah and a nice New Year. Mine was... strange.

I don't have a job right now. I'm doing what you might call regrouping. If I had a job, it wouldn't be wood-chopping. Too tedious. I like a challenge.

R.

February 15, 2012

R.-

What does it stand for? It's only been a few months, but I feel like I've known you a lot longer. I'm tired of writing to an initial. Does that make me weird?

This is not a good week for me. I probably shouldn't be writing you at all. Bad things tend to happen to me Valentine's week. Based on past luck, I will probably get run down by a runaway mailman after slipping this into the box.

Sigh.

Can you hear that?

It's a loud one.

I'm going to the cemetery today. I should have gone yesterday, but I couldn't. I don't know why.

I hope you're doing nothing tedious and everything challenging, and that life is shaping up the way you want.

Do you want to chat online sometime?

It's okay if you don't. I'm just being needy. At least that's what my family says...

-S.

March 1, 2012

Madame Sloth-

I'm sending my letter back in time. I hope you receive it February 13, so you can utilize my expert instructions. If not, there's always next year.

R. stands for Robert, if you insist on Knowing. It's not my favorite name, so I try not to use it often.

I heard your sigh. I thought, that sounded needy.

Kidding.

It sounded sad.

Why are you sad? I'm afraid I Know the answer, and that brings me to my instructions. (I wish I didn't Know them...)

I recommend at least one shot of a top shelf vodKa before getting in the car. It's better if you have someone else to drive you. A friend, perhaps? If you're not much of a vodka drinker, you could start with Snow Queen.

Yes, I realize you're not "legal," but I feel the situation should exempt you from the law. (I must insist you don't drive yourself, though, unless you skip this step).

On the way there, be careful with your music. You have to have music of some kind. Silence isn't recommended. Try something like The Strokes. The Stones would work, too. You want rock, and not the emo kind. Play it loud enough to drown out any thoughts. (If you drank enough Snow Queen, this will be less of an issue).

Don't look out the windows. When I do, I feel like I'm in a music video. The kind of shit video that's meant to be ironic when paired with a certain type of rock song. Your ~~drive~~ ride to the cemetery should not be imaginary music video fodder. Keep your eyes on the dash, or on the face of the person you're with.

Wear regular clothes. Nothing dressy. This is not a funeral. (You already did that.)

If you can pick the date, go with a day that's neither cloudy nor overly sunny. A cloudy day is just depressing, and a really sunny day seems like a slap in the face of the dead. Choose a day that's a little sunny, with some clouds. If you can't choose, and the day is extra sunny or rainy, consider adding another shot of vodka.

Do you have flowers or some other trinket? I should have mentioned earlier: put it in the back seat, in the floor. It's not that important. They'll never know you brought it. Whatever you do, don't hold it in your arms like it's a fucking baby.

Have your driver park you close to the grave. No walking. (The goal here is to minimize thinking time. Now that you don't have The Strokes, you've got to hurry).

Get out whatever you brought, if anything, and don't take your time walking over. Now is not the time to contemplate fate—neither yours nor that of the dead. (Note I didn't say dead person. You are not visiting a person. You are visiting a piece of stone. Or a drawer).

Walk quickly, and put your trinket down as soon as you reach the place.

I know I just said you're not visiting a person, but since I think you'll want to say some words, and most people don't talk to cement, pretend you are talking to that person on a SHIT day. You're mad at each other. Pissed off over something stupid, like they kneed you in the—okay, not that. (They stole your favorite thong? Lost your hair brush? Blasted you in the face with hair spray? Or maybe they broke your fucking heart.)

Call them a bastard or a bitch, tell them whatever you need to say, and get going. There is no reason to stay. Trust me on this. Get out, and don't look back.

When you make it back to the car, try to talk about whatever you were talking about on the ride over. (Hint: It needs to be everyday type of shit).

You may be tempted to go get some post-cemetery refreshments. I'd recommend against this. You don't need to talk about what you just did.

Get back to your life. Be glad you've got your thong, or your heart, or whatever. Spend the afternoon or evening doing homework, or (better yet) going out somewhere. Concerts are a good choice. They're loud, and most people are drunk. Clubs work, too. Don't try a regular bar, but if you do, get a booth with friends. Don't sit at the goddamned bar.

One more thing. When you go to sleep that night, be sure you've had some alcohol or even Xanax. If that's not your scene, fall asleep... I don't know. Reading. Or doing something else.

I think that's about it.

-R.

March 11, 2012

R.–

Hot damn, that was a good list. I usually go once a month, and my once a month in March will be this week. I'm so doing all of that. Except maybe the Snow Queen. Holy expensive alcohol, batman. I want to go to your house party!

When I was ten and my sister was five, she got hit by a car while getting off the bus from school. February 14, sooo... I'm not a hearts and chocolate kind of girl.

I would gladly give her all my thongs, even if they would be way inappropriate for a thirteen-year-old. I would even take a daily hair spray blast to the face. I would give her my boyfriend (if I had one) and even give her Snow Queen vodka.

What a fabulous big sister I would be.

Seriously, though, I appreciate your list. So much.

I like the name Robert. It's earnest.

Are you a college guy, Robert?

Are you still living in New York state? Are you from there?

I know—my stalkerish tendancies are coming out again! Also, I can't figure out how to spell tendencies. <- That looks right!

In all seriousness, I think of you a lot and wish the best for you. Please let me know if you ever need anything. Or want to chat. Or meet up. Or whatever. And if you don't, ignore my pushiness. I'm a take what I want kind of girl. I'm needy and wild and sometimes reckless. It's just the way I was made.

I hope that rubs off on you in all the right ways.

Xo,

Sloth

April 26, 2012

Sloth,

That fucking sucks, about your sister. I'll drink a shot of Snow Queen for her. It's a high-quality vodka, produced from organic wheat and spring water in Kazakhstan. She, like any discerning tween, would surely enjoy.

And you, too?

Buy yourself a thong. Sign up for a pen pal service. Several dozen cans of hair spray? Go wild. Be reckless.

-R.

(If there's not a VISA gift card in here, some asshole stole it.)

May 24, 2012

R.

Generous man, with good taste. I enjoyed the Snow Queen immensely. On the 14th, I had my friend drive me to the cemetery, where I left a shot on my sister's headstone. It was a semi-cloudy day. I didn't listen to The Strokes, but to The Unicorns, "Sea Ghost." It did the job. Afterward, I went to another friend's house to play pool. I fell asleep that night watching X-Men: First Class. I should have written you back sooner, but have been so busy getting ready for college! Squeeeee! I'm not going too far from home, but I'm excited anyway. It'll be nice to get out of my dumb small town and be onto other things!

I hope you're doing great and are enjoying college/hiking/clubbing whatever is your thing. I still think about you a lot. In a totally non-stalkerish way. Please keep in touch. I will continue sending the same way as always. I have the feeling you'd prefer that to email or IM chatting.

-Sloth

P.S. I'm glad it was you. <3

June 16, 2012

Sloth,

I hope you enjoy college. I hear Georgia has some great educational opportunities for its residents. I am... living life. It's a shock I'm not sure I'll ever get over.

Feel free to continue corresponding at your convenience. BTM has my address, and will for a while I believe.

P.S.—Your feeling of gladness is reciprocated. Also, multiplied.

Yours,

R.

October 7, 2012

Wow, it's been a long time! I can't believe how long it's been. I came across your last letter the other day and was surprised to see the date. How the hell are you?

I'm in my second semester of college, and I'm loving it! I found a job in my college town and worked my way through summer semester. I already knew my way around by the start of fall semester, so that was nice. I live in the dorms, but it's not as bad as I thought it would be. I kind of like my roommates.

It's so bizarre how much partying there is all the time here. Don't get me wrong—it's fun—but if I did it all the time I'd be flunking out of school. I have to keep my grades up for my sorority. Yeah... I joined a sorority. I know, I know. The clichés are sometimes true. But it was a good way for me to meet new friends. I'm trying to be a different person than I was in high school. Not in any major way or anything... In the normal way, I guess.

I'd love to know what you're doing. I hope B.T.M. has your address as long as I want it. I would be so sad if a letter came back to me.

Sloth

November 3, 2012

Sloth-

A college girl. I can't picture it. What does a college girl named Sloth look like?

(Your stalkerish tendencies may have rubbed off on me. I'm only just noticing.)

I'm glad you're enjoying yourself.

I'm in college too, actually. I, too, am enjoying it. Lots of opportunities to drink Snow Queen and read obscure poetry. (Don't knock it. The two go well together).

I hope you have a good holiday and keep in touch.

-R.

P.S. I did a shot for you 8/7.

January 10, 2013

R.—

Every time I see someone drinking Snow Queen, I think of you. It doesn't happen often. Grey Goose is the preferred vodka on my campus. I guess because it's more affordable. (I can verify it definitely isn't as good!)

What are you studying? I'm undecided, which I guess is typical for someone my age. I like a lot of things, but I don't know what I would want to do forever. It's a long time. I'm caving under the pressure, know what I mean?

Spring semester just started (I'm a sophomore now!), and I'm already dreading going home for the summer. My family has limited finances, so I don't think I can stay here even if I work. There are worse things, I guess! I have a younger sister (the middle one) who will be glad to steal my thongs.

How funny—I drank a shot of Snow Queen for you 8/7 also. Maybe in an alternate reality, we were drinking them together.

<3 Sloth

P.S. A college girl named Sloth looks lovely. Probably dressed in a gown for formal. Possibly giddy from too much vyvance or "Mary Jane". Don't knock it. It's a good look on me.

April 1, 2013

Sloth,

Do I ever get to know your real name? (All I was given was A.W.) Maybe next 8/7 we could make it happen. This year, I'm going to the Baltic Sea with my dad.

Sigh.

Did you hear that one?

He is... not the most exemplary father.

In my opinion.

There are others. Some differ. Some do not.

Be careful with the mixing of various goodies. I'd hate to lose ~~access to~~ you.

My major is English.

-R.

P.S. Really. Be careful. Especially if you're hanging out with frat guys.

May 30, 2013

R.-

Whew! School's out, and I'm "home." It's really just my mom and grandma, and my sister. I've only been here a few days, and it already feels like forever. Maybe your dad sucks, but the Baltic Sea? That's so cool. I want a postcard. Can you do that? Send to me internationally without problems? I'd love it. Maybe a picture too. Just kidding. You don't have to. I know that may be too much for you, and I'm okay with that. My stalkerish tendencies are being bred out of me over time. Is that a good thing? I don't know...

Weird is good. I still think that.

I wonder what you're doing now. Summer mini-mester? More traveling? Consider me your girl if you're ever in need of a pen pal!

Thanks for trying to look out for me. I am careful. Pretty clean, too. Drugs are kind of boring after all. Although I still want to try acid at least once...

I hope you're having a great summer so far.

-Sloth

P.S. I would tell you my name, but it's so lame, I'm afraid it would put you to sleep. I have an interesting middle name. Maybe next note, I'll tell you that.

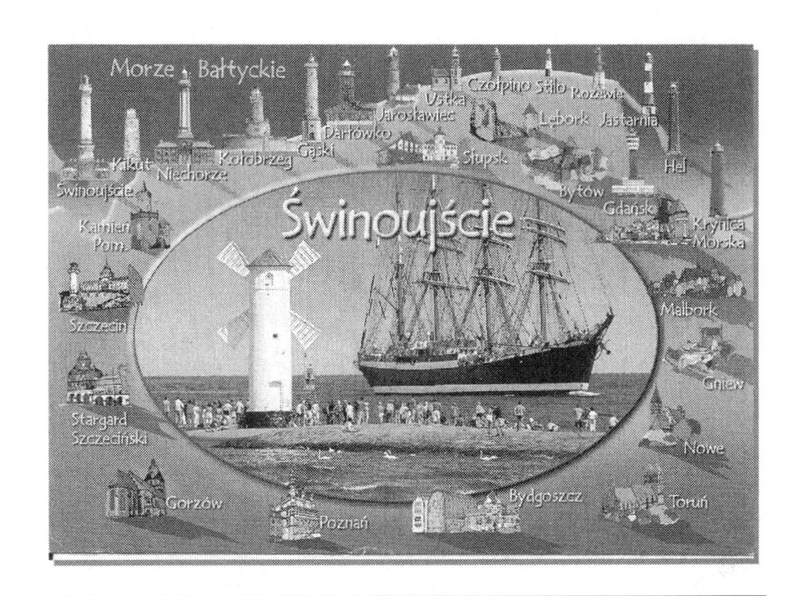

August 7, 2013

Sloth-

I wish I knew your boring name.

This is a postcard from Świnoujście, close to the German border, where I'm drinking at a little bar called Still Waters.

Here's to you...

R.

September 4, 2013

R.-

I LOVE the post card. I bet it's beautiful there! I hope you had a fabulous summer, and that your dad really outdid himself with uncharacteristic awesomeness.

My summer was... interesting. It went by faster than I thought.

I'm back at school now, living in the sorority quarters for the end of my sophomore and beginning of my junior year. It's kind of insane, but I think I might like it. I'm a girl of the people. I'm not good by myself. I need friends and boys, and yes, even a little drama.

I have a feeling I'm the yang to your yin. Or something like that.

I still picture you chopping wood in a quiet forest with icicles in your nose. ;)

Tonight I'm going on a date with my big crush from last year. I promise I'll be careful, even though he seems like a nice guy. I'm not really looking for anything serious. I have to focus on my major: art!

Keep in touch, and take care.

-Sloth

(Legally known as Autumn)

November 21, 2013

This guy reminded me of you. Hope you're having a nice ~~semester~~ autumn.

-R.

December 16, 2013

This one made me think of you! I had a very nice semester. You? Have a fabulous Xmas or Hanukah. How do I still not know which one?

Xo,

Sloth (Please Lord, never use the "A" word).

January 25, 2014

Sloth,

Please lord? I'll answer to that. Happy New Year.

R.

March 9, 2014

R.-

I'm going to let you off the hook for that one. I'm a Southern girl, remember? 'Please Lord' is something we say. It's like... an old "sayin". How's your year going? Is there some hot, R-loving babe calling you Lord? ;) I hope so.

-S.

April 1, 2014

Seventeen of them. Some call me Lord, others Master, and still more Lucifer.

When are you going to choose a name for me?

Happy April Fools'.

-R.

P.S. Does your school have a good art program? Mine does.

April 28, 2014

My Dear R.~

What a bad, bad boy. Guy? Man? How the hell old are you anyway? I'm thinking you must be in grad school. My school does have a good art program. Very good, in fact. Sadly, I am no longer in it. I have changed my major to art counseling. Don't laugh. It's a very serious field. Lots of balloon animals and papier mache. I look good in a dirty apron.

How's the English going? Going to be a professor or something? Me thinks it would suit your God complex.

-S.

July 10, 2014

R.-

I'm going to assume my note got lost in transit. Had to happen sometime I guess. Hope your summer is going well. Want to meet up 8/7? I'm game...

S.

August 9, 2014

I'm embarrassed to admit, I'm feeling a little dissed. Hope you're doing well. Drop me a post card? Even a blank one would do.

Xox

S.

ONE

September 2014

Cleo

I MIGHT AS WELL BE A VAMPIRE. That's how much time I've been spending in my closet lately. Being a college girl, constantly surrounded by dumb college guys, I can already hear all of the dumb-college-guy-caliber comments, so let me say, for the record: I'm not gay (I still fly the flag), and I'm also not rubbing one out.

I'm in here writing letters I then shred, and packaging one of the Seven Wonders of the World into Mason Jars. Also, obsessively Googleing the name "Robert," paired with a few key phrases.

Weird, I know. But weird is not a bad thing.

The letters are personal. Private. I don't write them very eloquently, but that's okay, because no one is ever going to read them. I can't seem to make myself mail any of them. It's a good thing, I guess. A practical thing. But every time I listen to the grinding sound my shredder makes, I find myself rubbing my chest, because it hurts a little.

The name "Robert"—well, that's personal, too.

As for the wonder, and the Mason jars... it's business, baby. My business.

Yeah. I have my own business. I'm proud of that. I never have to ask Mom or Grans for money. I never have to want for anything material. Sometimes I buy things I know my sister Mary Claire wants, pull off the tags, and mail them home, posing them as "second-hand." One day soon, I hope to set up a

Chattahoochee College grant for a hearing impaired student from my hometown. Yeah, you guessed it: Mary Claire.

I do business on the black market, but I keep it as classy as possible. When I deliver orders, I have everything all cute and tidy: product inside a baggie, tied at the top with a little strip of ribbon (sometimes I even do different sorority colors), then the baggie tucked into a Mason jar with an adorable colored lid. (Sometimes, I make the lid match the ribbon—*if* that's possible, given my limited selection of colored Mason jar lids).

Like most things I do these days, I make dealing drugs look effortless. And it is—mostly.

For the record, it's not really "drugs." It's weed, which is legal in some states and will probably be legal everywhere in another decade. That makes me a trailblazer.

Getting my cute Mason jars organized and ready to blaze is no easy task. For starters, my bedroom is the size of a square of Chiclet chewing gum, and located in a sorority house, which is officially drug free. Even worse, it's wedged between the bedrooms of Milasy and Stephanie—my sorority's president and vice president, neither of whom, you might have guessed, is showing up for any pro-marijuana rallies.

So yeah. I have to be covert. And that means packaging in my closet. It's not a big closet. It's where my desk is, and also where I keep my LELO. The walls are bright pink, courtesy of the last Tri Gam treasurer.

Right now, I've got less than thirty minutes until our Wednesday night chapter meeting, and here I am: slaving away over my precious buds. Picking out stems and seeds that Kennard told me wouldn't be there this time. Freaking Kennard. Medical grade my tight, tanned ass. This shit is barely even mid-grade. Bitches like Holly and Neda will probably try to get a discount. I can't do discounts. Not this week or any week.

I look down at myself: at my Seven jeans, my Gucci boots, my pink Kors sweater. These things don't buy themselves. I need money to survive here, in this lifestyle. Without my dealing, I've got nothing but a scholarship and a room down at the mold-infested swamp dorms. I might have good grades, and I might go to a lot of trouble to keep myself in good physical condition, but you think the campus' most exclusive sorority would let me in if I wasn't forking over giant quantities of the green stuff? (Not *that* green stuff. I'm talking about Benjamins). Not a chance in hell.

People here think I'm a rich girl. A rich, delinquent girl who likes pushing boundaries and breaking rules. It's *so* not true. I was the girl found crying in the first grade bathroom because I wasn't coordinated enough to put one foot *right* in front of the other as the students in my class filed, in a line, from our class room to the lunch room.

My mother is a seamstress, and my dad died when his eighteen-wheeler rolled over, hauling logs from Dawson up to Memphis. Mary Claire gets free lunch at school. I did, too. And it was fine—for high school. I made up for being poor as dirt by being reasonably well-put-together and doing really well in gymnastics and concert band. Oh, and dating Brandt Kessler, a doctor's son. But college is different. Poor girls don't rush, and on my campus, girls who don't rush have a hard time getting noticed. After a lifetime on the outside, window-shopping, I want to be an insider here at Chattahoochee College. So when I graduate, I can start a life that doesn't include a sewing table.

I place the last of my Mason jars in a little row on the edge of my desk and mentally tick off my regulars. My sorority regulars, that is.

Holly buys half an eighth a week, and so do Megan, Kelsey, Lora, Chole, Amber, Ricci, Katy Peterson, Hannah, Solena, and Lindsey. They all get charged $65 instead of my regular $70. Greek discount. Neda only buys a three-fourths of a gram, because she says when she smokes at the same time she's Vyvancing, she gets a rash. I charge her $50, because geez, I've gotta make some money off her. And then I've got a bunch of quarter-ounce customers. I walk my fingers over these jars: Julie, Sarah, Molly, other Molly, Forrest, Anna Maria, Christy,

Elizabeth, Joanna, and Jordan. These chicks are where I make some real money. I make them cough up $145 a jar for a quarter of an ounce. More, when the weed is really good.

This week, it's pretty much my norm: some barely mid-grade diesels, purchased from Kennard, my old across-the-street neighbor down in Albany. Chattahoochee College sits right on the Alabama-Georgia line—about one hundred miles southwest of Atlanta, and one hundred miles northwest of my hometown of Albany, Georgia. Every Sunday afternoon, I drive an hour and a half home in my ancient, white Mazda Miata, and drive back up with several grocery bags full of my Grans' cookies and brownies, plus a pound of bud concealed in patterned Tupperware.

I peek into the portable cake carrier on my closet floor and cringe.

Just like last week, I'm running through my stash too fast. I take the Ziploc freezer bag out of the cake carrier and sit it on the scales that stand on the carpet, in the nook under my desk. These are adjusted for the weight of the bag, and...

Shit. After I get rid of all my Mason jars tonight, and if I sell about a fourth a pound tomorrow at the bars, I'll be running really low. And I still have to make it through the Friday frat parties, and there's a home game this weekend, which means I could make a mint at Saturday tailgates. But I'll almost definitely be out by the Saturday night post-game frat bashes.

It happened last week, and I used up all my emergency, just-incase-Kennard-dies-suddenly stash.

I guess I should be glad. I'm growing my client base. Instead, I feel anxious.

I pick up my phone and scroll to "K.C.," but I don't dial. K.C. is this sketchy guy I met at a bar last year. When I get really low, I can buy a few ounces from him, but I don't like to. He's not like... *cop* sketchy. He's more the looks-only-at-my-boobs kind of sketchy. Let's just say I don't want to be alone with him in a broken elevator.

I rub my lipsticked lips together and decide I won't call K.C. unless I get a surprise order tonight. At this point, almost all the girls in my sorority and our BFF sororities know I deal, and so do some of their boyfriends, so I've got about a dozen frat clients. I also deal to some people from my classes. Add that to a handful of townie adults, plus my yoga instructor and a few guys at the ten-minute oil change place downtown... and I've got a pretty big client list. For a one-girl operation.

I look once more at the digital clock on my desk, then grab my Kate Spade overnight bag—the one that looks like a big, straw purse—and dump its contents—a tube of toothpaste and some PJ pants—onto the floor. I grab the PJ pants and put them back in, because I just remembered these dumb jars always clank together. I add a sleeveless shirt and some running shorts to the bag, to keep the Mason jars from bumping each other as I move. Then I hustle out of my room, into the shared living area of the "officers' suite." It's empty except for our leather couch and chair, the fluffy rug, the round coffee table. Because everyone else is already downstairs at chapter.

Oops.

I amble down the rubber-lined, hardwood stairs, moving from the top story of our four-columned antebellum house to the large parlor on the first story. I know it's weird, but I've found that when I'm late, moving fast makes me feel more stressed out. So I pretend I'm right on time and focus on the motion of my feet.

When I reach the bottom of the stairs, I hear Milasy's drawl from around the corner and confirm that the meeting has already started. I move through the foyer, through the small, square doorway, built at a time when no one gave a damn about an open floor plan, and get a straight-line view of Milasy and Steph, sitting on one of the antique sofas in the parlor. Their backs are pencil-straight, their ankles crossed. I stand behind the crowd of perfume-sprayed, lotion-slathered Tri Gams and try to paste an interested—or at least neutral—expression on my face. Milasy talks about our grades. Steph remind us (as she does *every* week) that ladies drink alcohol from plastic Solo cups instead of beer bottles or cans. Cassie tells us to prepare to vote on our Thanksgiving and Christmas charity events next week, and then she stands on her tiptoes and looks around the room for me.

Her brown eyes meet mine, and we share a conspiratory smile. Cassie is Type-B, and more like me than Steph and Milasy. She's the officer most likely to be late at any given time.

I square my shoulders and project my voice, and tell the room full of Tri Gams that they only have another week to pay first semester dues. After that, I sink back into myself and allow my mind to wander. Which it does, right back to my current read: a novella called *The Private Club*, by one of my favorite romance authors, J.S. Cooper. Mmmmm.

I remain in la-la land until my good friend Lora elbows me. I jump and apparently gasp, too, because a few girls in front of us turn around to see what's up. When everyone has settled down again and I've had a few seconds to get over my embarrassing outburst, Lora leans over and whispers, "What's in your bag, lady? Cake?" She wiggles her brows and grins.

She knows what's in the bag, but her comment reminds me: We've got a cakewalk right after this in the student center. Shit!

How am I supposed to hand out my bud at an organized event—one where I'll need to oversee the three girls who'll be handling the cash boxes?

That's really annoying. I can't believe I forgot. I rub my head. I didn't even bring a freakin' cake.

After the meeting winds down—all the low-fat snacks have been eaten, all the lemonade lite sipped—I chat with Milasy, Steph, and Cassie. Nothing interesting. Just the usual business stuff that sometimes makes me wonder why I even joined a sorority. I'm reminded almost instantly, when I walk with some of my pot posse across campus, toward the William Harrison Memorial Student Center.

On the long trek there, as we migrate across brick walkways and under giant, moss-strewn oaks, I manage to drop three Mason jars into three oversized purses, and receive three cash payments. In the chaos of everybody trying to fit through the glass doors on the front of the student center, a two-story brick eyesore from the seventies, I dole out two more jars and get two more wads of cash.

I'm trying to strategize how to get the rest of my illicit goods where they need to go when I step into the carpeted common room and stop in my tracks.

There are guys here. Like... a lot of guys.

I glance at Lora, and she arches her brows. "You don't remember we're doing this with Sig Alpha?"

I chew my lower lip. "No, I did."

She elbows me. "Pants on fire. I can tell you're surprised. Don't worry, though. Harrison said Brennan was skipping."

I let a slow breath out and nod.

Harrison is Lora's boyfriend, and until the end of June, Brennan was mine. Both guys are Sig Alphas, but Harrison is the president. Meaning he'll definitely be here.

I'm glad Brennan won't. Our breakup... sucked. So yeah.

I give Lora a paste-on smile. "That's good."

"The best," she says, bumping my shoulder.

Despite this first-floor common area being the most logical place to hold a cakewalk, we're not cakewalking here because Milasy couldn't book it. I can't remember why, but the cakewalk is in a large study hall on the second floor. I'm pretty sure it's near some bathrooms, plus a lot of little conference rooms, which works out perfectly for me.

We ascend the stairs slowly, as Lora and a few of the other junior girls chat about the effectiveness of the Diva Cup. The yucky conversation ends when we reach the top of the stairs, walk between two giant ferns on either side of the staircase, and behold the sprawling study area.

It's got industrial mauve carpet and is normally cluttered with couches, recliners, and tables. Tonight, the furniture is pushed up against the gray cinderblock walls. A chunk of the floor is partitioned into masking-tape squares for the cakewalk. All around the squares are fold-out tables bearing cakes and refreshments.

I make a beeline for the younger girls who'll be working the cash boxes, and give them specific instructions for how I want them to keep track of everything.

Then I walk around the bustling room, smiling and chatting like the biggest thing on my mind is how much money this dumb cakewalk makes. I'm also looking for Brennan, who indeed seems to have skipped tonight's event. Thank the Lord.

After a few minutes, I slip into the bathroom with two clients. I emerge with fresh lipstick, then chat with Steph about her disastrous calculus exam while the guys set up the sound system. I don't really remember what a cakewalk entails: some sort of hop-scotch kind of thing and numbered slips of paper, plus a boom box. A quick look at the tables around the cakewalk floor reveals two dozen or more cakes, and I guess people think this is a cool pastime, because girls and guys from other sororities and frats start spilling into the room.

I catch the gazes of my clients and begin subtly steering them into the bathroom or the conference rooms. Milasy is playing announcer, so she definitely doesn't notice. I don't think anyone else does, either. Sometimes I feel stares from the guys, but that's normal, I tell myself. I'm wearing jeans that make my ass look awesome, and I'm newly single too.

I take care of Jordan, Elizabeth, Julie, Forrest, Kelsey, Chloe, Ricci, Sarah, Molly, other Molly, Joanna, Anna Maria, Solena, Christy, and Neda, all in various conference rooms, before Lora and I go into the ladies' room—not because the conference rooms are a bad place to do this, but because both she and I need to pee.

"You making bank, girl?" she asks from the other side of a stall wall.

"You know it," I say.

"You little twat."

"*You* are. Jealous," I tack on.

She snorts. "I don't need that money."

True. Lora's dad is a lumber tycoon, and on the school's board of trustees.

"You wish you were buying yourself Louboutins for Christmas like I am."

"I'll steal my mom's." She giggles.

"Or steal mine."

When Lora and I have washed our hands with the school's citrus-scented soap and I've got her money added to the growing wad in the inside pocket of my bag, we latch arms and walk back out to cakewalk central.

"Win a cake for me," I tell her.

"Good luck with your shit, girlie."

I watch blonde-haired, pixie-small Lora walk across the crowded room toward Harrison—a tall, dark-haired hottie who plays soccer for our school and has a complete, pervert obsession with taking pics of Lora's ass and putting them on Tumblr.

Harrison and I are still cool, I think, but I've noticed he doesn't talk to me much since Brennan and I split, and when Lora hangs out with him, I'm never invited. I guess it makes sense, since I'd be a third wheel without Brennan... but it's still kind of sad.

I spot Megan by a window that overlooks the quad, chatting in a group of junior and senior Sig Alphas. I walk up behind her, smack her butt, and hiss into her ear: "Room one-A in five."

She giggles as she walks through the door seven minutes later. "I feel like I'm on a covert mission!"

I smile. "You are."

She gets her weed, I get my money, and then I have to talk down her nerves for a full two minutes.

"There're so many people here! Next time I want you to drop it off at my room again like last time...."

I slip out a minute after her and repeat my covert message to Katy, who wraps her arm around my waist and tells me I look hot in my jeans.

"I'm not waiting five. I'll go with you now, sistah."

So she does, and takes her Mason jar without a lot of fuss, probably owing to her status as the provost's daughter. Also, Katy's older sister, Belle, was expelled from school last spring semester for trying to bribe a professor with a blow job, so I think Katy figures nothing she does could top that.

The last person I have to slip away with is Foster. I forgot her earlier, but I always bring an extra Mason jar for that very reason. I text Foster to meet me in conference room 1B. I slip into the small room, filled with faux wood tables, and sink down into one of the plastic chairs surrounding them. I pull open the 'notes' feature on my iPhone and confirm that I've gotten everyone but Amber, Hannah, and Lindsey, all of whom I can catch on the walk back to the house.

The bit with Foster is... not fast. She hangs around *forever* telling me about how much weight she's gained since she started smoking pot again. She pulls a can of Sprite out of her purse and holds it out to me like it's a poisonous snake.

"It's my weakness. Take it! It'll go straight to my thighs."

I laugh, but take it. "Foster, it's a beverage."

"One with corn syrup!"

I shrug and pop the top as she elbows her way out the door. In the quiet of the little room, I take a minute for myself: to sip the Sprite and thumb through my overnight bag.

One minute, I'm peering into one of my remaining Mason jars, wondering if I over-measured. The next, I'm blinking into the dark.

"Ummm... huh?"

When the room remains pitch-black, I slide my arm into the straps of my bag and stand up slowly. Must be a power-outage. "Shit."

I walk slowly toward the door, and when I'm almost there, my face bounces off of something hard.

The lights flick on, shocking my eyes so I can't see at first. I blink a few times—and find myself staring at a wide, male chest.

TWO

ONE STEP BACK, and the chest becomes a full-fledged male. Not just any male, but Kellan fucking Walsh.

Motherfucker.

Fuck shit.

Shit fuck.

This is bad, like really, really bad.

Kellan Walsh is the Lex Luthor of Cleoland—as well as the golden boy of Chattahoochee College.

He drives a jet black Escalade. He has a Crest-white smile. He dyes his hair with gold dust. Okay, maybe not really, but it looks that way, especially in the sun. When he walks, he swaggers. When he touches a girl's arm at a party or a bar, he puts a spell on her. I've seen it happen with my own two eyes.

Take Katy, for example. First weekend back-to-school, at a party, she was being her normal self—in Katy's case, this meant guzzling her second "goldfish bowl" martini, swinging her hips around like Elvis, swaying her wide, swimmer's shoulders to a Lady Gaga dance remix, and singing off-key. Then Kellan Walsh showed up.

He was dressed to the nines, because that's the only way Kellan Walsh dresses. I think that night he was wearing slacks and an expensive-looking button-up, with the sleeves rolled up to show off his muscular forearms. He looked like some kind of... lion, or tiger. Maybe a rare yellow leopard. He tipped his head at Katy, and in five minutes—FIVE MINUTES *FLAT*, I'm telling you—she'd climbed into the Sexcalade with him.

He took her to a hotel. Not to his room at the frat house, but a hotel, as if she was a hooker.

That alone wouldn't be cause for concern, just revulsion. But, in addition to being campus playboy and soccer player extraordinaire, Kellan Walsh is also our school's SGA president. Which means he has a lot of influence over my fate as a student here.

Sound like a tough spot? He's also a champion of our campus' zero tolerance drug policy.

Yeahhhh.

As my eyes adjust to the light he's just flipped on, I take another small step back and run my gaze up and down him. Perfectly put together. Of course. Navy slacks and a pale pink Polo hug his body like... clothes draped over the world's most flawless body. I'm a back and shoulders girl, and *shit*, he's wide. I usually don't get this close to him but... gawd. His soft cotton shirt is stretching to fit across the width of him. My eyes trail down his ripped chest and gawk at the width difference between his shoulders and his hips. His hips are... square and sharp and delectable. I know from seeing him in soccer shorts that behind them, there's a nice, taut ass. Underneath his slacks are muscled thighs. And in between his legs... At games, when he runs...

I swallow and tug my gaze up to his face. His blue eyes demand my attention first. They're gorgeous—the color of deep ocean water. Looking at me, they seem to see everything; they're the eyes of a demigod, peering into my soul. I take in the rest of his face: the faintly feline shape of his high cheekbones; his heavenly lips, which beg to be bitten; the smooth line of his jaw; his healthy tan. He definitely looks angelic. Like an angel who would rip your panties with the strength of his immortal hands.

Oh, God.

My eyes flit up again, needing to get away from that face of his, and run into his wavy-messy blond hair.

I grit my teeth and step away.

His eyes, on mine, are shrewd. They track me as I move. My pulse quickens—and quickens more, and *What the hell is wrong with you Cleo!?*

I lift my bag up my shoulder and try to make my face like Mandy, a sophomore Tri Gam who is the most cliché sorority girl I've ever known: wide-eyed and wondering, just an innocent girl startled by Kellan's male antics. He sneaked into the room when I wasn't paying attention! He flipped the light switch and I was like OMGz!

But *did* he sneak in? I didn't hear the door open or close. Was he in here the whole time?

My pulse kicks up a notch.

He seems too close. I take another step back. Then I glare at him for good measure.

You're doing nothing wrong, Cleo! You're a liberator. Fight big pharma... Weed is medicine! A more relaxed student population is good for everyone! Rah rah rah!

I wrap my fingers around the thin straps of my bag and give him skeptical frown. What the hell is he doing in here?

"Were you spying on me?" I look him over once more, this time focusing more on his clothes than his delectable body. The slacks look tailor-made. The pink dress shirt is definitely straining across his shoulders.

As if he can read my lustful thoughts and wants to taunt me, he steps closer. His gaze hardens. Another step, and I can see the sexy stubble on his face. A third step, and he's close enough for me to smell his cinnamony breath. He folds his arms over his chest and breaks the silence with a voice like low thunder. "I think a better question is, what are you doing in here, Miss Whatley?"

I blink a few times, mostly because that voice is seriously panty-melting. No need for him to know I think so, though, so I toss my long, brown hair over my shoulder and fix him with a perfectly peeved stare. "What does it look like? I was taking a break in here, minding my own business and you popped up! Were you spying on me? Cause that's creepy."

"Minding your business, huh?" He tucks his lips down into a scowly, frowny, judgy look. He arches his brows. "Mind if I take a look in that bag?"

My heart forgets its rhythm. "What?" I swallow. "Is that a joke?"

He shakes his head. "No joke, Cleo."

I take a step back and try to think fast. To look outraged. To treat him like the creep he clearly is. "Of course I'm not letting you look in my purse." I shift my shoulder so the purse is more behind me. "I can't believe you would even ask."

I look him up and down, hoping to find him lacking in some way—but he's flawless. Long legs with strong thighs evident through the fabric of his pants, abs so flat I could bounce a penny off them; shoulders that seem three times as wide as mine. And his face. I could look at it all day. Scratch that, I could glare at it all day.

"This whole thing is totally creeping me out, Walsh."

His face is tight and serious. His voice is a menacing purr. "There's a reason that I'm asking, Whatley."

"What's that?" I hold my head up high and pull out a look I used a lot in high school: the you-can-talk-shit-about-me-but-I-don't-care-because-I'm-better-than-you special. Behind the look, my head is spinning. I watch his lips move, focusing more on them than on his words.

"I'm asking, Cleo, because I was told you were dealing drugs on campus."

I could let those words sink in. Let them freak me out. I choose not to. Instead, I shove his words away and let my mouth move.

"Psshhh! Is that a joke?" An awkward laugh tumbles out of my mouth, and my head shakes frantically, like I'm starring in a reproduction of *The Exorcist*. "Me? Dealing *drugs*? I'd get kicked out of Triple Gam so fast my head would spin! Drugs are for losers."

I shut my mouth and reel a little. *For losers?* God, I'm such an idiot! I loosen my shoulders and try to pull myself out of this. "Look, Kellan—Kellar? Walsh. I know your last name is Walsh, so that's what I'm calling you. *Walsh*, I understand your stance on drugs. I've read your columns in *The Bobcat*."

He writes a monthly column for the student newspaper. I hate his politics, which is one of the reasons I sometimes read his weekly column in the student paper—just to wave my fist at him. The other: his mug shot. It's 2D amazingness.

He smirks, like he knows what I'm thinking.

"Yeah. I know how straight-laced you are. Except when you're abducting my friends from bars."

His brows shoot up. Every one of his features, from his flaring nostrils to his electric blue eyes, screams *warning*.

"Not abducting," I quickly correct. "I mean... I guess they go with you." My gaze, trained on his face, loses its footing and flits down over his chest. I jerk it back up.

"Here's the thing, Kellan: It's pretty shitty to accuse a random student of doing something that could get her expelled. Do you have some evidence you'd like to show me? Or are you just going on hearsay? And who made you the—"

He takes a smooth step toward me, and his nearness makes my legs forget their mission. *Move, Cleo, move!* But I'm too late. His hand has closed around the straps of my bag.

I try to side-step him, but his grip is strong. He snatches it off my shoulder.

"No!"

I lunge for him, but he thrusts the bag up over his head. As I jump up and down, cursing him and hitting his muscular arms and chest, the motherfucker has the nerve to laugh at me.

It's a low laugh, the kind of laugh that settles in between your legs in other circumstances.

Not right now because he's digging through my bag! He's holding up a Mason jar! MotherFUCK! He frowns at it. This one has a light blue top. It's for a Tri Gam.

His long arm holds it way above my reach and shakes it slightly.

"What's in here?"

"GIVE IT BACK, *right* now! It's *mine*!" I'm straight-up yelling, but he doesn't even spare me a glance.

He shakes the jar again, and the round, half-dollar-sized buds inside the baggie bump against the glass. I clench my teeth.

He brings the jar down, and I make a grab for it. Instead of getting it, I get a fistful of his muscular shoulder. He laughs again.

"Cleo... Calm down." He opens the lid and I freeze. My heart stops. My blood runs cold. "I assume you have an explanation for this... what do the kids call it? Weed?"

I drag a deep breath into my lungs. I blink frantically, frowning. Then I widen my eyes. Innocence. "Yes. Of course I do. It isn't weed." The words just roll out. Like a boulder someone pushed off a hill, once I've got my story moving, there's no stopping me.

He arches a brow, and I grab the Mason jar from him. I hold it out in front of me and shake my head. "This isn't weed."

Arched brows. Pursed lips. "No?"

I shake the jar, causing the heady-sour scent of marijuana to waft up into my face. "You see... there's actually a story here. An impressive story, about this... stuff. Not a story for the newspaper kind of story," I babble. "More a fun times around the campfire sort of story. But trust me, this is definitely not weed."

"No?"

"Nope." I grin maniacally and open the baggie. I pinch off a piece of one of the buds with sweaty, trembling fingertips and hold it over my head, as if it's a prize. "I made it in organic chemistry lab. It's a project. That's my major." It's not, but how would he know? "To catch criminals. It looks like marijuana, and it smells like marijuana..." I seal the baggie. Toss it up and catch it. "But it's not. You want to experience my product in a hands-on way?"

I hold it out to him and find his face expressionless. He takes the bag. Unzips it. Inhales.

I'm counting on him to not recognize marijuana. I'm counting on him to be the bastion of morality he seems to be.

I'm counting on him to be gullible.

I'm not counting on that knowing smile. A wolfish smile. I'm not counting on the shrewdness of his eyes, or the subtle way he leans in.

His smile broadens, revealing sharp, white teeth. Another deep breath into the baggie; his wide shoulders rise, then relax. "You're right. It does smell just like marijuana."

I nod. "Got an 'A' on my project with it. Can I have it back now?"

He blinks. "I'm sure you did."

I reach for the bud, but he draws it back.

"So what is it, exactly?"

"It's an oregano-based herb. Kind of like, you know, oregano on steroids."

He holds it up in the fluorescent light. The crystals on the buds glitter a little—promises of fun times for someone else, and cash for me.

"Wonder if it tastes like weed," he muses.

"It doesn't," I say quickly. "So I've been told."

He bites off a small piece. Frowns. Chews a few times on his front teeth. I swear to God, I almost faint. His eyes find mine. "It tastes like marijuana."

"Like you would know." I shoot him a ridiculing look—a sure sign that I'm all out of moves.

He holds up what remains of the piece he bit, then reaches into his pocket and retrieves a shiny Zippo. His mouth flattens and his brows scrunch in concentration. "I wonder if it burns like weed."

I pluck it from his fingers. "NO! What's *wrong* with you? You'll set off the smoke alarms!"

He looks again into the bag then smirks at me. But it's not a smirk; it's like... a smug, aggressive look. One that says, "Got ya."

"Cleo. You have four jars of this. Why?"

I lock my jaw and debate not answering. His hard eyes force me. "For class," I breathe.

"I don't believe you."

"That's not my fault." I loosen my shoulders and recover some of my cool. I wonder if this would be easier if he weren't so damn hot. A guy with a patchy goatee, or a guy with really bad acne, *him* I'd be schooling in privacy and all sorts of noble-sounding principles. "I'm sure someone like you could never see the point in creating a good synthetic. Pretty soon, this stuff will transform the drug market. Cops will use it all the time. My professor thinks it's incredible."

He laughs again, and I'm ready. I jump and snatch my overnight bag from his careless hand. The jars clink together as I whirl on my heel and dash toward the door, desperate to get away from him. Desperate to hide in my room for the rest of fall semester, curled in the fetal position, waiting for the hammer to fall.

I'm almost to the door when strong fingers close around my arm. He tugs me, so I'm forced to turn around. Holds me in place, so I have no choice but to look up, into his eyes.

"We both know this shit is real. Tell me who you got it from, and maybe I'll forget this happened."

Blood roars in my head. "Is that a joke? I get it from class, because it's a class project, like I said." I throw his hand off my arm.

He grabs my upper arm again with stern fingers. His eyes are wide and blue. "Like I said, I don't believe you." His face hardens. "If I catch you dealing on campus again, I'll make sure you get expelled." He stares into my eyes. "Do I make myself clear?"

I nod mutely.

He looks me up and down, from my pink sweater to my ass-hugging jeans. "I'd never have guessed. Someone like you..." He rubs his forehead, appearing thoughtful. "You know you need to empty that bag before you leave."

"Yeah, right!"

"Maybe I ought to talk to Milasy. Let her know what kind of person is managing her chapter's books."

I'm outraged, but there's nothing I can do. Stupid Mr. Perfect could never understand this. Why I would do it. Why I can't just have Daddy buy me a fifty thousand dollar SUV. All he knows is his stupid rules.

I open the bag, and he points to the nearest table.

I can feel my heart flutter in my throat as I place the first jar atop the faux wood. I line them up in a neat row, and then I stare at them in disbelief. I can't leave them here. I think of the money, and I kind of want to screech.

My gaze finds Kellan, standing with his arms folded. His model-perfect face is cold, as if *I've* wronged *him.*

"So..." I want to leave, I just want to leave, but I can't. I look into his eyes, then at my jars. Then back at him, with hesitation—because I don't want to see his traitorous face. I don't want to know what he's thinking, though I have to ask. "Um, you're not really going to tell anybody, are you?"

His wicked lips curve up on one side. It's not a smile, but something derisive and mean. "Get out of here," he says.

I tuck tail and go.

THREE

Cleo

I'M SORRY TO REPORT, it's been This Week Vs. My Self-Esteem.

What happened Wednesday night with Kellan Walsh... sucked. I'd be lying if I didn't admit it shook me up. The loss of product, the hawk-like way he just made off with it. I keep blaming myself for not pressing the issue more—for not insisting it was fake marijuana and fleeing the scene or something—but deep down, I know I didn't really have that option.

Obviously, he's an uptight, rule-following prick who would have told Milasy everything he knew. And Milasy would have looked into the situation to keep Tri Gam's good name intact. Honestly, I'm pretty sure Milasy already knows I deal, but she looks the other way because I keep it discreet. Or I *did.*

It bugs the hell out of me that, since that moment, I've done nothing but worry he'll tell Milasy. What would Milasy do? Would she kick me out? She would have to, wouldn't she? And what about Kellan Asshole Walsh? Is he like, BFF with our college's president, Dr. Walker? Could Kellan go to some administrator and just get me expelled like *BAM*?

All day Thursday, I'm haunted by these questions. And by my rapidly dwindling stash. Kellan jacked so much of my shit, I'm almost out, and when I call Kennard Thursday afternoon (almost in tears, though he doesn't know that) he tells me he can't get me more on such short notice.

Perfect.

I spend some time pacing my room, fanaticizing about kicking Kellan Walsh between the legs. I bet it would be easy to make my mark because the size of the target would be... My face burns. Why does he do this to me? Why am I so aware of his body when I know he's a first-rate bastard? Perfect Kellan has no idea what it's like to need money so badly you'd go to the blood bank and sell your platelets. I bet he never saw the back of his mom's legs bruised from sitting on the same uncushioned wood bench for twelve and thirteen hours at a time, with just two bathroom breaks per day. He's never felt hunger cramps, or forced himself to eat something he hated because the need for calories meant more than the food's taste. Aside from his obvious case of silver-spoon syndrome, he's also an idiot, with no understanding of societal shifts. If he was smarter, he would know marijuana is no big deal. It's going to be legal everywhere soon. It isn't a real drug. It's just some stupid herb. I don't even smoke it. Too boring. It just makes me fall asleep.

These are the thoughts clanging around in my head Thursday night as I study for a calculus test and worry about how many customers I'll lose because of my dry spell. I'm chewing on the tip of my 'I Sloth You' pen when I get a text from Steph.

'Break into my room n get my birth control! Nitestand drawer!!! Double d8 going gr8! Bring to La Femme. Gonna need it 2nite. Please x10!!!'

Who can resist an SOS like that? Not this bro. So I throw on my unwashed blue jeans and a red Fall Ball t-shirt and drive down to the little French place on the river. I pull my hair into a clip and start the sandy trek from the parking area to the restaurant's wraparound deck. Dave Matthews Band strums through the humid river air. Moss dangles from the oaks over my head. Between tree branches, I can see the placid river: wide and shallow here, reflecting moon glow. The night feels saccharine and strange, a perfect picture from the book of someone else's life.

As I step over the tree roots that are famous for tripping drunk La Femme patrons, I promise myself I'll get in and out of here. No lingering, even if I see someone I know. I'm in a weird mood, and besides, I have studying to do.

I'm berating myself for being too withdrawn post-Brennan, for not being as close to Lora as I once was, or as tight with

Milasy and Steph as I was last year, while I cross the crowd-packed deck. A cute guy with an eyebrow piercing pushes the restaurant's back door open for me, and I step into the atrium dining area—the one with glass walls and ceilings.

As soon as I'm fully inside the candle-lit, plant-filled atrium, I spot Neda at a two-seater table. Across from her is... *Brennan*?

Holy hell, that's totally him. Brennan is tall and lean, with burnt copper hair he wears all shaggy, down around his ears. I'd know the back of his head and his bony shoulders anywhere, including at a candle-lit table across from Neda.

That bitch!

What do I care, I ask myself as I stride through the glass room. I don't want Brennan. He's a douchebag. I want more than Brennan. And if there's nothing more than Brennan, I want no one.

I take three stairs up to the glossy, mahogany bar/band stand area of La Femme and text Steph to meet me in the bathroom. I'm leaning against the sinks when she bustles through the door, lipsticked, earringed, and wearing a black skirt-shirt set with stylish boots. I give her a low whistle. She throws her arms around me.

"Thank you, honey."

I sniff her blonde curls. "Are you drunk, Steph?"

She pulls back and grins. "Am I?" Her eyes trail down my face. She licks her lips, still beaming like a fool.

I laugh. "Hell yes, you are—Miss Twelve Hours." Steph is only taking twelve class hours this semester (so, four classes, all of which are easy) and I love teasing her about it.

She slaps my cheek lightly. "You're bust—" She giggles. "You're just bitter, Cleo. Bitter..." She waves the birth control packet. "But you got my lady stuff. I'm happy."

I help Steph take one of the little pills with sink water, and then I point her in the direction where I think her date is waiting.

"Laters, baby," I call out behind her.

She rolls her head around at me. She grins, wide and glassy-eyed, as she saunters off. Steph is a major *Fifty Shades of Grey* fan. She even got me a signed paperback to share the love.

I came in through the back entrance of the restaurant, but because of Neda and Brennan making googly eyes in the atrium, I decide I'll leave via the front doors. I stifle a yawn with my palm over my mouth and make my way through the crowd swarming the bar. La Femme is a high-end restaurant, but we're still in a college town—so the bar will never be anything but a college hangout. Especially on a Thursday night.

I make it past a thick plague of Kappa Alphas, sipping whiskey and chugging Bud Lite, and talking about the rodeo next weekend. Someone's stray hand brushes my ass, but I'm too tired to care. Too wrapped up in analyzing how I feel about seeing Neda and Brennan on a date. I'm lost in thought, wondering if I never settle on another boyfriend, can I be a goldfish lady instead of a cat lady—when I pass the reservations podium.

And there he is: fucking Kellan. Perfect Kellan, with his stubble-shadowed jaw, his stunning eyes, his luscious lips. And that hair. I mean, Jesus, is it blond enough? Soft enough? What is he, a Ken doll? He's wearing a navy blazer over a white dress shirt, with straight-front khakis, a leather belt, and expensive-looking low-top leather boots.

The blazer must have been tailored for his big shoulders, because it makes him look Red Carpet-ready. The khakis look designer, too—wrinkle-proof and perfectly fitted. My gaze lingers on his powerful-looking thighs before I jerk it back up to his face. He's leaning over the podium now, looking at the schedule book, clearly overstepping his bounds. No waiter is manning the podium. Who crowned Kellan Walsh king?

The sight of him here, dressed like the deity of some minor kingdom, sniffing around the podium like he owns La Femme, sends my heartbeat kicking up into my sinuses.

Maybe he can hear it, because at that moment, he lifts his eyes to mine. They burn through me, damning, even as his lips pull into a tight smile. But it's not a smile—at all. It's an un-smile, every bit as condemning as his gemstone eyes.

And for a second, I feel shame.

As soon as it rises, it collapses. I've got nothing to be ashamed of, at least not anything he can peg me with. Irritation turns to anger, which, like always, makes me brave.

I smile back, a big, shit-eating grin. "Hi, Walsh," I chirp as I brush past him.

"Whatley."

Even his smooth, crisp, California voice is flawless, I think as I cut through the wait line and push out the doors. I stand on the porch for a moment, searching the parking lot for his Sexcalade. Almost immediately, I tell myself I don't care how he got here.

I skirt the building, choosing a trek that takes me right past the dumpster, where I narrowly avoid stepping on a stray eggshell. I cut between two palm trees, find the worn grass path to the outer parking lot, and race through the grove of big oak trees along the river's shore.

The image of the candlelight on Brennan's face and the curve of Kellan Walsh's lips must sear themselves into my synapses, because I see them both in my dreams after I go home, eat nearly an entire re-heated chicken pizza, and fall into a cheese coma.

I run through my stash Friday morning, due in no small part to Kellan Asshole Walsh. I call Kennard again, and in addition to telling me 'no', he now seems annoyed.

Out of desperation, I call someone Lora recommends. His name is Matt, and he's a junior in finance. His magic power: He's a dealer who occasionally sells large amounts to other dealers.

On the phone, Matt sounds nice. He has a New Orleans accent and the kind of relaxed bass voice that makes me think he's going to be fat. We agree to meet midafternoon Friday in the parking lot of the local industrial park. I'm so nervous, I consider asking Milasy for one of her anxiety pills before leaving. Since I never take anything anymore, I probably couldn't drive, though, so in the end, I hop into my car and drive the four miles to the industrial park blaring the free U2 album that popped up on my iPhone some months back.

I find Matt's hunter green Four Runner where he said I would, in front of a biotech headquarters. I park beside him and unlock my doors. Then I watch with my breath held as a lanky, brown-haired guy in Wranglers, a ripped t-shirt, and work boots climbs into my passenger seat.

Matt is soft-spoken and relaxed, and he seems perfectly non-threatening. He's happy to take the wad of cash I have on hand and give me two ounces, triple Ziplocked. The only problem is, he won't sell me more until we meet up at one of his safe houses.

I snort. "Safe for who, you?"

He shrugs. "C'mon, Cleo. You know a guy's gotta watch himself," he drawls.

I sigh. "If you say so."

After we shoot the shit for a few minutes—I find out that Matt is from Metairie, a little town outside New Orleans—he invites me to call him anytime. I just smile and tell him, "Thanks."

Friday evening passes in a blur of frat parties, where I hand out pot to the few people I owe and try to avoid worrying about Kellan Walsh. If he was going to do something, he'd have already done it.

Once I'm back at the house, and safely in my room, I strip down and let my naked body enjoy the cool air. I take a seat at the desk inside my closet and dial Kennard.

"Hey, Kennard. I'm so sorry to bother you again, but I really need some more. Like... really bad. It's an emergency for me. So Sunday... can I get a little more than my usual?"

"Psshhh." I can see Kennard's brown eyes roll. "I got nothing. I'm all out. My guy's gone. I don't know where he went."

And just like that, my supply is gone. I'm up all night, feeling ill about my drought.

I toss around in bed, considering other high-dollar occupations. I could be a stripper—but I'm not phony enough. As Milasy has pointed out to me in more than one 'sorority ambassador' situation, I'm not very good at feigning interest—or anything, for that matter.

I never could convince Brennan that his ineffectual tongue-flicking felt good to me on the one or two occasions I forced him between my legs. There's no way I could grin for a guy with body odor and wag my barely clad ass in his face.

Maybe I could sell a... what? Selling organs and other bodily fluids on the black market is illegal, so not that. I could sell my eggs... but that takes time. I don't have time. A few weeks without my regular income could pull me under. Okay—not a few weeks; I do have some savings, but it would be gone in a month or two.

Shit.

I'm out of bed at 5:15 AM. I shower, brush and floss my teeth, work on cross-stitching a quote that, when I started cross-stitching it, I believed was attributed to Vonnegut. Since I started my project, I found it's actually not Vonnegut, but some anon poetry-book person going by the name "pleasefindthis."

"Be soft. Do not let the world make you hard. Do not let the pain make you hate. Do not let the bitterness steal your sweetness."

I arch my brows at the sentiment—which doesn't exactly jibe with my mood right now—and put the piece aside after forming the "n" in pain. I debate going for a run, going for a swim, and working on a canvas before I finally give in and, a little after 8 AM, shoot my new friend Matt a text.

He calls me immediately and tells me we can meet up in the afternoon. He gives me an address in the middle of nowhere. I know it's the middle of nowhere, because Google maps, which I've pulled up on my MacBook, has never heard of the address. I'll have to go on Matt's directions.

"Four-thirty okay with you?" he asks.

I bite my lip, staring at the spot on the Google map where I think his place is located. "So it's down near the river, kinda south of town?"

"My friend's place. Yeah, by the river."

I tap my fingers on my chin. "Hmmm."

"You good for it?"

"I don't know," I say slowly. "I don't usually go to strangers' houses without taking someone with me. Especially strangers like you."

He laughs. "You gonna bring someone with you?"

"I've got another idea."

A few minutes later, I receive a texted photo of Matt's license. I shoot it to Lora, along with a text: 'Hope I can trust your homeboy. Meeting up at 4:30 at a house on a dirt road off that county road with the big, red barn. Send a search party if u don't hear from me by 7.'

I wriggle into my favorite black stretch jeans, pull a loose red blouse over my head, and slip into my silver Manolos. I drive through at my bank, at College Corner, and withdraw three thousand dollars. Then I point myself south, toward where the river weaves its way between the Alabama and Georgia lines.

The drive is shady and nice, with lots of pastures, big trees, and a few glimpses of the winding river. I have the top down on my Miata, and I'm feeling kind of excited. If I can start buying from Matt, it will be even better than Kennard. For one, no weekend trips to Albany. Assuming Matt's not lying to me, or a freaking cop, he's got a big supply. To top it off, on our first and only deal, he was cheaper than Kennard—and the shit was higher quality. Like... a lot higher.

I turn down the dirt road Matt mentioned, and my car starts bouncing. Some of the dust I'm kicking up ends up in my mouth, and I wish I'd left my car's top up. I take it a little slower, shut my mouth, and squint, then look down at the directions I punched into my phone's notepad.

The dirt road forks, and the dirt gets a little wetter—like it's rained out this way recently. I'm going so slow, I can hear the river rushing through the trees somewhere nearby.

Matt seems nice, like a normal guy. A good ole boy. I hope he really is.

Finally, I see my signal: a large, brown mailbox tacked onto the side of a towering oak. The road forks yet again. I veer right, and the sound of the rushing river amplifies. A black bird flies overhead, sailing up into the fluffy, white clouds then dipping down, where he soars ahead of my car.

I drive between a few pecan trees, and there it is: an elegant brick mansion situated in the middle of a lush, green pasture. There's a spacious porch, overflowing with plants and rocking chairs, plus four stately, round, white columns. Classic Southern plantation digs.

This is nice.

Like... really nice.

I strain to see how many cars are parked in front, but there are too many trees to get a count. I drive slowly, telling myself that if it seems sketchy, I can simply turn around and leave.

When I get to the end of the drive, I see two cars, plus a motorcycle. The porch is scattered with white rocking chairs, topped by ceiling fans, and framed by big azalea bushes. Maybe the safe house is owned by a little old lady.

I spot a humming bird feeder hanging from the limb of a mid-sized Maple tree, and that seals the deal for me. This place is fine. I'm going in. I park my car beside an SUV with our school's sticker on the back and spend a moment finger-brushing my hair.

Then I grab my bag, step out onto the red dirt ground, and walk up to the porch. I've got a little .357 Taurus tucked into my jeans pocket. I'd hate to use it, but I'm a good shot, and I need to be able to protect myself if Matt's friends turn out to be creepers.

I hold my breath and ring the doorbell.

Panic swells in my throat. What kind of people live so far out by the river? My eyes are searching through the glass panes framing the sleek wood door, looking into a wide, hardwood hallway for Matt's round face and redneck clothes.

As I'm watching for him, something comes over my eyes. Hands. I whirl. I *try* to whirl, but my captor does that for me, spinning me on my heels as my hand flails for my gun. "What the—"

"Cleo Whatley." The hand moves. I blink at—*KELLAN WALSH!*

"Oh *fuck*."

I try to change my course of action—what I want to do is *run*—but my hand is already in motion. I've grabbed my gun and I can't seem to stop my arm's trajectory. The nose of my Taurus comes in line with Kellan's collarbone.

His eyes don't even widen. He rips the gun from my hand like a professional fighter.

His face is hard as he snatches my wrists, thrusts them over my head, and uses his legs and his free arm to nudge me toward the door. I don't even see him open it before I'm jerked through doorway.

"What are—"

"Quiet," he snarls.

The next few minutes are surreal. My dazed mind marvels at how strong and deft he is as I am dragged down a high-gloss, hardwood hallway that runs alongside an elaborate staircase. *Better Homes & Gardens* comes to life around me as I'm spirited through a flawless kitchen and hauled into an enormous living area with top-notch furnishings, Oriental rugs, and yawning ceilings striped with exposed wood beams and long, glass skylights.

He sets me on my feet behind a white suede couch, still holding my wrists tight enough to bruise. It's weird to see Perfect Kellan look so... furious.

Fuck, he's glaring daggers at me.

"Where is Matt?" I screech, jerking against his hold.

Who would have thought that pretty face could be so cold? I hold his gaze, praying it will soften. When it doesn't, my heart throbs sickly. "Let me go!"

He shakes his head and locks his jaw. "I want an explanation, Cleo."

"What are you doing here?" I bleat.

"This is my house."

FOUR

Cleo

I'M BREATHING HARD AND FAST, like I just snorted something. With my arms above my head and his angry face so close to mine, I feel tears sting the corners of my eyes.

"W-what do you mean... your house?"

I hear a thud from somewhere in the rooms behind us, and my heart stops. All the blood must leave my head, because the living room careens around me. Am I busted? I can't breathe. I jerk against his hands, around my wrists, because I want to grab my throat. He lets me go abruptly, but before I can regain my balance, he scoops me up and throws me over his back.

He stalks toward some built-in bookshelves, then cuts between a wing-backed chair and a pretty, stone fireplace. Stairs. There's another staircase here at the back of the house. Kellan seems to be taking the stairs two at a time.

A frenzied sob bursts from my throat. "This is a set up!"

"Calm down," he snaps.

My mind races as my cheek slaps the fabric of his shirt. I get a bird's eye-view of the living area below and marvel at how extravagant it is, even as I wonder: where is Matt, did Matt sell me out, what will Kellan do to me? And why the hell did I say 'this is a set up?' *That* was fucking stupid.

The bounce of Kellan's footsteps levels off, and the dark wood staircase with its plush, green runner morphs into the flat plane of a hall.

I take in the décor—wine-colored walls that stretch to tall ceilings, framed by elaborate crown molding; contemporary abstract landscape paintings mounted between doors; a table with a lamp and palm tree beside a large bay window—while my arms flail in the air. I don't want to grasp his back despite my need for balance.

Fucking Matt. My stomach clenches as I question Lora, too. I'm feeling about three strides from barfing when he curves slightly to the right, pushes one of those schmancy wood doors open, and steps inside... a bedroom. My heartbeat throbs in my eyes as I blink at a plush, tan rug, and the bottom half of a dresser. I struggle to lift my head, catching a glimpse of tall, plum-colored walls, a giant Monet reprod, and the top half of a burly oak dresser.

I'm filled with *what-the-fuck* as Kellan lowers me onto the rug. It's a big bedroom, dominated by an enormous canopy bed, but that's all I note before my eyes are glued to him. He's standing right in front of me with his arms folded, his face set in a stern, avenging look. With his well-built body clad in a pale blue button-up, dark jeans, and brown leather boots, he looks as righteous as ever: Chattahoochee College's very own morality enforcer.

He also looks pissed off to behold me. Like I've wronged him. This makes me feel both angry and breathlessly afraid. "Why'd you bring me up here?" I manage in a froggy voice.

I glance again around the bedroom.

The wall in front of me is nothing but a sheet of glass, offering a stunning view of the tops of pines, and the river rushing over rocks below them. Above the treetops, the pale sky stretches on and on, broken only by a soaring hawk.

I roll my gaze around the room, taking in its deep plum walls, the high ceilings. There's even a fancy indention at the center of the ceiling, something that looks right out of a home and garden magazine. And to my left is the bed: a deliciously masculine oak monstrosity, with tree-trunk posts, a deep green duvet, and curtains that drop down around it.

A bed for fucking.

I'm still shaking slightly, so I fold my own arms, mirroring his stance. "I want my gun back." I wait a beat for him to speak, and when he doesn't, I scoff, as if all I feel right now is irritation. "Where is Matt?"

My eyes flick to the window-wall. I notice there's a balcony outside it. Something about the balcony makes my knees wobble. Or maybe it's that bad look on his face.

Shit—I'm starting to feel faint.

His jaw flexes, and I may be going insane, because I think I see some of the hardness melt off his features.

"Matt's not here right now."

"He set me up." There's no way around that fact, although I wish there was. I pulled a gun on Kellan Walsh. I'm at his fucking house, loaded down with wads of cash. A horrible thought steamrolls me. "Are you a secret agent? Like an... FBI?"

He laughs at that. The asshole actually laughs. He takes a small step closer to me, his eyes never leaving mine. "You think I am?"

"God, just fucking tell me. Don't keep playing games."

He's close enough to touch me now. His arms uncross. His face goes calmly neutral as he shifts his gaze around the room. It pauses on a wing-backed chair in a corner on the opposite side of the bed. I freeze as Kellan steps toward me. He steps around me. He strides over to the wing-backed chair, hefts it over his shoulder, and brings it to me.

He sets it near the foot of the bed and waves at it. "Sit down."

I shake my head. Out of nowhere, tears spring into my eyes. "Don't drag this out. It's cruel."

I grit my teeth as hot saliva pools in my mouth—as if my tears are being redirected.

"Sit down," he says, more sharply.

I do. I don't know why. I tuck my arms around myself and fix my gaze on the glass wall. The balcony is stone—expensive-looking, as if gargoyles ought to perch on its stone railing. I can see the river gleam between the pines. I'm so damn fucked. I'm so stupid. I drop my head into my hands, because the tears are falling and I hate to be caught crying.

"Cleo?" He sighs, as if he's irritated. I feel his hand close on my shoulder. "Look at me."

I can't. "Just let me leave," I whisper to my knees.

Why did this happen? Matt seemed nice. I wipe my eyes and look up at Kellan. "Did you guys set me up for... some reason?"

His eyes, on mine, are calm and blue. I find no malice there. Also, no outrage at the question, at my insinuation that Kellan Perfect Walsh is in cahoots with Matt, a known unsavory.

Kellan shifts his weight. His gaze drops to his feet, then drags back up to mine. "Not in the way you think."

"What does that mean?"

He lifts his chin. He tilts his head at something past me. "See that vase?"

I turn around. I half expect something hard to come down on my head, but Kellan just waits while my gaze drifts over the built-in bookshelves lining most of the left wall of the room. Just beyond the mini library, set close to the corner by the top, right bedpost, is an antique wash table—also oak—that holds, among other items, a black glass vase.

"Yes," I rasp. I see the vase.

"Go get it."

I turn back to him, so I can see his face. Perfection. Warmth spreads through me, chased by nervous cold. He nods toward the vase.

"Why?" I whisper.

"Just do it."

"Where's my gun?"

He reaches down and pulls it from his left boot like a cowboy. He holds it out to me. I swallow as I take it.

It's too light. Fear rips through me. "You disarmed my gun?"

He huffs a laugh. "Of course. You shoot, I bleed—and we're a long way from a decent hospital."

"I want my bullets back!"

He nods past me. "Go get the vase, Cleo."

"Are you going to give my bullets back?" I tuck the gun into the waist of my pants.

"Drop back by here one day, without the gun."

I glare at him and walk around the foot of the bed, past the curtained side of it, and to the table. The vase is vaguely fishbowl shaped, about that size as well, and it looks empty. As soon as I pick it up, I can feel it's not. There's something fuzzy in the bottom. After only a second, I realize..."It's my stuff."

A glance behind me reveals that Kellan's got his poker face on. I reach in and curl my hand around my long lost nuggets—but... they're not nuggets. This is... one long bud? I draw it out and frown down at it. "I don't understand."

I bring it to my nose. Inhale its sweety-sour scent.

"Can you smell a hint of grape?"

I set the vase down on the bed. "I'm confused..."

He flicks his fingers. "Come here, Cleo."

I don't know what I'm expecting, but my hands are shaking. Kellan doesn't take the bud from me. He nods down at the brown chair I was in before, and I find I have the urge to do as he asks. "Have a seat," he orders.

"Not until you tell me what's going on." Even as I say that, I'm sitting.

"That strain's called The Grape Escape. It'll knock you on your ass. Unlike the swag you sell."

I frown down at the long bud. Back at Kellan. *Unlike that shit you sell...* "Are you saying you... ?" I shake my head. "I must be missing something."

His lips smooth into a thin line, revealing dimples on each side of his glorious mouth. His brows lift as his face takes on a pensive slant. "I'll throw you a bone, Whatley. Matt's with me."

I blink a bunch of times. I can't stop myself. Somehow, what he said makes even less sense than me being set up. "He's... ? Matt's... are you saying you're—?" I laugh. "Are you saying *you're* a drug dealer?"

"I'm not a dealer. Matt is." His lips remain pressed together, and his blue eyes seem to twinkle, as if he's in on a big joke.

"Are you a supplier? A grower? The money man? Are you a fucking cop, Kellan?" My voice trembles. "Where's Matt?" I jump up out of the chair. "I want to know what's going on!"

"What do you think?"

"I don't know, but you need to tell me." My breath hisses out my nostrils. "I don't like surprises."

"I don't either," he says, stepping close enough so I can smell his cinnamony breath. "So imagine my surprise when one of my guys told me he was losing clients to a sorority girl. A pretty girl with a nose ring and long, dark hair."

His words are like drop-kicks to my chest. I hold my hands up while I try to comprehend. And then I do, and I see motherfucking *red.* "You're a dealer. You're a *fucking* dealer! What the *fuck*?"

He shakes his head, rubbing his mouth. "Matt's a dealer. Not me."

"You're a grower!"

He shakes his perfect blond head. "Soil's too rocky out here."

"You must think I don't know anything. No one grows it outside."

"Most don't," he agrees. "You and I know that plants grown outside tend to yield higher bud counts."

"So you *are* a grower!"

He shakes his head.

"You're a money man. You loan money to a dealer—"

He shakes his head. "I don't loan my money out to anyone."

I watch him bring his hands together, lining up his fingertips as his face takes on a thoughtful slant. "I'll make this straightforward, Cleo. On the condition that, if you ever tell anyone about our encounter here today, you'll come to regret it."

"That's a little fucking creepy," I snap, though I want to wail and flee. This is a fucking mess. I'm scared. I keep fear off my face, instead acting annoyed. "What's your problem?"

He shakes his head. "Those sort of threats come with the business, right? I'm protecting my interests."

"So you *are* in the weed business! Holy fucking *shit.*"

A soft smile flits over his lips. He lifts his brows. "I have a proposition for you," he says softly.

"I cannot *believe* you did that!" I laugh, even as my heart is beating hard from pure, old-fashioned rage. "You scared me shitless, you asshole. You're a fucking double-timing liar—and you stole my shit!"

He takes a smooth step back. Holds up his hands. "Whoa there."

"Whoa my ass! You took my shit! You ruined my business. Now I'm—" I suck air in.

"Now you're what?"

"I won't be your competition anymore," I rasp. My vision blurs from furious tears. "What you did led me to call my regular person. I must have sketched him out or just plain pissed him off, because now he isn't dealing to me anymore." I whirl around and lean against the bed's footboard. I'm breathing so hard, I'm kind of worried I might pass out.

I feel his hand on my back. On the lower part, the curve of my spine just above my ass. It's an intimate gesture, one that lets me know immediately he's as controlling and enticing as I ever heard.

"Stop it." I whirl.

He smirks—gentle, as if he understands why I'm upset and only wants to alleviate my anxiety. "I'm your SGA president, Cleo," he says patiently. "I wouldn't lead you astray."

"That's bullshit! You threatened me! You *lied*. You're such a big fat liar! You're insane!" I take a step away from him, away from the bed. "I should leave right now. I mean, *damnit*."

"Are you sure?" He takes a small step toward me. "There's lot of money on the table. You can earn more working with me than you can on your own."

I snort. "I could never work for you."

"Fine—that's not my offer."

"What is?"

"Working with me."

FIVE

MY EYES ROLL UP AND DOWN his body. Kellan Perfect Walsh *isn't.* He's a drug dealer. Who wants me to work with him. My mind spins at the crazy shift in our dynamic, and as it does, I realize I feel... tempted.

Shit.

I don't even stop to analyze my feelings. I snap, "No way. You must be insane," and make a beeline for the door.

He's on my heels. My ears pique, but he doesn't speak. Good. I close my hand around the doorknob, but my hand's shaking too badly to turn it. As I fumble with the knob, my traitorous eyes slide back to his handsome face.

"Just hear me," he says softly.

I turn around and press my back against the door. "It doesn't matter what you say, Kellan. My answer's no."

"Then no harm in hearing me, is there?"

I shrug. The answer is 'yes' but I'm not telling him that. My temptation is a secret. Secret shame.

"So if you decided to try dealing for me, the first thing we would do is, you'd live here for a few weeks," he says calmly. "We would get to know each other. Come to trust each other."

I scoff, even as my mouth goes dry. Living with Perfect Kellan... I shake my head. "I wouldn't live with you if I was homeless."

He closes the gap between us and looks down at me. "There's a lot of money in this, Cleo. You could still be part of your sorority. Still be treasurer, even." He smirks, as if the idea of me as treasurer is amusing. "But for a couple of weeks, you would live here. And during that time, I would train you."

He rolls his shoulders. He looks tense, as if discussing this is taxing and he needs to loosen up. "I'm not a grower and I'm not a dealer. I'm an operation. I supply to everyone working campus, like Matt, and even to a lot of the town too. And I've got a steady supply of medical grade shit."

I snort, so he can't tell I'm stunned. "I've heard that before."

He nods. "But have you seen it?"

He's looking at my hands, and I realize I'm still holding the bud. I run it under my nose once more, breathing deeply as I try to think.

I don't trust this guy as far as I can throw him. Which isn't far. He's bulky as hell and the sad fact is, I haven't lifted my puny five-pound arm weights in months.

When he touches my hand that's holding the bud, I start to sweat. Not just because I don't trust him. Because he's very attractive, and for some inconvenient reason, my body reacts to his.

"What makes you think I'd ever live here with you?" I ask.

I don't give two shits why he thinks I would live here. In fact, I'm sure he probably doesn't think I'd do it at all. He just wants to prolong my time here while he tries to decide how to keep me from running off and squealing—because he can surely see now that sharing his dirty little secret with me was a mistake.

But I ask the question because I want him to think I'm considering it. I turn the bud over in my hand, prompting him to move his fingers off me.

His mouth twitches. "Would you believe me if I said I make a mean crème brûlée?"

I snort. I don't know what I believe, but Kellan in an apron isn't it. It dawns on me: I have no proof that he's a dealer. He could be playing me.

"I don't," he says, shrugging. "I'm an ice cream and instant mac guy."

I can't picture perfect Kellan eating instant macaroni, but I don't say so. "And if I told you I would do it? What's the next step?" I force a tiny smile. It's all for show, to buy me a minute to think, but that doesn't stop my cheeks and neck from flushing like they always do when I'm aroused.

My stomach flips, but I hold my smile for a few seconds. With my free hand, I rearrange my hair. "Do you treat all your prospective dealers this way? Matt... whoever else? Do they all get an invite to stay in one of your rooms here?"

"What do you think?" He smirks.

"I don't think so."

There are so many things I would say right here if I wasn't pretending to go along with this ridiculous idea of his. For starters, why the hell would I want to live with him? I can't deny he's hot as hell, and now that I know he's a chameleon, he's interesting too—but he's also scary. Normal people don't have so much... duality.

(I know what you're thinking. You're pointing your finger. But I'm not in the student government, and sometimes, on Saturdays when I'm at the house painting my toe nails, I wear a tie-dyed Grateful Dead shirt. Yeah. The kind with the little dancing bears. I'm a total pot dealer at heart).

"They didn't have to live here," he says finally. "Neither do you. It's an option. Can you see yourself staying here?"

"I don't know." I try to sound uncertain—like an idiot. "I think I'd miss my friends at the Tri Gam house."

"I could make you forget about them."

IS KELLAN WALSH PROPOSITIONING ME?

I breathe in through my mouth. "How?"

He doesn't move, but I just know. I can feel the hum of tension in the air between us, and in that second, I get a wonderful idea. A devious idea.

He steps a little closer to me, sending my pulse racing. That reaction to him isn't fake. His wide chest is inches from my breasts. I step forward.

My breasts mash against his chest as our hips brush. Half a heartbeat later, I feel his dick pressing against my lower belly. Wow... it's totally hard.

Oh my God.

His hands come up and frame my face. His eyes, on mine, are hypnotic.

"I'm not going to lie to you. I want to fuck you, Cleopatra. That would be part of you staying with me. I'll teach you how I do things and help you make more money. We fuck in between."

I press my lips together. Holy fucking shit. I struggle to steer my mind back to my plan.

Kellan strokes his thumb over my lip, and I shudder—a real, live, turned-on shudder.

"Kellan..." I twine my arms around his neck and move in closer for a kiss. And when his soft, warm tongue separates my lips and strokes into my mouth, I imagine it between my legs.

I'm already wet for him.

That's why it's easy for me to tug him over to the bed. Easy for me to grab his collar and tug at his shirt, prompting him to pull it over his head. Easy for me to wriggle my way out of my red blouse, giving him access to my pale pink bra, the lacy one that makes my boobs look huge.

I have no trouble lying back on the mattress as he frees my breasts and sucks one of them into his mouth.

"Cleo... Fuck, you're gorgeous."

I run my hands up his chest—a god's chest: ripped and warm. I gasp at the pleasure of his tongue swirling around my nipple.

I gasp again when his hand unbuttons my gray jeans. He tugs them down my hips, then his fingers push past my panties and find my hot, slick skin. He spreads me open just enough to push a finger inside.

I grab at his crotch, feeling how ridiculously huge he is. I imagine him shoving it inside of me, and then his hands are pulling my pants off. His mouth is kissing down my belly as he adds another finger, stretching me so tight I can't help moaning.

"You're wet, Cleo. So wet for me. Let me make you feel good."

And I decide right then, I will.

I will definitely let him make me feel good.

I grip his golden hair as he bends over my pussy. I claw his shoulders as he flicks his tongue, rolling it down my swollen slit while his fingers surge inside me, teasing till I'm breathless, panting, grinding senselessly against his mouth.

He eats my pussy like no one ever has before, licking my clit firmly but gently, a glorious feline lapping milk, while his fingers pump inside me, skilled and rhythmic.

I come panting his name. Lie there feeling like my world has just been torn apart. When I open my eyes, his shirt is on again. He's standing by the bed, looking down on me as if he owns me. And for a second, I think I understand why so many girls succumb to him.

I giggle. The sound echoes through my hollow head. "Damn, you're... damn."

"What do you say?" He raises one eyebrow.

I fake-grin, and pull my pants back on. "I think I might be game, but I want to get more information first."

What do you need?" He's deadly serious. If I wasn't already on edge, I would be now. My skin tingles. My heart pounds. My clit throbs.

I leave my shirt on the bed—a necessary sacrifice, I've decided—and slide off the mattress. I close the distance between the two of us with one stride and press my palms against his chest. "I want to suck your dick first, Kellan. Feel you in my mouth. That's how I'll really know if this is worth it for me."

I can see the surprise on his face. The arousal in his eyes. He nods once. "Come with me."

He pulls me over to the wing-backed chair and sinks down into it. He unfastens his pants and tugs them down, revealing an enormous, straining cock. I give myself a minute to behold its perfect shape and thick, outlandish size. To appreciate the nice, big balls that hang beneath it.

I think, if I liked him, I would definitely enjoy getting him off.

"Kneel," he orders.

With a hungry smile, I do.

"Put your mouth around me, and I'll tell you how I like it done." So bossy. I kind of like that, given what I'm setting up here. *Boss me around, baby. You just tell me how you like it.*

I decide to tease him a little first. I try to wrap my fingers around him, and of course, he's too thick. I encircle his shaft, just under the plump head, and feel him jerk a little. Damn, that's hot. I run my hands up and down him, heady at the softness of his warm skin over the stiff erection.

I can feel him take a deep breath as I explore him with my hands. The trick here is to be gentle: a light touch as I roam under his balls—he makes a delicious, throaty sound—and travel up his shaft, where I rub my thumb under the rim of his head, right there where it meets the underside of his shaft. I don't know what this little hot spot is called, but when I stroke it softly, guys go crazy.

Like right now. I feel his thighs tense as he blows his breath out. His hands tighten on my shoulders as I trace my fingertip around the rim of his head. I grip him with my other hand and start to pump... He grunts, hands clenching.

"Fuck..."

I pump his shaft and lick him there—one soft, slow lap at that sweet little indention on the underside of his head. He moans, and it's too soon to give him more. Instead I trail around the rim again, exquisitely soft and light... a tease, designed to make him brainless.

And it works. He lifts his hips. "Oh fuckkk." He squeezes my shoulders hard enough to hurt. I twirl my tongue under his head... and open wide... and close my lips around him. Fuck, he's big. I-can-barely-fit-my-lips-around-him big.

I don't have room to twirl my tongue around him, so instead I use my lips—rubbing them just underneath the rim of his head, which is pushed against my tongue.

I feel him inhale. Exhale. His legs are shaking. "More." He shifts a little, and I'm surprised to find he's holding back. He wants to slam that big dick down my throat—I *know* he does—

but he's trying to be polite. The effort costs him, clearly. One big hand tunnels into my hair and tightens, pulling harshly as I stroke his shaft and suction my mouth around his head.

He groans. My eyes flick to his face, finding it rapt and tense.

"Your throat," he moans. "Suck me... down into your throat."

I cup one hand under his balls and keep pumping his cock. I'm gripping harder now, stroking faster. As I roll his full sac in my hand, his hips tremble. I hum a little, just to be a tease.

His eyes flip open. He looks wasted. Drugged. "Deeper," he growls.

I suck my cheeks in around him, easing him carefully deeper as he wraps his hand around my head. My eyes begin to water. He's so big and thick. I've got his head completely in my mouth now, and I can feel the pressure at the back of my tongue. To truly take him in, I'll have to open wide and gobble down his cock.

I take him deeper, looking up at him as saliva floods my mouth. His eyes are heavy-lidded... almost shut, long lashes tipped down. I can see some color in his cheeks that wasn't there before. His perfect lips are slightly parted.

I take still of him and feel his legs spread wider. Fuck, they're muscular. I stroke my fingers over his sac, and his cock rewards me with a soft throb I can feel against my cheeks.

Oh yeah. He really wants this.

Deeper and I'm almost gagging. I taste something salty. His fingers stroke my scalp.

He moans and shudders. I'm deep-throating him. *Go me!*

I shut my eyes and focus on relaxing my throat, while one of my hands grips his hard hip. The other strokes his balls, which pull taut as he settles deep in my throat. Tears slide down my cheeks as I swallow against his length and suck my mouth tightly around his base, until he's thrusting those granite-carved hips; making me gag around his huge girth; rocking into my throat as he pants and flexes his legs and I suck air in through my nose.

I look up at him once more. He's beautiful. Perfection, really, even more so as he comes undone. His cock is so responsive.

Swelling when I suction my cheeks around the base of him, leaking salty pre-cum when I suck and swallow deeper.

His fingers quiver in my hair and he starts snarling... talking dirty. Calling me his *fucking whore*, his *cock-tease*, *slut*, even as he slumps back in the chair, more swollen-cock-that-needs-to-come than guy.

His body trembles as I give the best blow job I've ever given. "'M... gonna make that pussy... pay for this," he pants. He grasps my breast and pushes further down my throat.

So aroused... I'm surprised to find that even I feel hot and bothered.

So it's a shame what I'm going to do. What I must do, to ensure my safe departure, and also to get some insurance: a way to invalidate his story if he tries to set me up.

I swallow one more time against his thick head—something all men seem to love—and focus my mouth around the base of him. I taste another drip of pre-cum. His hands, now threaded through my hair, curl into fists as he thrusts into my throat. He groans loudly. Grunts. I feel a flash of sheer lust, imagining his huge dick in my pussy. Damn, he's close. *I'm* close. I realize with a bolt of shock that I am wet and throbbing too.

And then, as I suck my cheeks in hard and grasp his sac, his hips buck; he spurts like a fountain down my throat. His body shudders mightily, and I marvel at the moisture that's pooled in between my thighs. I've never enjoyed giving blow jobs, but this was something else.

I stare down at him as I stand up. His eyes are closed, his head leaned back against the chair.

But his legs are wide open—cock still mostly hard, his balls hanging without a care.

His eyes peek open too, right then, confirming my hunch that Kellan Walsh is not someone who relaxes for long. His gaze connects with mine. I grin.

And then, before he or I can speak, before another proposition can be made or another kinky phrase exchanged, I ram my knee between his legs.

I hear him grunt, but I am on the move, grabbing my shirt and shoes and darting out the door, dashing down the hall and down the stairs. Down the stairs and to my car. I hit the driver's side so hard it hurts my ribs. I hoist myself over the door and fumble with my keys. I'm cranking the car before I catch my breath, gassing it as my head spins.

I glance behind me, half expecting to see his Sexcalade bouncing down the dirt drive after me. Half expecting to see him in my back seat.

But... nothing.

Nothing as I leave his dirt road.

Nothing as I pull over to put my shirt and shoes on.

Nothing on the drive home.

Nothing as I contemplate if he was really what he said. If he really wanted what he said, or if he was simply playing me.

Nothing as I shower, study, slip into my bed.

And then my phone lights up.

SIX

Kellan

I'M SUCH A FUCKING LIAR.

I think the thing about it that bothers me most is how weak it makes me feel.

I tick them off:

Would she believe me if I told her I make a damn good crème brûlée? I'm not sure why I asked. It doesn't matter if she'd believe me, because I can. I'm a great motherfucking cook. I cooked for my brothers for years. But after I told her that, I backed away from it. I don't even know why. Scratch that: yes I do.

My second dumb lie: ice cream. I hate the shit, so why did I say that? Having her in my house made me uneasy. As much as I want her here so we can fuck ourselves into oblivion, I can't stand having anyone close. Everything about me is... forbidden. So many reasons.

So I told her things about *him*.

I rub my temples, but the pressure only gets worse. The deep green canopy I'm staring at seems to sag a little lower over me.

Lie three: Leading her to believe, even for a moment, that any dealer has ever lived with me to be 'trained'. There was Nessa, for that one night—but I let her go. I didn't even fuck her. At times, I've almost wished I had. But it wasn't like that with us. It's still not. Oh, I wish it was. I wish it could be. Not because I would want to ruin our friendship that way, but because it would mean...

I close my eyes, and I remember the cool glass wall against my forearm. I remember how hot the cell phone was, pressed against my ear. I can hear the awful sound that came out of my throat April 29 when they called to tell me: the first domino that fell in this last chain of events.

I moved out of this bedroom because I couldn't stand to see the window anymore. Because, after that moment four months ago, I dismissed my then-sub, Gina, without a single word, and told myself she'd be the last.

There were other lies today as well. The way I set Cleo up to come to my place. Having Matt tell Lora, Cleo's friend, that he deals to other dealers sometimes. Intentionally omitting that if Cleo moves in with me, she'll spend most of her time cuffed, suspended, or spread-eagle on the middle of this bed. On weekends, she'll watch the sun rise and go down as she hangs here, getting fucked as often as I want to fuck her.

I'm not finished with this. I just... can't be.

I swing my legs off the side of the bed and allow my toes to luxuriate in the thick rug before I grab my black silk robe from a hook on the door. I try the balcony, but despite its generous size, there's not enough space. I feel pinned in. Edgy. It's a problem I have often.

I go downstairs and grab a shake out of the refrigerator. Drink it down and fuck with my phone.

I'm still wired, so it's the workout room, down in the basement. I run for twenty-seven minutes before my heart starts beating too hard, then hop off, pace around, lift some weights, and hit the elliptical for another numbing forty minutes.

I'm climbing up the stairs when I give in.

I read once that everyone has a finite supply of willpower, and tonight I've used up all of mine. Not going after Cleo and giving her the whipping she earned. Not calling one of the girls on my list of dirty fucks.

I pull up the text feature first, but I know as soon as I see it that I'm not going to text Cleo.

I need to hear her voice.

I punch her number in and sit at the top of the front staircase, looking down on the foyer: a dark cavern, sparkled and polished—all for naught. No one who comes here cares about those sorts of things.

No one but me.

I like order.

Cleo lets it ring so many times, I'm surprised when the ringing gives way to silence. A little rush jolts through my body when I realize she's breathing into the phone.

"Cleo."

It takes her a moment to answer, and when she does, she sounds... young. "It's me."

I curl my fingers around the phone, remembering how good she tasted on my fingers. My dick hardens, and as it does, my balls draw up and ache. I ignore the pain and focus on the pleasure. My hand drifts down and wraps around the thick head of my dick. I tug and grin, imagining how I'm going to discipline Miss Whatley as soon as I get the chance.

"What do you have to say for yourself?" I ask.

I know she's got something to say to me. Otherwise she wouldn't have answered my call. I wait a minute, stroking myself through the opening of my robe.

Finally she says, "What do you have to say for *yourself*? You made me feel cornered and set up. I don't trust you. If you try to rat me out, I'll say you lured me to your house and tried to force me. The bruise between your legs can back me up."

I laugh—a low hoot, surprising myself. "Can it?"

"Yeah, it can. I don't like you, Kellan. I don't want to talk to you again."

"Tell me—how does your pussy feel? My cock is wounded. Even now, as it salutes you, it feels... misunderstood. Discarded."

"Are you really trying to sexy talk me after what happened today?"

"No trying to. I am. Don't tell me you don't like it."

"Is that a threat?" Her voice is high, like she really thinks it might be.

"Cleo. Cleo, Cleo... We've gotten off on the wrong foot, I'm afraid. If you think I would hurt you, I'm forced to wonder if you're fanaticizing. I'd never hurt a woman who didn't beg for it."

"What does that mean?" she whispers.

"Have you ever been whipped?"

"No." Her voice is still a whisper.

"Have you ever had your cunt spanked?"

"No."

"Ever been bound?"

She hesitates.

"You have." My pulse quickens.

"Not really. My ex tried to tie me to the bed posts with one of his ties."

"What did you think of it?" My throat is so dry, the words stick a little.

"It was fun I guess, but he wasn't very good at knots. I got out in like ten seconds."

"Maybe you're just good at escaping."

"Maybe." Another pause. "Kellan, can I go now? I'm sorry I offended your dick or whatever. I did that because I was freaked out. Thank you for not following me, and for not threatening me or being any weirder. I enjoyed..." She fumbles for the words.

I stroke my cock. "You enjoyed my mouth on your pussy?"

"Yeah," she murmurs. "If you have to put it that way."

"My tongue in your slit? My lips on your clit? I know you enjoyed it. I'd like to do it again."

"Not happening."

"What will it take? How many bricks?"

"You want to pay me like a prostitute, with marijuana?"

"I'd make an exchange involving that, yes." I add, "Don't say it on the phone, Cleo."

"And you would get what?" She scoffs. "My body?"

I picture her lying in her bed, shirtless with her nipples hard, cradling a phone to her cheek. "And I would get.... a bunch of free weed?"

"Exactly. And you give me a cut of what you sell."

"How big a cut?" she asks.

"Sixty."

She scoffs. "That doesn't sound so great for me."

"You have no overhead. You pay me nothing. It's all profit to you."

She sighs. "Thereby making me a whore."

"My whore. I treat my whores better than most men treat their wives. I should add... you would get my body, too."

I went with an arrogant voice, and it did the trick. She giggles.

I arch a brow as I stroke my aching dick. "What's so funny, Cleo?"

"I can't believe I'm talking about this. With Kellan Walsh of all people."

I lean back against the wall and lift my legs up onto the second-story floor. I raise my knees and spread my legs slightly. "The insults keep coming."

She snorts. "You're an uptight, rule-following douche—or so I thought."

"I do make a strong—and wrong—first impression."

I hear her yawn. "I never thought I'd be discussing stuff like this with you. I can't believe you called me after I got you in the balls."

"I didn't call to chat." I'm going for stern, but I feel like I can hear a smile when she says, "What did you call to do?"

I imagine her pussy, spread open—pink and dripping. "I wanted to give you one more chance to work with me. To live with me. To be fucked by me."

"Your arrogance astonishes me, Mr. Walsh."

I try to analyze her voice and find it curious. Soft and feminine and definitely curious, despite claiming she was scared.

She wants me.

Just like I want her.

"Let me make you come—right now. With just my words. When I do, you'll move in with me."

Cleo

Damnit, but his voice is really sexy. It's the kind of voice that pervert hypnotists use... right before they tell you to strip off all your clothes.

Just a voice on the other end of the line. Not a person. That's what I tell myself.

"Where are you, Cleo?" it purrs. "Tell me, are you in your bed?"

"Yes." I've got a soft fleece blanket tucked around me, and I'm looking up at the glow stars on my ceiling.

"Tell me what you're wearing," he instructs.

I hesitate while my heart pounds, pumping blood to the growing heat between my legs.

Should I lie?

I open my mouth, and the truth tumbles out. "Just a t-shirt."

"Take it off for me, Cleo."

My hand, between my legs, pauses as I argue with myself. I would probably be masturbating even if I wasn't on the phone with him, so I'm not doing this for him. I'm just... horny right now. Yeah. He might be crazy and a total ass, but I do think he's hot. So what if I use his deep voice to get myself off?

"Are you naked, Cleo?"

"Yes," I lie. "I'm naked."

"You're not naked. Take your shirt off, Cleo. Take it off now, or I'll come and do it for you."

My eyes widen, and I'm not sure if I should laugh or cream my panties. "You're good, Walsh."

"That's Master Walsh to you. Pull your shirt over your head and cup your breasts, Cleo."

I put the phone down, and yeah, I'm doing it. I pull my shirt over my head, and my hair falls around my shoulders. The cool stream of air from my box fan makes my nipples harden.

I sink into the covers, holding the phone to my ear like a sixth grade girl talking past curfew on a school night.

"What do the sheets feel like against your skin?" his voice rumbles.

I stroke my hand down the inside of my thigh. "It's not a sheet. It's fleece."

He purrs, just like a tiger. "So it's soft."

"It is."

"Is it cold in your room?"

"Now that I'm naked it is." Reality slices through my fantasy, sending a pulse of fear through me. Making me feel vulnerable, like tomorrow I'm going to find a recording of our conversation posted on the campus forums.

"Are your nipples hard?"

I bite my lip. "I'm not telling until I know something about you."

"What do you want to know?"

My stomach twists a little. I still can't believe I'm doing this with him. I could stop right now, but... I can't seem to say the words. In fact, I hear myself ask, "What are you wearing?"

"A robe."

"What color is it?" I whisper.

"Black. And silk."

My cheeks burn as I imagine his glorious body draped in a black robe. How it would hang off his huge, ripped shoulders. If I was there, I could part it and see his six-pack... and his happy trail.

"I'm sitting at the top of the stairs in a dark house, but I think I'll get up and go back to your room now. Getting up..." I hear the sound of fabric swishing, followed by his deliciously low voice. "My cock is so hard, it's bouncing as I walk. I've got my hand around the head of it. Put your hand between your legs, Cleo."

I imagine his perfect cock as I slide my hand back down between my thighs.

"Touch yourself," he orders. "Rub your fingertips over your clit—lightly—and then stroke down. Nudge your finger in between your lips so you can feel how soft you are. So warm and wet, aren't you? Glide your fingers through your wetness."

My fingertip circles my clit, almost on its own.

"Good girl. Don't be shy. You're fucking sexy, naked with your fingers in your pussy. My cock is aching for that tight, wet pussy. Slide one finger down and push a finger into yourself. It feels like velvet inside, doesn't it Cleo? Push in—all the way. Do you like that?"

God—for shame. I push my finger up inside myself, and it's all I can do to swallow back a moan.

"Tell me, Cleo—do you like to be finger-fucked?"

Heat sweeps through me, and every inch of my skin tingles with sweat.

"Yes," I whisper.

"Clench around your finger. Clamp that pussy down on it. Are you doing that?"

I nod.

"Now drag your finger out. Not fast. Slowly."

Damn me, I'm doing what he says. My clit feels warm and swollen.

"You're empty now. All wet with no dick to fill you up," his low voice whispers. "Push your finger back into your cunt. Then slide it out. I want you to fuck yourself. Like I would do if I was there."

I close my eyes. I imagine my finger is his finger. I'm so wet.

"My robe is coming off, Cleo. I hung it on the door, and I'm walking to my—to your bed. I'm on it now, Cleo. I'm naked. Can you see my chest and shoulders? Can you see my dick? I'm stroking it. Squeezing it. It's hard. Getting harder."

I rub circles around my clit, tensing my legs. "Does it... hurt?"

"I'm sore, but you didn't break it, Cleo. It's ready for that pussy."

I picture his hard length standing at attention, long and thick and striped with veins. His hand around it, stroking as his balls bounce underneath.

"Can you stroke your clit with your thumb while you slide another finger inside? I want you to feel full, so when you close your eyes and imagine my cock, you can almost feel it. Almost." He laughs, a low, throaty sound that turns me on even more. "Are your fingers in your pussy, Cleo?"

I've been holding back, but now I spread my legs and push two fingers in. My clit throbs, and I can't swallow my moan.

"Your pretty lips are around my cock. Now you're taking it down your soft throat. I'm thrusting in and out of your mouth, pushing myself down your throat, because I'm getting close. Do you have a vibrator?"

I can't speak, so I just swallow. I lie still for a minute, with my fingers in my pussy and my thumb stroking my swollen clit. Then I reach over to my nightstand drawer and pull my little bullet out.

"I trust you've got your vibrator in hand. Blow on it a couple times. Get it nice and warm, and then position it right over your clit. You're throbbing, aren't you Cleo? I can smell how wet you are."

He's right. I'm practically gushing.

"I'm wet, too. I'm so fucking hard for you, I'm leaking. I'm so hard it almost hurts. My balls are drawing up and that does hurts, Cleo. That's your fault. But it's a good hurt."

I drag my finger through my pussy lips and swirl it over my clit. I'm starting to pant, so I angle the phone away from my mouth.

"Turn on your vibrator. If you pulled your fingers out of your pussy, I want you to stuff them back in, nice and deep. Unless you have a dildo. Do you have a dildo?"

"No," I rasp.

"Stuff yourself. Two fingers. Shove in as far as you can go and imagine my dick buried deep inside you. I'm thrusting in and out of you. Then I'm dragging my tongue over your clit. Rub the vibrator over yourself and feel my tongue. It's soft and hot. I'm teasing you. I'm lapping down around your cunt. Licking back up to your clit, so everything is soft and slick."

I squeeze my eyes shut. Work my fingers in and out of myself. Hold the bullet to my clit.

"I'm thrusting into you. Slamming my hips into yours straining to get deeper. You spread your legs as far as they can spread and I bury myself in you."

"Yes," I pant. I don't mean to. I just... can't help myself.

"I'm coming now, Cleo."

I hear a low, rough groan—and that's all it takes for me. I roll over the edge with a little gasp, and I hear Kellan's chuckle. "Did you come, Cleo?"

I shut my eyes and breathe as he says, "I blew my load imagining that pussy. This is the last time I'm going to imagine it."

I shake my head and curl over on my side, hugging myself as all the tingles work themselves out of me. "You're wrong," I say. "I didn't come."

Another laugh. "I heard you panting. You're lying."

"That's not true." I can't believe I did that. Holy shit.

"Tomorrow, Cleo. Pack your bags."

SEVEN

Cleo

R.-

This is my school's campus. See? We ARE known for our art program.

I miss you...

I'm surprised how much.

-S.

It's 7:48 a.m. when I drop the post card in one of the campus mail bins and trudge toward my first class: calculus for business. I plan to start my own learn-to-paint shop, so I know I'll need some business skills. I just don't understand why calculus is necessary. And I definitely don't understand why they put the sorority houses on the east side of campus when so many science and math buildings are on the far west side.

That's a lie. I do. Sexist bastards.

I look down at my feet as I walk—at my ankle-high leather boots and black leggings. I'm wearing a black shawl, too, with a black shirt underneath. All black today. Because it suits my mood.

I feel... weighted. As if there's an itty-bitty black hole behind my sternum, collapsing me from the inside out. I just want to sink down to the ground. And spread my legs. And think of...

Damn.

Maybe I'm ovulating today? Because I want him. Like... I totally, illogically, inappropriately want that asshole, Kellan Walsh, inside me. Right now.

I cross an arm over my chest to try to hold this feeling inside, where it's safe. I feel so much the opposite today. As if something small and soft could break me. Maybe it's the clouds. The puffy, dark gray clouds riding low over the campus's stately brick buildings remind me of the instructions Robert sent me what feels like forever ago: not a sunny day, and not a cloudy one. I inhale deeply and feel the pressure in my chest again.

I'm worried—okay?

Anyone in my shoes would be.

Nothing will be right again until I get another note from "R." Or until BTM returns my call or my letters. Until then, I'm waiting. I hate waiting.

I follow the curve of the wide, brick concourse, cutting a flat path beneath mossy oaks, between bike racks and pebble paths. I shift my thoughts to Kellan Walsh, where they're safer.

It's official: I'm bespelled, just like the others. On paper he screams "horrible idea," but in experience... well, he screams horrible idea, but also "hot fuck." I didn't think of myself as someone extra susceptible to the whims of my pussy, but I guess with the right guy, anyone can be swayed.

Why is he the right guy? I don't have a clue.

Right *dick*, I correct myself. I only want him for that gorgeous cock of his. And his sexy voice. And that body...

Fuck.

I arrive at the Braun Mathematics Building in a crap mood and stop in the doorway to pull my shoulder-length, brown-black hair into a pencil twist. Like everything today, it feels heavy.

I literally drag my feet the rest of the way to Room 120. I pull my iPhone out of my bag and check it before I step into the classroom.

Nothing. *Yet.* I have a feeling I'll hear from Kellan sometime today. Or see him. And when I do... I shake my head. I have no idea how I will handle seeing him in person after last night.

I sigh, and actually relax a little as I open the door, because at least in here I can turn my thoughts to something concrete.

I push through the door with my right elbow, curling my fist toward my wrist to avoid picking up germs: my new worst fear. Then I step onto the bottom level of a stadium-style lecture hall and freeze like a burglar in a spotlight.

The room is quiet. Everyone is bent over, scribbling with pencils. As my eyes across desk after desk, all I see light blue paper on each. Scantrons. Because today is test day. SHIT.

I spot my hump-backed, seventy-year-old professor, Dr. Marx, behind the podium, and I walk slowly over to him. My hand feels numb as I take a test booklet and a Scantron of my own.

How the hell did I forget this? I've actually been studying lately, and using my day planner.

I am screwed. So screwed. I'm a disaster at math on my best day, and this is not my best day. Not at all.

I take a seat on the fourth row up and try to remember how the grade for this class is calculated. I'm pretty sure it's calculated by averaging four tests and an overall pop quiz average. This test is going to be one-fifth of my grade.

I slide into my seat with a hard knot in the back of my throat. I'm surprised to find I'm blinking against tears by the time I get my name bubbled in.

The moment I open the booklet, the classroom door creaks open. I look over then blink a few times, just to be sure I'm not hallucinating. But... nope. Standing there in the doorway, holding a manila folder, looking tall and broad and flawless in charcoal slacks and a dapper charcoal vest over a crisp-looking button-up, is Kellan Walsh.

What the fucking fuck?

My head pounds, and all of a sudden, I can't seem to remember how to breathe or even be here in this room.

Awareness returns to me slowly, centered between my legs. My vag is pounding. Throbbing, really. It's hot and eager, ignited by the sight of Kellan Walsh. Like one of Pavlov's dogs. How totally humiliating.

Kellan steps fully into the classroom, like he wants to go ahead and get rid of any hope I have the he's just a very Kellan-looking person. My eyes run from his golden blond hair down his heavy chest—which I have to admit, looks amazing in that vest—to the podium, where Dr. Marx is peering at Kellan curiously.

I look down at my Scantron and bubble in a random "C" for question number one while Kellan and Dr. Marx talk with their heads leaned close together. I see some of my female classmates watching Kellan longingly, and I'm shocked to find I want to throat-punch them. Then Dr. Marx nods twice and looks in my direction. "Come," he beckons.

I pick up all my things, including the test papers, and walk toward the podium in slow-motion. All I can think of is last night, in my bed. How wet and shaky I was when we finished. How I couldn't fall asleep without using my LELO wand and replaying his dirty words in my head.

Kellan folds his arms over his broad chest and keeps his eyes on the rows of desks directly in front of him as I close the distance between us. Then he shifts his gaze to me the way a man might look from his bowl of cereal to the text of a newspaper article. His face is completely apathetic.

"Miss Whatley," he murmurs, when I'm close enough that only I, and maybe Dr. Marx, can hear. His gaze rolls up and down me, casually assessing.

"What are you doing here?" I choke.

The corners of his mouth quirk. His lips press together and twist slightly up, a sly expression that shows he's enjoying my ruffled feathers. His blue eyes tug at mine. "Can you step into the hall, please, Miss Whatley?"

My heart hammers like a drum as we move toward the door. I feel his fingers on my lower back—pressuring or guiding me?

He reaches around me to push the door open, and I can feel the gentle sensation of him shadowing me as we move into the hall. It's empty now that class has started—fliers on a nearby bulletin board no longer flapping in the breeze that busy bodies make; the shiny, gray and maroon checkered floor tiles glinting beneath shoe scuffs.

I tell myself that despite his ridiculous plan, and no matter what he says, I will hold strong and keep my panties on. I turn slowly to face him, wearing my best poker face. "What are you doing here?" I ask curtly.

It's such a lie, the 'hold strong' bit. His eyes are so, so blue. They're like the ocean. His lips curve up a little, and I want to bite them. Lick them. I can feel my nipples harden. I thought that was just a line from romance novels, but for real, they actually harden at the sight of this bastard.

"What do you think?" he practically purrs. Something deep in my belly tucks into a little bow for him.

"I'm not sure I want to know," I say flatly.

He offers a gentle smile I'm not expecting, then reaches out to touch a loose strand of my hair. "Cleo... Don't worry. I'm not the asshole today. I'm the prince." A satisfied grin breaks over his lips, and his face goes from beautiful to breathtaking.

Deep breaths, bitch.

I arch one eyebrow and hug my books closer to my pounding chest. "Why are you really here?"

"I've got an independent study this period. I'm helping the provost film a commercial. I need students." His greedy eyes rake up and down me. He takes some of my shawl between his fingers as his flirty mouth curves up again. "You look good in black, Cleo."

"I'm sure that's what the provost wants." I roll my eyes. "A girl in a shitty mood, dressed in all black."

"It's what I want," he says in a low voice.

My heart trips, then starts beating off-beat.

I laugh, ridiculously awkward. "No charming me," I warn. Except that isn't true, is it? He made me come last night—on the frickin' phone!

He catches my hand, his long, strong fingers weaving through mine before I have the chance to pull away. "Walk with me, Cleo. No strings."

I want to pry my fingers from his, but our hands are locked together, palm to palm. His hand is warm and strong. The close contact reminds me of how lonely I've been since Brennan. Just for the basic things, like hugs and hands. That's the only reason I let him tug me gently down the hall, toward the front entrance of the building. That, and I want to confirm for myself in the light of day that he's really not an FBI agent. If he doesn't bust me now, I can believe he's actually a drug overlord.

Our forearms brush as we move. The curve of my hip touches his thigh. I try not to sweat. He seems calm—completely unaffected. FBI-like... ?

"You can re-take your test," he tells me. "I'll get your excuse."

He looks down at me out of the corner of his eye, a smug smile curving his lips. At least, I imagine he's smug.

I feel the word "thanks" form on my tongue, but I clamp my mouth shut before it can roll out.

I glance down at our joined hands. His wrist is bent a little. His fingers grip mine, light but firm—an easy cradle. They're long and elegant. The angles of his wrist and forearm are the same. He's just... well-hewn. Andddd, I'm lusting after a forearm. I'm in such big fucking trouble.

"You got Marx for cal?" Kellan asks as we pass closed classroom doors. My boots and his black leather shoes echo around us.

I'm hyper-aware of my damp fingers in his, so it takes me a moment to remember he asked me a question. I nod. "Business calculus."

"You're going into business?"

"Yeah." My voice sounds high and forced.

It's his damn hand.

His fingers shift in mine, tickling my palm, and heat shoots up my arm. We reach the building's front corridor, where a stairwell leads up to two more levels of classrooms and a row of glass doors leads outside. His thumb strokes the back of my hand.

"What sort of business?" He leans forward to push one of the doors open with his free hand. He flattens his broad back against it, and I squeeze through beside him while my pulse pounds in my head.

Outside, sunlight is streaming through the clouds: a soft, cool, filmy light that seems to set the scene for something serious. The pearly glow flickers through the trees, making a shadowy kaleidoscope of leaf-shapes that flickers across Kellan's face and shoulders.

"Psychology," I fudge. I don't want to get into my real ambitions with him. I have a feeling he wouldn't get it.

I look around at the wide, brick concourse out ahead, empty because everyone is in class; at the impeccably manicured lawns that spread out underneath giant, mossy oaks. The lawns and flower beds are striped by pebble walking paths.

He leads me toward the nearest trail, curling between rows of massive azalea bushes. Despite all my reservations, I follow.

My forearm brushes his, and suddenly I just can't keep touching him. Not without bursting into flames. I wriggle my fingers impatiently, and his hand relaxes to free mine. He stops moving, and we stand there on the shaded trail, watching each other. He looks like a real prince in his vest-suit thing.

I feel like a pumpkin.

He trails a finger lightly down my forearm. "Relax, Cleo." His voice is stern and soft. "I won't bite—this time." He winks, and I roll my eyes, despite the increase in my heart rate.

He walks, and my traitorous feet follow.

"You're a senior?" he asks, glancing back at me.

My stomach writhes under his blue gaze. "Yeah."

"So, grad school after this?"

The azaleas on each side of the path rise up around us, fluffy green bushes taller even than Kellan. The feeling of privacy makes my head buzz. Makes me sound breathless when I say, "It's one of the reasons I need money."

I search his face for hidden motives, but he's looking at me the same way he was before: with sincere interest, as if he's interviewing me for an important job. "What will you do with your degree?" he asks, in his resonant voice.

"Help kids." Kids like my sister and me. After our youngest sister, Olive, died, Mary Claire and I both struggled. We had a hard time in school, and an even harder time at home. Our house was so gloomy. Both my grandmother and my mom cried all the time. My mom closed her sewing shop and took a factory job. Grans started cleaning houses when she could. Mary Claire and I were on our own. To understand why Olive was taken and we weren't. To make sense of the knowledge that we'd never, ever see her freckled face again. For years, I would go to the cemetery on the fourteenth of every month, because she died on the fourteenth. Mary Claire has never been. She just can't go.

Neither of us ever got "therapy," because we couldn't afford it. At our elementary school, there was one counselor, and she was busy helping with the kids who acted out.

My business will target kids like us. I'll do private art classes, and I'll charge my patrons... aggressively. I'll make the classes really fun. I'll make my clients feel like artists, and ensure they're able to take home a nice canvas. Then I'll use some of the money to offer free art classes to kids who've experienced tragedy. I talked to the local school superintendent here in Chattahoochee, and she said a plan like mine would definitely work in most school districts.

I look up at perfect Kellan, and I know I can't tell him all that. He'd never understand.

I give him an easy little shrug. "Kids with troubles," I say. "I'm going to help them."

"That's a noble calling."

"I should warn you, I have a sensitive bullshit-o-meter." I lift my eyes from the ground and find him staring at me earnestly. He's all blue eyes, cheekbones, and lips. Anger wars with desire inside me, tightening my chest. "It's got to be better than your criminal plans."

He slants his gaze down at me. "You're probably right."

Curiosity seeps through me. I only fight it for a minute before loosening my tight shoulders and asking, "What are your plans seriously? More of what you do right now? And you really do... what you said yesterday?"

He places a finger over my lips and looks into my eyes. His are so... intense. Almost hungry. I do this weird, mini-shiver thing, but he doesn't seem to notice as he draws his hand away from my mouth and turns back to the path ahead. "Yes, Cleo. I really do. And... I don't have plans," he says, walking. His eyes are on the pebbles. His hands have disappeared into his pockets.

"Nothing?"

"Just keep thumbing through my wads," he says. One corner of his mouth lifts, but it's not a smile.

"Investing," he adds, like it's an afterthought. Our little path turns east, toward Taylor Hall, the tall, brick pre-Civil War administrative building.

I'm aware of his body, just a foot or so from mine. How quiet he suddenly is. How big—and also graceful. Like an athlete. Which makes sense, because he is. I keep forgetting Mr. Perfect plays soccer. I glance at his legs. I can see thick muscle through his slacks.

My eyes move back up him, over his lean waist and his muscular chest and shoulders. My throat is dry. I swallow. What were we talking about?

Our future plans.

I wonder what his really are. I wonder why he's so intent on doing business with me. Could it really be as simple as it seems on the surface? Eliminate the competition—which just happens to be me? I should probably ask more questions.

"Do you do just the... um... M.J.?" I glance at the tall bushes that line our path, as if anyone is actually around. "Or more stuff, too?"

"You're curious?" He gives me his beautiful, blue eagle eye.

"Isn't that part of why we're talking? Because you want to work together?"

His eyes darken. He stops walking, his arm brushing mine as he reaches up to touch my shoulder. "I made you come, Cleo. We both know that. We are going to work together."

His low words drive the air out of my lungs. I can't tear my eyes away from his. I gobble at the air like a goldfish on sidewalk.

"Is that why you got me out of class?" I feel a swell of warmth between my legs and suck another breath in. "Kellan—no." I shake my head, finally finding my equilibrium. I step away, forcing his hand off my shoulder. "There's no way I'm living at your house. I don't want to deal for you either. No offense, but... no. My answer is the same. No way."

He brings a hand to his heart. The intensity of a few moments ago falls away, leaving a thick blanket of charm that makes my chest feel fuzzy. "You wound me."

I give a hoarse laugh. "You're hot and everything. You've got a really sexy voice, you're the kind of guy that people post in my slutty Facebook group but—"

His brows arch. "Slutty Facebook group?" An instant grin spreads over his face. "Cleo—tell."

My face heats so fast, my eyes actually sting. I slam my palm against my forehead. "Never mind. Forget I said that. Please."

"Are you an admin there?"

I take another step back and put my hands up again. "Slow down, Pervo. It's not like you're going to get to see. It's a group for women. Smuffins," I tell him, smiling just a little. I pull my shawl up and show him my long-sleeved black t-shirt, with its little, white Smuffin logo—an artful marriage of an "S" and a heart.

"That's the logo?" He's still grinning. Maybe smirking.

I laugh a little, real this time. "That's the logo. It's a women's perv group. Totally amazing. Very fun. It's more than that, too. It's sort of like... a group of friends, who read and talk about girl shit. And smut." I drop the shawl, feeling a little too exposed. "Anyway, they'd totally drool over a Kellan Walsh .gif, but that doesn't mean I want to live with you. Or even screw you. No offense."

"I am offended," he says gravely. "You tell me you only like me for my looks, and they don't even make up for my perceived... shortcomings? Is that it?" He looks mortally offended, and I scoff.

"You're a—I won't say what," I hiss, "but we both know it." I cut my eyes at him. "Let's just put it this way: You're the wolf, and I'm a lamb."

"*Twilight* fan girl?" He makes air quotes around 'fan girl'. His brows are arched.

"Familiar with the movie?"

We're walking again, having fallen into an easy pace, still winding through the azaleas toward the Taylor building.

"*Book*," he tells me. "Actually, book*s*." He smiles a little, looking secretive—and way too handsome.

"Did you read it for a girl?"

"A woman."

I rake my eyes down his body and try to imagine her: the woman-not-girl who got a guy like Kellan Walsh to read the *Twilight* books.

"Her name is Dr. Merchant," he says, with a quirk of his lower lip.

"You took her 'Guide to Modern Publishing?' Color me shocked."

"The blows keep coming."

I snort, trying desperately to pretend my heart's not pounding every time his eyes meet mine. Trying to pretend I think about him what I should: that he's a liar, a phony, and a threat. "Why would you want to write and sell a book?"

Again, the eagle eye. I can't tell what he's feeling. "Maybe I was thinking of writing my memoir."

I throw my head back. "A comedian, too!"

His lips twist into a smile; he's smirking at me even as he shakes his head. "You think so low of me."

I nod. "That's why I'm not going to live with you. Or do you."

He gives me a sidelong, thoughtful look. "You said you struggle with math?"

"I hate it. Why?"

We're in sight of Taylor now. It looms above us, a dark brick building with two huge towers. Pines sway gently around it.

"I've got another deal for you."

My heart thumps. "Oh boy."

He holds a hand up. "What are you studying now? What specifically?"

"Intro to basic antiderivatives and—damnit, what are they called? Indefinite integrals! And I already know where you're going with this. Even if you can perform lobotomies, I'm not changing my mind."

"What if I enlighten you completely? Make you a math whiz."

I snort. "No one's that good."

"I'm a finance major, Cleo. That means I'm a god at math. You need help, so let's see if I can help you." He catches my elbow with his fingers, and I look into his eyes.

"Give me two hours. Just two. If I don't change things for you, then the deal is off. I'll let you back out of our agreement from last night."

My gaze dips to the ground. To our feet, standing so close together. I don't know what would be the best move. All I do know is that he throws me off. He makes me nervous. "I have an officers' meeting tonight," I tell him lamely.

He waves at his clothes. "I have a trustee selection committee meeting. After that?"

I step away, drawing my elbow out of his hand. I'm not sure if I should sign on for the study session just to call his bluff, or if I should simply *run.* I smooth a hand over my hair, a nervous gesture I thought I left behind with freshman year. "My meeting isn't over until seven-thirty."

"I'll be by to get you then."

I rub my lips together, and finally work up the nerve to look him in the eye again. "I don't think that's a good idea."

His face turns serious—gravely so. "It's because of yesterday," he says. "I scared you."

"No shit, Sherlock. I thought I was getting busted. Then I find out you're some drug lord. Yeah." I shrug, feeling annoyed all over again. "That's not fun."

He lifts my hand and surprises me by kissing the back of it. "I know you're surprised. I know I must seem—"

"Shady? Very."

He shakes his head. "I can make this work for you. I can make it easy."

Looking up into his earnest face, it seems improbable enough to almost make me laugh. "I don't believe you, Kellan. I shouldn't hang out with you, even to study. You stress me out."

His face is unreadable again, his full lips pressed together. "If you're as bad as you say, tonight will be the end of it. I don't help you, you go back to dealing swag."

"Or not dealing," I correct. "That's what will happen."

"It won't happen." He rolls his shoulders and grins his arrogant grin. "I'll be at your place at seven forty. Then, the library." He narrows his eyes into a funny little winky face, then points his finger and thumb into a gun shape.

"I'm coming armed," I call over my shoulder.

My heart is still pounding when I walk out of the garden, into the parking lot behind Taylor.

EIGHT

Kellan

THE USC/ARIZONA GAME goes to commercial, and I lean back against the couch in my living room. The ceiling in this room is striped with skylights, so I'm staring up at my reflection in the glass: my arms crossed behind my head, my sleeves rolled up to my elbows, so my forearms are on display. I shut my eyes and I can see my right one stretched in front of me. I can smell the grass. The dirt. The sweat. I can feel the gallop of my heart.

The game I'm watching now is recorded on DVD. It's from the Trojans' 2012 football season. In May, I ordered everything from 2010 forward, but I only started watching them last week.

I'm calling this game a loss for the Trojans. That's the worst part of watching recorded games: the sense of inevitability when you can feel a loss coming. There's no changing fate when it's already been sealed.

And with that thought hanging around my neck, I turn the game off and reach onto the mahogany end table beside the couch. I keep a stack of post cards by the coasters where I sit my iced tea. Also a fountain pen.

Most of the time, after I pick a card and prop it on my thigh, I can't write a word. My hand freezes. My throat feels thick, as I stare down at the paper. This time, like almost every time before it, my fingers, wrapped around the pen, are cold and still.

What can I say? I've got nothing for her.

Fury rises in me: sharp, then suffocating.

I crush the card—a picture of CC's campus in autumn—in my fist and stab the pen into the couch cushion. I watch the ink spill out of it, creating a small, black cloud on the cappuccino suede.

I duck down over my lap and curl my arm around my head and take deep breaths. Now, before I lose my nerve, I grab a fresh, clean post card and try the pen's bent tip against it.

I'm surprised it works. It's my surprise that jars me into action, so I'm able to write a few words. Five... six... seven.

That's all I can.

I fold the card into my back pocket, stand up, and stretch. I look at the stairs that lead from the living area up to my room. I could change clothes, but I don't feel like trudging upstairs.

I walk into the kitchen, where I serve myself some ravioli and slam back a shake. I grab a few sticks of beef jerky for the road and a glass of sweet tea. I might be a Southern transplant, but I love this shit.

I grab my bag off the front staircase, then open the top drawer of the massive, Victorian-era table beside the stairs. I pull out a couple of notebooks, an extra calculator, and my old Calculus 1 text book. I sling the items into my bag and pull the front door shut without locking it or setting the alarm.

It's a cool night—cool for September in Georgia. The air feels lighter than it has in months. It's breezy on my cheeks; taunting me with all that I can't have.

I press "unlock" on my Escalade's key fob, climb into the front seat, and turn around so I can lean into the back. There's a white laundry basket on the seat behind mine, filled with thick, pink fleece blankets. Manning must have dropped it off while I was watching the game.

I had to call and let him know I wouldn't be at the trustee meeting—I dipped out early—and to bring it here instead. I guess I shouldn't be surprised he did what I asked, when I asked for it. He's my manager of operations, and efficiency is his middle name. Actually, Manning is. He's Adam Manning Smith—and using an alias just like I am.

I can smell what's in the blankets as I drive. I roll the windows down, jack the heat up, and listen to The Doors. And then the Dead. And then the Stones. And then The Strokes. And then nothing.

I'm too damn edgy.

Because I need her: Cleopatra Whatley.

I can't decide if it's her impertinence, her blasé, or my own urge to circumvent both and make her submit to me in every way—but I ache when I imagine her in the glass-walled room upstairs.

I park in the U-shaped lot behind the Tri Gam house and carry the basket under my left arm. I'm not afraid of getting caught. Not now. I've lost fear.

I open the front door and climb the old ass, creaky stairs like I own the place. The "executive suite" is on the front of the second story, arranged around a rocking-chair littered balcony that juts over the first-floor porch. If my sources are correct, there's one door that leads to the "suite," which houses all the officers' bedrooms. I knock twice and listen to light footfall, hoping it's Cleo's.

The door opens, and Milasy appears. She's got a pretty, oval face, with deep brown eyes and glossy, straight black hair. She sees me and smiles. "Kellan. How's it going?"

"I'm here for Cleo," I say. My lips are caught between a smile and a smirk.

Milasy looks me over. I can see the approval on her face, followed by her curiosity. "She's got you doing her laundry?" She seems to think this is unlikely. Then her face lights up. "Is there a puppy hidden in there?"

I decide on smirk. "Not a puppy," I tell her.

"Okay. Well come on in." I step inside a small but nicely adorned living area, and Milasy points to a hallway just beyond the kitchen on my right. "She's down the hall there, on the right."

"Thank you, Milasy."

My long legs carry me through the living-kitchen area quickly enough. The hall is short: only a few strides. I stand on the lilac carpet outside Cleo's door and knock twice. When the door swishes open, I smell her before I see her: some kind of soft perfume that reminds me a little of tea leaves. At first, she's just a curtain of dark hair. Then she swings it back behind her shoulders and I see her face.

Her green eyes are wide, long-lashed, and topped by thin, elegant brows. Her cheeks are high and always just a little pink. Her lips are slightly parted with surprise.

My cock stiffens.

"Kellan?" She's holding a letter, which she lowers as her gaze sweeps me. She frowns at the basket, like she thinks I've got a snake inside.

I surprise her and myself, leaning over and rubbing my thumb along her lower lip. "Cleo..."

She jerks back. "Stop! And come inside, I guess."

She steps back, and I step inside her room. The first thing I notice is it's blue: green-blue. It reminds me immediately of the ocean, viewed from high atop a cliff. And that reminds me of home. My chest aches.

I roll my gaze around, noting a white iron bed with way too many plush blankets and quilts. It's more blanket pile than bed. There's a yellow dresser, topped with various frames, and a full-length mirror on one wall. A night stand with a delicate, yellow-shaded lamp, casting cheery, amber light across the room. A window, decked in gauzy red curtains. And on the ceiling, glow stars. Belatedly, I notice that the walls are dotted with canvases. I step closer to the nearest.

It's an abstract painting: red, maroon, and purple. But something juts out of it. I lean in closer and realize there are strips of paper melded into the bold oil strokes. A quick glance around confirms that the other canvases are similar: lovely abstract art, with strips of paper—and maybe even small objects—melded in.

I reach out, compelled to touch, but at the last second, I sideline my hand to the wall outside the frame. I look at Cleo with my eyebrows raised. "Is this your art?"

She glares at me. "Are you a critic, too?"

I remember her calling me a comedian earlier and feel a twist of excitement. This girl is fiery. Complicated. Sexy. Taking her home will be rewarding in so many ways.

I look again at the red, maroon, and purple piece before me. I look more closely at the strips of paper. I catch the words "Though absent long... But oft, in lonely rooms..." and my chest tightens so it hurts to talk.

"'Tintern Abbey'?"

She steps closer. "I'm surprised you know it, math nerd."

Wordsworth was my mother's great-great-great grandfather, but I see no reason to share that factoid with her. My mother was an artist, and while I have none of that talent, I'm not bad with words—finance is a double-major, along with English—but again, what's the point?

If she wants to see me as a math nerd, I can roll with that. There's not much point in me sharing anything. Conversely, there's not much point in me holding anything back...

"I'm a Wordsworth fan," I tell her simply.

These words in her painting, I can't stop staring at them. It's like they've grown, until they fill my vision, and I feel the need to write.

I'd like to write about her body. Which means I need to see it again. I turn around and find her still holding the letter.

"What's that?" I ask.

She cradles it against her chest. "Private Cleo business."

I find myself chuckling at her puckered lips. "That sounds dirty."

"Maybe if you have a dirty mind." She sets it on the edge of her dresser with some reluctance, and I close my hands around her waist, turning her toward the spot on her rug where I sat the laundry basket.

"A gift for you," I murmur by her ear.

She crouches down, forcing my greedy hands to release her. "Blankets?"

She reaches into the basket, and I walk around to stand at the foot of her bed, so I can see her face as she digs... ah, she found it. Her eyes pop open wider. Her jaw drops.

"Holy shit! Are you kidding me? Is this a *brick*?"

I nod, and she pulls out a pound of weed, wrapped dozens of times over in Saran Wrap. It's about the shape of a masonry brick.

She "Ooooos" and "Aaaaaahs" over it, and I hold my poker face, even though I want to smile. "I told you I'd take care of you."

She drops it on her bed and runs her hands over it reverently.

"Smitten?"

Her eyes crinkle as she beams. "It's my baby," she croons. "My weed baby. What do I owe you?" She looks a little worried, so I'm happy to tell her, "Nothing. It's a show of good faith."

Her eyebrows jut up, and the smile falls off her face. "And if monkey can't learn math?"

"Then you got lucky. Or your clients will come find my guys when you run through this, so I get all your ex-clients."

She comes at me, and I'm stunned to feel her arms around me. "Thank you for this!" She presses her cheek against my chest and squeezes me around the waist. "I'll give you fifty percent at *least*, I swear!" She releases me, still grinning like a little fool, and I feel a tug in my gut as she turns back toward her gift. "It smells like heaven."

"So do you," I say to her slim shoulders. "You smell like tea."

She turns back around and smiles at me, a mega-watt grin that streams charm through the little room like sunlight. "I wear Green Tea perfume. You've got a good nose."

"Part of the job," I kid.

"I want to know more about it," she says eagerly.

"My nose?" I'm surprised to find myself smiling again. I press my lips together, because my cheeks are aching.

"The job, silly."

I arch my brows. "Does this mean we're... associates?"

I'm actually thinking of making her my partner, but it's too soon to tell her.

I fold my arms over my chest and watch her leggings stretch over her nice, round ass as she stashes the brick under her bed. She ignores my 'associates' comment as she turns and sifts through the basket. "Snuggly blankets." She presses her face into one of them. "They smell like fresh detergent."

"They are freshly detergenterized."

"By you?"

"Who else?" I ask. For some reason, I want her to think I laundered them myself. "I'm courting you, Cleo. You said you like fleece."

"When did I say that?" she asks, almost accusingly.

"Last night." I run my eyes over her bed, and Cleo's cheeks stain red.

"I don't like to be embarrassed," she says. She leans her butt against the mattress and her green eyes peer into mine.

"So don't be."

"I was going to do that anyway," she says softly.

By "that" I assume she means "masturbate," not "have phone sex." I can tell she's trying to be casual and failing. Even her neck is red now. I'm surprised I'm having this effect on her.

She recently got out of a relationship with Brennan. That guy is boring, and a douche. Maybe he just never really did it for her.

I assume she was referencing him; the guy who bound her wrists with his tie. I wonder if it was on this very bed... I grit my teeth. I can't stand to imagine her body stretched out under his.

Instead I ask, "What else don't you like? Teach me your mysterious ways."

Her green eyes blink, wide and more solemn than this moment calls for. "I don't like surprises."

The intensity of her expression makes me smile a little, teasingly. Cleo seems, to me, like exactly the sort of girl who would enjoy a nice surprise. "So I need to promise never to surprise you?"

She nods, chewing her lip. "Unless it's good. Like that." She nods to where she tucked the brick under the bed.

I've got nothing good at all, so I promise, "No more surprises."

She seems appeased by that, as if she's moved past whatever serious moment had its claws in her.

"Sixty-five percent," she says lightly, grabbing a leather book bag from one of the bed's posts. "Because that deal of yours is so not happening. I can barely add two plus two. You'll see."

I reach down to work the bag's strap from her fingers.

"Don't think that wins you any points," she warns. She grabs a water bottle off the dresser, stuffs the letter she had earlier into her bag, and sprays the room with linen-scented air freshener, while I check out her art again. I like the bold brush strokes and the way that she blends color. The texture of the paper adds a 3D effect.

The one I'm looking at now is Sylvia Plath. The colors are a translucent sort of jade, pale gold, and, in a few places, milky white. Running jagged and clear, horizontally, through the middle of the canvas, is a line I recognize immediately and, after a long second, place as a line from the poem, "Daddy."

"So I never could tell where you put your foot, your root, I never could talk to you..."

Where in the Wordsworth-inspired painting, the colors are a blunt amalgam, making any intention beyond the feeling of discord difficult to discern, the colors here are elegant; almost ghostly. They fade in and out of each other, like billowing clouds backlight by glowing light.

The pale spots—clouds—are beautiful. Blooming. Swelling into whatever they will be. The painting stirs a feeling of inevitability, and catches something at the bottom of my throat, so it's hard to draw my next breath.

I look up and find her staring at me with a poker face. "Criticism?" she snips.

I shake my head. "It's lovely." I want to say more, to rave about the particular feeling she just thrust into my chest, but I can't find the words. I'm only good with words on paper, so I just stand there, hoping that I look sincere.

"Thank you," she says eventually. She sniffs, standing a little straighter. "I don't like fake compliments, you know."

"Then you'll be glad to learn, I don't like blowing smoke up asses." I hold her gaze for a moment, just to show her I mean it. Then I hold out my arm, and she slides her tiny hand between the crease of my forearm and my bicep.

I walk her down the creaking stairs and out onto the porch, down the stairs into the lawn, then through the lamp-lit, car-filled parking lot. A balmy, grass-scented breeze tosses her dark hair, filling my nose with her light, sweet scent.

"That's your car, right?" she asks, as we approach the Escalade. A street lamp shines off the hood, making the black paint look like wet ink.

I nod. It belonged to my father first, but that's just another thing not to mention. He's not someone I care to talk about.

"You know it's called the Sexcalade," she says as I steer her around the hood and toward the passenger's door.

"What?" I stop with my hand stretched toward the handle.

Cleo gives me a smirk that has a distinctly chastising tilt to it. "People call this thing the Sexcalade. Because the last four months."

"The last four months." I repeat the words once more in my head, trying to make sense of them. The last four months are significant to me personally, but I don't associate them with sex. In fact, I've never had so little. I pull her door open, and in her soft, prim, Southern drawl she says, "Before that, you didn't ever seem to go out hooking up with people."

She hoists her small self neatly into my passenger's seat, and I press my lips together. So that's what people think. I guess I shouldn't be surprised that I got noticed.

After I dismissed Gina, my last submissive, I thought I could terminate all sex. I made it all of thirty-seven hours before I admitted that would never work. So I started bar-hopping.

I always took the women I picked up to hotels. I couldn't fuck them how I like, because word would get around—as evidenced by Cleo, looking smugly down her nose at me right now. I fucked them hard and fast and sent them on their way. They may have told their friends I like it rough, but they couldn't say they didn't enjoy it.

All those liquored, perfumed, ropeless fucks weren't satisfying. By coincidence, about the time I started to feel restless, I was sniffing out my "rival." She's been my distraction ever since. Everything about her, from her slow, casual gait to the way she throws her head back when she laughs—like a bad actress on a sitcom—strums some cord inside me.

I think I knew earlier than I've been willing to admit that I need Cleo in my windowed room.

I walk around the car without corroborating her story about the "Sexcalade" and slide behind the wheel. I can feel her watching me. I ignore the urge to meet her eyes as I back out of the spot.

It doesn't matter why I was never seen out socially with women, then suddenly was. She doesn't need to know. Keeping Cleo in the dark about me is the only way I can know her.

I pull out of the parking lot onto a crosswalk-striped campus street. She crosses her legs and props her hands on her knee. She looks at me, and I can feel her expectation hanging in the shadows.

"So that's kind of weird, right?" she asks me, in a chipper, prodding tone. "Aren't you going to tell me why you didn't you date before four months ago?"

My throat stings with the question. Four months. It's hard to believe it's been that long. I wish I had met Cleo before. I want to have her thoroughly, and now I'm worried that there won't be time.

I keep my feelings off my face, because, again—she doesn't need to know this shit. I twist my lips into a smug smile and try to project the Kellan Walsh she thinks she knows. "Maybe I was in a committed relationship."

Her pretty face twists skeptically. "Were you?"

I laugh. "That's Kellan business, don't you think?"

I turn into the narrow drive that leads around the side of the huge, brick library building.

"I thought we're doing business *together*," Cleo replies.

"Are you committing to that?"

She hmphs.

"That's what I thought."

I find a spot on the second level of the parking deck and notice the thought of Cleo doing business with me has taken some of the tension out of my shoulders. More and more, I think she's exactly right for what I have in mind. It gives me peace.

I walk around the front of the car and open her door. She sashays out, her black shawl fluttering behind her as her boots click against the cement. Like every time I'm near her, it's a struggle not to touch her in some way.

She turns around to face me as I shut the passenger's side door. "Were you?" she asks, hand on her hip. She looks like a superhero with that ridiculous long shawl and those boots. "Were you with someone before? Honesty, Kellan. If you want to work with me..." She licks her soft, pink lips. My cock twitches.

I trail my hand down her lower arm, catching her by the wrist and tugging her lightly toward a covered breezeway that adjoins the parking deck to the side of the library.

"I was," I say as I slide my fingers through hers. It's not a lie—exactly. "I was always with someone else before."

Sometimes several someones. The relationships were always regular; mutually beneficial and bordering on official at times. So much neater and tidier than what I'm doing now with Cleo. So much more... sound—in every way.

She frowns at my answer, as if she's turning it over in her head and isn't sure what to make of it. Then she looks down at our joined hands. "For a domineering prick, you're pretty big into hand-holding, aren't you?"

I grin, and quickly roll my lips together. "You're mine for now," I murmur to the top of her dark head. She tries to pull ahead of me, but I ignore that fact and focus on the warmth of her hand in mine, on her small-but-curvy body. I tighten my grip and force her to break her fast stride. She looks back at me, and I bring her hand to my lips. "I want to keep you close."

She snorts and increases her pace until she's dragging me behind her. I'm surprised to find I'm feeling... lighter. The weight that seemed ever-present on my shoulders seems to have drifted off—at least until I see the mail bin at the top of the library's brick steps.

Emptiness yawns inside me: a crushing need for what I can't have.

As Cleo flounces to the glass doors, I drop another half-step behind. I slide the post card out of my back pocket and reach around behind her to toss it inside.

She spins, a blur of black fabric to match her raven hair. "Did you just mail a letter?" she demands. It's the same tone she uses for everything: some funky blend of incredulity and amusement—as if she's ready and waiting to comment on any toe I put out of place.

I murmur, "Kellan business."

Pain cries through me, and I tell myself to try to forget about the postcard. After all, there is no address on it: no mailing, no return. It, like the few others I've written since May, will be discarded.

And still, the words echo in my mind.

I'm sorry, Sloth.

I'm so sorry.

NINE

Cleo

"HOLY SHIT, I THINK I GET IT!"

I give Kellan my surprised bug eyes, which probably scare the crap out of him, because we're sitting thigh-to-thigh on a narrow, padded bench in one of those little closet-rooms-for-rent inside the library.

He's got his right ankle resting atop his left knee, and my calculus textbook spread over his muscular calf and thigh. He's only been at it for about thirty minutes, and most of the time I've been distracted by his huge shoulders edging into my space as he gestures to the pages. But just now, something clicked inside my head.

"So... to find an antiderivatives for a function *f*, just reverse the process for differentiation?"

The corners of his mouth twitch. He nods slowly as his eyes twinkle.

"So you can usually find an antiderivatives by reversing the power rule. And the indefinite integral is like... a reference to all the different antiderivatives of a single continuous function. Because there isn't just one. There's a bunch of different ones. Even an infinite number?"

His grins smugly. "I told you."

"I can't believe it. I mean... Cannot. Believe. It." I bump his shoulder with mine. "Kellan, you should be a math teacher. A professor!"

He snorts.

"Seriously! How did you know how to explain it to me? I'm an idiot with this stuff. I wasn't even good at algebra."

He looks down at me through his long lashes, and I feel my body temperature spike. With his deep blue eyes, his high cheekbones, and those sculpted lips, he's just so... striking. His skin is smooth and tanned, with just a little stubble on his jaw and cheeks—more than most college guys have, I can't help noting. His hair is short and soft-looking, and just a little wavy: the just-rolled-out-of-bed look, which contrasts nicely with his dressy clothes.

He lifts a shoulder, and I swear that simple motion makes sweat pop out on my forehead. "You caught on fast," he says.

"Yeah, cause you have serious skills."

He shakes his head.

"Too cool for school?" I tease. I'm getting better at hiding my awkwardness from him, I think.

And immediately I think *maybe not*, because he's just... staring at me. My cheeks and neck are red now. I can feel them burning.

"I won," he says softly. His eyes are steady on my face.

A shiver runs across my shoulders, the kind of chill I felt once when someone was looking at me through my bedroom window back at home. I feel breathless. Helpless. Like a rabbit in the eyes of a coyote, I can only pant here, frozen.

I lick my lips, trying to think of what to say. When nothing comes to mind—because I can't decide what I want and my heart is beating too loud for me to think anyway—I shrug and, in a strange, high voice, say, "I don't understand it *all*..."

"I won, Cleo."

I watch his jaw tighten as he casts his eyes away from my face and down to the space between us. I study his hair as he reaches out and grabs a strand of fringe hanging from my shawl. He rubs it gently in his fingertips. When he looks back into my eyes, his luscious mouth is frowning.

"I really make you nervous."

"You really do."

I can't help noticing he briefly looks away. His eyes are on the brown carpet below our feet as his fingers travel smoothly up my forearm, caressing the inside of my elbow before running up my shoulder. His thumb strokes the hot skin of my neck, and then his gaze is back on mine.

"Don't be nervous," he says, rough but soft. My heart pounds as he finds my throat with his mouth. "I'll be careful with you."

This is a bad idea. It's all I can think, but the words stick in my throat as his mouth moves softly, gently, warmly over my jaw.

"Give me a few weeks." Hot breath tingles over my throat. "Three."

I'm panting now. I feel his thumb over my nipple, making it harden through my bra.

"Why?" I rasp.

"Because I need you." His tongue traces my ear. "I've got you in me, Cleo. Now I need to get you out."

He squeezes my breast, and I feel a burst of warmth between my legs. "That's what I'm scared of."

"What?" He nibbles my earlobe.

"Being subject to your... whims, or whatever." The word fades into a gasp as he kisses my throat, hard then tickling.

"This is a business plan, Cleo." He kisses my chin and finds my lips, his low words blowing warm into my mouth. "I won't be living here in Chattahoochee for much longer," he breathes. "I want to get you settled before I leave."

He drags his lips over my cheeks, my nose, my brow, until my stomach is somewhere below my knees.

"How do you know... I plan to stay?" I ask him as he strokes the skin above my shirt collar. My voice quakes so much, it sounds almost like a sob.

"Do you?" While his eyes burn into mine, his hands smooth my hair back firmly off my forehead, a soothing motion one might use to calm a child.

"I haven't decided yet."

"Would you deal long-term, Cleo? Would you run dealers? Or do you just want something temporary? Something easy?"

The word 'easy' makes my neck flush. He snakes an arm around me, pulling me against his warm, hard chest as his hand delves between my legs. He flattens his palm against the inside of my thigh and presses, light but firm, until my legs swing open.

"I don't know," I whisper.

"The pay is good," he murmurs to my hair. "The three weeks you're at my place, I'll make it twelve K." His mouth covers mine, and he kisses me so hard and well, it makes me dizzy.

"What?" I break away. My heart is racing. "Why?"

His hands frame my face. "That's thirty-six thousand dollars, Cleo. Deal to your regulars, and sleep in my windowed room."

One hand slides down to stroke my neck, his fingers dragging lightly over flaming skin. I can feel his forehead brush my cheek as he runs his lips along my jaw.

He breathes, "You are beautiful... you make me want..."

His lips trail down my throat, tickling. When he nears the indention of my collar bone, I feel the soft heat of his tongue and mouth. He moves slowly... softly... taking great care as he sucks my throat—increasing the force until my skin feels like it's bruising and my body like a rope about to snap.

His arm snakes underneath my shawl, and I feel the weight of his wide palm spread over my thigh. His fingers burn through the cotton of my leggings, then drift to the crease between my legs.

I grip his shoulder. "Kellan..."

I clench my teeth as he settles his fingertips on me, tracing my most tender place as if he's learning braille.

His mouth sucks toward the collar of my shirt.

I grip the solid muscle of his shoulder. "I—I can't."

His thumb strokes the line of my lips. His fingers part them; he's working his way inside, teasing against the fabric of my leggings.

With the hand still between my legs, he wraps his other arm around me and he pulls me onto his lap. The arm that's not across my belly, reaching between my legs, is around my chest, kneading my breast. His hard length presses against my backside.

The cotton of my leggings is wet and pliant. The pressure of his fingers is just right, making me lift my hips. I swallow back a moan.

"Kellan... I *can't*—" If I do this with him, I'll be snared. I can tell already, from the way I feel about him. He's a dangerous temptation, in so many ways. I don't need that. Don't want that, I try to tell myself.

"Tell me 'no,' Cleo."

He rocks himself against me, then peels down the waist of my leggings so he can reach inside. His palm brushes my mound as his fingers find their mark. He strokes down toward my center. His finger smears my slickness, making me quiver and pant.

"It's okay..." he rumbles. "Focus on my fingers."

He spreads my lips and glides down through my moisture... skating. Then he's dipping down and curving. His fingertip is pushing into me. He adds another, shoves them deep.

I groan and buck against him.

"That's right."

He shifts his hips, so his huge cock pushes harder against my ass.

"Cleo... You're so warm inside... so tight." His fingers wriggle deeper. I let my legs fall open. I can't help it. He pushes even deeper as he whispers filth into my ear and glides his thumb over my clit. My body catches fire.

I feel the outline of him pressed against my ass: the long, thick shaft; the plump, round head.

I feel his fingers curl inside me.

"Ahhhhh." I don't mean to make a sound, but a moan spills out, turning the air around us into honey.

"You like getting finger-fucked," he growls. "You love it."

His thumb glides up and down my slit, then rolls around my swollen clit. I rock my hips, pushing my ass against his hardness.

"What if I rub a little faster... here?" His thumb drags, heavy and slick, over my swollen nub. "What if I quit teasing you," his low voice whispers, "and try something like this?"

He bends his wrist a little, and I can feel another finger push inside. "I can feel how much I'm stretching you," he whispers in my ear.

"*Oh.*" He's right. I'm full. *So* full. I feel both paralyzed and electrified. Like I'm gripping a live wire.

He pumps his fingers, shoving them in, then dragging them slowly out. I arch my back. "Oh God, please..."

His thumb, encircling my clit, is deft and slick. I rock mindlessly against him.

"So full..."

He pulls his fingers almost out, the tips of them only just inside... teasing. I clench, wanting him deeper.

"Say my name," he orders.

"Kellan," I pant.

All three fingers thrust at once. My pleasure squirts against his expert hand.

"Deeper." My voice cracks.

He slides out a little. Strokes back in.

His thumb is playing in my moisture, painting my clit. My throbbing clit.

His fingers stroke against my walls, making me dizzy.

"You want my cock inside you. You can't take much more. You're so tight, Cleo. So greedy. Look how fat this clit is. Your cunt is so tight around my fingers, I can barely move them."

He demonstrates, and I groan and arch my back. I'm clutching his arm. Wrapping my feet around his calves. I throw my head back, panting.

"I love you like this. So helpless. I bet you would do anything to keep my fingers inside you. Would you call me Master?"

My mind struggles to think beyond the pleasure in between my legs.

"Call me Master, Cleo."

I clutch his hand. I'm rocking against him, desperate to feel his fingers deeper. He's right: I'm so needy I'm about to scream.

He pulls one finger out. His thumb, stroking my clit, freezes in place. He pulls out a second finger, and I bark out, "Master!"

"That's right."

I'm aware of the pressure of his length against my backside. He draws his third finger out and I whimper. He huffs, a smoky sound, and eases me down to the floor.

I'm on my knees, my shawl hanging around me, my leggings pushed down past my hips. I feel him join me on the carpet. His chest brushes my shoulders. His arms wrap around me and his fingers trace the band of my leggings. Goosebumps cover my back.

His fingers sweep back into my leggings; he peels them down further. He pauses when he gets them to my knees, and his fingertips dance over my ass. His dick is a velvet sword, brandished against my backside as he pulls my boots off, then slides the leggings off my feet. I hear a whoosh as he tosses them behind us.

His hands grasp my shoulders. "Get down on your hands and knees and show me that ass."

He reaches between my thighs, stroking through my wetness as I hear a rip, and then a snap of latex.

I press my palms against the carpet and thrust my ass into the air. I no longer remember why I thought this was a bad idea. I'm so wet, I'm gushing on his fingers. He pushes two of them inside me and then starts to pump, delicious pressure given and removed at his will.

My clit throbs with my heartbeat, and he strokes it sometimes, gliding mercilessly over me while he rubs his huge, condom-sheathed cock against my ass. I center on how stiff and long he is, the head of him rubbing up and down my crack.

He draws his fingers from my folds, then plays at my clit with practiced grace. I sag down on my elbows as my knees tremble.

"That's right," he murmurs, rubbing his length along my ass. "Open those legs for me."

His voice is so smooth. Hypnotizing. I obey him frantically, spreading my legs a little more. He hooks two thick fingers into my pussy, finding my G-spot and rubbing slowly.

"Kellan..."

His fingers writhe inside me, moving all at once in slightly different directions. With the small part of my brain that isn't drugged numb by the writhing of his hand, I can feel pressure against my asshole.

"God!"

He rubs his thumb in a warm, wet circle, making my muddled mind race with want. With fear.

"Relax," he purrs. "You're going to like this."

And then, at the same time the pressure gives and his thumb invades my virgin hole, he stuffs his big, thick dick into my cunt.

Stars explode behind my eyes.

I slide down to the floor.

He twines an arm around my hips, pinning me against him as he thrusts so hard and deep my eyes roll back into my head—then drags out slowly, inch by hard, thick inch, then punches in. I screech, because I'm not sure I can take him... but I am. Thrust in—my toes curl—slow draw out. I clench around the head of him.

"More," I whimper.

"Told you." The words are warm and husky on my nape.

He thrusts again—and my legs quiver. I've never felt so full: as if I'm stretched around him. He's so deep... When he moves in and out, my body melts around him.

"Oh my God..."

"You're tight," he rasps. "You're like a fucking... virgin." And it kills me, how his voice shakes on the word.

I clench around him and he moans. He pushes deeper, freezing there for a long moment. I feel him trembling behind me—feel him take a deep, slow breath—and then he drags his cock back out and slams in hard.

I gasp, he groans—a symphony of sin.

The arm that's holding me against him tightens and he starts to fuck like a machine. His cock is a piston, pumping in and out with so much grace and force my body can't withstand it. I'd be in a puddle on the carpet were he not holding me against him.

I can feel myself shaking... sweating; hear my own moans rise up in the room. They mingle with his loud breathing, the moans he makes when I clamp down around him.

His finger, buried in my backside, jerks with every thrust. Finally accustomed to his length and girth, I'm hungry for him: clamping as he draws out, pushing back against him as he plunges in. It's never been like this...

"You're... a fucking... slut," he groans. "Tight cunt... Cleo. Goddamn... ah, *Cleo...*"

"Fuck me," I whisper.

"Yes... oh *fuck.*"

My palms graze the carpet as I sag forward. The arm around my hips tightens, his hand gripping my hipbone. His cock batters me... and it's incredible; it's merciless; it's terrible. I'm getting sensitive—so sensitive. I can feel my clit throbbing... my pussy roaring as he uses it so hard tears pop into my eyes.

Somewhere far away, I hear his low breaths turn to mostly groans... I feel him strain against his pleasure: sweating, shaking. He shoves his thumb deeper and pounds so hard and fast I feel a drop of sweat land on my back. I try to clamp my thighs around him... anything. Fuck—anything to get him... just a little deeper.

"Fuck!"

He's so hard now... I gasp each time he fills me up, momentum building like an ocean wave... I want him deeper... need him deeper. I push back against him, and the world goes white and hot. I'm almost there... my clit is pounding like its own heartbeat.

His cock is like a punch..."I want it..."

"Yes... fuck. Ohh God." He pounds so hard I fumble forward and his hand on my hip slides down to my thigh.

He snarls and grabs me back against him, in and out... another in... he shoves so hard I feel my eyes roll back.

And then I feel him twitch inside me. It's the most erotic thing I've ever felt: the way his cock pulses, then swells as he comes, panting and clutching my hip.

"Oh God." His voice is hoarse: delicious.

I come in the rush of a tsunami overtaking islands.

As I pulse around him, I feel his thighs tremble. "Oh *fuck...*"

His chest pumps against my backside, and then his forehead drops down to my back. He's shaking hard—his legs, his hips. He's like an animal, spent and ravaged by adrenaline. His forehead nuzzles me, digging into my back in time with his ragged breaths. And I'm surprised to find: I love it. That I did this to him. That I made him as crazy as he made me.

The feeling spreads through me like melting butter. I feel warm and sleepy. Kind of—no, not *kind of*—GOOD.

My head begins to whirl... the room is tilting. I can't breathe. I feel the weight of him move off me and I feel him sliding out.

He says, "fuck." He sounds surprised, I think as I blink wet eyelashes in the dark.

He clears his throat, and when he speaks, his voice sounds stronger than I thought it would. "Press down against me, Cleo." I'm so dazed, at first I'm not sure what he means. "My finger. Bear down against it." I do what he asks, and seconds later, I am startlingly empty.

I can hear him rustling behind me. I push up on my elbows, turn myself around, toward the little bench... but I can't seem to move. I lie there on the carpet like a turtle in its shell. My heart is beating way too hard. My eyes cast up, I clutch my shawl around myself. I can see the outline of his body, darker than the dark. He's bending down, combing the floor—for his clothes? Mine?

I imagine Kellan pulling my leggings back over my feet... tugging them up my calves. The way his long-lashed eyes would crinkle slightly as he stretched the fabric over my thighs, the way his lips would curve into that perfect, cocky smile. The smile morphs: gentler. His hands are warm and kind. As if he wants me, more than just my body.

I'm insane. Obviously, he's driven me insane with sex. I mean... my God above, his dick is something else. I feel deflowered. My lips curl into a mad little smile. I shake my head. I just got my brains fucked out. By Kellan Walsh. I blink at his moving form and wonder *who the fuck is he?* Why did I react this way?

The sex was just intense. That's what I tell myself as I get to my feet. My cheeks and neck are hot, my body is unsteady, but the sex we had was so intense, of course I would react differently. I've been with other guys. Kellan's more intense. It's messing with my head.

I step over to the wall beside the door and drag my palm along it, feeling for a light switch. When the room lights up, I draw my first deep breath since being pulled atop his lap.

See? I'm totally good now. When I turn around, things will be just the way they were while we were studying. Just business. Okay—maybe some occasional heart-thumping... but definitely nothing serious. These squishy-wishy feelings I've been having in the last few minutes: they'll be gone. Because I don't even know him. And what I do know, I don't like. There's no reason I should feel drawn to him in any way.

I stand there facing the wall, breathing slowly, and allow myself to admit that I've been lonely. Really lonely. The kind of lonely that always feels like after Olive died, when Mom and Grans were never home and I would find Mary Claire standing in the street "on accident," and I would curl up in my bed at night and pray for someone to come take me to another house. Any time life gets quiet, the image of that sharpens in my memory. I start needing things I can't get. Things I think maybe no one ever gets. Things that don't have names.

So maybe I've been a little like that lately.

So his hands on me felt good. No big deal.

Deep breath... blow it out my nose... five, four, three, two, one...

I turn slowly and it's almost a shock to see him there. My nerves spark as I look him over: Kellan in his unzipped slacks. He's freaking beautiful. And perfect. Those wide shoulders, and his heavy chest—that look is one I love. The way his abs are dusted with gold-brown hair, trailing down...

I jerk my eyes up to his face and find his mouth curved into a gentle, sideways smile. His eyes seem to twinkle. Is that a smug look? Happy? His smile widens and I realize that it's both. He's pleased with himself, and he looks also pleased with me. *I had you, and I liked you. Yeah, you.* That's what his face says.

My leggings are draped around one of his forearms; there's a tissue in his hand. He steps to me. I tell myself to look down at my feet, but my eyes look to his eyes. Low-lidded. He looks satiated. His hand, clutching the tissue, raises.

"I would have cleaned you up." He trails the tissue along my chin, the motion soft and teasing. And he smirks. It's... intimate, that smirk. As if he knows me.

"I'll take care of you while you're with me. You'll like it," he says. He drops a light kiss on my forehead, and I take a step back.

"When I'm with you, my ass." I hold my hands out, as if his tissue will hurt me. "I'm not going with you! I'm not going to your house. I can't do this. This." I wave wildly at the room, then snatch my leggings from his arm. "I'm not a crazy person, Kellan Walsh, you make me feel crazy!"

When my eyes return to his face, I'm surprised to find he looks thoughtful—almost relaxed; the bastard. "You're a person who likes pleasure," he says, reaching for my shoulder. I step back, though it doesn't get his eyes off mine. "What's so crazy about that?"

I blink at him, because it's too hard to explain. "I know guys like you," I stammer. Guys like Kellan Walsh are bad for girls like me. It's a cliché, even. "Doing this in here—" having wild sex in the library—"it's not my thing. I'm not that kind of girl. I know you've been with tons of them. You've got the wrong girl, Kellan."

He chuckles, tilting his head a little to one side. He folds his arms. "Oh, Cleo. You have no idea what kind of girl I like. You are my kind of girl. And you know what I think?" His sea blue eyes look through me. "I think you're surprised how much you liked what we just did."

It's true. There is nothing I can say to deny that, and I'm too strung out to lie. I shake my head. "I told you, I don't like surprises."

"I thought surprises were okay as long as they're good," he says. His face is hung between emotions, totally unreadable to me. So I'm honest. I turn slightly away and yank my leggings on as I say, "Maybe they aren't. Maybe they're never okay."

I turn back around to face him just as his face tightens, unreadable to gravely serious. "Someone hurt you," he says, low. "Tell me who. Did you lose someone, Cleo?"

"What are you talking about?" My voice rises, then cracks.

He blinks, and stares right through me. Right down to my bones. "It was a surprise, wasn't it? Was it your dad?"

My throat knots as my pulse goes haywire. "How... do you know that?"

"The poem in the painting." His eyes blink again. "That Plath poem. A Post It note from 'Mom' was in your textbook, so I know she's still around." His gaze pulls at mine as his lips fold down, apologetic now, remorseful. "It was just a guess."

Uncanny. I push the thought away and focus on his chest. His stupid, gorgeous chest. "I don't like you guessing."

"Why not?"

"I don't like you."

He steps closer to me, moving cautiously, as if he knows I'm a flight risk. "I don't think that's true." He wraps an arm around my back and spreads his hand over my shoulder blade. He brings me gently against him, so my breasts press against his warm, hard abs, and then—before I can move away—he smooths his thumb along my jaw, tipping my head up. His mouth finds mine. He kisses me so gently I drift toward the ceiling. I grab onto him, his elbow, and pull away panting.

His thumb brushes my lips. "Three weeks, Cleo." His eyes burn. "Three weeks you're mine. We'll start tomorrow."

I whirl away from him and push through the door, spin back around to grab my bag. He stands there, fastening his pants, although his eyes are stuck to mine. My mouth flails as I throw my bag over my shoulder; tell him "no" again. But I can't breathe. I've got no moves, no words—but I can feel his eyes on my back as I flee.

I jog the whole way to the Tri Gam house, pulling all my leg muscles and making my chest over-tight. When I reach the top of the stairs, I find Milasy holding the brick.

TEN

Kellan

THE BREEZINESS OF THE afternoon is gone. The night is heavy and still. It's neither cold nor hot, but tension warms me as I stand on the balcony outside the windowed room, watching the treetops as they sway.

All I can think about is Cleo.

Tomorrow, I will bring her here.

It hasn't been like this before. Not the urgency. Everything is different now. I am different now.

Cleo is a relapse. Bringing Cleo here is letting go. No more logic. No more restraint. Finished. The word swells to fill my head. I let it have me—giving myself over as I shut my eyes and touch the cement railing.

Moments later, the phone rings. I pull it from my pocket and blink at the name I knew would flash across my screen: *PACE.*

I never answer on the first ring, even though I always know when he'll be calling. I want Pace to feel that I am difficult to contact—always one ring out of reach. It's important: the control. Not just because I enjoy control, but because Pace is so closely aligned with Robert.

I bring the phone to my ear and let the static fill my head while I wait for him to speak.

"Kellan?"

"Pace."

An ocean breeze whips over his phone's receiver, muffling his question: "How's it going, man?"

I let my gaze fall through the pines, landing on the gushing river below. It's narrow here—not even the width of a tennis court—so the water is fast-moving.

Pace gets my point and clears his throat. "Got some teddy bears coming your way. Double nickel and penny. You ready for 'em?"

"Always."

"They're good bears." He pauses, as if thinking. As if we haven't had this conversation thirty times before. He adds, "Made in America."

I roll my eyes. Pace and his love of talking in code. I can only assume that 'Made in America' means the weed he's bringing me from California is higher quality than what he usually sends.

"Sounds good. I'll be ready."

This is where I'd choose to end the conversation, but my cousin never can just let things be. Pace is an awkward motherfucker. Coming up on fifty, he's a beach bum with nothing to his name except a lot of good intentions. I like Pace well enough—as kids, we called him Uncle Pace—but these phone chats can get tedious.

"You doing okay?" he asks after a silence.

I shut my eyes. "Fine." The word is sharp.

"Really?" he asks.

Fucking Pace.

"Just checking, dude," he says defensively. "Robert has been sniffing my ass crack, wanting to know if you've decided anything."

"I don't want to talk about this, Pace."

"I know, but—"

"Fuck him," I growl.

"You just... you can't say that, man. Robert is—"

"Who do you work with, him or me?"

It's a simple question with a complex answer. I'm not being fair to Pace. Not that I really give a fuck. He's not being fair to me, either.

I hear him breathing. Biding time as he tries to figure out how to broach forbidden subjects. I hear the phone brush the scruff of his beard, followed by his low voice saying, "Whitney called him. She said she hasn't been able to get up with you."

Whitney. Of course.

My fingers rearrange themselves around my phone. "I haven't noticed any missed calls from her," I lie. Whitney has been calling weekly for three months.

"You've got everyone all stirred up," Pace says in his low-but-nasally voice. "Man, I'm worried too. Don't get all butt hurt, but we all have the same horse in the race. We're a motherfucking family." In a low voice, he says: "No one wants to see you wind up like Lyon."

The mention of my brother makes my eyeballs ache. Pressure builds inside my head. I suck a deep breath back and clutch the phone. "Don't go there, Pace. *Ever.* You have a problem with Robert, deal with it. He's your burden—not mine."

I hear a shuffling sound: Pace's flip-flops on that little deck that hangs over the beach. He puffs some smoke out; I can hear his breath. "I just want to help you, man."

"You can't, so stop trying."

I want to punch him in the teeth. I want to roar at him. I can't believe he mentioned Ly. Instead, I say, "Till one-one, then."

The shipment will arrive at the old toy warehouse on Fifty-First Street on the eleventh of September. That's what he meant by "teddy bears" and his made-up drug trafficking code, "double nickel and a penny," as code for the eleventh.

"Next week," he says finally. He sounds defeated.

I still feel enraged.

I slide the phone into my pocket and stalk down to the basement. I tear into the punching bag that dangles from the ceiling, and imagine that it's Pace's pug-dog face. It turns into my father's face, and then Ly's. Which is almost indistinguishable from mine.

I'm tired of fighting. I'm so tired of fighting me.

I wait until the darkest part of night to go to Nessa's house.

Cleo

September 9, 2014

R~

Okay. Deep breath. So... I did something I probably shouldn't have done. Please don't be too mad at me.

It was stupid. It was a breach of trust. I know. But I was desperate. After all that time, you just stopped writing me, and I was worried. At this point, I'm pretty sure this letter is irrelevant completely, or you really are an icy cold stunna, in which case you don't care that I'm worried past the point of logic. (I'm not sure which scenario I'd prefer... probably the 'stunna' option).

But OKAY. I placed this stupid call to BTM and said you'd told me you would be out of the country for a few months. I said I had been writing you through them, but I didn't think my letters had been reaching you.

"What address do you have for him?" I asked them. "Is it in America or England? Because I think you're sending my letters to the wrong place."

That was the ruse: That I at least knew what country you were in, and they didn't.

The girl on the phone seemed young, almost as young as me, and I tried to sound really casual and friendly so she'd tell me the address she had for you.

"Who?" she said. She was clearly confused.

I said, "Robert. The person I've been writing to? How can you not know his name?"

I was sort of a bitch, and she totally fell for it.

She was all like, "Oh yeah, right. Robert... D. Yep, that's your guy."

She asked for my address and said, "I'm not sure I can do this," and I was all like, "Trust me, you can. C'mon, Lainey," (that was her name) "this isn't the secret service!"

I laughed like a phony bitch, and today I got a print-out with your information on it.

Robert D. The last address she had on you was a P.O. Box in Alabama. Are you KIDDING me?

You live in Alabama, and I haven't met you yet?!

Please tell me you just think I'm annoying. That's okay with me. Tell me now that you've grown out of our correspondence. Maybe you're engaged, or with the Peace Corps. The Marines. That would be so hot. Everybody likes a sexy man in uniform, and I know you're a sexy man.

See? I'm flirting shamelessly.

Just reply to me.

Did you know my name is Autumn Cleopatra Whatley? What do you think? You know a fucking Cleopatra. C'mon and tell me that that isn't cool as hell.

Actually... tell me more than that. I need your advice.

I've gotten into some trouble with the head of my sorority, and I'm unofficially kicked out. I'm going to keep on serving in my role as an officer, because the president wants to keep this hush-hush, but I'm not allowed to stay at the house or do anything fun.

I'm in trouble because I AM trouble. I regularly do something most people wouldn't approve of. Something I started doing for money (which I needed and also wanted) and have kept up because it's exciting, and adds some light to my boring little world.

And why does my world need light? Because I'm kind of gray at heart. I used to think I was exciting and original—nothing gray about me—but as I've gotten older I realize I'm just one of billions of people here on planet Earth, and I feel like a boat without an anchor.

I guess I'm kind of lonely. I can hear you gagging. First world problems, right? I know.

I've met a new guy, and he's going to help my first world problems go away. I can feel it. He leads this ridiculous double life. I'm about to live with him for three weeks, because we made this deal.

Would you like to write me there? Please?

I'll mark his address as the return, because I don't trust my sorority president not to go through all my mail now that she's mad at me.

I want to end this letter with something profound. Because I don't know where you are or what you're doing, and I feel the need to make some sense of things.

And you know what, Robert D., the wood chopper?

I don't have a thing to say. I don't know the first thing that's profound. My younger sister, who is deaf and goes to a deaf high school, is sleeping with her teaching assistant. My youngest sister's grave doesn't even have fake flowers by it, because people steal those. (I know, you warned me not to try that anyway, but my mom did, and they get stolen every time). I just broke up with a guy who used to call me "bebe" like for real (think baby but more like beh-beh) and believed me every time I faked it during sex.

TMI?

I know. That's my other middle name.

When I get upset, I get a little crazy. It can be a good thing and a bad thing, but it's more bad than good I guess.

Just so you know, I'm considering going to this little town's post office and figuring out where you really live. I need information. I'm in knots, and not the good kind.

-Shamelessly Sloth.

P.S. If I don't hear from you this time, I won't write again. I swear. And I'll probably only hunt you down if a series of terrible events *occurs in my life, and I need an anchor. Let's hope it doesn't come to that.*

Just reply, please!

ELEVEN

Kellan

I'M UP BEFORE THE SUN, pacing the balcony outside the glass-walled room. Gulping chilly air into my lungs.

My knuckles are bruised from my assault on the punching bag. My body screams for sleep, because I stood outside Nessa's window for three hours last night: a silent ghost, eviscerated. Now I'm drinking coffee—black and hot.

After a while outside, listening to the river slosh below, watching the pines tip in the breeze, I pull on some basketball shorts and go down to the basement. Fifty minutes on the treadmill, and it doesn't tame my hunger. I do my weight routine for longer than my usual, making sure that by the time I'm done, all my muscles are shredded. Then I make myself two waffles and choke down every bite.

I wander back up to the room: her room. I take a small, black remote out of the night stand drawer and press the button that makes the middle part of the indented ceiling retract. I take the canopy off the bed and lower the harness down to the mattress. I caress the ropes and smooth the sheets and rub my cock as I imagine Cleo lying right here, her wrists and ankles bound to the four ends of my X-bar, her wet, pink pussy ripe and ready for me.

When I realize I'm going to stay hard until I see her, I sink down on the edge of the mattress and stroke myself off, remembering the way her pussy clenched around my cock on the floor at the library.

When I'm done, I put the harness and spreader away and leave the room with my pulse hammering in my ears.

I need to shower and get dressed. Focus. I've got things to do this morning.

I shower quickly, and dress in khakis and a plaid button-up: the preppy shit that helps me blend in on campus. Then I walk into the bedroom I've been using, pluck a brass key off the duvet, lift up the Native American blanket that hangs on one wall of my room, and step to the mahogany door hidden behind it. I slide the key into its custom keyhole. My feet feel heavy as I turn the doorknob and step inside my sanctuary.

The room is small: no bigger than a half-bath. The wall I face as I step in is smooth and beige. Cashmere, the paint was called. Built-in bookshelves indent the tiny wall on my right. I had them built because I wanted to like something about this space, but I could never place a book on them.

The wall on my left is not a wall but stacked cabinets and a small counter. The four-foot slab of granite is black, with tiny veins of gold. The cabinets above the counter are dark and glossy, stretching to the ceiling. They contain my arsenal of secrets.

I run my hands over the cold granite. As always, I try not to look into the mirror, but my eyes betray me. As I meet my own gaze, the far-off echo of a hopeful spark strikes in my chest. I look into the eyes and wait to see the face transform. The mouth should smile—a dimpled smile. The eyes should crinkle. The face should relax, the way mine only ever does if I've had a good, long hit and held it in my lungs for several seconds.

If you never met him, you would never understand the way this face could look. My mouth tugs down into a deep and dimpled frown, and I wrench my gaze up to the cabinets.

I pull a door open.

"You fucking with me, Drake?"

"No sir."

"Well... fuck. I can't believe that. I just can't believe that you... You're sure? You sure you're sure? You got more than one person telling you this, and it's not a mistake? It's not your—being paranoid because of... ?"

I shake my head. "I'm sure, coach."

"I'm gonna keep this to myself. I want to see you both next fall."

I can hear the words, echoing off lockers. I don't know why my mind chose to regurgitate them now.

I shake my head.

My gaze rises to my right hand, and I use it to pull the first canister out. I set it on the countertop and get a second, third, and fourth.

I sweep my eyes over the array. The things inside this cabinet are as essential as they are horrible.

I take one of them in my hand and feel the smooth, slick plastic under my fingers. I take the top off and empty its contents onto the granite.

I sift through them. They whisper as I push them around. There are guidelines for this, but I always tweak them. Fuck the rules. Where I am, they don't apply.

I gather the ones I need into a pile, then put the cap back on. I store the container back inside the cabinet and repeat the process eleven more times.

Then I close the cabinet doors, leaving most of their contents untouched. Those things I will need later, if it gets that far.

Three more minutes in the small room, one long gulp of soothing water and a splash on my hot face, and I'm back in my bedroom.

I rub a hand through my hair, run my fingers over my brows, where want of sleep already tugs at me. Then I hurry down the stairs.

I've got an eighth of an ounce in a vacuum-sealed bag under the sink. I toss that into my messenger bag, grab the books and notebooks I need, and let a deep breath out as I shut the door behind me.

Next time I'm here, I won't be alone. If I play my cards right, I might never be alone again.

Three sharp raps jerk me out of sleep. I shoot up, slamming my forehead against the underside of the study table that dominates my little library room.

It's the same room I was in with Kellan Walsh, so the first thing I think about after my eyes focus on the green cinderblock wall and my palms flatten out on the rough, industrial carpet, is the feeling of him driving into me. For a heart-racing second, I'm immobilized. Lust is the brightest color mixing on my mind's easel.

Fear becomes brighter. On the other side of the door, I envision furious police, a snarling drug dog, my mother's devastated face, a gossipy library monitor who somehow saw Kellan and me fucking like animals on a hidden camera...

I scramble out from under the table and straighten with a wince. I'm dizzier than a kid at a carnival, and my mouth is painfully dry. My hands shake as I try to right my twisted leggings, tug down my rumpled Smuffins shirt, and straighten the big, black shawl that's doubled as my blanket. I'm not wearing a bra.

I grit my teeth as The Man knocks again. "Just a second, please!"

My Vera Bradley overnight bag sits, unzipped and barfing up my favorite outfits, on the padded bench where Kellan had me in his lap last night. Beside it is my book bag, crammed with my laptop, day planner, and text books. I wrangle with the overnight bag until it's zipped, tug the shawl away from my body with a prayer that my nipples aren't hard, and drag my tangled hair into the rubber band around my wrist. I take a shallow breath and pull the door open.

When I see Kellan, my stomach somersaults. He's wearing a blue and white gingham button-up with a pair of straight-front khakis that look like they were made for his trim hips and long, strong legs. His blond hair looks a little messy and a lot soft. His stubble-shadowed jaw and the gorgeous planes of his face remind me why he has his way with so many girls.

But it's his eyes that drop an anchor to my soul. Something about the way they fix on my face. There's concern there, born not of alarm but interest. It makes his gaze soft.

For an intoxicating moment, I wonder what it would be like to be cared for by him. But that fades as I remind myself I'm being unrealistic. Fantasizing. I have the desire to be cared for in this silly, over-the-top, romance novel sort of way... But the guy standing in front of me wants a sex deal. If there's a real person somewhere underneath his sharp clothes and Spartan body, I'll never know it.

He makes my panties wet and—yes—he piques my curiosity, but so what?

I break my gaze away from his and cast it down to the grease-stained paper bag he's holding. Is that for me?

He doesn't notice me eyeing the bag. He's too busy noticing my situation. His eyes trail up and down my sore body, checking me out. When they meet mine, they are wide with incredulity.

"You slept here."

I clamp my teeth down on my lip and let my eyes wander to his shoes. What do I say to him?

"What happened?"

I look from his shoes to my socked feet. There's a hole above my right foot's pinkie toe. "Milasy... found the brick."

In the thick silence that follows, I focus on the motion of my ribcage, moving much more gently than my frenzied mind.

When I get the nerve to look back up, I find his fingers curled around the door frame. "Did you tell her where you got it?"

"No. Of course not." I wrap my arms around myself. "I'd never do that."

His shoulders slacken. His face relaxes as he steps toward me. I take a step back into the room, allowing him to fill it up. His husky voice says, "That's good, Cleo."

He's so wide, so tall—and I can smell him. Shaving cream and something earthy; spicy; rich; the way I imagine "warm" should smell. The back of his hand comes up to brush my cheek. "You slept on the floor." I feel myself flush as his fingers trace the little pock marks the carpet made on my cheek.

"Cleo," he says, low and taut. His eyes press mine. "You should have called."

I draw my face away from his hand. Not just because his fingers are making me dizzy, but because there's something in the tenor of his voice that strikes a painful chord inside my chest. "You're not my superhero, Kellan."

He frowns. "You don't think I would have helped?"

"You already know how I feel about you. You're a predator, remember? An opportunist. Clearly." I turn around and lift my book bag off the bench. "I don't know what to do now," I say, aiming to fill silence. "I won't be able to work with you if people know I deal. I'll have to find a—"

"Milasy's going to rat?"

"Well, no." I adjust the book bag's straps and shake my head. "She said she'd tell people something came up with me. Some other obligation that's keeping me away from the sorority. I can go to chapter meetings and stuff, but nothing fun. And I had to give her some of my stuff. Like, purses and things. One of my favorite pairs of boots."

His mouth opens. "She took your things?"

I nod.

Kellan's jaw clenches. As quickly as I see his anger, he extinguishes it. "That's bullshit." Well, most of it. "I can help you get your things back. And I think Milasy will keep it to herself."

"Why?"

He shrugs.

"She said if I get caught by anyone else—she mentioned you specifically," I say with a roll of my eyes, "then I'd be kicked out of Tri Gam. She even checked the records that I kept as treasurer. It's so insulting. I did it on my own. I started my business from nothing. I didn't steal a bunch of rich girls' money."

I raise my hand to cover my mouth, because seriously, I never planned to say all that to him. I cover my whole face with my hand, only lowering it when I hear him laughing softly. "Righteous indignation." He reaches out and cups my cheek. "You know your face gets red."

I pull away from his warm touch and lean my butt against the little table. "This whole thing is such a mess. I feel like I can't deal at all since she knows... and is mad and stuff. But I don't know what I'll do without the income. I make a lot of cracks about 'I need a Coach bag' and stuff like that, but the truth is I'm not even sure that I could stay here at CC without that money. I get literally nothing from home. My mom and grandmother both think I live off grants. My plan for years has been to have a little nest egg for Mary Claire—for my little sis—*before* she goes to college, so she doesn't have to—"

Kellan shakes his head dismissively. "Don't worry, Cleo. I'll take care of Milasy."

"How?"

He grabs my overnight bag off the bench, pulls my book bag off my back, and shoulders them both. He pushes the door open. "Let's get out of here, okay?"

I'm not sure if that means he doesn't want to talk here or he doesn't plan to tell me about Milasy, but I have the strange thought, as we walk through a common area, that Milasy finding the brick has altered the course of my life. I'm not sure how much yet, but without a doubt, it has.

If I'd been sleeping in my room at the house this morning, I wouldn't have let Kellan in. Not because I don't want him, but because deep down, I know he's only using me. For my body, for my business—for both? It doesn't matter. He doesn't care about me. I'm just a means to an end.

And I don't know if I can handle knowing that when his soft eyes are on me.

TWELVE

I'VE THOUGHT ABOUT IT—Kellan's offer. Which may not even be on the table anymore. But if it is... it's probably too much money to pass up.

Money isn't everything, of course, but it's a lot. If money's never been scarce—if you've never helped your mom search every crevice of everything in the house for change to put gas in her '91 Accord—maybe you wouldn't understand, but when you have no means, you have no choices. Even something as simple as choosing the high-quality deodorant at the grocery store was revolutionary for me after I first started dealing. Being able to grab a snack I want at a gas station, or buy one notebook for each of my school subjects, rather than a five-subject spiral notebook that would have to work for all my classes.

You know how they say 'it's the little things?' It *so* is. Like eating cheese. Not the boring, WIC-approved kind, but the good stuff: asiago, halloumi, Havarti. When you have one pair of shoes and it rains, guess what? They start to stink, because you have to wear them the next day, and the next day, and the next. Life goes on, but I don't like stinky shoes. I like crackers. Do you know how expensive a box of Cheese-Its is? Plus or minus four dollars. What about jeans? I like jeans that fit my curves in all the right ways; not the cheap ones. I like painting on canvases that don't come from the discard pile behind Michael's. Almost all my art from high school is on ripped canvas.

But it's the little things that other people notice, too. They didn't see my mom working sixty hours a week to make rent on our little house, they only saw the second-hand clothes she bought me. They saw the perma-sweat-stained strap of my one and only bra when it peeked out of my shirt. They could see past my pathetic attempts to dress myself up with my one nice jacket I got for Christmas the year before, or the earrings that belonged to my great aunt.

I don't want to look second-rate.

I don't want to always be reaching.

I don't want to be a cashier, or a gas station clerk, or a mill worker. I'm so close to all my goals, I can't give up now. Even if I have to spend a couple weeks at Kellan's illicit river mansion, sticking my ass into the air for him.

It's not as if I'll mind *that.* Sharing my body with him can be done without too much heartache, I think, if I can manage to remember the limitations of our arrangement.

A strand of hair falls into my eyes, and I swipe it off my face. In doing so, I get a glimpse of Kellan, striding a half foot in front of me. He's got my backpack slung over one muscled shoulder and my overnight bag hanging from the other. I notice, as I pull ahead to walk beside him, that he's still holding the sack.

My stomach rumbles at the sight of those grease stains. "What's in there?" I ask.

He looks down, as if he's only just remembered he's carrying it. He gives me a small, lopsided smile—a smile that feels distracted, as if he's only peeking out at me from wherever he is inside his head. "You'll see."

He holds his free hand out, and I stare down at his forearm. The skin on the inside of his arm is smooth and pale, softness stretched over taut muscle.

I glance at his eyes. They're steely and blue. I keep waiting for them to start to seem less gorgeous—and I'm still waiting. He raises his brows disapprovingly, urging me with just that look to take his hand, and me being me, I fold after only a moment.

"Skittish," he murmurs, closing his fingers around mine.

"What?"

"You're skittish. Like a deer."

With a tug of my hand, he steers me to the right, toward a wall of bookshelves stretching from floor to ceiling.

I open my mouth to tell him I'm not a deer. I'm a sloth. It's my longstanding nick name, from back in middle school, when I was pudgy and took forever getting ready to go places, but I get the feeling he'd give me grief for it. Instead I tell him, "I'm not skittish. I'm suspicious."

"Don't be," he says.

We walk through an opening in the wall of books and toward one of the library's outer walls. Punched into it is a door I've never noticed before. We stop in front of it, and I look to Kellan, who is pressing some numbers into a keypad beside it. It opens with a soft click, and he ushers me into a tiny kitchen, with the same cinderblock walls as the rest of the library's rooms. These are painted mauve and adorned with half a dozen of those cheesy inspirational posters that always seem like jokes to me.

I inhale the lingering scent of peanut butter and bananas as Kellan releases my hand, shifts my bags down onto the floor, and steps over to the microwave. I admire his broad back as he sets the paper bag inside. My eyes roll from his shoulders to his ass. I don't want to stare, but I can't seem to help myself. I've seen him at soccer games a few times, and I always noticed his golden god looks, as well as his model-hot mug shot in the school paper... but up close and personal like this—damn. He's hot enough to take my breath away.

He punches a few buttons, then turns back around to me. I barely jerk my gaze away in time to avoid notice. He smirks a little, and I arch a cool eyebrow as my pulse skitters. "What? You have a sticker on your ass."

His lips curve into that radiant smile. "A sticker?"

I nod placidly. "Want me to get it off?"

His eyes dance. "Oh—I do."

"Okay, well turn around."

He turns around, and... there's no sticker, of course. When he asks to see it in a moment, I'll be empty-handed. Before I can stop myself, I draw my hand away, then slap his ass as hard as I can.

I hear him suck his breath in, and he whirls around, his face a riot of intensity. He catches both my wrists in one of his big hands and steers me to the brick wall with his hips. "Cleo." He sinks his teeth into my neck. He kisses me roughly down to my collar bone, and my body convulses in a shiver.

He bites me again near my throat, and I feel heat swell between my legs.

"I'm going to have to punish you for that," he murmurs to my neck. He raises my arms above my head and pushes my wrists into the wall.

I giggle softly. "Just getting the sticker off."

"I'm sure." He rocks his hips into mine, and his thickness juts against my lower belly. I swallow a moan, unwilling to give him that satisfaction. I clamp down on my lower lip so hard it stings.

"Tonight," he murmurs.

Then he releases my arms and turns back to the microwave. I'm thrilled to see his shoulders are heaving. I'm breathless and light-headed as I watch his back, trolling my gaze along his muscular arms as he pulls the bag out. So intently am I watching his body, I actually jump when the kitchen door opens and Laura Lancaster, the SGA secretary, breezes in.

"Kellan!" She smiles. Her perfume permeates the room as her eyes widen. "Kellan's *friend*." I've seen Laura around—she's a Phi Mu who always smells like she bathed in Coco Chanel—and I remember her being friendly. At this moment, she looks excited enough to launch herself into the stratosphere.

I look to Kellan for a clue to how to behave. He's leaning casually against the counter where the microwave sits, the hand that just bound both my wrists hanging loosely from his pants pocket. "Laura, this is Cleo." He waves at me. "Cleo, I think you probably know Laura." He tilts his head toward her.

I nod. "Hey, Laura."

"Hi." She gives me a warm smile and then she sniffs the air. "Something smells delish."

Kellan reaches into the bag and draws out the biggest croissant I've ever seen. It's fluffy and greasy, and it looks like it's been rolled in sand. Brown sugar, I realize as my mouth waters.

"Want one?" he asks Laura.

She shakes her head and smacks her curvy hip. "My next class is intermediate tennis. My ass does *so* not need a yummy. But thanks anyway."

"More for us." Kellan winks. "See ya later." He's flawlessly cool as he grabs my bags, then presses his hand against my lower back and guides me toward the door.

The scent of the buttery croissant makes my mouth water as we step out of the room, back into the bookshelf forest. "Is that cinnamon?" I sigh. "Oh God, I can smell the butter. Gimme!"

He rips off a piece, and we both stop walking as his fingers bring it to my mouth. Taking it from him is surprisingly erotic. Sweat pops out all over my body, so I make a big show of falling sideways, almost into a bookshelf, to distract from my reaction.

"Swoon! Oh holy God, this is the best shit I've ever put into my mouth. Where did it come from?"

His lips curve, into a smile or smirk; I can't tell which, but he's handsome as hell, and I'm alarmed to find that I'm pleased the smile or smirk is all for me.

"You've never been to the Fifth Street Bakery?" he asks as we start moving toward the side door of the library.

"I've heard of it," I say defensively.

We pass a long row of copy machines and printers, and now I know he's smirking. His blue eyes seem to twinkle at me. "You don't leave campus much, do you, Cleo?"

"I do sometimes." I wave my booted foot. "For pedicures and stuff like that."

His smirk turns into an amused little smile. Almost as soon as it plays across his lips, he presses them together, going serious in the span of half a second. His eyes are unreadable as he holds out his hand.

I feel lit up all over, like a light bulb. Despite the dynamic we started with—me, kicking him in the balls—now I'm writhing under his gaze. The last thing on earth I want is for him to know this, so I force myself to scoff as if he's lost his mind. "I'm supposed to hold your hand again?"

"It *is* the hand that feeds you, Cleo." Definitely a smirk this time.

"Pshhh. I can feed myself."

I snatch the bag from him and open it, finding four more butter-coated croissants inside, plus the other half of the one I already sampled. I take that one and shove it in my mouth, then grin at him around the flaky bread.

Kellan pushes a finger in between my lips, shoving the rest of it into my mouth. I squeeze my eyes shut, trying not to laugh.

"Good look for you—the foie gras." I open my eyes in time to see him smiling at me like we're old friends. The moment I smile back, he rubs his lips together, making his frown-dimples show; shutting it down.

Looks like I'm not the only one who's skittish.

THIRTEEN

I'M HYPER-AWARE OF HIS long strides as we move past the media center, toward a row of glass exit doors. He pushes one open, and I step into a little entryway corridor, lined with newspaper machines.

I toss my gaze back at him as I push the next door open, this one leading to the cement breezeway.

"Aren't you supposed to let me get that for you?" he asks.

I hold the door for him and fall in step beside him as we walk down the breezeway, toward the parking deck. All around the cement walkway, flowers, trees, and bushes sway in a gentle breeze.

"It's a shame that you're both bad and from not the South," I say. "I think if those two factors were removed, you could be a Southern gentleman."

Now it's his turn to laugh. "Cleo, Cleo..." He grabs my hand and folds his fingers around mine. "What makes me so bad?"

I look him over, hair to low-top boots. "Um, everything? I mean, sure you *look* like a rule-following golden boy, but that's clearly a ruse."

He runs his free hand through his hair and laughs, maybe self-consciously. "I look like everyone else here."

I shake my head as we walk into the gum-pocked stairwell that leads down into the deck. "That's where you're wrong. You dress like everyone else here, yeah. But unlike them you look perfect."

Ugh. I want to swallow "perfect" back down as soon as the word somersaults from my mouth. My eyes fly to his face, waiting for him to laugh at me or tease me. I'm surprised, because he looks... wounded. His mouth is soft and uncertain, curved downward just slightly. His brows are drawn down low over his eyes, which look darker than usual in the shadow of the stairwell.

"Perfect?" The corner of his mouth tugs up a little, and I'm positive: My 'perfect' comment made him sad. What the hell? I take a deep breath, trying to guess at *why*s, and trying to keep things casual, so he doesn't know I'm analyzing him.

"Yeah, Kell." I tighten my grip on his hand a little. "You're pretty. I assume that's not news to you."

"Cleo Whatley thinks I'm pretty?" We walk into the second level of the parking deck, and I can feel him regain his equilibrium as his fingers play with mine. "That's news."

"Yeah, right." I snort.

"You think your opinion doesn't matter to me?"

I hear a beeping sound, and a few cars ahead of us, his Escalade's lights flash. "I think you're a whore, so right, you probably don't care."

He walks me to the passenger's side, opening it for me while still shouldering my bags. I slide my fingers out of his, or try to. He catches them again and nuzzles my shoulder with his forehead, urging me back against the passenger's seat. I feel his chest brush mine, and then his lips are on mine, warm and soft.

"Cleo—even whores have feelings," he breathes against my cheek.

He pulls away just enough so I can see his smirk. He leans down to kiss me in between my brows, and then he's disentangling from me. I give him what I pray looks like a cool-headed, doubtful smirk of my own before climbing up into my seat. He shuts the door behind me, quickly deposits my bags in the back seat, then strides to the driver's side.

I watch him walking, and I can't help but admire the utility of his movements. He's so graceful.

Half the campus calls him the golden god, so at least it's not just me. And still—how embarrassing. I told him I thought he was perfect. I have a few heartbeats to wonder at his strange reaction before he opens the driver's door and slides in. He fills the space so thoroughly, I find myself shrinking in my seat. I wrap my hand around the top of the croissant bag in my lap.

He buckles his seat belt, then his eyes flick over me. "Buckle up for safety, Cleo."

"Right," I murmur. I pull the belt across my lap, feeling self-conscious as I snap it into place. What's wrong with me? I need to screw my head on straight.

Kellan shifts the car into reverse, and as he looks over his shoulder, his gaze flickers down to a to-go coffee cup between us.

"For you." His blue eyes find my own. "A café mocha."

My pulse picks up, ridiculously, and again I struggle to exude a calm, cool vibe. "Good call." I smile. "Chocolate is a win with me." I pick it up and take a long swallow as the car glides backward out of the space. "Damn." I exhale slowly. "There was whipped cream in here, wasn't there? It must have melted, but I can totally taste it."

His mouth curves a little, and I thump his muscular forearm. "Aren't you full of surprises?"

He doesn't reply, and I notice we're driving up the ramp instead of down.

"Where are we going?" I ask.

"Your car."

I rifle in the croissant bag as we drive out of the shadows and onto the top story of the deck. "You know where I'm parked? Wait a minute... how'd you find me here in the first place?"

"I went to the Tri Gam house, and one of the girls—Steph, I think—told me you weren't there. I checked around and saw your car here."

"Why were you looking for me?"

He brakes behind my Miata, and his eyes meet mine head-on. "Why do you think, Cleo?"

"I don't know," I whisper.

"Yes you do." His hand encases mine, just briefly, before releasing it. "Give me your keys and I'll get it out of your car." *It* being the brick.

I fish my keys out of my bag, refusing to meet his eyes as I hand them over.

"You got anything else in there? I'd like to leave your car here until later."

"Why?" I ask suspiciously.

"You worried I'm being shady?" He smirks.

"Yes."

"I'm not. At least not in a way that'll bother you."

I wonder what the hell that means as I hand him my keys. "Get the books out... and the canvases." For some reason, I don't like the idea of him looking at my art again. It feels too personal. Everything about this new arrangement does. Do I like it? Do I hate it? Do I have a choice? I can't tell. That worries me.

Kellan disappears inside my car, emerging a minute later with the laundry basket, my favorite three paintings, and a small mountain of paperbacks. He packs the items carefully into the rear seats, and I watch the ripple of his back and shoulders in the rear-view.

I must be insane, planning to spend any time at his place. I must be looking for trouble. I must want... I don't know. Bad things. Also, money. I roll my eyes at myself.

When he slides into the driver's seat, his lips are pulled into a teasing smile that makes my neck flush, only emphasizing the trouble that I'm in. "Don't tell me you've never heard of e-readers."

I square my shoulders and give a haughty little sniff as he starts driving. "E-books are good for reading in class or bed, but in every other scenario a paperback is superior."

His smile broadens. "Did I see Fifty Shades of Grey beside The Sound and the Fury?"

My lips twitch. I press them flat. "And if you did?"

"I'd say you're a... ?" He lifts my shawl up and frowns at the symbol on my shirt. "Smurfin?"

"Smuffin," I say primly, taking my shawl from his hand and smoothing it back down. He looks like he's about to tease me—

eyes mischievous, lips working themselves into a joke—and suddenly I feel a little too exposed. "Where are we going?" I ask before he gets a chance to say anything more.

"You'll see." He pulls onto one of the roads that cuts through central campus.

"I have a class in twenty minutes."

He strokes his fingertips over my knee, casual, as if he's been doing it for years. "I'll get you a note."

I work to breathe around the weight of his hand on my knee. "Why do I need a note?"

He slides his gaze to mine. "You don't want an unexcused absence."

Sighing, I move my knee out of his reach. Last night's showdown with Milasy was pretty draining, so maybe it would be good to skip. I shake my head at myself. "I probably look like I've been through the wringer. Maybe that's a good call."

He steers through downtown, keeping his gaze on the road. "You look perfect, Cleo. It's your eyes that give you away."

I rub my fingers over them. "My eyes look puffy?"

"Your eyes look tired."

I take a bite out of my croissant and try to work out why it bothers me—what he just said. I'm sure I *do* look tired. That shouldn't be news to me. Then I remember what he said before that. He said I look perfect. Somehow, in the moment, I missed that. But now it's slithering around my head, confusing me.

Or maybe I'm not confused. Maybe I just don't like it.

I shouldn't have said *he* looked perfect. He doesn't need to know I think that much of his looks. Looks aren't all that important anyway. It was just me being me, talking before thinking.

But why did he say it back to me? Was it intentional, or coincidence?

He pulls onto Main Street, and we pass the cute boutiques, wannabe coffee shops and so-so bars that make up Chattahoochee's little downtown. I wonder if he was flirting.

I think "no," mostly because there's no reason to flirt. It's been established that we aren't exactly peanut butter and honey personality-wise, but at this point, it's also pretty clear we want sexy times with each other.

Maybe I'm not even bothered that he said I look perfect. I think it's the *way* he said it. Yes. Like he meant it. It's the way he said my eyes look tired, too. As if he cares.

I can live with him, I guess. I can take the free housing he's offering; not just free housing, but housing I'm actually being paid to occupy. I can swallow my pride and pocket his money.

But I don't need lines crossed.

Because the truth is, I *do* think Kellan Walsh looks perfect—even as I know I shouldn't dwell on that. Because I'm in kind of a weird place right now, and he's got those eyes—that smile—that make me feel as if he really cares. Holding my hand... I shake my head. That has to stop.

From now on, I need to keep my mouth shut. Try to avoid talking to him. Try to avoid connecting.

"Cleo?"

I jump so high, I spill coffee on my shawl. I jerk my gaze to Kellan's. "Yes?"

"I asked you if Milasy's the only one who knows, who's not your client."

I glance around, trying to get my bearings, and find we're on the south east side of town. We pass a police precinct, and my stomach twists uncomfortably.

"Yeah, she is. I think she is. Actually—" I huff—"she probably told Steph." I rub my eyes, which really do feel puffy.

Kellan nods, and I chew the inside of my cheek. My gaze tugs to the mirror on my side of the car. I watch the police precinct shrink behind us. How weird that Kellan is a law-breaker. I can't seem to reconcile that with his day-to-day existence: SGA president; frat boy. Why masquerade like that? Doesn't it get tiring? I look over at him. With his beautiful, blank face pointed toward the road and one long-fingered hand draped around the wheel, he looks more politico than kingpin. I picture myself unbuttoning that dress shirt. I lick my lips and blow my breath out. "Have you ever had any trouble with the cops?"

He makes a right onto a bumpy county road that takes us out into the country. His mouth tightens fractionally. "They know the alias I use, but they don't know it's me. There've been a few close calls."

"What's your alias?"

He shakes his head.

"Aw, c'mon."

He slides his eyes from the road to mine. "Tonight."

"Tonight?"

"I'll whisper it between your legs."

My cheeks and neck burn. It takes effort to avoid squirming in my seat. He makes me so hot. So flustered. A thousand things line up to spill out of my mouth. I swallow hard and pick the most concrete one. "You still want me to help you deal?"

"I can handle Milasy, Cleo. Nothing will get out." He turns onto a highway that runs south of town.

"So... same offer?" I'm kind of surprised. Surprised and relieved as hell. I guess he can tell, because he lifts one eyebrow.

"You are what I want. And you haven't changed."

I grab a fistful of my shawl and squeeze it in my right hand. Why does he want me? Sex. But it isn't just for sex. It's business, too. He doesn't want me stealing any more of his clients. But I told him my supply has dried up. So... it can't be that. Right?

I look out the window, struggling to keep my questions off my face. This is just another reason not to warm up to him, not even a little. I don't trust him.

We're surrounded by verdant, green peanut fields; I imagine myself small, a child, running through them. I look down the red-dirt plow lines streaked between tufts of crop, trying to feel hypnotized by the subtle shifting of the lines as our road curves.

"Is it because I'm a pain in your ass?" I murmur.

"What?"

I move my gaze from the peanut fields to the winding road ahead of us. It's framed by tall pines. "Is that why you want me?" I ask. "Because... I'm not overly impressed with you—like everyone else is?"

I wonder at his face, but I refuse to look at it. I just sit there, acting self-contained: the kind of girl that kicks guys in the balls. I'm her, too, after all. She just tends to go away when he says certain things.

With my eyes on the thick trees, his voice comes as a shock. "I watched you for a while before I found you in the union that day."

This... is a surprise. A troubling surprise.

He must notice my tension, because he hastens to add, "I wasn't creeping on you. I was keeping track of the competition. To start with. But I liked you pretty quickly. I think it's... the way you moved. From class to class. I noticed that you stop a lot. You stop to look at things. I think you're forgetful," he says, his lips quirking, "because you pause a lot and kneel down and open up your bag to get things—like that glossy shit girls put on their lips. And you'll put it on right there. When you lean down, your hair falls in your eyes. You push it away, and it's hilarious because I can see as you bat it away that you're pissed off that it dared to get in your eyes in the first place.

"You'd throw your book bag back on, and sometimes you would run if you were late. One time I saw you smoke a cigarette. I don't know why you did it that day, but I could tell you were enjoying yourself, because you let your head hang back. You were standing under a tree—that willow, by the south quad pond. You sat under it and pulled your knees up, and I could see what you were thinking almost. You're what you seem to be, Cleo."

Unlike him.

I watch his shoulders rise and fall. He's going to say more. I realize I'm hungry for it. I wait, frozen, for another morsel—something to help me piece Kellan together. But he looks pensive. Like someone else just said all that, and now he's noticed, he closes his lips.

FOURTEEN

Kellan

I SAID TOO MUCH. I know it right away, because she clasps her hands together like she's praying, and she doesn't move at all.

Finally, when I've sat in silence for a few moments, she looks down at her lap and asks, "Where are we going, Kellan?"

I shouldn't have told her that I followed her. What the fuck was that about? Goddamn.

"I thought I'd show you a grow house. I have to go there anyway. And after that, we'll go to my place."

Her eyes shift over me, and then back to the road. "Okay."

But she's not sure. I can tell she isn't. Regret stings me, sharp and unexpected. "You think I'm an asshole."

Her gaze drags over me, and then flits away. "I think you're the wolf."

"I'm not the wolf." I squeeze the wheel. "Okay, maybe I am, but you're not a lamb, Cleo. You're a... dog."

Her eyes fly to mine, wide with her already familiar indignation. "I'm not a dog! No way. Did you really just say that?" She goes full-on girl and bats her lashes in prim fury. "That's an insult. Dogs are... loyal and comical, and sleepy. They chew on things and pee in public. Trust me, I am nothing like a dog."

I laugh, and turn left under a bent pecan tree, onto the dirt road that is Pecan Way. "Dogs are man's best friend, Cleo."

She shakes her head. "So I'm a sleepy, loyal, drooling, chewing, flea-ridden yard dog, and you're a wolf. And how is this better than me being a lamb?"

"You're almost just like me, Cleo. But you're the good version. You're the version people want to take home, and to bed." I give her what I hope is a devastating smile, and Cleo smirks back.

"I'm going to let this drop, Walsh, but it's not over. I'm not a dog. I can't stand drool or silent farts. To be completely honest, I'm really more a cat person. They groom themselves and stay out of the way. Loyalty—whatever that is? Cats give as good as they get."

As we bump over the red dirt road that streaks beneath a copse of pecan trees, I wonder why she thinks she should only give as good as she gets. After watching her from afar for so long—after trying so many labels on her, from scared to treacherous to clueless—I'm almost surprised to find that Cleo Whatley is a real person. She's nothing like I thought.

I remember her mouth around my cock and grit my teeth. I want to make it up to her. To take back all the observations I shared. I'm fucking weird sometimes—I know this. I shouldn't have said something so strange. Certainly not if I want her staying at my house.

I think again about the amount of money I agreed to pay her and have to rub my lips together to keep from laughing.

"You know that you have dimples when you frown, but not when you smile—right?"

"I've been told."

"That's kind of weird."

We pass a crooked green mailbox. There's an old farmhouse at the end of that driveway, with an even older farmer pulling weeds. I shrug. "I'm weird. Not scary weird." I look her in the eye. "I followed you to get an idea of how much you were dealing, Cleo. That's all."

She snorts. "Hashtag: were there any signs?"

My mouth curves up without permission. "You're different... than I thought."

"I hope that's a compliment."

"Mostly."

She scoffs.

We pass a few more mail boxes mounted on a giant piece of plywood, and I veer right at a "Y" in the road, following Pecan as it rolls onward, deeper into thick, oak-pine forest.

"How am I different than you thought?" she asks.

I can't help smirking. "More difficult."

"How?"

I shrug. "Just are." I realize I'm being more forthcoming with her than I've been with any girl in years. It's... inappropriate. A moment later, I'm relieved to see the pale blue mailbox to the right, followed a few feet later by a thin, dirt drive that curves into some trees.

"I'm a ninja," Cleo says as I turn.

I press my lips together, suppressing a bark of unexpected laughter. "What?"

"That groin kick is my least fancy move. I've got more where that came from." She sits up straighter and arches her brows at me. "In other words, don't try anything sketchy, unknown guy with whom I'm driving into the woods."

I rub my temples. "Would it help if you drove?"

She shrugs. "Probably."

I pull over on a red dirt shoulder, and she cuts her eyes at me. "You sure? Your car is worth like, more than my family's house."

Shit—could that be true? I've got no damn clue what to say about poverty, having never experienced it myself, so I shrug. "Just a bunch of glass and metal."

I watch her neck as she drives. I watch her shoulders. She seems tense. I smooth my hand over my pants and glance over at her, then I set my eyes back on the road. "There's a stray at my place. Black cat. A 'she,' I think."

I watch her delicate brows lift. "Oh yeah?"

"Mm-hmm."

She smiles at me, bright and unexpected. "Can I adopt her?"

"She's kind of mangy. She might be sick."

Cleo shrugs. “I don’t care. I’ll take her to the vet and make her better.”

“If we can get her.”

“I think we can,” she says.

I tuck my thumb inside my fingers. “Do you consider yourself an optimist, Cleo?”

“I don’t know,” she says, braking a little as we reach a fissure in the dirt road. “People say glass half empty, glass half full like it’s so easy to just pick one. I think things are more complicated. My full might be different from yours. Or maybe all the glass is, is a glass.”

“You think this cat will be your new pet?” I manage a smile.

“My Eight Ball tells me ‘very likely.’”

“And if we catch her and we have to put her down instead?”

I watch her throat as she swallows. Her skin is pale there—pale and smooth as satin. “I don’t know. I wish you wouldn’t say that.”

“It makes you sad to think about putting down a feral cat you’ve never even met?”

Her tongue darts over her lips. Then she slides her gaze to me. “I think pain should be reserved for something painful. Not a fucking hypothetical.”

She seems angry as we roll on through the trees. Like she’s sure I’m fucking with her head.

I *am* fucking with her head. I don’t mean to, but I can’t seem to help myself.

This close to... everything that’s coming, I find myself strung taut. It’s not like you might think. I can feel myself becoming more... exacting. More thorough. As if force of will can help me.

Cleo’s green gaze wanders over me, and my chest tingles like it’s waking up from sleep. “If you know the cat’s gender,” she says, “then you must have touched her.”

“That was a gamble,” I admit.

“Why?”

“She could have been rabid. Could have clawed me.”

Cleo shrugs. “I’m all about gambles.”

“Then you are an optimist.”

She shrugs again. "You think the cat will be hard to catch?"

I shake my head. "She's pretty friendly for a stray."

She smiles. "Then it's settled. She'll be the third in our crime unit. I'm naming her Helen."

I can't help smiling at the thought of Cleo with a cat. For some reason, I have the feeling they'd get into some trouble. "Helen—of Troy?"

She shakes her head. "For Helen Keller." After a minute, she says, "My sisters w—they're deaf."

"They can't hear anything?" For reasons unexamined, this shocks me.

She nods, tightening her hands on the wheel as we lurch over the bumpy road. "My parents both had a gene for it, even though neither one of them are. Were," she corrects. Her mouth tightens.

I think about how she reacted to my guessing that her father died and feel a tender wave of curiosity rise in me. I want to ask, but I don't dare. Losing my Mom and Ly has taught me to tread lightly where loss is concerned. Shit, my own damn life has taught me that. I swallow a deep breath and let my eyes drift to her hands. "Does that mean you know sign language?"

"Yep."

I turn that over in my head. Last time I tried to learn sign language... I swallow. "Show me something." *Anything*, I want to plead.

"The sign for 'fuck you' is this," she says, pushing her knees into the bottom of the wheel as she holds two fingers up, almost like a peace sign, touches the tip of one to her nose, and then moves her hand out and up, making a classic "okay" symbol.

I laugh.

She grins. "Want to see the sign for whore?" She folds her hand in a little and runs it along the side of her chin.

She follows the curve of the driveway to the right, and I watch her face as the house comes into view. It's a whitewashed two-story with a wide brick porch and Manning's Harley in the dirt out front.

"Welcome to nine-one-one Pecan."

Her lips quirk at the corners. "A pecan emergency?"

I shake my head, fighting my own smile. "The address. It's nine-one-one Pecan Way."

"Oh. So who lives here?" She pushes her dark hair out of her face as she steers around the bike and pulls up right next to the porch.

"It's a private residence, registered to a woman named Rose Cole."

"Who is that?" Cleo asks, shifting the Escalade into park.

"She's dead. It's phony paperwork."

She twists her lips. "Makes sense. I guess if you're lying about something of this caliber, you have to go big."

I nod. A slow spinning sensation starts at the base of my throat and crawls up the back of my head, until I feel so dizzy, I'm forced to lean over my lap and touch my fingers to my forehead.

FIFTEEN

Cleo

KELLAN LOWERS HIS HEAD INTO his hand and, with his long, strong fingers, rubs his brow. He inhales deeply, making his thick shoulders rise, and then he exhales, and his back seem to slacken.

"Is something wrong?" I look down on his neck and shoulders, admiring how tanned and thick he is; the way his hair is shorn to different lengths as it tapers to his nape.

I'm just starting to get nervous when he lifts his head. His eyes are clear and blue and void. "Everything's fine."

But the look on his face is just so weird. I don't believe him. "Are you like... frustrated or something?"

He glances at his cell phone, cradled in the palm of his big hand, then looks back up and me. His cheeks are sucked in as he shakes his head. "No." He loosens his jaw, so he looks a little less uptight. "Come on." He smiles wanly as he nods at the house. "Let's go in."

"You're really doing this? You're going to let me see a grow house?" I'm both excited and nervous. Excited because forbidden things are always exciting. Nervous because I'm hopping off the fence now. Going into Kellan's grow house will put me firmly in his camp. His illicit, dirty-monied camp.

I wonder again what a work relationship between the two of us will look like as I watch him stride around the car's hood. His button-up shifts over his chest and shoulders as he moves. My eyes search his face. The pretty lips. The deep blue eyes. The scruffy jaw. What kind of guy is he? Where did he come from? What's his family like? As if he's seeking to reassure me, his features gentle as he peers into my window.

I smile a little while my stomach flutters.

Then he pulls the door open and before I have a chance to swing my legs out of the Escalade, he lifts me out and sets me down beside him on the dirt drive.

His eyes roll up and down me, settling on my Armani boots.

"You're in it for the money, aren't you?" He smirks.

I put a hand on my hip. "What does that mean, pray tell?"

"I can spot expensive leather." His eyes crinkle as his lips curve into a funny smile.

"It takes a greedy cow to know one."

He laughs. "A greedy cow?"

I shrug as we start moving toward the porch. "I see it as a cow. A hungry cow, gobbling down green grass. That's me, at least. I'm new money. The newest."

"The first in your family with means," he says as we approach the wide porch.

"The veeery first."

As we climb the stairs, his left hand hovers behind my elbow. Protective? Possessive? Whatever his intentions are, they're throwing me off my game.

"Unlike you," I say belatedly as I step onto the brick porch. I'm fishing for personal information, eager to confirm my guess that Kellan was born with a silver spoon in his mouth. But he's focused on something else. Something on the roof over the porch. I'm about to ask if he's having a seizure when the door swings open, revealing a short, skinny, ginger guy who looks like he stepped right out of the halls of my old middle school.

"Manning," Kellan says warmly. I glance at the spot I think Kellan was staring at, and after a second I spy a discreet security camera. Of course.

Kellan clasps the guy's upper arm in some kind of dude hug, but the ginger guy isn't paying attention. He's sizing me up. It's as if he's trying to let his facial expression and his body language alone tell me he doesn't like me.

"Why is she here?" the ginger asks. He's got one of the deepest drawls I've ever heard, the kind of voice I imagine basset hounds would have if they spoke.

"Manning, this is Cleo. She's getting a tour. I wanted to make some space for the teddy bears and check on the Silent Stalker."

I frown, looking from Kellan to the guy he calls Manning. Teddy bears? Silent Stalker? I could not be more confused.

"Whatever you say, bro." Manning takes a step back into the foyer. I notice he's wearing big, clomping work boots. And ratty jeans. And a Lynyrd Skynyrd shirt.

Kellan's hand finds mine. I look down. Our fingers tangle, and he squeezes lightly.

His eyes are on his friend, who reaches over to a coat rack in front of a flight of stairs and grabs a Crimson Tide baseball cap. He fits it onto his head. As he adjusts the bill, Kellan's eyes never leave his face.

"Don't worry, dude. Cleo's on the D-team now."

The D-team?

Manning shrugs. "If you say so, bro."

"He does," I interject.

Manning quirks a brow at me, and I flash him a winning smile. "If Kellan trusts me, you should too," I point out.

He snorts. "Kellan don't trust you," he drawls.

I feign hurt, and look from our joined hands to Kellan's face. "Is this true, Kello?"

He frowns and twists his mouth: confused, amused, or both.

I shrug. "Sounds like Jello, and everyone likes Jello."

"I don't." Kellan makes a face.

"He don't trust anybody," Manning says cryptically. His thick country drawl makes my accent sound almost Midwestern in comparison.

"Then it's a good thing I'm somebody." I wink.

"He probably don't even trust ole Truman," Manning says. I frown, and at that very second, I hear something clicking against hardwood, followed by a soft jingle. At the end of the hall stretching past the staircase, I see a flash of reddish brown.

A resonant bark echoes through the foyer, and a dog with a jingling collar sails comically toward us. A blood hound, I realize as it launches itself at Kellan.

"WOOF! WOOF!"

Kellan drops my hand and throws his arms around the dog, who's lost all doggy decorum and jumped up on him, huge paws on Kellan's chest.

There's mud caked on the dog's paws. Every time the big beast shifts its weight, it smears mud on the front of Kellan's button-up. And still, he leans in close and rubs the blood hound's floppy ears.

"Tru." He clasps the dog's head.

The dog paws at him, leaving deep mud streaks down each of Kellan's pecs. I notice Manning staring at me and shut my gaping mouth. Our gazes boomerang to Kellan.

His hands around the dog's nape loosen, and the dog sinks to his haunches, head held high. His tail thumps against the floor.

"This is your dog?" I ask Kellan, leaning down to rub his wrinkly forehead. I sink into a crouch. "Truman, hi." I tip his face up to mine and peer into his doggy eyes. "What a pretty boy you are. Just like your owner. Such a pretty boy..."

Manning chuckles. "Maybe I do like her."

"You do," I smile. I stroke the dog's soft head and softer ears. "Pretty boy. You're so pretty."

"Call 'im handsome," Manning says. He laughs again then says, "I'm gonna run to the feed and seed. Y'all be here a while?"

"An hour or so," Kellan says.

"Catch you girls later. Keep your yap shut, snake bit."

Manning disappears out the door, and I look up at Kellan. "Snake bit?"

He rolls his eyes, despite an amused smile. "I told him that your name was Cleopatra."

I smile. Snake bit. Makes sense; Cleopatra was killed by a snake. "I'm a queen, what can I say?"

I rise, because the hardwood floor is making my knees ache. I watch Truman shift his lithe, muscular body, so he's lounging at Kellan's feet.

"He's beautiful," I say sincerely.

Kellan leans down to rub the dog's ears again. I watch the easy way his fingers stroke the dog's head. It's a practiced movement—no doubt.

"He's been staying here with your friend?"

Kellan lifts the dog's floppy ear, squeezing it lightly. The dog lets out a comically long breath, and Kellan nods, his face stuck somewhere between sad and stoic. He doesn't look at me when he says, "I go out of town sometimes."

I open my mouth to ask why the dog can't stay at his house alone, but I don't want to be annoying.

Kellan stands, and his dog circles both of us, tail thumping my leg as he nuzzles my knees.

"Hi, sweetheart," I croon, stroking his back. "Are you named after President Truman?"

Kellan snorts. "Capote."

I look up at him. "You named your dog after Truman Capote?"

He folds his arms over his chest and arches a brow at me.

"Well, well. I guess your dad does read," I say to Truman.

"C'mon," Kellan says. He waves me past the staircase on our right and down the hall. I sweep my gaze over the crown molding lining the high ceilings as I follow him. From where we stand, it looks like the hall dead-ends into a living area.

Truman trails behind us, making me remember the dog we used to have when I was little. Her name was Honeycomb, because she was always trying to eat bees. She was a black lab, and she ran away the month after my sister Olive died. I use to think our crying was too much for poor Honeycomb. Our grieving sent her running for the hills.

I watch Kellan's face as we move down the hall.

"Can we take him home? I'd feel so much better with a guard dog." I smile cheekily. "He can keep me from getting offed by a rival drug lord."

He runs his eyes over me. Solemnity weights his features. "You worried about that?"

I nod. "Are you surprised by this?"

The hallway dead-ends at a living area with cappuccino walls, brown curtains, two teal couches with chevron-patterned pillows, and a huge brick fireplace. To the left is a modern-looking kitchen, with granite countertops and stainless steel appliances. To the right, another hall—the floor of this one lined with a burgundy runner.

We drift up behind the nearest couch, and Kellan wraps his hand around the spine of it. He surveys the room, looking pensive. "Not many people know where I live, Cleo. My dealers are students."

I glance down at Truman, who's smacking Kellan's calf with his ever-wagging tail. "So they're all non-threatening and presumed loyal."

"It's not perfect, but I pay them well and I keep tabs on them."

"Hmm." I lean against the back of the couch and look around the room, which resembles a family room; it's nothing like the drug den I expected.

He props his hip against the couch's back and leans a little closer to me. I watch his hand come up. I shiver as he drags his thumb along my lower lip.

He smiles a predatory smile. "So sensitive."

I arch away from him. "Yeah, when people touch my mouth."

"You had a Tru hair on it."

My cheeks go hot for absolutely no good reason. "Well thanks I guess."

He smiles at me, and it's a weird smile—one I don't understand, because it seems so sad. I wait there silently for an explanation. I wait for him to open up to me, to tell me what is on his mind. But Kellan doesn't.

I feel useless. Clueless. My eyes wander around the room, noting the Glade Plug-Ins beside the entertainment center, and to the right of a potted palm.

I wave at the massive brick fireplace, filled with a pretty, iron candle stand, and topped with a dozen half-burned white candles. "Are you sure this place is what you said it was?" I ask him finally.

He puts his arm part-way around me, clasping my shoulder and turning me toward the hall with the runner.

"Come with me."

His strange, sad air and sparse words have got me nervous, but I'm soothed a little by the Thomas Kinkade prints on the hall walls. They're quaint and country, framed in cedar. One shows a barn, another a waterfall, the third a proud-looking black lab surrounded by dead ducks. The ceiling overhead is striped with a thin skylight, casting filmy light into the shadows.

When we reach the first door, cut into the left-hand wall, Kellan delves into his pocket. I see his key ring come out, and am momentarily distracted by it. The angle of the Escalade is such that I can't see it dangling from the ignition, so I'm surprised that it's... a rodent? I blink—and blink again as he inserts a key into the deadbolt on the door, then wraps his hand around the handle and tugs the door toward his chest.

It looks almost like a little, pewter sloth. Is it a sloth? I swear it is.

Before I get the chance to ask, the door swings open, and I brace myself for what I'll see. Part of me expects to find a Pottery Barn-style bedroom with bookshelves filled with bud-stuffed Mason jars. I picture an old-fashioned smoking parlor with Victorian-era couches and bong-bearing end tables. I'm imagining high-gloss antiques. Something sensual yet homey.

So I blink when I behold what looks like the outdoor garden section at our local Wal-Mart. Instead of palms, ferns, azaleas, or lilies, every plant inside this room is marijuana. Some are tall and some are short, but all are endowed with fragrant, palmate leaves.

I hear the dull hum of a generator somewhere nearby and take a deep breath of humid, pot-scented air. I run my gaze down to the far end of the room, which is roughly the size of a basketball court. So many plants! There's too much fluffy green for me to see exactly how they're potted. They're planted in three thick rows that look at least five feet wide: two rows along the rectangular room's two outer walls, and another row down the room's middle. Two cement aisles stretch between the three rows.

Between the mini forests of the leafy green plants, I can see the cement aisles are water-stained and littered with coils of hoses, bags of fertilizer, and familiar gardening utensils, like shovels and mini rakes.

I turn to Kellan with my mouth open. "Holy *shit*, this is a grow house."

SIXTEEN

I LOOK TO MY RIGHT, where the nearest row of plants dances in a breeze made by huge, wall-mounted fans. Their blades whirl slowly. The plants' thin leaves wag.

I turn back to Kellan. "I'm just... *wow*. This is so... WOW. This is incredible! How much weed is in here?"

He smirks. "Enough."

"Enough for everyone! Enough for the whole school, the whole *town*."

I reach out to fondle the plant nearest to me, but curl my fingers before I touch its leaves. I wonder what a plant is worth. I'm so clumsy—I don't want to injure it.

I look around the space once more, this time noticing the ceiling, home to an army of tire-sized heat bulbs. I guess that's why this room feels a little like the inside of a tanning bed.

Each time my gaze roams, I notice something new, from rows of mysterious mechanical gauges along the room's two shorter walls to the arrangement of the marijuana plants. Now that I've had a minute to look, I can see they're potted individually atop elevated wooden platforms.

I turn back to Kellan. "This is so legit. I don't know why, but... I'm surprised."

I can't tell if he looks smug or bored with all my gushing. Ever since we came into the grow house, I've had a hard time reading him. Hell, I guess I've always had a hard time reading him.

"Where are you from?" I ask him. "I think your guest column I read in the student paper said California? One of the ritzy glitzy cities?"

One brow arches. "Ritzy glitzy?"

I shrug. "If the shoe fits... So am I right? Are you from California? L.A. maybe?"

His brows draw together. "Why do you ask?"

"Just wondering how long you've lived in this area. I'd think it would take time to create something like this."

He lifts a shoulder. "You'd be surprised."

Mounted on the ceiling to my right is a big, flat-screen TV. It's protected by some kind of plastic wrap, but through the hazy cover, I can see alternating views of the inside and the outside of the house. Mounted on another spot on the ceiling is some kind of clock counting down in red, digitalized numbers.

"What's that?" I point to the clock.

"It has to do with adjusting carbon dioxide in the room."

I blink, because beyond the basic association between plants and carbon dioxide, I can't summon an intelligent comment.

"Does Manning run this?"

"We do," Kellan says, shifting his feet.

I hold my arms out. "I'm surprised you trusted me enough to show me this. It's crazy impressive, Kellan. You're legit as hell."

One side of his mouth quirks up, like he's amused by my praise. "Walk around if you want. You can touch the plants. Just be gentle—if you can manage that."

I stick my tongue out. "When called for. I only see one douchebag in this room, and I think I've already dealt with him."

I whirl around, halfway hoping Kellan chase me. When my self-restraint runs dry and I look over my shoulder, I find him smiling, definitely amused.

The cocky fucker.

I walk up and down the room a bunch of times, pretending I'm on a documentary and marveling at the plants. Many are taller than I am. They're so green. So... real. The marijuana I bought from Kennard came in several large, round containers—a little like the canisters that zip from the bank to the drive-through line. To me, weed has always seemed almost synthetic. Sometimes the crystals have an orange tint, other times a purple hue. They have various scents and there are various strains. But I never bother much with that, or give much thought to where it came from. So I'm surprised to see it in its raw plant form. It looks so innocent and unassuming.

I stop in front of a particularly tall, spindly plant on a platform labeled TIGER'S CLAW. After rubbing my fingertip along one of its soft, thin leaves, I let my gaze wander to the far end of the room. Kellan's in the same spot he was a few minutes ago: standing in front of a platform of smaller plants. His head is bowed, as if he's inspecting them. I'm admiring the width of his shoulders like the girl perv I am when he crouches, poking at the soil in one of the pots. A jolt of lust bursts through me, thinking of his fingers poking something else. I take a long, deep breath and look away.

I don't know why he gets me so damn hot. It's probably the mystery. He's a golden god from California, who is both SGA president and some kind of drug kingpin, who's never appeared around our town with any woman—until the last four months.

And one of the only things I know about his personality is that after I busted his balls, he called me hours later for some panty-melting phone sex. That, and he's willing to pay me like a prostitute to... well, prostitute. Except it isn't prostitution, because it's not just about the money for me. It's about this weed business, and it's about those thick, hard shoulders, too.

The more I think about the deal he's offered, the more I think that this could work out really well for me. *Could.*

When I make my way back to Kellan, he's standing again, staring pensively down at the plants, one hand cupped loosely over his mouth. I stop slightly behind him, checking the label in front of the platform: SILENT STALKER. Hmm.

"What ya thinking about, Farmer Kello?"

He lowers his hand. His mouth twitches on one side, revealing the ghost of a dimple. "Farmer Kello?" His expression is hung between disapproval and amusement.

I smile and nod. "All you need is a straw hat and some overalls."

"Is that all?" He gives me a wicked look that goes straight to my panties, but it fades after a breath into a smirk that, this time, features the reappearance of that adorably handsome dimple. In that heartbeat, he looks so unlike the Kellan Walsh I usually know, I'm buoyed by affection. I throw my arms around his waist and press my cheek against his back.

"I know where your grow house is, na na na na na naaaa!" I squeeze him. "It makes me happy that you brought me here."

He sets his hands on mine. I can feel the hesitation in the way they flutter for a moment before settling. "Does it?" he says, sounding serious.

I nod against his hard, warm back. "I like to be trusted. I'm a trustworthy person. You'll find out."

He cuts his eyes over his shoulder. "How?"

Nervous elation coils under my ribs—from the weight of his gaze at such a close proximity. I shrug and try to keep my voice light. "When rival drug dealers kidnap me and hold me for ransom, they'll have to torture me for, like, seven hours straight before I reveal this address." I wink, as if my hands aren't shaking slightly as they rest atop his hips. Maybe he senses that in me: the giddy nerves, the banked hunger. Because at that moment, he turns to face me. My hands brush the top of his slacks as his rise up to cup my face. His fingers stroke into my hair.

"I won't let you get kidnapped, Cleo."

"Because you'll loan me Truman," I joke weakly.

"No—because I'm going to take care of you. Like I said."

For one hard heartbeat, I wonder if he's joking. The guileless intensity of his face, the way he's stroking my hair: as if it's second-nature to him to touch me gently... It's easier to imagine he's about to grin and add "in bed" to the end of that earnest-sounding declaration. I wait for it, but his expression never changes.

With one final, light stroke of his thumb over my brow, he lowers his hands and takes a half step back.

My heart gives a few slow, off-beat *thu-WUNK*s before I realize I'm staring. I spin around, because damnit, when I get embarrassed, my feet move without permission. "Wait, where's Truman?" I turn back around to Kellan with my arms out. "Did we lose him somewhere?"

God, my awkwardness is so obvious. I glance around the room, and when I'm brave enough to look at Kellan, he's smirking. This one is curved upward at the corners, as if he thinks I'm funny but has something against the act of smiling.

"Truman's not allowed in here. He knows it."

"Aw, that's kind of sad."

Again, that smirk—but this time it seems pained. "You like him."

"I've always been obsessed with hounds, and Truman is like... a proto-hound."

Kellan laughs. At least it should have been a laugh. He turns it into a weird, low laugh-cough thing, covering his mouth with his hand and shaking his head.

"Bow wow WOW." I lift my brows coyly and get a real laugh. It's just a raspy huff of air, but it's a laugh for sure. I beam proudly.

As the smile slips from his face, he sticks his hands in his pockets. His eyes move over me. They're deep and blue, round and serious, and just as quickly as they move down me, they shift away. He looks to the floor, although there's nothing there. It's as if he *needs* to get his eyes off me.

I'm scrambling for a way to draw him out again when he turns and starts walking down the cement aisle.

My stomach flips, and all the giddiness I felt comes crashing down.

Did I do something wrong?

I stare at his back, and all I can think about is rushing after him.

I'm not insane, right? That *was* weird.

Yes, of course it was weird. Twenty-one years of being female lets me know why, too. I shake my head. If Kellan Walsh didn't just now get scared off because he felt too close to me, then I'm a monkey's auntie.

My stomach clenches as I remember what his friend said—Manning. About how Kellan doesn't trust people.

I watch him moving down the cement aisle between the plants. He's probably thirty feet away by now. The angle of the lighting has him looking slightly shadowed: a lone figure defined mostly by big shoulders and a broad back. I watch him stop, pull some leaves into his hand and bring his nose down to them. I watch him as he crouches down to touch the soil.

If I stare hard enough, will he look back at me?

A less confident Cleo would start feeling insecure now. Like she'd overstepped some invisible bounds. Like she'd been too obviously *trying*. I take a deep, slow breath and tell myself this Cleo is beyond that.

I walk slowly, at a steady pace, toward Kellan. I tell myself that I'll be patient. Wait him out. I'll be living with him, so I can watch him. I'll find out what makes him tick. Why laughing at my stupid joke made him clam up like he'd just confessed some deep, dark secret.

I notice my hands are in fists. I loosen them and flex my fingers. I need to take this thing with him one moment at a time. I can do that. If anyone knows the tenets of mindful living, it should be Cleo Whatley, future art therapist.

I practice as I move. Listening to the sounds of the room: fan blades spinning, and their echo through the large space. The smell of the plants: bitter yet sweet, like fresh-cut garden weeds mixed with some kind of citrus fruit. The warm, heavy air on my cheeks and arms. I redirect my mind from Kellan by looking at the plants. Noting which ones are tall, and which ones smaller. I note the names of various strains of marijuana as I pass the plant-filled platforms.

VIOLET VIPER. KILLER CROCK. APPLE ASTEROID. By the time I reach GRAVE YARD DAISY, I'm feeling calm again. I pass THE BIG SLEEP and am pretty sure I've found a pattern in the plant names. I nod to myself as I remember SILENT STALKER. All the names are morbid.

Curiosity slings through me. I thought marijuana was a happy thing.

By the time I catch up to Kellan, he's at the front left corner of the room, just a few feet from the door through which we entered. To the right of the door is a slab of corkboard countertop, stretched under a row of cedar cabinets. His luscious back stretches as he reaches into one of them.

I stand behind him as he fiddles with something inside the cabinet.

"Hey," I murmur.

He turns to look at me, lifting his brows in acknowledgment. His mouth is twisted, like he's irritated by whatever he's trying to do.

"Having trouble?"

He shifts his weight, leaning over the counter as his muscular arm fishes deeper inside the cabinet. "This is one of our water tanks," he says over his shoulder. "There's a hose that runs off through this wall," he says, pointing, "pumping fertilizer. One of our newer strains didn't like the cocktail we were using, so I changed it up. But the new shit's clogging all the tubing."

"Ugh. That sounds annoying."

I think I see him nod, but I can't tell. His attention is definitely on his task.

I look down at my boots, but who am I kidding? My eyes are starving for him, and with his back turned, I'm free to gawk without consequence. The first place my pervy gaze goes is his ass, but I don't want to be a freak, so as soon as I eyeball-hug his taut buns, I drag my eyes up his back. I watch his muscles shift under his shirt. My fingers drift to my cell phone, tucked into the waist of my leggings. I smile, wondering if he would notice me nabbing a little .gif footage for the Smuffins group.

I roll my eyes at myself. We're in a grow house—*hello*, Cleo.

As I admire the cords of muscle in his neck, the golden hair that blows a little in the light breeze of the fans, I wonder why a rich boy like him would turn to dealing drugs. Does he like the risk? Or was he even a rich boy at all before he started dealing? Maybe he's like me—but I don't think so. He seems... well-bred. I'd bet my lumpy little nest egg that a guy like Kellan Walsh knows when to use the two-pronged mini fork.

When my brain finally tires of imagining Kellan in a tux, his long fingers clutching a teeny tiny spoon, I let my breath out and decide to risk interrupting him.

"Soooo, these are your strains?" I ask. "Like... *yours* yours?"

"Some are," he says, still yanking on the tube. I admire his strong jaw-line, evident because he's clenching his teeth. He pulls his arm out of the cabinet and turns to face me, shocking me again with his beauty. He leans his hips against the counter. I have to force my eyes to stay on his.

"Most of our strains started in California. But we've been cross-breeding long enough that we do have our own stuff now." He shuts the cabinet door and nods at the one leading back into the hall. "Come this way."

I follow him back into the hall, marveling that such an amazing grow room is attached to such a normal-looking house. He steps over to a door on the other side of the hall, then pauses to fish his phone out of his pocket.

He hunches over it, his face bathed in blue light.

"Just a second," he says tightly.

"What's the matter?"

A few long seconds later, he stuffs the phone back into his pocket and pushes this new door open without meeting my eyes. "Dealer drama."

SEVENTEEN

HE STEPS INTO THE ROOM, and I follow, so close I can feel his body heat. I don't realize I'm holding my breath until I let it out. I'm not sure what I was expecting, but I'm relieved to find this room looks much like a stock room—and it's empty, save us.

Floor-to-ceiling plywood shelves line all four walls, and another row of shelving splits the room in half. The shelves are stacked with large, blue plastic bins. Two cement aisles running long ways down the room are dotted with tables and weird-looking iron machines. For chopping up the crop and weighing it and stuff?

I look at Kellan, who's still clutching his phone.

"This is the stock room. Pretty straightforward," he says, without looking up.

When it seems he isn't going to say more, I turn away from him, drifting slowly down the aisle.

He seemed so solicitous before we got here, but since we walked into the house, he's been acting "off." So maybe his mood took a turn. So what? What's bothering me? I try to think, but all I can come up with is the gnawing feeling that I don't really know what he wants. Yes, he wants to get rid of the competition—if I could even be called that. Yes, he seems to want my body. Those things, I understand. But I'm still not sure why he wants me to live with him. Why he wanted it enough to offer to pay me so exorbitantly. His reticence about the dealer drama underscores what truly bothers me about Kellan: his secrets.

The double life he's living is... really double. He's Chattahoochee College's golden boy, but he runs dealers and was able to lift a gun off me. Why *is* he paying me to live with him? He said it was so we could learn to work together, then later acted like it was more for sex. But is it really? Why pay me so much? Why, why, why? What am I missing here?

I fold my arms and inhale deeply. Exhale slowly. I imagine I can feel his eyes burning my back. I stand there another moment, trying to decide if I should mention my concerns and ultimately deciding not to. I do need to stay with him for at least a night or two, after all. Until I can see if Milasy will cool down about the brick. And so I have a little time to try to figure Kellan out.

After that, if I still feel like there's too much I don't know, I'll figure out a new solution to my homelessness. If there's any way I can feel okay—or even good—about this weird thing between him and me, I'll stay. Because I'd really like that money, and if I'm being honest with myself, I'd like to find out more about him, too.

"Cleo." He touches my shoulder. "You're jumpy." His fingers squeeze as his blue eyes search the waters of my own. "Tell me why."

I bite my lip. Because you make me feel unsteady. Because I don't know if I can trust you. Because I want to find out all your secrets. I say the first thing that pops into my head. "Do you hide weed in teddy bears?"

He gives a raspy laugh. His lips twitch, like he wants to smile—but by now I know he won't. "Is that what's bothering you, Cleo?"

Sensation tingles under his hand, trickling hotly through my torso like the first wave of anesthesia. I take a small step back and try to pin down my racing thoughts.

Ah, hell. "What's bothering me is... I don't know why you trusted me with this. Enough to bring me here." It's not all that's bothering me, but it's something tangible I can lob at him.

He tilts his head, not blinking as he looks at me.

I press my lips together, mirroring him. "I guess I just don't understand. Why get this involved with me at all? Don't get me wrong," I add, "I'll deal your stuff, but I don't see why you need me to know so much about your business. Or to live with you. Like, why you want me to."

He blinks, owlish and unreadable.

"You're paying me so much..." I exhale. "It can't just be for sex. I guess I just... feel weird about it. I don't get it."

I let my breath out.

"I don't either," he says, low. "I don't think I *should*, but I'm going to anyway. Do you know why?" He lifts his brows.

I shake my head.

"I don't either. If I dismissed you now, and you never stayed at my house, would you keep this place a secret, Cleo?"

"Of course," I nod. "I don't want to get you busted."

"Why?" His voice is sharp.

I glare at him, because he's dodging my questions... leading me down bunny trails. I can feel it. "Why wouldn't I tell? Because I'm not an asshole. Are you?"

"I'm not that kind of asshole. Come here, Cleo. Let me show you something." He walks to a thick steel door beside the place where the wall seems to fold or lift up to accommodate a hook up to an 18-wheeler. He pushes the door open.

I can see the pines sprawl out behind him as I step closer.

"See that?" His left hand touches down on my back as his right points at the woods. I notice two lines of red dirt snaking through the pine straw: tire tracks. I nod. "It leads back to some hunting land off Highway 231. That's a big truck. Dump truck. You know what's in the truck?"

I shake my head.

"Fertilizer. Real black market shit, just what we need to grow our stuff. Comes up all the way from South America. Dude who brings it—he works for some bad guys." His eyes meet mine. "Do you know why I told you?"

"No."

"I'm telling you, Cleo, because I choose to trust you. If you really want in, I'll tell you more. But I need to know that first. I don't think *you* know that yet. That's why I brought you here. I want you to see it—so you can know what you're maybe getting into if you decide to do more than just deal my stuff."

"More than deal?"

He nods. "You'll make your mind up and if you want in, then we'll talk some more. I think we could work together. Really work together."

My stomach flutters. I want to ask what that means, but I'm too nervous. "Will there be an initiation?" I ask. I'm mostly teasing, trying to shift the tone of things a little—but he must not hear the light tone in my voice.

His eyes harden and his voice yawns down an octave. "Do you want to be hazed?"

I press my lips together. "No."

"Are you sure?"

"No," I whisper.

"Don't tell me that."

"Okay..." My voice trembles. "I take it back."

He drops his head down like he's going to kiss my mouth, but he diverts his lips to my jaw. He kisses me so tenderly my stomach flutters. His mouth crawls, warm and moist, beneath my chin—and then he bites my neck. It's sharp and sudden, predatory. His teeth tear at my throat until my heart is pounding and I want to pull away. And then the pain is gone. His warm, soft mouth strokes me; his tongue soothes my stinging skin.

And when my legs begin to tremble, when I'm clinging to his shoulders, drunk from his strange ravishment, his teeth pierce me so hard I gasp.

"Cleo."

My own name thrums in my ears like an exaltation as he nips my neck. He drags it out. He makes it hurt. I clutch his shirt and lock my jaw to keep from crying out. I moan. He's going to hurt me!

And then his silken mouth, his graceful tongue.

He moves so fast, his hair tickles my chin. He moves like he's hungry: harsh, thorough—and yet the whole thing is so gentle,

I'm moaning with bliss. He trails down my throat and over my collarbone: nipping and then licking, marking with his teeth and following with his tongue and lips, biting and then soothing, punishing and stroking.

He sucks my tender throat between his teeth, and a moan spills from my lips.

In between my legs, I'm throbbing.

I wrap my hands around the back of his head, clutching him to me as I moan again. I've lost my mind... I press my hips against his thighs, gulping back air and exhaling in a low sigh. One of my hands trails down his nape and grips his shoulder as his mouth continues its assault on my throat.

"Kellan..."

He moves away. At first I think I've wrecked this, but he doesn't step back. Instead he tilts his forehead against mine, gives me a heavy-lidded smile, and plants a soft kiss on my lips.

When he lifts his mouth off mine, I press my lips against the base of his throat, pausing for a moment because at first, I'm sure that he will pull away.

He doesn't move.

I can hardly breathe. As I gaze at his smooth, tanned skin, I find his throat is marred by a small, horizontal scar. It's thin and pale, and looks like someone drew a dash over his jugular with a beige Sharpie. I roll my tongue over it and feel him shudder. *Yessss.*

His hands wrap around my head, his fingers tangling in my hair, then grasping my skull. I've never been a skilled lover, but this is different. My hunger leads me. I see his smooth throat as a canvas and I want to mark it. I kiss him softly at first, then so hard I hope it aches.

I'm rewarded by a hard catch of his breath, followed by a muttered, "fuck." He clutches my head tighter and presses his erection against my hip. I wait for him to move, to grind against me—in fact, I hold my breath for it—but he doesn't. He just juts against me, his throat still under my mouth, his chest frozen against mine. And then, after an exquisite second, he grabs my arms from around his neck and pulls them up over my head.

"What a little slut you are," he growls. Clamping his hand around my wrists, he pushes me toward a row of shelves. With my arms bound and my upper back against one of the Tupperware containers, I'm helpless—and panting so hard I feel almost panicked.

I can feel my face burn as he looks down on me.

"You like this, don't you?" His fingers tighten around my wrists. His head drops down. He kisses my mouth slow and hard, then bites the corner of my lips. "You like fucking around with me, don't you, Cleo baby?" He murmurs it against my cheek. "You were waiting for this. You're already wet for me." It's true, of course. I feel him hard against my lower belly, and I grit my teeth.

He takes my chin in his fingers, revealing my face. There's no point in answering. I know he can see it in my eyes. I can see my lust reflected back at me in his.

His face is so intense, I almost expect him to pull my leggings down and take me as I lean against the shelves.

Instead, his strong fingers release my wrists, and he drops down to his knees. He puts my shawl out of the way and claims my pussy with his wide mouth.

"Ohmygod!"

He closes his jaw just slightly, mouthing at me, and then I feel his voice vibrate. "You smell like sex, Cleo."

It takes everything I have to keep from rocking into his face. My legs quiver. My voice shakes so hard I can barely speak. "I haven't had a shower."

"You don't need one."

His mouth shifts against me, and there is his tongue. I know it by its lovely pressure; the feel of it is big and hot and damp. He settles it warmly over me—and then his lips are back, clamping on my throbbing sex as he blows into the fabric. I can feel the hot moisture against my skin.

"You want my mouth on your pussy. You want to feel my tongue between that slit, right where you're wet and throbbing, don't you, Cleo?"

Yes!

He puffs on me again, and I can feel the damp heat seep between my lips. I can't help it—I thrust myself at him.

"Cleo..." The pressure of his mouth is gone. I want to scream as he wraps an arm around my ass and looks down at my feet. "You're on your toes. So hungry..." His eyes find mine. His grin is arrogant; unhampered. "I bet you want my cock. It's okay." His fingers, pressed into the back of my thigh, loosen their grip. Begin to stroke. "There's no harm in wanting a big cock in your pussy. I think a good, plump pussy deserves a thick cock. I bet you do too..."

He rubs his lips against me through the fabric. I grip his shoulder.

"Say my name," he purrs.

"Kellan."

"What do you want, Cleo?" As he looks up at me, he blows another long, hot breath through my leggings.

I moan. "*Please*!"

He pushes his tongue against me. Moves away. "Please what, Cleo? Please *who*?"

"Take off my leggings!"

His fingers pluck at the elastic. "And?"

Eat me out. I can't say it. "Put your mouth..."

He lowers his mouth to my pussy and hovers there, just breathing. "Put it where?" he rumbles.

"There! Please..." I'm swaying, almost falling over.

"You want me to eat your pussy? Say it, Cleo. I want to hear you say, 'Kellan, I need you to eat my pussy.'"

His mouth gathers over me again, and he puffs one breath after another into the fabric, like he's doing CPR on my cunt. One time... two times... three. I'm so wet, I could die. His eyes flick up to mine, stern and expectant. I dig my nails into his shoulders.

When the fabric over me is soaked and sweat is beaded on my pussy, and the slickness in my slit is dripping like the icing off a cake, he stops and gazes up at me. "Last chance, Cleo. Tell me what you need, or I'll assume I'm doing this all wrong."

I grab his hair and yank hard. "Eat me out, Kellan. Eat my fucking pussy. Just do it right now!"

He laughs, pressing his mouth against me so I feel every vibration. Pleasure slices through me. I can feel it pulse deep in me, like I've magicked his cock right where I need it. Then he leans away, grins like a predator, and grabs my leggings at the seam that runs from the waist down to my crotch. With a quick jerk, he rips them open.

I can feel his warm, smooth forehead stroke down my lower belly, the bridge of his nose over my mound... Then his tongue parts my damp folds, delves inside, and—

"OH FUCK!"

That is all it takes.

EIGHTEEN

I REPOSSESS MYSELF SLOWLY, as if I'm waking from a long sleep. I flinch at first blink—at the stock room, with its glaring light and stark aesthetic. But I'm more shocked at where my face is: nestled in the crook of Kellan's chest and bicep. I blink a few times at the plaid of his shirt before my awareness shifts to the rest of my body. The first thing I feel is the hardness of his chest and thighs against me. The second: a cool sensation between my legs. It's as if—

Kellan ripped my leggings open.

Kellan. Ripped. My. Leggings. Open.

I lift my head off him. I want some distance, but his face is right in front of me. I'm about to take a big step back when his hands, tucked around my lower back, drift up my shoulders.

"Cleo?" He smiles at me. It's a small smile, but it's real. Instead of falling off his face the way they seem to do so often, it kind of sticks there. "Hi."

And even though we've probably only been standing here, tucked into each other, for a minute or two, it feels like something between us has shifted. I watch his face. He looks attentive. Interested. And, as a few more milliseconds tick by, kind of smug. Yes, definitely smug.

He smirks at me, and I feel the vibe between us settling back near our baseline. "How you feeling?"

I blush big time. And curse my father's name. (My mother doesn't blush; she says I got it from my dad). And feel ten times more awkward thinking of my dad right now.

"Damnit," I mumble.

The smirk turns smile-ish, complete with a crinkling at the corner of his eyes. "What's the matter? Tired?" He drawls the word, as if he's proud he wore me out, then briefly grins. My stomach lurches.

He rubs his hair back off his forehead, then looks at me for a long, heady second before the world starts turning again. He clasps my hand, lacing our fingers together.

"You want to try a new strain?"

I laugh as he pulls me toward the door. "I don't smoke."

He opens his mouth. "Of course not," he says richly. He smiles, fast and fleeting. "I don't either."

"Really?"

He pushes the door open, squeezing my hand as we walk back into the hall. "Rarely."

"Why not?"

His eyes fix on my face. "Why don't you?"

"I don't know. It makes me sleepy. I blab secrets and eat up all the donuts. It's not exactly conducive to doing good business—or making the grades I need to make."

"Are you on a scholarship?" he asks as he locks the stock room door behind us.

"How'd you know?"

He winks. "You just told me."

He unlocks the grow room again, and we step back into the warm, sweet-smelling air. "I kind of have to be. I make money from the dealing, but that pays my sorority dues and trips and t-shirts, and—" I wiggle my boot—"the pursuit of high fashion. Haircuts, electric toothbrushes, books and music. You know... the basics."

He nods. "You don't pay your tuition."

"Thankfully. It would be a big drain if I was."

With a stroke of his thumb over my knuckles, he releases my hand. I watch as he opens a cabinet under the countertop and pulls out a small, plastic box. From another cabinet, he grabs a few towels. He spreads them on the floor at the mouth of one of the aisles. Then he runs his hand along a panel of switches on the counter, and music comes on.

Classical music.

I smile. "Is this for the plants or us?"

His brows lift. "Are you mocking Chopin?"

"I wouldn't say mocking so much as... noting." I smile again, and sit down on the towels. "You're surprisingly geeky."

"I'll have you know the Nocturnes are a strain favorite." He sinks down beside me and opens the box. He takes out a blue and green, glass-blown pipe about the length of my hand. Then he pulls out a lighter and a bottle of water.

"Damn. The bud." He laughs a little, but he's gritting his teeth. He pulls his phone out of his pocket and looks down at it. Without looking back up at me, he says, "Can you grab something from that bin beside the Silent Stalker?"

There was a bin somewhere? "Sure," I say. "What am I looking for?"

Still looking down at his phone, he points toward the end of our aisle. "It's a bin with dried out stuff."

I bring back a bud that's about as long as my palm, and Kellan laughs.

I shrug, smiling. "I didn't know how much to get."

I sit down beside him, and his dancing blue eyes move over my face. "You know how to pack a pipe, right?"

"I'm not very good at it." I laugh lamely.

"Cleo, Cleo. How can you call yourself a dealer?" He shakes his head, then pats the space across from him. "I'll show you."

He sets the bud down on the towel and starts to pluck eraser-sized kernels off it, his expert fingertips stacking the little tufts inside the pipe's bowl with amazing speed. I think I maybe see his hands shaking, but I can't be sure. Still, it sets my mind in motion.

"Who was on the phone just now?" I ask.

"One of my guys." He lifts his eyes to mine. "It's nothing, trust me."

He sets one more tuft of weed into the bowl, then taps the side of it, knocking the little kernels of marijuana into the bottom.

"You're good at this."

"I used to smoke." He holds it out to me.

I bite my lip and squeeze my eyes shut. "Please don't laugh, but I don't know how to light it. One of my friends... My friend from home, he used to light it for me and cover up the hole on the side of the pipe for me. I would just suck in."

"Cleo—" his brows arch—"you can't be serious." His mouth pulls into a sort-of smile. "How do you vouch for your product?"

"I don't know. No one ever asks me to sample it or anything. And Lora tells me how it is. It's been like, years. Two summers ago I think is when I last smoked. And that was a few hits off a blunt, not from a pipe."

"Tell me more," he says, moving the lighter over the bowl. He looks at me over the pipe. "Why did you stop?"

I watch him flick the lighter and hold the flame over the bowl. The tiny pieces crinkle and snap, flaring red as he presses his thumb over the small hole on the side of the bowl and closes his lips around the business end of the pipe. His shoulders rise as he drags in. The bud in the small bowl pulses red and orange. I watch his chest expand as he pulls the smoke deep into his lungs.

Then he leans forward and cups his hands around my mouth. He blows his breath into the space between his hands. The smoke I suck in is warm and sweet and a little sour. I hold it in my own lungs, and my head feels immediately warmer. My eyelids feel heavier as soon as I exhale.

"Did you get some?" I hear his low voice, but my eyes are watering. I can't see his face.

I cough. And cough.

I feel something plastic pressed against my hand. A water bottle. Through bleary eyes, I see him twist the top off and hold it out. I take it and bring it to my mouth. I gulp until I start to choke. When I lower it, I'm smiling. Grinning.

I feel good. I look at him, to see if I can tell whether he's feeling as loose as I am. I can't tell. Too buzzy.

He looks fucking hot with the pipe raised to his lips. I watch his lashes kiss his cheeks, his lips close around the pipe, as he puts the lighter to the bowl again. He holds the flame until the marijuana glows, and his chest expands with a deep breath.

I'm so mesmerized by him, I'm startled when he sets the pipe down and leans toward me. He cups his hands around my face, and I get ready to inhale the smoke he's going to blow between his palms. I'm utterly unprepared for his mouth covering mine. For his soft, firm lips and the gentle puff of velvet air he blows into my mouth. His tongue strokes the inside of my lip, and pleasure whirrs through me. I fix my lips around his. Take a deep, long drag, pulling smoke from his mouth into my lungs.

My head spins like a moon around a planet.

I take another breath, and find the air is cold. Kellan moved away... while I wasn't noticing. I cough.

"Cleo..." I hear him smiling, even though my eyes are closed. His hand rests on my lower back.

I blink a few times. Cough some more. I see him smiling down at me, as if I'm viewing him inside a dream. This is dream Kellan. His face looks kinder. More relaxed. Silly perfect Kellan. "Cleo. Are you with me?"

"Maybe." I squeak. It turns into a giggle. "I like this..."

"Do you?" He's out in front of me now, smiling his lazy Kellan smile.

I nod, and the room shifts slightly, with its weird heat lamps and forest of green illegal plants. I'm grinning anyway. I laugh, because this shit is funny. "I forgot how much I like it," I say, leaning forward. "I want to do this every day!"

Kellan, who is sitting cross-legged in front of me, leans toward me, too. We're having a moment. His eyes are seeing me. So much seeing me. They're such blue eyes. They're really watching me. I watch his lips. They're such good lips. I want him to kiss me.

I realize I'm too tired to be sitting up. I want to lie down. I stroke the towels spread out under me. They feel soft. I try to stretch out on my side and end up flopping onto my stomach. *Ungraceful,*

Cleo! Not winning! My ribs dig into the cement. I roll onto my back. There are fans in the ceiling, too? Between the lamps! I never noticed this. Lights *and* fans. It's cold here on the floor.

I need to find a new position.

Kellan must have ESP, because here he is. He lifts me up, he lays me against him, he lowers my head into his lap. He's sitting cross-legged. My cheek is on his hard, hard thigh. His arm goes around me, just below my breasts, and his other hand sifts through my hair. I feel like high school on that field trip to the Atlanta Zoo with Alan McIntire. But this is better. Mmm, it's really better.

His fingers play along my hairline. I moan maybe. I'm not sure. It's hard to pay attention.

His fingers trail along my side. They go under my shirt! Oh my God, the goose bumps.

"Ohhh yes. Mmmm."

His hand spans my ribcage. It's a big hand. Strong but... really good at being soft. He traces my ribs with his fingertips.

I feel warm and tired and great.

His mouth is on mine. I didn't even see it coming. It's hot and soft and tastes like smoke. I pant against his lips.

"Cleo." He pushes the word into my mouth, then pulls away and nips my neck.

I grab his hair. He moans. I drag his mouth back up to mine. Our lips and tongues and teeth. I don't know how. I kiss him hard, as if there's someone else controlling me.

He's stroking my breasts, but that's not what I want. I push him away and roll over on my stomach. I push myself up on my arms. I'm smiling at him. He's looking serious. Angsty. I kind of want to giggle.

Instead, I lean over his lap... and he uncrosses his legs. His face is rapt. His eyes are pools of darkest blue.

I reach for his dick and find it through his slacks. I grab and squeeze.

NINETEEN

"CHRIST..."

I rub up and down it. He moans. Then he grabs me by the arms and pulls me onto his lap, so I'm straddling him. He presses down on my hand, keeping it over his bulge while his lips trail up my jaw. His mouth tickles. It's warm and wet. I shiver, but I can't get too distracted.

I go for his fly, but my fingers are so dumb right now. I can't make it work. I stroke his big dick through his pants. I want his dick. I shift my weight, so I can touch him with both hands, and I notice the soft bulge just below the base of his shaft. His balls. Oh, yes. I like the balls.

Under my spread legs, he stretches his out. I reach between my legs and push his thighs wider. Hard thighs. Mmmm. I reach down below his dick and—*there.* His balls are big and full. I cup my hand around them. *Must be careful...* I try to trace him from the soft bulge of his balls up his thick shaft, around his smooth, round head. I want to touch him—all of him.

He hisses. "That feels good."

He grabs a handful of my hair. He finds my mouth again, and together we stretch out on the floor. His hand works between my legs. I frame his dick with my fingers.

"Your pants..."

He unbuttons them, and I pull away from his kiss so I can find my brain enough to tug them down.

His hips. *Oh shit.*

His dick. *Fuck yes.*

This is a cock—not a dick. His cock is standing up, tenting his black boxer-briefs. He tugs his pants the rest of the way down, then pulls the elastic of his boxer-briefs out of the way. His cock springs up—a porno of my own.

"You *are* perfect." I laugh, curling my hand around his head. "Especially this."

"Likewise," he breathes. He's sucking on my nipple through my shirt and bra. I'm lying atop him—but I don't want to be. I want to be between his legs. I crawl down him, settling on my knees between his muscular thighs, and when he reaches for my shoulder, I evade.

I curl one hand around his shaft, caressing his velvety skin. I run my fingers under his heavy sac, then cup it in my palm and tug a little.

"Fuck," he breathes.

I tickle my fingertips over the tightening skin.

He grunts.

"They're getting tighter." I've never really played with this part of a guy before—but I always perv on well-hung guys when I'm watching Tumblr porn. I knead him a little more, lightly stroking my other palm over his plump head.

"Ah—Cleo. Fuck..."

I gather my courage and lean down to lick his sac. My tongue laps gently. I can feel it tighten. "You're so sensitive," I breathe against him, then tease him with the tip of my tongue.

"Fuck." His heavy thighs twitch. His hand comes down on my head. "Suck me, Cleo. *Now.*"

And wouldn't that be easy? So predictable. I wrap my hand around his shaft and stroke, glancing at his stricken face, then pull one of his balls into my mouth.

He barks.

Oh, *yes*. So hot! I suck him a little deeper, caressing with my tongue and cheeks. His groan hits me light a lightning bolt between my legs.

I think I could take the other one, too.

I open wider and use my fingertips to guide the fullness of his sac into my mouth. I use my lips and cheeks to tuck him in, exploring him with the tip of my tongue as I keep the gentle pressure of my cheeks around him.

I glance up to find his lips parted, his eyes rolled back. He's stroking his shaft, his big hand moving in a frenzy. I close my hand over his, then push his hand away as I maintain the steady rhythm. His fingers bite into my shoulders. I trail my tongue between the twin globes of his testicles, and he lets out a wicked groan.

More of that...

I want to see what I can do to him. I tighten my grip on his cock and pump faster. All the while I'm sucking gently on his swollen balls. I feel his thighs flex.

He moans again, like he's in pain.

I curve my hand around his slick head... ease his sac out of my mouth. His hands fist on my shoulders as I give his sac another warm, slow lick then flick my tongue over his taint.

He lifts his ass up off the floor.

"Cleo... *Fuck*. Your mouth is... God... please. Fuck...." His legs fall open, then clamp hard around my shoulders. "Cleo," he begs.

I lick his sac once more, just to feel him jump, and whirl my tongue back up his shaft. I curl the tip of it around his head, then draw away, just far enough away so he can feel the warmth of my breath on his erection.

"Oh, Kellan." I giggle wickedly. "You're wet."

There's a little pearl of pre-cum on the tip of him.

I love being a tease, so rather than suck his head into my mouth, I lean down and kiss his thighs. I kiss the smooth, pale skin as he thrusts his cock against my cheek. I suck on his thigh, my chin brushing his balls.

"You... little fucking whore," he snarls. But he's gasping between the words.

I grin and lift my head so I can see his face. He's completely wasted. Gone. His lids lift open, and his eyes look liquid. "Cleo—what... is this?" The words wobble. He twists my hair around his hand and shoves his cock at my mouth.

He's so hard now, his length is pressed against his abs. I pull it down and stroke it, fast and steady.

"Suck me. Jesus fucking Christ. *Now*... Cleo." He cups my head, fingers digging hard into my scalp. I just can't stop. After all his bossiness, I love that I can do this. I smile to myself and drop down to tease his balls again, but his thighs clamp around my ears. He thrusts his hips and pushes my face down, pressing his swollen head against my lips.

I open for him, sucking him in deep... then deeper, until I feel like I will choke. His palms cup the back of my head, pressing me in place, as I drool and work to rearrange my mouth and throat around him.

"More," he orders. "Take... it all." The words are rasped. I flick my gaze to him and find his eyebrows clenched, his jaw tight...

Yes.

I shut my eyes and take a long and careful breath. As I ease his plump head deeper down my throat, he tugs my hair. His hips tremble. "Cleo... Christ, that mouth..."

I bob my head, applying pressure with my cheeks as I move up and down his cock.

"Such a fucking slut," he moans. "My little tease. You love this don't you? Teasing me..."

I swallow gently and he thrusts, making me choke. He tugs my hair so hard I almost bite.

"That throat... so goddamned soft. You're such a... ahh." His head tilts back, and I can see his chest rise as he pants.

Stroking his balls, I take him deeper, until my eyes are streaming tears. I've given blow jobs before, but never one like this. He's buried so deep in my throat, every breath is a struggle for me. My jaw aches, even as I pulse and leak between my legs.

My tongue struggles to curl around his girth.

He moans, clutching my head.

I pull almost all the way off him, grab a quick breath, and slam him all back down my throat. I repeat a few times, till his legs are shaking badly and his breaths are ragged, fast and hard.

I swallow once more, taking him deep as my lips massage his shaft. "Fuck me, fuck..." I feel his balls draw up in my palm. I stroke the tender skin and swallow once more, hard, around his cock. I'm rewarded by a hard thrust of his hips. "Oh God... Oh—fuck Cleo!"

He tries to pull away. I clamp my mouth around him, suck him hard, and grab onto his hips. He breathes a harsh curse, then he's blowing in my mouth.

The marijuana does some magic on the moment—slows it down for me. I'm aware of my fingers clawing his hip as I swallow. I open my eyes while he's still pulsing down my throat.

He's leaned back on his elbows. His face is tilted to the ceiling; his eyes are shut; his mouth open.

He looks nothing like the Kellan I know. This one looks exultant. Free.

My prideful thoughts must echo through the ether, because a moment later, he grabs me by my hair and jerks his dick out of my mouth.

I sit up and wipe my chin. I'm so wet right now, I can feel it dripping down my legs. My cunt feels full and swollen... heavy. Empty. I can't even draw a full breath.

He blinks, looking shell-shocked. Maybe because I'm about to ask him to help me come, the harsh look on his face feels like a slap.

I know something is wrong when he fumbles to his feet and turns his back without meeting my eyes. He starts to pull his clothes on, moving quickly but clumsily, like someone trying to flee a one-night stand.

How embarrassing. Insulting. Rude.

I shift a little, so the fabric of my ripped leggings isn't pressing against my swollen, clit. It's still throbbing. I lick my lips. My mouth still tastes like him. Is that the problem? That I swallowed? I thought guys liked that. It hits me that I've done it for him twice now.

I put my hand over my chest and watch his back and shoulders ripple as he pulls his pants on. I take a few deep breaths and try my best to forget about my throbbing pussy.

Fuck his moods. I gave him a blow job because I wanted to. I was in control.

Why did I want to? Why did I enjoy it so much? Because... I feel this weird regard for him. An inexplicable... not fondness exactly. More like interest. I'm so damn interested in this guy. So attracted to him. So when I saw the chance, I guess I wanted to make him come undone. Not even want—I *needed* it. I don't know why he stokes such strange feelings in me, but I'm not going regret it now.

I remind myself that just before this, he was the one initiating things in the stock room. What was so wrong with me doing the same?

Doubts whirl through my head. I shut them down as I sit on my heels. I gave a fabulous blow job—no question about it. The way he jerked and writhed... the way his cockhead leaked a river... All those dirty words... the mindless moans. There is no denying it. He wanted what I gave him.

I want to hold out judgment, give him a few more minutes to collect himself and start acting normal again, but as he puts his shoes back on, I feel fury. Spurned fury, born of the embarrassment I just can't shake.

Did I read that wrong?

Is he sending mixed signals?

I thought half the point of this ridiculous acquaintanceship was messing around. Is Kellan some kind of blowjob hater?

The back of his biceps ripple as he gets the last boot on his foot. He straightens up, and my stomach curls into a little ball as he turns around to face me. I can tell he's trying to keep neutral, but his features are taut. Troubled.

I can't stand it, so I look down at the floor. I spot the remainder of the bud I plucked and scoop it up. It's a little nugget: no longer than my pinkie.

I drag my thumb over it, then find the nerve to hold it out to Kellan. He blinks down at it. He looks pissed off. No—he doesn't. His mouth twists, and I think that he looks desperately unhappy.

I curl my hand around the bud. He watches me without a word, without a breath.

I try to read his face, and when I can't, I feel the weight of everything I don't know about him. My heart is pounding as I whisper, "Why do you do this, Kellan?"

"Why do you?"

"I asked you first."

"I have a lot of reasons." He blinks. His handsome face is now on lockdown.

"Name one."

He shrugs, the motion quick and angry. "It should be legal. As medicine, for recreation. I give it to people who need it."

"You mean like people with ailments? Chemo patients and... whoever else?"

"Yes."

"Do you have a lot of people like that on your list? People who use it as medicine?"

He shifts his eyes away from me, then back. He locks his jaw, then holds my gaze for a long moment. "I sell so I can give it to the med patients for free."

"So... you're like Robin Hood." I look at his stark face, trying to find the kindness that I know is there. "How many of those patients do you have?"

"A lot." He sighs and rubs his brow, as if he has a headache.

I nod slowly, wishing I knew him well enough to ask what's wrong right now and get an honest answer.

His brows lift. "You disapprove?"

"No—I'm... surprised. Impressed, I guess." I stroke a fingertip over the nugget in my hand. "I used to want to be a nurse, but I was afraid hospitals would remind me too much of my dad and sister."

I watch his shoulders lift with one deep breath. He lets it out—and then his hands curl into fists.

"Let's get out of here, Cleo."

His voice is bitter.

I have no idea why.

TWENTY

Kellan

THIS IS NOT GOING AS PLANNED.

It's not Cleo's fault. It's mine.

I'm not doing this right. Maybe I *can't*.

I can.

I just have to focus. Like now. I'm driving. She's beside me. I don't need to talk to her. I haven't since we left Pecan, and why should I? The only way Cleo is different than the last girl hanging from my ropes is that there are more rules—for me. She's not one of my submissives, but I think I could work her into that role. As a stand-in, anyway.

I would love to break her down and make her mine. I would love to see her tanned skin marked. I'm hard just picturing her round ass in the air, her blushing cheeks against my sheets. The way her shoulder blades would draw together when I pull her arms behind her back and bind them at the wrists.

I want my cock to live inside her throat. Inside her cunt. Inside her ass. I bet she would feel good from behind. She's not a virgin but I'm guessing no one's been inside her ass. These Southern girls don't always go for that. Something about the Bible and sodomy, I think. Fucking literal interpretation if you ask me, but who would?

Cleo shifts in her seat. Can she feel my dirty thoughts? I almost hope she can.

But there's the rub. I need to refrain from lusting after her until it's time to get my rope out. I need to think of her as Cleo, possible business partner, until the need for her body becomes too great. I won't let myself think of her sweet pussy until we're walking up the stairs. Every other moment, it's just business.

I don't need her to be funny. I don't need her to be kind. I don't even need her to learn the logistics of stock and delivery—not really. When I go, I'll shut down the import part of my little supply chain, as well as the smaller grow house on LaMont. The Pecan house is all she and Manning will need to continue turning enough profit to supply my VIP clients—the ones with medical needs—and pay themselves enough to make it worth their while. I know it won't go on forever. I've got a plan for checking in on things, for discerning when Manning is ready to stop without asking him directly.

My hope for Cleo is that she can be the face of my enterprise for the VIPs and help Manning when he needs her—while padding her pocket book, of course. I'll put Matt in charge of all the dealers. I've already started laying groundwork for that, although I haven't told him. I won't until it's almost time for me to leave.

Cleo starts to hum.

My fingers twitch over the volume key on my steering wheel. This girl is all about the questions. I don't want to answer any, so I let her hum "Friend of the Devil" without mentioning it's one of my favorite Dead songs.

I think of Truman back at the Pecan house and I grit my teeth. I should have brought him with us. Manning doesn't want a dog, and Cleo was ready to write songs about him. Tomorrow maybe. I couldn't do it today. I don't know why. It doesn't matter.

I inhale deeply, working hard to keep my chest from rising with the effort. I may be unraveling, but I can fix it so Cleo never knows. I can keep my thirsts and all my pains a secret.

Three weeks. We said three weeks, but I may make it less. I may leave early. It wouldn't hurt her. Nothing about my situation will touch her. I make that promise to myself as I park the Escalade beside a pear tree and kill the engine. Midday sunlight streaks in through the windshield, playing over Cleo's heart-shaped face. After a minute of sitting there in silence, she casts her eyes to mine.

"Are you going to be this way the whole time I'm here?"

"What way?"

She lifts her brows. "A moody prick."

My mouth twitches. It wants to bloom into a smile. I clamp my lips down, giving her a stern look. "You think I'm a moody prick?"

She shrugs. "I think you're hot and cold. You say you're going to protect me, we get high and mess around, and then you just ignore me? That's annoying. I don't want a boyfriend, Kellan, but if we're going to mess around, you've gotta at least be cordial. I'm not *that* hard up for money, you know?"

So if I keep being "hot and cold," she'll leave. That's what she's saying.

I suck air in. Blow it out. "Fine."

"Fine?" she echoes. She's looking at me as if I have three heads. "What the hell does 'fine' mean?"

"It means fine. I'll keep it lukewarm, just for you."

She rolls her eyes. "Perfect."

I pop the knuckles of my left hand, enjoying the dull throb. "For the record... you look good choked on my cock." Too fucking good. I don't blow down any woman's throat. I seem to break that rule every time she puts her lips around my dick. I can't let it happen again.

She quirks one elegant brow. "Well, as long as there's that..." She rolls her eyes—but Cleo doesn't get it. I haven't accepted a blow job on a whim since I left USC in January 2011. Gillian came to see me in New York, but...

I shake my head. "It won't happen again like that. I don't get high," I tell her, forcing myself to meet her eyes. They're crystalline green—a color that I've hardly ever seen except on her. "I initiate what we do," I add. "Every time."

She shrugs. "Unless you don't."

"You want to get your pussy paddled?" The words spill from my lips as my dick stiffens.

"I don't *not* want to." She locks her jaw. Her eyes on mine are steely. Challenging.

Fuck me. "No?"

She thrusts her lower lip out. Fucking minx.

I breathe so deeply, I can feel my nostrils flare. "Do you want to get your pussy paddled, Cleo?"

"I don't care." Her eyes are emeralds; I can see the twinkle of rebellion there.

"Are you sure about that?"

The corner of her mouth wavers. Then she nods.

"Get out of the car then, Cleo. Go inside and wait up in your room."

Cleo

This is what we're doing, then. I don't know what. I don't know what it's called, but I can feel it taking shape inside me: something dangerous and beautiful.

I walk slowly up the stairs. I want to hear his footsteps, but the house is quiet and empty.

He told me to lie face down on the bed and take my leggings down. I spend a moment in the room, and then I go out on the balcony.

It's a windy day. The treetops sway slowly. Pine bristles tremble with orchestral restraint. All around their roots, the river spills—an open vein. The rushing water hurts my ears, like someone turned the volume too loud.

I wait for him with my hands on the cold stone railing. I daydream him behind me. The way he will scoop me up. Throw me over his shoulders. Take me to the bed.

I didn't plan on this. I didn't plan for how exciting things would be with him.

I hear him moving—really there now. I can't breathe. He grabs my elbows. I am whirled around. His face is cold and hard. I try to match his look.

"You're a defiant girl, Cleo. It's time for you to get your due."

"What's that?" I ask, smiling naughtily.

"I'll show you." His low voice is strained. His cock is bulging in his slacks. I smile wider.

With his hands around my elbows, he pulls me down to the cement balcony. He urges me onto my hands. He yanks my tattered leggings down, pulling so hard they get stuck on my boots.

My stomach twists as I remember when he tore them. Then he smacks my ass—so hard I yelp. I rock forward on my arms.

"That's for making me come down your throat."

"What?" I snap.

He smacks my ass again.

"Ungrateful bastard!"

He hits me again.

"You loved that! I could—"

Again. I screech.

He hits me one more time, then growls, "What's your safe word?"

"Hit me again," I taunt. I look over my shoulder, at his poised palm. Little bolts of glee race through me. My ass stings bad. My heart is racing. I think I kind of love making him growl.

"Pick a safe word." He sounds strained, as if pausing in mid-air like that is costing him. "One word to stop things—if it gets too much."

He slaps my ass again, and I pant.

"Safe word?" he prods.

"Sloth."

"What?"

"Sloth. My word is sloth, asshole."

I wag my ass a little. It burns like hell, but I am ready for his hand. This fucked up game—I'm in. I fucking adore making him react.

A drama queen, a needy little girl: that's what I was always called. I guess I am.

"Too scared?" I ask over my shoulder.

The breeze blows a strand of hair into my eyes. I look behind me.

No one's there.

PART II

Once you start to live outside yourself, it's all dangerous."

- Ernest Hemingway

ONE

Kellan

September 18, 2011

IT CAN'T BE TRUE. IT ISN'T TRUE. IT CAN'T BE TRUE.

It can't be true. It isn't true. It can't be true.

It can't be true. It isn't true. It can't be true.

I hold my forehead as the words spill through my brain. I wrap my other hand around the waist of my pants, keeping them from sagging.

It can't be true. It isn't true. It can't be true.

My hollow head and frenzied breathing keep out most of what's around me. I cling to the details I need. I'm in an elevator, going down. I don't have shoes.

It can't be true. It isn't true. It can't be true.

Is my jacket zipped? I look down.

It can't be true. It isn't true. It can't be true.

I need to zip it. Can't. I tuck its flaps together. Then I shove my hands under my arms and try to tamp my breathing down.

It can't be true. It isn't true. It can't be true.

It can't be true. It isn't true. It can't be true.

The elevator lurches to a stop. My elbow bumps the mirrored wall. Too suddenly, the doors swish open, revealing a glossy, glass-ceilinged lobby. My insides are dead to the familiar sounds and colors. Even the novel sight of people wearing jeans and sweaters, laughing and chatting, ignites no feeling in me.

It can't be true. It isn't true. It can't be true.

I try to quiet my gasping breaths. No dice. When the elevator bounces like the door's about to shut, I step onto the glossy tile.

My feet.

"Oh, *FUCK*."

For a minute, I forgot. I step from one foot to the other, trying to escape the pain. I grit my teeth so hard I hear a crack. I groan.

I start to walk.

There's a row of glass doors over on my left, past the information desks. I tuck my chin against my chest and shuffle toward them. My tongue finds the fault line on my tooth and traces up and down.

When I get through one of the glass doors, into the building's entry corridor, I'm forced to stop. Pain laps up my calves like streaks of fire. My breathing is so loud, a couple coming through the doors stops to stare. The woman reaches for me, but her husband yanks her arm down.

"Come on, Cindy..."

Good. I don't need anybody recognizing me. Thinking of me makes me think of him. I squeeze my eyes shut.

It can't be true. It isn't true. It can't be true.

It can't be true. It isn't true. It can't be true.

I use my shoulder to push through the next door and keep my hands pulled close to my body.

The moment that I step outside is indescribable. The sunlight is so white, the air electric. I forgot the stench of smog. It reaches into my throat, filling my nose with the memory of living. My lungs deflate. My eyes blur as I watch cars file by. Taxis line up by the curb, and people—out, then in. People on the sidewalk. So much movement. Adjusting a hair band, sipping coffee, unzipping a purse.

Purpose and intention. Both feel sharp.

It can't be true. It isn't true. It can't be true.

I disappear into the crowd, moving east. I've thought about this so many times, I know where I'm going, despite my current state.

I pull the jagged air into my lungs. Cement is cold beneath my aching feet. I pull my jacket closer.

I'm trying to move fast, but I'm so unsteady. People stare at me—of course they do. I look fresh out of a war zone.

It can't be true. It isn't true. It can't be true.

My mind swims: drinking in the chaos of Manhattan; reliving what just happened. I can't believe I'm really out here. Christ, I'm almost scared.

It can't be true. It isn't true. It can't be true.

I glance up the street and back behind me, looking for... what? A police officer? A frantic civilian?

One foot in front of the other... *Keep on moving, Kellan.* My lungs make a sound like tissue paper. The inside of my nose and throat is raw—raw and so painful, I'm starting to tremble and sweat.

It can't be true. It isn't true. It can't be true.

I think of what I'm running from. A moan escapes. A woman in front of me turns to look at me. Her eyes widen. She spins around, lengthens her strides.

It can't be true. It isn't true. It can't be true.

It can't be true. It isn't true. It can't be true.

It can't be true. It isn't true. It can't be true.

I'm moaning with every step I take now. Pain is a monsoon—drenching me inside and out. It's a reminder of the many risks I'm taking. When I was there, I was comfortably numb. When I was there...

It can't be true. It isn't true. It can't be true.

It can't be true. It isn't true. It can't be true.

Finally, the subway. Fear penetrates the thick fog of denial as I move down the filthy stairwell. I try not to touch the rail, but I can't descend without it. I wrap my fingers around the cool metal—consequences be damned.

It doesn't matter. Nothing matters now.

It can't be true. It isn't true. It can't be true.

I stick my dirty hand into the pocket of my jacket and flex my fingers, fumbling with my Metrocard. Somewhere nearby, a train thunders. I shiver. Inhale exhale. *Quiet, Kellan.*

It's a losing battle. I'm panting like a runner. People back away and stare. I hear someone whisper, "no shoes," and from another mouth, "addict."

It can't be true. It isn't true. It can't be true.

It can't be true. It isn't true. It can't be true.

My head is still so foggy, but I realize I need to choose somewhere to go.

It can't be true. It isn't true. It can't be true.

I can only think of one hotel right now: the Carlyle, where Lyon and I stayed with Dad before he said goodbye to us that day in November. Almost a year ago. I bring my fist to my mouth. I pull my hand down at the last minute.

Now the train is here. People moving.

I manage the two steps up without losing my balance. It smells... like dirty laundry and old fruit. I grab a nearby pole, close my eyes to bear the pain in my feet.

The train lurches. I clutch the pole and let my broken body sway and tremble with the rocking motion.

Time thins out and starts to twist around things like a string. I can't control the moaning. My knees can't hold my weight. I'm on the floor and there's a woman kneeling by me.

"Honey—you look ill. Are you okay?"

It can't be true. It isn't true. It can't be true.

I try to nod, even though the motion hurts my head.

"Would you like me to help you at the next stop?" she asks. "You're not an addict, are you? You're a veteran."

It can't be true. It isn't true. It can't be true.

I pinch the bridge of my nose. I swallow, using the razorblade sensation in the back of my throat to stay conscious.

"We're stopping now. You want me to help you off, honey, or call someone?"

I lick my cracked lips.

Hands and shoulders get me to my feet—maybe more than one set. I'm moving down the stairs. The hands let go. So much effort to stay standing. The next time I open my eyes, it's because tears are spilling from them. I'm swaying under an awning. I don't feel anything but pain.

"Come sit down, sir. Mr... ?"

"Walsh." My voice is so soft, I doubt she hears me—but the answer satisfies me. I will never be Kellan Drake again.

"Sit here." There's a bench. I slump onto it, keening like an animal. I hear the stranger tsk around me, murmuring to herself.

"Okay now, here's a cab for you," she says in soothing tones. "Where should I have him take you? How about the VA Hospital?"

"Hotel," I manage. I groan. "Cash."

"You know, my grandson is a Navy SEAL. I've got cash—about a hundred in my wallet. But look here, I see an ATM right over there across the way."

It can't be true. It isn't true. It can't be true.

I reach into my jacket and pull out my debit card. It feels strange in my fingers. I crack one lid and hold it out toward her shadow. "Zero three... zero... five."

"How much would you like?"

"Max," I croak.

I see a yellow cab through bleary eyes. I can't seem to focus on the shadow woman's face.

Maybe she's my mother, come to guide me through—

It can't be true. It isn't true. It can't be true.

I don't so much step as fall into the cab. The driver jets off. I can't remember if I told him where to go, or if I got my cash. The woman was...

I bend over. Clutch my head. I can't remember how I got into the cab, can only think of—

It can't be true. It isn't true. It can't be true.

It can't be true. It isn't true. It can't be true.

It can't be true. It isn't true. It can't be true.

I crack my eyes open to a view of beads hanging from a rear-view mirror. Underneath it, the city marching by. "Do you... have sanitizer?" I rasp. "Hand—"

A bottle is thrust into my hands. My fingers shake.

"Here!" The driver snatches it away. I blink and swallow. My throat *burns*.

The bottle lands in my lap, the top flipped open. I squeeze some out into my palm. The smell of alcohol consumes me.

The next time I open my eyes, we're at the Carlyle. My throat hurts so much, it's making things blur.

I can't go back. I won't.

I hand the man my debit card. He shakes his head. "She paid, before we leave."

I nod. *Okay*.

But I'm not okay. I can't get my legs to move. My head is spinning like a top. I start to cough. The short man comes around to help me. As he wraps his hand around my wrist and I try to shift my hips, my jacket flops open. His eyes fly to my chest, and then pop wide.

"Not here," he says, shaking his head. "This no the right place. You not get out here."

I laugh and struggle out, onto my feet and through the hotel's automatic doors. I stagger into the lobby like a bear into a palace. I find the nearest chair and list into it, sweating.

It can't be true. It isn't true. It can't be true.

It can't be true. It isn't true. It can't be true.

I try to focus. Breathe.

I guess somehow I get a room. I get a room with the wad of cash tucked into my jacket pocket, and manage to ride the elevator up to it.

When I open my eyes, the clock beside this strange bed says 11:49 PM.

My throat is dry. It hurts so much I start to shake.

My stomach is awash with nausea, even as my body screams for food. I roll over on my side and am surprised to find a tray beside me on the bed. With a trembling hand, I lift the receipt. My eyes seem wet. I can't read it.

I tear a piece of bread, but it's no use. As soon as I feel it in the back of my throat, I'm vomiting.

I feel the edge of panic start to fray around me.

Soon, someone will come...

I slide off the bed and crawl over to a chair beside the window. So dark outside. Maybe just stay here on the floor...

TWO

Cleo

September 10, 2014

I STEP THROUGH THE GLASS door slowly. Once, while I was still down on my hands and knees out on the balcony, I called his name. But that's the only time.

I look around the bedroom. That bed—sans canopy now—with its thick headboard and tree-sized posts. The vast expanse of hardwood, topped by rug. The lamps on shelves and tables, wearing dust.

The urge to call out for him pulls at me, but I don't want to give him the satisfaction. I straighten my shoulders and wait.

His arms come around me like a dream. His chest against my back, his hands cupping my hips. He turns me toward him, and we're like a wicked fairy tale. Me with the sick gallop of my heart. Him with his hard face, his staunch mouth.

The room is warm with sunlight. He carries me away from the gold glow, toward the shadow of the bed. He lays me on my back and folds my arms over my chest. My hands rest on my shoulders.

I wonder where he went before he hid behind me, in the curtains, but I don't think it really matters. It's a game we're playing. I want to stay in it, so I just lick my lips.

I keep my eyes fixed on the ceiling, even as I feel him moving just behind my line of sight. I hear him opening a drawer. The ceiling gives a groan, and then it opens. Fear deadens my limbs. I watch a metal fixture lower down over me. Ropes. I don't know what this means. My eyes try to tug toward him, but I don't let them. For reasons unknowable to me, I don't want him to see my nervousness.

A metal bar shaped like an X hovers over me, about five feet above the bed. Thick, white ropes hang down from each of its four ends.

Kellan comes into my line of sight, standing shirtless by the bed. He's grim and... different. I don't know exactly how, but I can sense a shift inside him—and it makes my heart pound harder, even though I wouldn't say I'm *scared.*

He climbs up on the bed and takes one of the ropes in hand.

"If you stay," he says slowly, "I'm going to bind your wrists and ankles. I'm going to fuck you until I'm tired." He blows his breath out. "It takes a long time, Cleo." He tightens his fist around the rope. "This is for me. I will make sure you enjoy it, but at some point, you'll get tired—and I'll want to keep going."

I whisper, "Try me."

I don't know why. Because I'm scared? Because I'm spurred by my ridiculous bravado? This same shadow, tucked inside me, laughs when police cruisers rotate through the parking lots on campus, booting tires... while I walk by, my straw bag swinging from my shoulders.

There's something bad about me. Years ago, before I learned to hide it, Grans would call it pride—but it's more than that. It's recklessness. It's sin.

This stupid bar, these stupid ropes, they're nothing. There's a part of me that needs to play this game with him. I didn't even know my dark spirit could rise to sex, but...

"Try me, Kellan."

"You want to do this?"

"Yeah." The word sounds nervous. The girl inside me, normal Cleo, *is* nervous, but I don't tell him that. I'm shaking a little as he watches me. He's serious and still. He's beautiful.

"What's your safe word, Cleo?"

"Sloth," I whisper.

"Is that a nickname?"

I nod and he slides his arms under mine, pulls me against his chest, and moves me over, so he can lower the X-bar down to the bed. When it's lying atop the sheets, he reaches down to the footboard for a slip of mattress he smooths over the X. This way I'll be lying on padding, with the X-shaped bar beneath them. The only purpose the bar will serve is to anchor the rope that will bind my ankles and wrists. He lays me down on the tuft of padding like a sacrifice.

He doesn't speak or even seem to breathe as he mounts my hips and begins to bind my right wrist.

My heart throbs in my ears. I start to look at him for lines, for the point where I would start if I were sketching him. I'd do his shoulder lines real smooth. I'd make his cheeks stand out the way they do right now. And pensive lips. I close my eyes and feel his fingers brushing my hand. Flexing and straining as he gets the rope just right.

I take a slow breath as that wrist is fully bound.

He shifts his weight, and I feel a bolt of something hot and satisfying. I love being under him. I think maybe this proximity is the best thing I've ever felt. How I can feel it when he takes a breath. How I can smell him. How it's foreign and I want to breathe it deeper. He's so pretty. He's so strange. He's got my left hand now.

"You're at my mercy," he murmurs.

I'm proud that I'm excited now, not scared.

He moves his heavy straddle down my hips, my thighs. He leans back on his heels and spreads my knees apart. His hands are gentle, running down my calves.

He coils the rope around my ankle. "Scaring you is not my goal."

"What is?" I whisper, peeking up at him.

His eyes bore through me, slide away. He lifts my right ankle and sets it down atop the rope. "Making you feel pain and pleasure—so you can enjoy them both. Have you ever gotten off from pain?"

The word burns through me. I shift my head a little, trying to escape the warm blush on my cheeks. A strand of hair falls in my face. I reach for it. The rope stops my wrist before my fingers even fully stretch.

Kellan's blue gaze presses on mine. I shift my eyes away, but feel his linger on me in a subtle show of dominance. I have to work to stop a smile from blooming on my face.

He finishes tying my ankle and I try to scissor my legs, just for the sensation of failure.

Kellan grins, wolfish. He's crouched at my feet in nothing but his khakis. He looks vibrant. Energized. And his upper body... damn. It's like a statue.

His dancing eyes elevate his beauty to an almost supernatural level. For once, his face looks... light. I scrutinize his features and find the word I'm looking for: jubilant.

He moves between my legs and leans to plant a kiss behind my knee. I thought seeing me bound would stoke him to a frenzy, but I didn't understand. Now that he has me where he wants me, he's relaxed.

He trails his warm mouth up and down my inner thighs until my pussy has its own heartbeat—and when he parts my lips and strokes me with his tongue, my hips buck off the bed.

His tongue rolls through my swollen slit. I push myself against his face. The ropes tug at my wrists and ankles. Pleasure sears me as his tongue laps at my sopping core. I try to scoot away. I moan. I rock forward.

"It's too soon to come, Cleo."

He teases at my entrance, stuffing his tongue inside, dragging it out. He laps up and down my folds. When I'm moaning, trembling and helpless, he scoops his hands under my ass. He shifts my hips up off the bed, tugs my ass cheeks apart, and meets my puckered entrance with his soft, wet lips. I gasp as he tries to push his tongue inside.

Into my dripping pussy, he stuffs a third finger.

"I like this little asshole, Cleo," he breathes against it. "One day soon, I'm going to work my way inside it."

For today, he lubes me with his tongue and pushes a pinkie finger in. It's overwhelming, being stretched back there, while three fingers writhe in my cunt and his slick, hot tongue teases my swollen clit.

I come hard and helpless, panting as my wrists jerk against their binds.

My chest is heaving when my brain reboots. I feel... electrified. I curl my fingers inward, pull against the ropes.

"Relax."

I do—because I want to show him I can handle this.

He licks my pussy once more, making me struggle against my binds, then tugs his pants down just below his rigid hips, revealing a mouth-watering treasure trail and his long, stiff dick.

It's fucking huge: a cock, for sure. It's so ridiculously... perfect—like everything about him. It could be a mold for a dildo company. He wraps his hand around it, loosely pumping up and down, and I think this should be a .gif, gracing Tumblr feeds.

He grins. His eyes look sleepy—hypnotized. He tips his weeping head toward me. "You want my cock inside your pussy, Cleo?"

I nod. Restraint, propriety... pride: all fall to the feet of lust.

He shifts on his knees and pulls a condom from the pocket of his pants, still bunched below his hips. Then he parts my folds with deft fingers. He swirls his swollen head through my slickness, pressing at my entrance long enough to make me moan.

He grabs my hips and nudges in. I freeze at the invasion, all my focus falling to my tender entrance. I'm soaked, but swollen too, and he's so big. It's a stretch, even just the tip of him.

I shift my hips a little at the sting.

He groans.

I writhe against him.

"Cleo... you're so fucking tight."

The sting sharpens as he pushes slowly in. Oh fuck, he can't get in. With a swift thrust of his hips, his head pops in. I moan.

I look down because I feel so full of him, but... it's just his head.

"Oh, shit," I pant.

His eyes hold mine as he pushes inside, inch by inch. I moan, clenching. I peek up at him, watching his face tighten as he settles. His eyes slip shut, and I can hear him swallow.

God—he feels so good. I bite my lip and try to keep myself from rocking against him yet.

He twists his hips a little, sending waves of bliss through me. He presses his palms on each side of my shoulders and stretches his glorious torso over me. With his eyes hot on mine, he shifts his hips, pressing the base of his dick against my clit. I let my breath out.

"Oh my God..."

I feel every inch of him—and that's enough. It's more than enough... until his forehead drops into the crevice of my neck. I feel his soft lips brush my shoulder. His voice drifts through me. "You're so tight..."

I love the rasp of it. The need.

"I like this," I say. It's all I can think of, and I mean it.

I nudge my chin into his hair. My heart beats hard. I whisper, "You're so big."

He punches deeper and my eyes roll back.

He draws out slowly.

Shoves back in.

"I would call you a slut. A little cock whore." He withdraws his hard length as his eyes hold mine. "But I don't think you are." He thrusts his head slowly back in, stretching my entrance. "You're not a whore, Cleo. You're playing slut—for me." His words flare like a match inside my chest.

He shoves his cock deeper inside me... rolls his hips. The base of his cock teases my clit.

I feel his hand against my throat. "Is it because I'm pretty?" he rasps.

I peek at him through my lashes, finding his face tight. He thrusts harder, deeper, and I come up off the bed.

His fingers press against my chin, lifting my head up. His eyes hold mine: searching.

Hard thrust in, then slow draw out... hard thrust in. I jerk around him, stretched so tight I can't help moaning.

"Master," I try, aiming to please.

He squeezes my hip. "This body is mine. No one else's. I'm gonna fuck you hard and use you up and treat you like my whore—and afterward, you're gonna tell me why you want me so much you've got tears coming out of your eyes."

He flexes his shoulders and finds a harder, deeper rhythm.

"What do you like about me?" His teeth nip my cheek. "Is it the money?" he purrs, his words punctuated by the hard thrusts of his cock. "Are you greedy, Cleo?"

I gasp, "Yes."

He kisses my lips tenderly, then sucks my neck so hard I moan. "Is it my body? My cock?"

"Your cock."

It's stretching me so wide, I'm gasping.

"It's because I make you come so hard. I can feel you squirt around me. I'm going to have to change the sheets."

My clit is throbbing. He shifts his weight, forcing himself deeper, so I feel... so full.

"Keep your eyes shut, Cleo. You're going to take what I give you. Keep on crying out. I like your little noises. I like shocking you."

His hands slide off my shoulders, and he punches in with so much force, I jerk against my binds.

He drops his head down, so I can only see the crown of it—gold-blond.

I feel his body curve slightly over mine. His knees dig into the mattress. His hands bare down against the sheets. Inside my softness, his cock gouges—making me feel empty and then full, empty and then bursting, empty and then—

He groans, a rough, dry sound, and I don't know what happens. I just... burst. I come so hard, my muscles burn. I come so hard, I feel the ropes bite.

I'm crying out and then he is. Just a husky bark, and then his warmth is pulsing in me. I squeeze my eyes shut. Squeeze my legs shut.

He's still in me.

"Oh God..."

Then he's pulling out. He's getting off the bed. There's a whisper of fabric as he pulls his pants back up. I feel the mattress shift, but can't tell where he went. My eyes are shut. My heart is beating so hard I feel strung out. Like he shot this lust into my veins. Tears drip from the corners of my eyes. Damnit, I feel... raw—and used.

I *am* his whore.

I listen to my blood roar in my ears and try to regulate my breathing while I wait for guilt to come, for shame.

I'm still waiting when I feel his weight indent the mattress. I peek my eyes open. As I peer into his handsome face, my chest heats. It's such a rush, it knocks my mind clean.

I like this, I realize. I like what we're doing here. The way he talks to me. It's dirty... but I crave it. More.

My mouth is already opening to goad him when I see what's in his hand: a LELO Ina.

His eyes, on mine, are wiser than I wish. He sees how wide he's cracked me open. And what's worse? He doesn't seem smug or excited. He just... looks at me. For one searching moment, his eyes hold mine. Saying... what? Intention curves through me, but I can't tell what kind.

Then he tugs his gaze down my belly. He scoots closer to me, settling between my legs. He stretches me open with two fingers and pushes the dildo into my swollen cunt. My eyes close in consent, so I can only feel his fingers position the clit piece. Vibrations sluice through me, forcing me to move my hips.

He pushes it deeper, and my mouth waters.

It starts to thrust. *It's thrusting on its own*—and I can't..."Oh!" Oh God! My muscles spasm.

"Hold on to it." His eyes are round and blue. "You're so damn slick. I'd hate to see it work its way out before you get the chance to come again."

He disappears for years or minutes. I try to clench the dildo inside me, and all the while, I want to push against it, urging its width deeper.

When he comes back, I'm curled slightly on my side, losing the battle. Only the smooth, round tip is still inside me, pulling at my tender folds. The tiny wand over my clit has slipped away, so I have to thrust my hips to feel its vibrations. Every thrust works the thick wand a little farther out of me. I'm panting like an animal.

Kellan chuckles as he watches me squirm.

"Help me! Let me come!"

I try to reach for him. The knots stop me. He climbs onto the bed as I flail, watching from above me with a coy smirk.

"You're ready?" he asks.

"Yes, please!"

I can't see. Oh—right: tears. Fuck me!

"That's a good girl." He wraps his hand around the base of the wand and shoves it back inside me. I moan.

"Does it feel as good as I do?" He shifts his hips, and I notice the huge hose of his dick straining against his pants.

He rubs his big palm up and down it. "You want this, don't you, Cleo?" He wraps his hand around his head and with his other hand, he pulls the dildo out of me.

My clit throbs so hard my legs fall open. I lift my hips and Kellan blurs.

He strokes my hair. "You want me to push inside your cunt. To fill you with my cock, give you every inch of me. Am I right, my little slut?"

My throat stings. "Yes..."

He leans down over me, and the ropes around my ankles tug as he adjusts the bar to spread my legs wider.

I watch him take his pants off. His dick is so huge, it has to curve to stay inside his charcoal boxer-briefs. My mouth waters as he frees it from the fabric. It springs up against his smooth, tanned six-pack. The girth makes me moan. The head of him is pearled with pre-cum.

"I can stuff you full of cock. My cock would love to stretch you open. I can see this cunt is hungry for me."

He leans down and runs his fingers through my sopping slit. My hips come off the bed.

I'm dying as I watch him roll another condom on, too slow. He spreads my lips. He edges closer to me, as if my pussy and his dick are connected by an invisible fuck string. Then he takes his monster cock in hand and rubs the swollen head against my core.

I scream.

"What a filthy little whore." His eyes burn mine. "Just aching for my cock, aren't you?"

"Yes, please. *Please!*"

He rubs his thumb over my clit.

"Oh God!"

He feeds his cock into me inch by slow, sweet inch. I look down and watch myself impaled. I'm stuffed so tight my hips feel compelled to move.

I shift my ass. He grits his teeth.

"Yes! *Yes...*"

With one smooth stroke, he punches in. I moan.

"Cleo." He thrusts. I groan. He presses my thighs apart, and it's like he knows—I'll have to spread more if I want to take him all.

"You're full already," he rasps. "I can feel you stretched around my cock. But that's not all of me, Cleo. Are you ready for me again?"

With his eyes on mine, he pushes deeper, stretching me exquisitely. Each shift of his huge cock sends a sweet ache surging through me.

My legs sag open. My eyelids drift to half-mast as I lift my hips to feel him move within me. "Fuck..."

"I'm not even moving yet."

"Please do," I pant.

"What do you need to say?"

"Please, Master. Please fuck me."

And he does. He fucks me twice in that position. When I'm sure my heart will burst—that I will die here, from another crashing orgasm—he repositions me. I'm on my stomach with my arms over my head. My nose and mouth press into the mattress. By the time he unbinds my wrists, the sun is setting.

THREE

Cleo

OH, SHIT.

I'm in the windowed room's en suite shower, and that's seriously all my brain can muster.

Shit.

I've washed every inch of my body with the thick bar of French lavender soap I found in its bow-tied, burlap wrapping, but I can't seem to turn the water off. I watch it slosh around my toes like mini rapids. Watch it all slide down the drain—until the steam starts fading. The water runs lukewarm, then cold.

I'm a card-carrying member of the Scorching Shower Lovers Club, so I turn the lever and grab my towel from the small tile bench built into the back of the shower.

I dry myself, then wrap my hair. I step over to a granite countertop and grab another fluffy towel for my body.

When I'm dry enough to touch my phone, I check for word from Kellan, but there's no text or missed call. After he untied me, I remember him cleaning me off with a warm, damp cloth and rubbing some oil on my shoulders. I guess I must have drifted off to sleep, because when I awoke, my cell phone was beside me on the pillow, and on the screen was a text he'd sent: **I'm 1 in your phone now. Call if you need. Gone to sort out some shit. Back later tonight. Food in the oven. Make yourself at home.**

That was around 6:30. It's 8:50 now. I consider texting him—but why? To be sure he's okay? Really?

Instead I unpack my toiletries, brush my teeth, smooth some olive oil lotion all over my body, and put on my favorite ragged gray sweatpants with a hot pink Greek Sing t-shirt. I drift around the windowed room, first averting my eyes from the bed, then staring at it from the safety of the balcony.

Shit.

That's still all I have.

Shit, that was amazing. Shit, that was crazy. Shit, that was intense. Shit, that Kellan Walsh. Just... fucking shit.

What am I doing?

That wasn't sex, I think as I descend the stairs. It was... ritual. Some kind of pleasure-pain ritual that blurred all my lines and took me somewhere new. Somewhere I can't walk without a bite of pain between my legs.

As I step into the swanky living room, I imagine my old Sunday School teacher, Mrs. Elvira, with her short, gray hair and baby doll-round hazel eyes.

"Sex should be for husband and a wife."

I know I don't agree with that, but I've always thought before now that it should at least be mutually satisfying.

But I *am* satisfied, I argue as I sit on his white couch. I'm so satisfied, I'm almost floating. Because Kellan Walsh tied me up and did everything short of smacking me in the face with his dick.

Do I like to be degraded?

I liked being bound.

I'm weird.

Is it weird?

It's a little weird.

I bite my lip and look down at the pale suede couch. A few inches away from me, there's a small black ink stain. I rub it with my fingertip. I'm satisfied, okay? Alarmingly so. But is that incidental? Did he *care* if I was? He told me that, though, didn't he? That he wanted to please me, but he was going to keep going until he got tired.

Is he some kind of sex addict?

I ponder this in the safety of his high-gloss kitchen. I'm pleased to find what's in the oven is some kind of ham, potato, and pineapple casserole. I have no idea who made it, but it's delicious. I pour myself a glass of lemonade and settle on the couch.

Should I call Lora? No. Calling Lora reminds me too much of yapping about Brennan. This thing with Kellan is... I don't know what, but for now, it's mine.

I find two remotes beside a stack of post cards on an end table. I tinker with them as I stuff my face.

"Damnit..." I'm a mess with technology. I manage to get the TV on, but it's got a mysterious blue screen. I screw around with the remote as I nom nom. Then I drag my sore self up and walk to the enormous TV.

Fucked and chucked... a little voice whispers.

Is that what he did? It's true he's gone now—but isn't that a coincidence? He had to go, to deal with something. I inhale deeply, and I can smell the faintest whiff of the vanilla-ish oil he rubbed into my shoulders.

I don't need to bother wondering what other people would think. The only thing I didn't like about the crazy sex we had was how overwhelmed I felt. But isn't that also what I *did* like? I feel like we rolled off a cliff together. Started falling. Maybe we don't have an emotional relationship to serve as a kind of safety net, but if it's only physical, do we even need one?

I bite my lip and turn on the DVD player. The screen remains blue. Because the DVD player is already on. Well okay, that explains things.

As I stare at the settings on the DVD player, something pops into my head: a memory from before I went into my post-sex sleep-haze thing.

"This body is mine. No one else's. I'm gonna fuck you hard and use you up—and afterward, you're gonna tell me why you want me so much you've got tears coming out of your eyes."

He's right. I want him so much it scares me. The worst part, I think as run my finger over the buttons: I know deep down that I don't want him for his money, or because he's hot, or because, in all his duality, he seems dangerous. There's no clear reason I want Kellan Walsh enough to let him lick my asshole.

No reason at all.

I ponder this as I turn the DVD player off and look down at the TV. Now the screen is black. I turn the DVD player on again: blue screen.

"Ugh."

Maybe I don't even care about watching TV. Maybe I'll call Lora after all.

I put my hands on my hips and let my eyes drift around the room. It's the first time I've really looked since I've been here, and I'm impressed by its opulence.

The rear wall, facing the river, is pretty much just windows, with a few giant potted plants in front of them. There are windows in the ceiling, too, strips of glass between exposed beams. The hardwood floor is beautiful and glossy, the walls a mint so soft it's almost white. But what really makes the room is the décor.

The white and brown suede chairs and sofas; the stained glass, Tiffany-style lamps; the enormous Oriental rug that's dominated by brown and blue and beige, with the occasional dash of red. There's a long, intricately carved cuckoo clock along that wall that leads to the kitchen. Adorning most of the space to the left of the clock is a huge... a reproduction of a famous Rousseau painting I happen to love. It's called *Negro Attacked by Jaguar.*

If I remember correctly from my art classes, this was one Rousseau painted near the end of his life. It's mostly jungle, with an orange-red sun, and in the center of the image is a shadow being pounced on by a tiger, which is standing on its hind legs, so it almost looks like it's dancing with the man. It's kind of hard to explain exactly what's so great about it, but I think it's all in the dimensions.

I wander over to it, because I want to see if I'm correct—that it's an actual painting. I walk around a claw-footed end table, and behind the couch, bare feet smacking against the hardwood floor—and yeah. It's definitely some kind of high-quality reprod.

I pick a spot at the edge of the painting and touch my finger to it. Then I stretch my arms out. The painting is at least three feet wider than my arm span. I tip my head up, because I just noticed a wall-mounted lamp above it—like the ones they have in museums—and as I do, the boom of a man's voice makes me jump.

I whirl toward the TV.

"What the..." Okay. I blow my breath out, laughing. Holy shit, that scared me, but it's just the TV coming on. Finally.

Football, I realize as I turn fully around.

The first thing I notice is, it's grainy. As if the film is from a while back, before filming things in high-def was the norm.

The second thing I notice: *Kellan.*

My eyes snap to him as he raises his arm to throw the ball. I'm mesmerized as I walk around the TV. Trojans... I walk closer to it. Holy fucking shit, that's USC? Kellan played for USC? He played football?

He turns as he completes the throw, and I blink at his number: 14. God, I can't believe that's Kellan. It *is* Kellan, playing fucking quarterback. So why is the name stretched across his shoulders DRAKE?

I walk closer to the TV. I figure out how to get the player open and I look at the DVD. I start to open drawers in the entertainment center, looking for the DVD's case. And then I find it: TROJANS: VAULT—2012.

I sit on the couch for twenty more minutes, watching Kellan move around the field. Soaking in every detail. I listen to the announcer talk about Kellan Drake, and I know as soon as I turn the DVD player off, I'm going to search my phone for Kellan Drake, USC student.

Questions whirl through my mind—like how a USC quarterback could blend into the fabric of our student body here at CC without attracting anyone's notice. Is it possible that I'm the only one who doesn't know about his past?

I watch as he jogs to the bench. He takes his helmet off. His hair is black. My pulse thuds in my throat. His hair is black, but that's his face. What the hell is going on? I pull my phone out and open up my browser window.

FOUR

Kellan

I DRIVE IN CIRCLES, blind to everything. My hands on the handles, the tilt of my body as the road curves—I move on memory. My mind is reeling, even as my body feels so good and satiated.

I didn't know.

I should have known.

I didn't know, and when I did, I let her stay.

It's wrong. So fucking wrong, to let her near me.

She won't find out, I want to scream—but if she did.

I don't care... can't care. And that's how I know I'm truly sick.

I shouldn't need anyone the way I need to string her up. It just confirms what a monster I've become.

"I'm Nessa."

"Kellan," I say teasingly.

"You deal weed, don't you?"

"Who's asking?"

She smiles. Her lips are blood red. Her skin is white.

I touch her auburn hair. "Is this stuff real?"

"My hair?" She laughs.

"It looks like a wig."

"No, it's mine." She smiles again.

"It's beautiful."

"Thank you."

"Why are you here? I've seen you before, at—"

"I want to help you with the... special cases. Someone told me what you do."

I look into her brown eyes. "Why?"

"Because I like to break the rules. And because I like to make a difference, you know?"

"Make a difference?"

"Don't judge." She smirks. "You don't know me. There's no type for Nessa."

"You're brave, to come to me like this."

She shrugs. "I trust you. We're not so different."

"If you want to deal for me, you'll have to live with me first."

I'm only teasing, so I'm surprised when she nods.

"That doesn't bother you?"

"Not much bothers me, Kellan. What is it they say? It's all small stuff."

I blink. "Except the big stuff."

I mean it as a perverse allusion. She takes it differently. Her deep brown irises seem to pool. She bites her lip, and I can almost taste her sorrow.

"I just want to feel like I can do something."

I nod, because I understand. I push open my front door—the one she just came through. "Come back tomorrow, Nessa. Bring your bags."

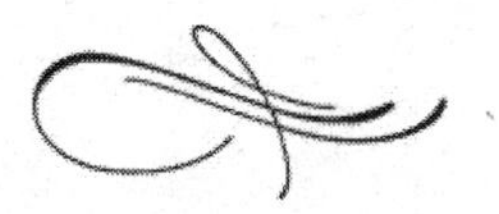

I fly down a busted county road that starts just south of the Chattahoochee city limits and juts northwest, curving through a ten-mile tuft of thick pine forest. The faded asphalt is spotted by moisture from a recent rain. I steer my new Ducati 899 Panigale into the pale trace worn on the dark road by cars' tires.

The speed limit is 55. I push the bike to 80, 85, 90 before I start to ease up on the juice.

It's dangerous, but then that's how I'm feeling.

If I lost control and wrecked, wouldn't that be preferable to what will happen if I don't?

My heart is pounding hard. Making me feel sick. But that's fitting, isn't it? What kind of monster would I be if I didn't feel ill?

I pick a firm-looking shoulder to veer off and angle the bike for a quick, ten-foot descent over battered grass, into a bed of pine needles. I park at the edge of an eternity of pines and swing off the bike's seat.

For a second, I just stand here, testing out my legs. Nothing about this night seems real, so it's almost surprising that I have a body—much less one that does the things I tell it to. My mind is back at home, curled up somewhere near Cleo.

Sloth... she says it is. Dear fuck.

I grab a freezer-sized Ziploc baggie from my pack, tuck it in the pocket of my black jacket, and step deeper into the trees. The entrance to Nessa's neighborhood is well lit, so I'm cutting through a fourth a mile of forest, using the light from the subdivision's welcome sign to signal my exit.

Every heavy footstep drives her through my head.

Sloth... Sloth... Sloth.

What are the odds?

What are the odds?

My mind should be on Nessa but it circles *her*. I wonder what the chances are, in numbers. Out of all the colleges in Georgia... How many students? How many of them female? Only one of them is her. What are the chances we would meet?

Well, you came here for her...

It's not entirely true. She was just a thought, a distant want. Yeah, I wrote to her—notebooks full—but that's not all. I've always liked the luscious South, starting with a family trip to St. Simon's Island the year before my mother died. Lyon and I were eight, and Barrett thirteen. We stayed for three weeks by the sea. My dad came just four days.

She's a dealer—Sloth is?

I can't reconcile it. It doesn't fit with my picture of her. And yet, it kind of does. I imagine her swinging her arms around, all jacked up on Vyvanse; I can see that black shawl flapping around her. Cleo, kneeling, making faces at Truman. I can see a younger Cleo, getting high and eating pizza.

Why is it so shocking? That a good person—a person whom I know to be inherently good and generous—would sell marijuana?

I don't want her getting caught.

If she was doing it anyway...

I don't want her anywhere near me. And yet—

And yet.

I see the white glow of the subdivision's sign, and step out of the woods in the shadow of two houses that I know don't have security lights. The lots in this neighborhood are about two acres each, and there are plenty of trees and hedges to hide behind as I make my way to Nessa's quiet circle.

Her house is a two-story dollhouse, painted deep lavender with mint green accents. It's a new home, but it's meant to look Victorian. Her parents bought it for her after the break she took last year.

I've been here dozens of times, but lately I just haunt the yard. Nessa always leaves the curtain open, just for me.

Tonight, I take my time among the hedges and the azaleas that encircle her house, moving from window to window on the balls of my feet. My heart pounds. I start to sweat. Tonight will shape up different from those prior nights. I haven't done the deed yet, but I can tell I will. It's... both strange and not. It's natural and deplorable.

It's me, making good on a promise.

I find Nessa in a little library, framed by floor-length burlap curtains. She's wearing blue sweatpants, a giant white Auburn University sweatshirt—probably one of her father's—and fuzzy yellow socks. She's sitting on a sea blue couch, blaring Broken

Bells from the speakers of her iPhone and moving her shoulders to the beat.

I watch her as she checks her phone—looking for a message from Ryan, her on-again-off-again?—As she runs her fingers through her tight curls. As she paints her toe-nails some greenish color that's not clear to me through glass, and from this distance. I fall into a calm as I watch her balance her checkbook, a habit I know her mom demands. I watch her drink peppermint water. Take her Kindle from a desk and read a book.

After seven weeks of this, I know her habits. Nessa has ADD, and now that she's withdrawn from school again, she seems to drift through evenings, moving from one thing to the other, trying to entertain herself without really seeming settled.

After more than an hour peeking through her window, I walk around the house again and mess with a flimsy window in her first-floor half bath. I know from past visits that I could open it without much trouble, but I'm pretty sure that's not the way I'll go. Why would I, when I have a key?

I walk through the dewy grass behind the house, where she keeps her garbage cans as well as a small, baby blue bicycle. My pulse is racing as I re-approach the little study room she's in.

Nessa is still there. Now she's drinking coffee from an owl mug.

I think of Cleo. Sloth. I'm hoping that the guilt I feel over not sending her away tonight will distract me from the lead ball in my gut right now, but no such luck.

There's no hiding from tonight—not even behind the shock of Sloth. Tonight has been a long time coming. I just couldn't get the balls to do it for these last few weeks.

I tilt my head back, look up at the moon. The stars. I can see so many of them out here, miles away from city lights. Even Chattahoochee, an old mill town-turned-college-town of thirty thousand, doesn't put off enough light to really blot out the stars. Not like where I'm from.

Somewhere nearby, a dog barks.

I hold my breath and listen. It's quiet after the dog settles, nothing but the sound of trees moving and the low hum of traffic, somewhere miles away. I picture Nessa standing out here with me, smiling that faint smile of hers. That smile that said *I have a secret.*

Like my secret.

I can't think long of that, can't think at all of that, so I start walking, around the edge of Nessa's porch, toward the giant magnolia tree in the middle of her soft, green lawn.

The thing is massive, only a little shorter than the roofline of her house. I turn my body sideways and I work my way between its branches. Its limbs press against my back and shoulders, come around my hips, until I'm hidden by its waxy, oval leaves.

Once I'm settled in, I hold my body still, trying to be sure I know my own mind.

Can I do this?

I can do this.

I pull my phone out of my pants pocket. I can do this, but first...

I rub my thumb over the screen, calling up the picture I took of Cleo a few months ago on the concourse. I clench my aching jaw and peer down at her. After this is over, I can go back to her.

Wrong wrong wrong.

After this is over, I can fuck her.

It's wrong—because of who I am, my situation; it's even more wrong because of who she is, and what she is to me—but I know already I will keep her for at least a few more nights. Because I have to. Because I'll need her after this.

Despite my own assurances, air whistles through my teeth. Blood booms like a drum between my ears.

I rub my brows—a little too hard. My fingers curl into fists. I think numbly of Lyon.

Lyon, Ly... please help.

After almost an hour of this madness, I dial Nessa. She answers wordlessly. I breathe into the phone. Swallow. "You know why I'm calling," I rasp.

"Yes."

"What are you doing, Nessa?"

"Dancing." She sounds nervous. "Just drinking a little wine."

"Oh yeah. What kind?"

"Hmmmm... honestly, I don't know," she giggles. "It's red, and it was the most expensive bottle they had at the store."

"Be sure to save a glass for me."

"I will."

I exhale slowly. I'm surprised by the strength of my desire to tell her about Cleo. Sloth.

But this isn't about that. Or about me.

"Do anything special tonight?" I ask.

"I saw a shooting star."

My stomach clenches. "Yeah?"

"Yep."

"Did you make a wish?"

"I did."

I swallow hard, willing my throat not to close up on me. "Was it that I'd call," I tease. My voice is strange—but Nessa understands.

I can hear her gentle smile. "It was about you. You know what."

"That I would call you?" I ask, even though I know that's not what she wished for. "Then, wish granted."

She laughs a little, but says nothing, and soon there's a silence.

"I should let you go," I say.

"See you soon."

"... Goodnight."

"Goodnight Kellan."

I wait almost two more hours, to be sure she is asleep. Usually, she has trouble. But the wine and the Ambien will help.

The lights have been off for almost two hours now.

I move from the tree to her porch in half a heartbeat, my shoulders curled in as my key slides silently into her lock. I turn the knob and slip inside.

I'm in the two-story foyer, with an oak staircase I take two steps at a time. I pause on the top stair. Listen.

Nessa is asleep, not in the master bedroom, which she feels is too big and uses for storage, but in the larger of the two bedrooms down the hall to my right.

I pass a family portrait: Nessa with her mom and dad, dressed in their church clothes. To my left is a framed photo of Nessa with her best friend, Hope. On the right, a pressed, framed rose from Ryan.

I pass a closet door. I look down and—

"Fuck!"

I throw my arms out, trying to keep my balance, while Nessa's cat, Cheshire, dashes off, then doubles back, his tail waving, to look at me. I lower my hand, but I can't make myself crouch down and pet him.

"Sorry," I murmur silently.

I move slowly, walking softly. I don't want to wake her up. I don't think she'll wake up.

Stay asleep, Nessa. Stay asleep.

Her bedroom door is slightly ajar. Thoughtful.

The room is dark, but the blinds are open, letting in starlight.

I pause at the threshold. The Ziploc bag feels heavy when I pull it from my pocket. It's melded around the small cylinder inside.

Taking care to be quiet, I peel the 'zipper' open. I stick my fingertips inside, grasping the end of the syringe. I dig a little deeper, until I can feel the cool glass of a vial I mixed up just for Nessa.

I'm surprised my fingers work. Amazing, what can be endured when choices are so limited. I stick the needle in, draw the plunger. My jaw aches, a precursor to tears. A scream builds in my chest. I lock it there, where it belongs.

I step over her pink polka-dotted rug. My limbs feel heavy, as if I've sampled Nessa's cocktail.

I take half-steps, past her feet, her knees, until I'm level with her hips. Under the lilac covers, she is just a lump. It strikes me that is all she'll ever be again. My eye twitches.

Nessa's bed has a large, carved headboard her mother had imported from Italy, if I remember. I can't see much of the carving, even here, beside her, but I stare up at it for a minute, because I want to see what's on it. My eyes never fully adjust to the darkness, as deep down I know they won't. I've got acquired night blindness. All I'm doing standing here is waiting.

Long enough, apparently, for Cheshire to come join us.

Shit.

I take long, steady strides toward the door and scoop the cat up. "C'mon... Stay quiet," I murmur to his soft head as I spirit him down the hall, toward the stairs. I set him down and stroke his neck and back. He arches to my hand. "That's it. Good boy." My voice quavers. Cheshire perches like a gymnast on the bannister.

When I return to Nessa, she's rolled over on her right side, with her back to me. I take a deep breath. I position the syringe between my fingers and lean over her. My hand hovers by her neck. Her hair is in my way. I move it slowly, relishing the softness of her curls. My fingers tremble. I will them still.

The jugular is not a mystery when you've dealt with it as much as I have. I locate hers with a gentle touch. She doesn't stir. It takes a moment to position the needle, and when I've done that, I plunge quickly in.

Nessa's breath hitches, and for a horrifying moment I think she's going to wake up just to die.

But she doesn't. The cocktail includes Midazolam, a sedative. Also, Dilaudid. So much of both drugs, the truth is, Nessa doesn't have a chance. And still, I stay. I wrap a copper curl around my finger and, with my arms still propped on her bed, I sink down to my knees. Her breaths go shallow. Shallow. *Quiet.*

When I fear the sound of my own heart will drive me mad, I get up and go.

FIVE

Kellan

September 20, 2011

"TAKE THOSE CLOTHES OFF—EVERYTHING... is what Arethea said. And then you've gotta put them in this bin." She points at the big, yellow garbage can, shoved into the corner of the bathroom. I can see her arm jut out, even though my eyes are focused on the floor. "You know the drill," she adds softly.

My gaze breaks away from the tile and throws itself at Whitney's face. In another life—one I lived just days ago—this girl's wide smile and mismatched green and blue eyes heralded homestyle comforts. Whitney Marsh: knitter of beanies and floppy socks. Whitney Marsh: Pinterest-a-holic. This girl can make a turkey out of an Oreo, a Hershey's Kiss, and candy corn. When life gives Whitney lemons, she makes lemonade in every color of the rainbow, sweetens it with Stevia, and donates the proceeds to childhood cancer. In a few more years, Whitney Marsh is going to help autistic children learn to talk through special iPad apps. She's Methodist. A little Marxist, which she won't reveal until she's had a few stiff drinks. Whitney was a virgin until my brother.

And so it's strange that she's my prison warden now.

Her mismatched eyes reach out to mine, so warm the heat of them threatens the ice I'm using as a shield. I shift my eyes away. They sink like anchors to the floor.

I shrug my shoulders, grateful that the simple motion sends my jacket falling to the blue tile.

"Jacket," she says in a quiet, tired voice. I'm not looking, but I sense her pick it up and put it in the bin.

I bend to remove my shoes, then change my mind and straighten slowly back up.

"Do you need some help?" I hear the fabric of her clothes swish as she steps toward me.

I turn away from her. I bend again, reach for my shoes, and end up on my ass. The cold of the tile bleeds through the fabric of my pants. I tug the shoes off, then the socks.

I hear the soles of her Chucks *mnnchh* against the floor behind me. I hear her scoop my shoes up. The bag inside the bin crinkles as she deposits them inside. Unsanitary: everything on me.

"I'm going to step around you, Kellan. Turn the shower on. Just do the same thing with your pants. I'll get them off the floor."

I clutch my head.

"I can help you up if you want. Do you want me to?" Motherfuck, she's right behind me.

"No," I growl.

I clench my jaw. I can't believe she's even here with me—but that's Whitney. Compulsively dependable. Like a sister... that my brother fucks.

FUCK*ED*.

"Go away," I snap.

I hear her retreat over by the door. I don't feel any guilt, although I know I should.

I get to my feet without her help and drop my running pants. I hope to fuck she isn't looking. That's just... weird.

I look over at the shower stall. The door is open, and now that the water's been running for a minute, a familiar, acrid scent leaks across the small bathroom, wafting to the low ceiling in bluish tufts of steam.

My knees feel weak as I try to figure out where she is now, within the room. I can feel her eyes on me. I hear her soft sniff.

"Go on, Kellan. You can get in. I'm not looking."

Stepping into the shower is a hard thing for me. I'm too tired to discern why, but my chest aches as I do it. The water is lukewarm, like always. Might as well be freezing. I shiver and step under the chemical water.

I don't move, just let it roll over me. They should really make this water warmer. I deserve warm water, I think numbly.

I sense Whitney move in front of the rippled glass door.

"Kellan?" she calls.

What the hell is wrong with her?

"I'm out here, but I can't see you. I'm sorry to corner you like this, but I'm going to talk. You need to listen."

I snort, pulling steam into my nose. The chemicals in the water burn into my sinuses like cocaine.

"I need you to hear me. Okay, Kellan?"

I shut my eyes.

"You made a bad choice, K. I get you lost your cool... but you might have ruined this whole thing in doing that. Have you thought about what that *means*? Is that what you even *want*? To force yourself into a corner?" Her voice echoes through the tiny room. "Is that what you want?" Her voice is breathy quiet; shrill. Because she's on the verge of tears. "I want to know. Is that what you want, Kellan? To just... give up?"

I look down at myself. I hate everything about my life right now—including her. So I tell her, "Go the fuck away. And Whitney? Don't come back."

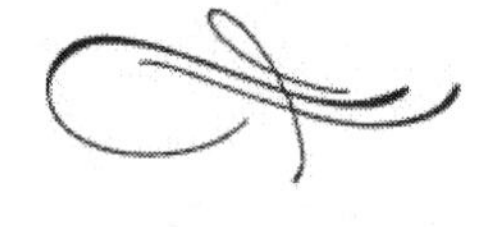

Cleo

September 11, 2014

I want a dog... but I don't have one. I don't think I... pet him on the head. He's warm. Soft hair.

"Roll over."

I'm supposed to tell him that, I thought?

Mmm.

I roll over, mashing my breasts into the mattress and sinking back down into sleep.

I crack open my eyes because I'm being tickled. My arms...

I try to move them and I find I can't.

Fear slices through my grumpiness. I try again to move, and as my eyes blink, I spot Kellan. He's lording over me. It's dark. I'm on my back now, and Kellan—

"Ahh."

I look down and find his head is pushed against my entrance.

"Oh God." My voice is low and hoarse with sleep.

He pushes in a little, making me grunt.

"I can't move," I whimper. I'm so sleepy.

"You're not going anywhere." His voice is low—a nighttime voice.

He's shadowed by the moonlight spilling through the windows. His thick shaft pushes in a fraction more, and I inhale. Now that I'm waking up a little more, I can smell him: sweat and male. I can see his face: so taught and solemn. I wonder how his outing went. I don't even remember falling asleep.

I drop my legs open a little wider, and his hand closes around my hip. He rocks gently against me until my body welcomes more of him.

"You're so damn tight." His hand trails up my arm. "You're gonna take in all of me—deep into your pussy, then your throat."

He strokes my belly gently, sending chills over my skin; making my inner muscles clench around his hard length.

"I need to be inside you... have to be." His eyes on mine are soulful and intense, as if it really is a *need*, and not a want.

He thrusts once, hard and deep, and he's in up to the hilt. I've got every inch of him inside me, forcing me open, rearranging me with his invasion. He starts to rock his hips, and I can feel the bulb of his head way deep inside me, teasing the same nerves that alight when his finger's in my backside.

"You feel so good," he rasps. His free hand crawls slowly down my ribs. "So fucking good, that pussy, Cleo..." He rocks into me, finding a rhythm that is steady and slow, with deep, almost punishing thrusts and slick pulls as he rocks away from me... then plunges deliciously back in.

His gaze on my face never falters. His fingers twist my nipple as he pumps his big cock in and out of me.

I arch against him. My clit throbs.

"You feel so good," I whisper. "The way you stretch me..." This pleasure combined with the grogginess from sleeping. I sigh, thrusting my hips toward him.

"You like being stuffed with my cock."

"Not gonna lie..." I try to reach out for his shoulder, but my hands are tied. Oh... right. I smile up at him. "I love your big cock."

"My little slut..."

I rock myself against him and I sigh, relaxing my shoulders despite the tightness of the bind around my wrists. Kellan strokes a thumb over my clit. My toes curl.

And then he pulls out of me.

My eyes widen. "What?"

He smiles down at me as I'm... lifted off the bed? I'm instantly confused, because Kellan is still right in front of me. If he's not lifting me...

He rises on his knees and smiles grimly.

My eyes dart down my torso.

"Holy fuck."

I'm strung up like an animal after a hunt. I'm in some kind of harness...

Straps are holding me upright, pulling me slowly upward. I glance up, observing with my eyes what my body already senses: I'm hanging from a rope that disappears into a dark hole in the ceiling.

"Oh my God, Kellan." How the fuck did I not notice this?

The harness is wrapped around my waist, between my legs, over my shoulders. My arms must be bound to the rope I'm hanging from; they're still stretched above my head. I didn't notice it before but—

"Ahhh." The little moan pops out my lips.

As my weight is lifted fully off the bed and balanced by the harness, my legs sway a little, and I notice something... in my—

"Oh God."

In my ass!

I squirm in my restraints, feeling panicked as I hang there, swaying above the bed like a trapeze artist with a—

"Kellan, what did you..."

I clench around whatever's lodged in me. It starts to vibrate. For a moment, I see stars. Then I'm able to focus, to look down at the bed. Just a few feet below me, Kellan is sitting up on his knees, grinning wickedly as he holds a small remote. He rises a little higher on his knees, so his face is level with my pussy.

I try to stretch my legs, to brush the balls of my feet against the bedding. To get some control. He's got me just high enough that I can't really stand. I bend my knees, lifting my legs and feet up and tucking them behind my butt. My ass throbs. I have to swallow back a moan. The harness around my crotch pulls a little, but it's not unpleasant pressure. I look down again. The rope that makes the harness looks like it's coated with a softer fabric.

"What do you think of your predicament?" he murmurs. He wraps his hand around my calf and strokes. "Does it feel good, the surprise I left you?"

The pressure in my ass might be delicious. I can't tell. I've started shaking. I tug air into my lungs. "W-what is this thing? I thought we were having sex?"

"Oh yes. I'm going to fuck you, Cleo."

"I don't..." I roll my hips into the air and close my eyes, my body swaying gently from the ceiling. My ass is so full. God, it's hard to think. "I don't get it," I cry.

He runs his palms over my thighs, stilling my swaying body. "Let me show you."

He takes out a longer, silver remote and I am lifted slightly higher. My pussy clenches as the nerves inside me sizzle from the pressure in my ass.

"You can almost touch the bed," he says, looking down at my feet. Dangling as they are, just my toes brush the mattress. "But you can't. What do you think the purpose of this is, Cleo?"

He presses a button on the black remote, and what's inside my backside thumps against my tender walls.

I moan.

"Let me show you."

He rises into a crouch and grabs my hips. He lowers his head between my legs and drags his warm tongue through my sopping folds.

"I can do *this*," he drags his tongue over my swollen flesh, "and you can't move—at all."

I try to shift my hips and swing my legs to prove him wrong, but to no avail. The roar of pleasure in my backside and his slick tongue on my pussy has my legs feeling so weak.

"Oh God..."

"I was going to fuck that pussy, but I wanted you helpless first." He shoves two fingers into me. I can feel the plug in my backside crescendo, making my hips buck against his fingers.

"Ahhh!"

I stretch my feet again to get a foothold on the bed, but all I manage to do is close my legs around his face, bringing his writhing tongue deeper into me. He flicks against my entrance.

I curl and straighten my legs.

"That's right, baby. Struggle. Show me how crazy my tongue makes you."

He adds another finger, and my arms jerk.

"I want to touch you too," I gasp.

"Oh, this?" He leans away from me, and I can see his cock standing against his abs. Pre-cum glistens in the darkness.

"You'll touch this. Just your mouth. But now it's my turn."

He drags his long, slick tongue between my puffy lips and opens his mouth wider, feasting on me while I screech and throb. He whirls his tongue through my slickness, thumping lightly over my clit, then pushing inside my hungry cunt. My asshole pulses at the whims of what's inside it.

Somewhere far away, I'm aware of his fingers pulling out of me, of him adjusting the angle of the harness and lowering me back down to the bed. He eases my legs out in front of me and ensures I'm sitting firmly on the bed before he stops the churning of the rope above me. I'm on my ass in a semi-reclined position—with my arms still stretched above my head.

He nudges his hand between my thighs and glides two fingers back inside me. He flexes them, and he must brush my G-spot, because the jolt of bliss is so intense, I come up off the bed.

"Oh shit!"

With one fingertip still curled against the tender spot, another writhing against my inner walls, he gives my pussy a slow, warm tongue-kiss.

I jerk in the ropes. I can feel my moisture seep out over his lips.

"You're clenching tight around my finger. You're so wet and swollen. I think you're getting ready to come soon." He licks me, from where I'm dripping around his fingers up to my throbbing clit. "How do you feel, with your thighs drenched and your pussy stuffed? That ass of yours is so damn full. Do you feel the egg inside you... ?"

He makes a lazy circle around my clit with the tip of his tongue. I moan loudly. "I can smell you, Cleo, taste you. You can't help it, can you? You're so wet, so close."

I feel him drag his mouth down my sopping slit. His puffy lips tease over me as his fingers, stretching me inside, push deeper. He's right about how wet I am. I'm dripping down my thighs. I buck my hips, trying and failing to press myself against his hot tongue. I need release, but I can't move. "Oh please..."

The rhythm of his probing quickens and he rolls his tongue over me, lapping... oh God..."Oh God! FUCK fuck!" I come screaming. Kellan groans into my folds, sending pleasure back through me. "Oh God..."

While I'm still panting from the onslaught, pressing my thighs together and letting my head loll back between my raised arms, he reaches back under me, parts my ass cheeks with the base of his hand, and rolls two fingertips over my well-lubed sphincter.

I gasp because I'm stretched already, stuffed full of whatever he put there while I slept. His fingertips stretch me even more, until it hurts—so good my pussy throbs. His fingers stroke in deeper. I moan as he draws the warm egg out.

"Oh *God*."

I feel like... some kind of fuck toy.

My asshole throbs as I sag; the binds around my upper body keep me suspended, swaying.

"You're dripping everywhere, Cleo. I don't think I've ever seen a wetter pussy..." With his fingers still in my pussy, Kellan lifts my ankles to his shoulders, and I feel a different pressure at my backside. Something bigger...

"Kellan," I pant.

His fingers, in my pussy, wriggle encouragingly. "Relax and take a deep breath, Cleo."

I do as he says, and let out a low grunt-groan as something thick and hard slides into my ass. It spreads me wide, stinging even as the pressure of it inside lights up all my nerve endings. At first the sensations tell me it's his cock, but then I sway a little in the harness, and I realize that's not possible.

His fingers, still inside my pussy, stroke. I press my heels against his shoulders, trembling slightly as I move my ass in time with the throbbing pressure inside.

Kellan slides his fingers out of me, and I want to scream. He lets my legs down, comes between them, parts my puffy lips with his fingers, and wraps one arm around me, holding my lower body in place while he works his hard, thick cock into my cunt.

I'm at his total mercy. Swaying slightly. Stuffed. Invaded. His arms coil around my waist to keep me locked against him as he fucks me... brutally. So hard and good I start to cry.

"You're so big..."

"You're so tight."

"It hurts," I gasp.

He pauses his thrusting, long enough to look me in the eye.

"It's good," I moan.

"It hurts me good, too."

His arms around me squeeze a little, and he clasps his mouth down on my throat. His thrusts are hard—so hard and deep. I feel the frenzy of his breathing in my breasts.

He thrusts harder, and I groan.

He squeezes my hips as his cock plunders me, moving with strong, punishing strokes. I'm so aroused, I feel almost ill. Then he slides his hand down my flank, walks his fingers over my ass cheek, and pushes his palm hard against the end of the dildo.

I see stars.

He barks, low and loud, and I can feel his dick surge inside me, followed by the warm rush of his cum filling the condom.

He lowers me onto the mattress and then frees me from the harness. He licks me up and down my swollen slit, and then he wipes me with a warm, damp cloth.

He rubs my temples and my forehead. He kisses my hair, and whispers, "Thank you, Cleo. Sloth."

And when I'm half asleep, he leaves.

He doesn't know I'm awake when he comes back. He doesn't know I feel him wrap his arms and legs around me.

SIX

IF THAT WAS NO-ATTACHMENTS sex with an acquaintance, I don't want to make love, ever.

I wake up like a Georgia kid on a snow day: excited as hell, a little daunted—oh, and really sore everywhere below the belt from kinky sex and a big dildo.

For a while I just lie there, looking at the canopy and wondering what it says about Mr. Perfect that he bothered to put the damn thing back up after harness time was over. When I finally get the energy to roll from my back onto my side, I realize I *really* have something to chew on.

I'm not crazy. I swear. But... these sheets are not the same as they were. Right, like I'm saying they are not the same set of sheets I last saw on this bed. Those were cream. These are brown.

No, like seriously.

Oh my God, did he change them? Because of me? The thought makes my cheeks burn.

I throw an arm over my head, and wonder if I can sneak out of his house and run away.

Where is he now?

I remember him slipping onto the bed with me and curling himself around me. I was almost asleep at the time, but I held off going totally under for a little while, just so I could feel him tucked around me. Brennan didn't do that. He never wanted to touch me unless it was for sex.

But... Kellan clearly did. He might have waited until I was asleep to do it, but he needed that. He needed to be close to me. He didn't get the pleasure of my arms around him, making him feel held and sheltered, but he got whatever pleasure can be derived from sheltering another.

Why did he do it?

Was he feeling lonely? Sad? After our sexcapade, did he simply want to pay some kind of homage to my body?

I slip out of bed and cool air wraps around my skin. I look around the bedroom, cast in shadows, and then walk over to the balcony and pull the brownish curtains open. Sunlight soaks the room in gold.

Something about the sunlight jars my memory, and my mouth drops open as I remember what I learned about Kellan before going to sleep the first time last night. I inhale deeply, still shocked. Kellan was a quarterback. A freshman at the University of Southern California, an alumnus of some swanky Beverly Hills high school, and when the star QB got hurt after USC's first game of the 2010 season, the Trojans' coach let Kellan start. And he was crazy good. I read his stats. Once I started looking at his pictures, with that black hair, I even kind of remembered a beautiful, blue-eyed player with "DRAKE" across his back.

I go over to the door, behind which I dumped my bags, and find them propped on luggage racks. Kellan played fabulously until January 2011, and that's where his story takes a dark turn. Around four-thirty in the morning on a Saturday night, he got into an awful fight at a bar in downtown Los Angeles.

He and the guy—who turned out to be a fellow Trojan: a lineman named Joshua Franks—got thrown out of the club, but the fight continued in a parking garage. By the time someone called the cops, Franks had a fractured cheek, a concussion, and so many punches to one side of his head, he later went deaf in that ear.

Franks was shit-faced, and had allegedly been the one to start the fight. Kellan wasn't drunk at all, and at the end of the night, he didn't have a scratch on him.

I try to see it all inside my head as I poke through my duffel, searching for my favorite sleeveless, purple nightgown. I can't see

Kellan being violent. Beating someone so... repeatedly? I can't see him doing that. I pull the nightgown over my head and try to decide why. I think it's because he seems so measured now. So in control of things. *So in control of me...*

My gaze careens around the room, trying to reconcile this drug lord's palace—and its prince—with a dark-haired college football quarterback, beating a teammate in a fit of rage in L.A.

Kellan is a bad guy.

That's how it seems.

If I told Lora everything I know about him, she would tell me to leave his house and stay away.

Instead I put on my night gown, followed by my fluffy, hot pink bathrobe, which has been taking up approximately thirty percent of the space inside my duffel. I take a moment to relish the familiar feel of my clothes.

Then I look around the room for what I had on last night, because I want to launder it. It's nowhere in sight, and I notice while I search for it that the ceiling looks normal again. The ropes and pulleys must be tucked behind the indention at the center of the ceiling.

Kellan Walsh... who the hell are you?

My mind spins like the wheel of a bike, fast at first, then settling into a slow coast as I step into the bathroom, where I find my clothes in a brown wicker hamper. I brush and floss my teeth, smooth my hair down, and go back into the bedroom, squinting a little at the brilliant sunlight. I'm thinking of heading downstairs when I spot my *Thomas* on the wall over the bookshelf across the room.

What the hell?

I turn slowly around the room and notice *Grans* on an easel in the corner by the wing-backed chair.

I let my breath out. The third painting, one I kept under my bed until I left the house, is called *Olive*, and it's nowhere to be found. But these two...

I walk over to *Grans* and marvel at the easel it's on. Kellan just had an easel hanging around? This one is the one he asked about in my room, the one with lines from "Tintern Abbey"—which so happens to be one of my grandmother's favorite poems.

I walk over to the bookshelf with my eyes fixed on *Thomas*. My dad's name was Thomas, and this painting truly is for him. Under the paint are slivers of a card he wrote to me, a love note he wrote my mother when they meet in high school, and a button from one of his shirts. Sprinkled over the paint, so sparsely it's not noticeable, are the soft, soft hairs I got from his beard trimmer and hid in an oval locket that I stole from Grans after he died.

I was only seven, but I had a sense that I should keep every fragment of my dad that I could find. When my mother decided to have him cremated, I stole some of the ashes, too. I stirred them into the paint for *Thomas*, and I don't care who thinks it's weird or gross. This is probably my favorite painting. I did it in high school. It was the first piece of art that ever really meant something to me.

Kellan hung it on the wall for me while I slept.

I'm still thinking about this as I pad downstairs in my pink robe.

The living area is radiant with sunlight, drifting in from the skylights in the ceiling and flooding through the wall of windows that faces the river. Before my foot touches down on the dark hardwood, I hear the frenzied click of dogs' nails, and Truman bounds across the rug, tail wagging, ears flouncing.

"Hi, boy." I crouch down and tug one of his ears into my hand. "What soft ears you have. How are you?"

On a whim, I wrap my arms around him: thick and warm and soft and panting. I love dogs because they warm the soul without the baggage of another human.

"C'mon boy... where's your daddy?"

I find Kellan in the kitchen, making pancakes. At first I can't see much of him because he's standing behind an island, so I step around it. I find he's dressed more casually than I've ever seen him, in a pair of loose, charcoal lounge pants and a white undershirt that emphasizes his beautiful body—and his gold-blond hair.

I smile a little, and he arches a brow at me. "Daddy?"

I laugh. "You are kind of his dad. Unless you're his brother?"

He scowls. "No."

He pushes a plate of bacon at me as I walk back around the island and take a seat at the bar.

His hair looks messy, and there's some delicious scruff on his jaw. I can't help noticing his eyes look tired. I feel a pang of guilt for not asking how his night went, although it's not as if I actually could have. I was already in the harness when he woke me up.

"Okay, bro," I tease. "Then dad it is."

"I'm not his dad." He flips a pancake.

"Adoptive dad?" I want him to smile, but he just gives me a blank look.

"Things must not have gone very well last night on your... um, errand."

I see the muscle of his jaw clench. He doesn't even lift his gaze to me.

"Okayyy. Well cool beans." I grab two pieces of bacon off the plate and get up to get myself a drink. If he's going to be a moody butthead, maybe I'll go have my breakfast somewhere else. I can sit on the balcony and continue reading news stories about Kellan Drake.

I grab a Mason jar out of a cabinet and a glass pitcher out of the refrigerator. I set it on the countertop.

"You should try some lemons in your water," I advise. Just filling the silence, I guess. (Cleo Whatley: always awkward).

He doesn't reply, and my feelings war with each other. Part of me feels sorry for him, part of me is irritated that he's still so moody—especially after our night last night. Part of me feels pessimistic, like I'll never really get to know him, and still another part wants to erect a wall around myself.

I pour some water into my glass and feel the warm weight of his hand around my wrist. I look down, then get the nerve to glance up at his face.

"I'm sorry," he says. His blue eyes hold mine.

"What for?"

"For being a dick." He lets me go and runs his hands through his hair. He lets a little breath out, like he's been holding it. "Bad night."

His voice sounds thick—emotional, even. His cuts his eyes away and then turns back around toward the skillet. The pancakes sizzle, but he doesn't pick the spatula up. I can't even see him breathing.

Shit.

I turn around and lean against the counter. "Anything you want to talk about? You have a roomie now, you know."

I look at his broad shoulders, imagining them in a jersey. Bare and goosebumped while he stands on a surfboard. I imagine them tucked around me last night... the way he pressed his face into my hair.

I have the urge to wrap my arms around his waist again, but I think of his reaction last time at the grow house. And that's how I know I should.

Is this what he does with other girls, too? Just fucks them, and if they make him laugh or wrap their arms around him, they get pushed away?

I put my hand on his back, then realize I want more and press my cheek against it.

He goes very still. So still I can hear his heartbeat.

I kiss him through his shirt, and then I wrap an arm around his waist.

"Don't be pissed," I whisper. "You seem sad. I like hugging you... I'm a hugger."

I smell something burning, and I lean around him to find the pancake smoking.

I slide my arm from around his waist and kiss his bicep. "I didn't mean to make you burn the food."

"You didn't," he says gruffly.

I walk around the bar and take a seat on the stool right in front of him. I find myself waiting for his eyes to meet mine. He looks everywhere but at me as he finishes the pancakes, smears butter on them, and brings out a small cup of hot syrup from the microwave.

He puts three on a plate for me and sets it in front of me, still without looking in my eyes. Then he turns around to open the refrigerator. He takes out some fresh-looking strawberries and sets them in front of me as well.

"Thank you," I say, as he finally looks me in the face. "Are you going to have some too?"

He shakes his head and mumbles something about working out.

I puzzle over this as he walks slowly toward the living area. He opens a door that looks like a closet door, situated between the kitchen and the living room, and disappears into it.

I eat slowly.

Should I ask him about football? Should I tell him what I saw? And what I read? I want to know the answers to my questions, but do I really *have* to have them? He's clearly in a shitty mood. I don't want to make things worse. Although of course, I want to know.

I finish eating, clean and wash my plate, and when he's still not back, I can't help myself. I follow him through the door, which leads down to a basement.

At the bottom of the stairs, I find a nice home gym, and Kellan running on a treadmill, pouring sweat.

He glances at me, then straight ahead. I'm not sure if I should feel irritated by how he's acting, or sorry for him. I go with sorry. If I knew him even just a little better, I would ask what's up. As it is, I stick my hands in the pockets of my robe and stand there feeling like some awkward stalker.

"This is really nice down here. I guess this is how you stay in shape for soccer."

"Yeah."

"Don't you guys have a game in a few days?"

"Yeah." His gaze flicks to mine, and I see effort on his face. He's trying to be... not an ass. Which I appreciate, even as I wonder why he has to try so hard. "You a fan?" he asks. His voice is rough, the words slightly panted.

My throat tightens with the secret I'm keeping—about his past. "I'm a fan of how you look in your uniform," I say slyly.

"Is that right?" He slows his pace.

I nod as the air around us starts to prickle. "I used to appreciate you as eye candy even though I thought you were a jerk."

"And now?" He steps off the treadmill and closes the distance between us with three steps. He seems so tall. He looks very serious, considering we're teasing.

"Now I don't know." My heart gives a long, unsteady beat. "You seem... really hard to read. I don't know what I think of you."

"It doesn't matter," he says, folding his arms. Any emotions I might have seen on his face are locked away now. "Tonight, we'll be going somewhere. It will be a chance for me to show you another aspect of our business."

"Are you getting a shipment or something?"

"You'll see."

I nod, and when silence spreads between us, I can't stop myself from prying. "So what about last night? What did you have to do?"

"It was nothing," he says softly.

Sweat rolls down his temple. I put my finger on his shirt, where it's stuck to the middle of his chest. "Do you do this every day?" I step slightly closer as I ask.

He nods.

I stroke his chest, then ease my hand away. "How long do you run?"

"I try to do aerobic shit for at least ninety minutes."

"Holy hell. Ninety minutes? You're like, training," I say, stepping a little bit away.

He raises his brows.

I take another small step back, establishing a safe distance between the two of us. Then I take a deep breath. "Can I ask you a question?"

He plucks a towel off a weight machine and wipes his forehead, not quite meeting my eyes as he says, "You have that ability."

"Will you promise not to be growly about it?"

"Growly?" He smirks—but it's a ridiculing smirk. Like he thinks I'm crazy. Like he isn't close enough with me to tease.

I plunge right on ahead, keeping things casual even as my pulse picks up. "Yep, growly."

He stares at me. "Is something wrong, Cleo?"

"No," I hedge. "But I... last night, I saw a DVD of you playing football." I search his handsome face. "You had black hair, and you were playing for USC. Your last name wasn't Walsh. Your jersey said Drake."

I know I've hit on something, because his face stays absolutely neutral and his jaw tightens. He doesn't move, just stares right through me.

"Kellan?"

SEVEN

Kellan

IT ALMOST FEELS RIGHT—that Cleo found it. Sloth. I let her in my house, of course she finds the DVD of me playing.

This girl has got some fucking link to me. I've heard of it before: a soul tie, that's what Whitney used to call it. When people's souls just know each other. Maybe that's Cleo and me. Sloth and "R."

As I cooked her breakfast this morning, I wished I knew more about her than chicken pizza. Tonight before we meet Pace to look over the stuff, I thought about taking her for pizza. I can't let her stay the full three weeks now that I know who she is—but I'm not sending her away quite yet.

Call it selfish. You'd be right.

I look down at her, and I try to imagine Cleo writing me the letters.

I didn't really go to sleep last night. After I slipped into the windowed room and held her for a little while, I re-read every one of them. Before the sun rose, I went and got Truman. Got her some strawberries from the farmers' market. Stared at her art.

Cleo.

Sloth.

I'm not in a good place, but having her here... it eases me a little.

"You watched my DVD?" I ask.

She nods.

"What did you think of it?"

"Your name was Kellan Drake. You had black hair."

I smirk and run a hand back through my sweaty locks. "Which do you prefer?"

"I think the blond is really your hair. Is that right?"

I nod. I have a memory of Lyon snickering at the black dye stains all over my neck the day I did it—to disguise myself at a game of flag football with the senior dudes from our rival high school. I can hear his laughter.

"That's right," I rasp.

"Why did you dye it?"

"For a dare." It's not entirely true, but I don't want to recount the flag football game. Don't want to think about it—*him*.

She chews her lip. Her brows are drawn together. "What about your name? Which one is real?"

I remember the stench of heavy perfume, and an older lady's gentle hands on my shoulders. The way I fell into the cab that day, the first day I told someone my name was Walsh. "Walsh was my mother's maiden name," I tell Cleo now. "It's my middle name."

"So your real last name is Drake?"

I nod. I'm not telling her much more, but I don't see the point in lying about these basic facts. I don't think BTM ever told her anything about me. She doesn't know anything but what I told her in my letters: that my name is Robert. Which is, of course, untrue.

"Why'd you change it?" she asks.

The truth of my change in surname is not just the need for privacy once I came back from New York and started college here, but what happened before that. All the many things that made me feel like leaving Kellan Drake behind. Things Cleo can never know—lest she should find out how the two of us are linked.

I would never put her through that.

"Something happened," I say slowly. "Something that made it so... I couldn't be that person anymore."

"Was that something an assault charge?" she whispers.

My stomach clenches as my pulse pounds behind my eyes. "What do you know about that, Cleo?" I rasp.

"I Googled you." She looks nervous—and guilty.

"And you read I was suspended from the Trojans for a bar fight."

She nods quickly.

I nod with her, trying to decide what if anything to add to that.

"What else did you read?" I need to know if any of the articles mentioned Lyon. His situation.

"That's all. You had some killer stats when you were a senior at private school. You played first string as a freshman after Mark Waldon tore his ACL." I nod, because those are facts. "And?"

"And then you got into a fight that night. You weren't drunk—that's what the story said—but you were at a bar in L.A. at like... closing time. And you got into it with this guy, this other player. It said he lost his hearing," she says in a whisper.

I grit my teeth. Fear swells in me. Worry—about what Cleo thinks of that.

"It happened in January," she adds, as if I need reminding.

"Yes."

Her green eyes widen just a little. "So you really did it?"

"Do you think they lied?" I snap.

She shrugs. "Sometimes people do. Or there are disputes. Someone remembers one thing, someone else remembers something different. Keeps lawyers in business, you know?"

Not in my case. Everything the papers reported about that night was true. Franks did lose his hearing in his left ear. Like both Lyon and me, he never returned to the field. My father found a way to settle out of court.

Franks runs a vineyard now. And the truth of that story is, it took me years to feel sorry for what I did to that fuck.

I nod at her comment about lawyers. I'm starting to feel twitchy now. I want this subject dropped—but Cleo doesn't notice. She shifts her stance a little, digging her hands deeper into the pockets of her fluffy robe, and tilts her head.

"So you moved here and changed your name?"

I shrug. I wipe my face again. "Looks like it."

"Did you? Is that how it happened?" she asks. Her tone tells me everything I need to know about the likelihood she'll let this drop.

I smooth the irritation off my face and try to appear forthcoming. Or like not a fucking liar who's deceiving her about almost everything.

"I did some traveling first—but yes," I say. "I left USC and ended up here."

I turn back toward the treadmill, eager to get back on it and run from those green eyes. After last night—after I wrapped my arms around her and used her heat to warm myself—after she hugged me in the kitchen—and after this line of questioning—I've decided it's a bad thing that the universe brought the two of us together in person. I should send her packing right now, but I'm finding I'm not strong enough. If she learns more about my past, I'll have to find the strength somewhere. Until then... For just a little longer...

I step onto the treadmill and start the belt back moving, even as part of me is waiting for her words.

She walks over by me. I keep my eyes down as I start to run. She wraps her hand around the treadmill's grip bar. "Kellan, I'm so sorry. That sucks."

I turn, confused. "What sucks?"

"You lost... your life. I mean, you had to like playing football, right? You probably loved it. And after you got suspended, you must not have been able to go back. The news didn't say anything about that—I didn't Google much, because I wanted to ask you instead of prying on the internet—but I know that when something is a huge part of your life and you have to give it up, it always sucks. That is, if you loved it."

My throat closes off, my body's own acknowledgement that what she said is true—on so many levels. I swallow and nod. I bite my cheek as I lengthen my strides.

"Did you play a long time?" she asks warmly. "I wanted to read profiles about you, but like I said, I didn't want to snoop."

"Except right now?" I huff a laugh—and am surprised. That I'm able to. After last night...

"Except right now." She smiles. "You're right here in the flesh. The legendary Kellan Drake-Walsh-Charitable Kingpin-SGA President. I can't resist a few questions. Maybe an autograph." She tugs on her t-shirt. "You know," she smiles, "the Sharpie-on-cleavage."

That gets a chuckle out of me. "Bring me the Sharpie."

"I just might."

I push my body from a jog into a run. Her gaze moves with me. "Thank you for being honest with me. I know you didn't have to tell me, but I like to know where you came from."

I snort. If there's anything I'm not, it's honest.

"No biggie," I say, as I stretch my legs into a more punishing pace.

"You know... I won't tell. I swear. No one here knows that you played football, do they?"

"Nope." Our soccer team sucks too much to get me any exposure. Which has been a good thing. I'd have never played if that wasn't true. Don't need any sports press sniffing around.

"Well I won't tell a soul. Not even my best friends. Maybe just Truman."

I jerk my head in a nod.

Now that she's standing silently off to my side, and not distracting me with her questions and her pretty voice, the pain inside my chest flares to life again.

I run faster.

Harder.

"My first class is ten. When's yours today?" she asks.

"Eleven."

"Okay. Well I guess I'll drive myself then."

"Don't. I'll take you."

She looks surprised. "You would have some time to waste."

I shake my head. "I have to go to the dentist at 10:30, so it works."

"Yuck. I hate the dentist. Do you have a cavity?"

I smirk at her. "What do you think?"

"I think your teeth look pretty perfect. Is it just a cleaning?" she asks.

"Cleaning." I nod. "Now get out of here."

"I want to work out too," she pouts.

"Later."

She turns to go. At the bottom of the stairs, she turns back to me. "Kellan?"

"Yeah."

"Last night was—crazy. Like the wolf."

She walks back upstairs, and I laugh. That's me. I'm crazy like the wolf.

EIGHT

Cleo

MY SCHOOL DAY IS DOMINATED by a run-in with Milasy. I pass her on the concourse and can't miss the Gucci boots she has on—mine: the tan ones that are knee-high. I'm walking with Lora, talking for the first time since the other night, and Milasy glares at her as if she's doing something wrong.

Before I can even ask Lora what's up, Milasy is in front of us, with her hands on her hips and her dark hair flowing in the humid breeze.

"Lora—what did we talk about?" she asks, not looking at me.

"Yeah I know, but—"

"But?" Milasy asks.

"Cleo is my lab partner," Lora lies.

Milasy's face is unreadable, so I'm surprised when she says, "Find another partner."

As soon as she stalks off, Lora pulls me into the nearest building—an aviation science lab—and tells me Milasy has told some of the Tri-Gams that I'm blacklisted.

"She didn't tell us why, just that you're sort of like... suspended. I was going to tell you..." Lora bites her lip.

"It's fine," I say—even though it isn't. Lora is supposed to be my good friend. I don't think I've missed a single call from her in the last day or two. Nor has she sought me out, except a few minutes ago when we bumped into each other on our walk to the west side of campus.

We part ways outside the aviation lab, and Lora promises to call me later.

As soon as I get into my next class, Art as Self-Expression, another Tri-Gam, Sally, asks about my grandmother.

"What?" I frown.

"Milasy told us you've been home a lot, because she's... Well, Milasy says she's not doing so good."

Perfect.

Another girl, a freshman named Christine, confirms this as I leave that class. She pats me on the arm as we pass one another in the lobby of the psych building and says, "I'm thinking of you, darlin'."

I plant myself under my favorite willow tree to kill a little time before my next class, biology II, and as I step inside that classroom, my phone vibrates with a text from Kellan.

'Pick u up at 4:30 behind Taylor?'

'PLEASE.'

When I drag my tired ass into the parking lot at 4:32, he's waiting in the Sexcalade. I experience a bolt of glee, like a lab rat presented with a carrot.

I slide into the passenger's seat and quickly size him up. He looks nice: same dark jeans and emerald green button-up he had on when he dropped me off, so I can't explain why the sight of him makes my heart do backflips. I notice his hair is a little wind-blown, I guess because he has his window down.

I give him a small smile. "How was your day?"

He lifts a shoulder. "How was yours?"

I drop my head into my hand. "It was tedious and tiring. I'm grumpy. And can't wait to get away from campus."

"I know something you might like." He looks surprisingly light-hearted.

"Well, what is it?"

"You like pizza?"

"Who doesn't?"

We drive the short distance to Mama McCalister's in companionable silence. He parks behind the restaurant and comes around and opens my door. I smirk at him, but it slips into a smile as I check him out again. He looks more casual frat boy than usual today. And either way, "You make a good Southerner."

He smiles a gentle smile for me, then he helps me over a big crack in the parking lot's asphalt. As we approach the door, he keeps my hand in his.

He picks a booth in the back, and when a lustful-looking waitress sashays over five seconds later, he orders chicken pizza.

"Chicken pizza? Are you kidding me?"

"What can I say?" He smiles. "Chicken? Pizza? It works. You agree?"

"Hell yes, it's my very favorite thing ever."

He smiles again (clearly he is going for a record). "Ever?" He leans across the table. "Even better than my harness?" he asks in a low voice.

My cheeks and neck burn. "That was dirty. Dirty-dealing. Unfair. Scandalous."

"Wait until you see what I have for you today," he says.

I'm blushing so much I'm worried tears might spill over. "Not in public," I hiss.

He grins wickedly.

"Your teeth look nice and white. How was the dentist?"

"I got a good report. A cleaning too."

He sits back in his seat and I notice, now that he's not smiling, how tired his face looks.

"How about your other situation? With the... you know... the you-know-whos?"

"The you-know-whos?" He smirks. "Sounds like some Dr. Seuss there."

"I love Dr. Seuss. Look!" I lift my shirt sleeve. "It's YOU."

He frowns and leans across the table. "Is that some kind of code?"

I laugh. "No, this little guy is from *Oh, the Places You'll Go* by Dr. Seuss. It's one of my favorite books ever. YOU is the star."

The tattoo is on the inside of my bicep.

He wiggles his brows and rests his hands atop the table. "So will you succeed?"

"Yes, I will indeed." I laugh happily. "I can see I've misjudged you. Not only do you read, but you seem to read a variety of things."

A troubled look passes over his face, but it's gone quickly. "I'm a Seuss buff," he says.

"Really?"

"Maybe."

I give him a curious look, but he just lifts a brow, and I know he's not going to tell me what he meant by that.

"Do you have any tats?" I try.

"Don't you want to know."

"I do."

He leans his elbows on the table. "I do."

"Are they on your booty?" I giggle. I don't know why, but I'm feeling a little silly now that I've made my escape from campus, and at the moment I just want to make him laugh.

"No." He laughs, a low, dry sound, but still a laugh, and I feel like a champion. "My ass is ink-free."

"Mine too."

"Yes—I'm aware of that."

I bite my lip and look down at the table, hoping he won't notice my face flush. I can't believe the sex we had last night. I had no idea that it could be that way—and with an almost-stranger.

"Is the illustrious 'You' your only tat?" he asks.

"I've got one more."

His brows come together. "Really? It must be well-hidden."

I blush a little, thinking he's seen almost all my hiding spots—even in between my ass cheeks. God.

"I guess so." I lift my wavy hair up off my neck. "It's right back here, can you see that?" I point to the spot. "Kind of behind my ear."

He leans forward again, and I get a silly little thrill from being the one to dictate what he does, even for such a small moment. He reaches out and traces his finger over the soft skin just behind my ear, where curving text spreads over the area where my sisters' cochlear implants sit: 'HEAR NO EVIL.'

The server arrives bearing bread sticks and water, and Kellan sits back in his seat. I notice that his face looks very serious. Almost angry. As the blonde girl sets the breadsticks on our table, his eyes never leave my face.

"Pizza should be out soon. Can I get you anything else?" the server asks.

I look at Kellan. He inhales.

"Beverage?" he asks me. He means in addition to the water she just brought.

"I'd also like a medium lemonade," I tell the server. Her eyes brush over Kellan. "You?"

His gaze is still on me. He wrenches it away and lifts it to her. "Sweet tea."

The waitress saunters off, and I grin. "Sweet tea? You like sweet tea?"

The corner of his mouth twitches, but he doesn't smile—or even smirk. "Y'all got that one right."

I giggle. "You don't say it right."

"Say what right?"

"Y'all."

"How do you say it?" He looks sullen, like he wants to be stormy but I keep interrupting the storm with sunshine.

"It's supposed to be *y'all*—so like if you were going to say 'awww, that puppy is so cute,' you need that 'awww' sound in there. Kind of like..." I clear my throat and use a low voice. "Y'awwwwllll." I smile. "What you say is more a 'yal.'"

Now he smirks. "You mean a y'all?"

I shake my head. "There's a subtle difference. Not so subtle even." I tuck my hair behind my right ear, where the tattoo is.

"Yesterday," he says slowly. "You mentioned hospitals. And your dad and sister. I know your dad passed away." His lips rub together, like he's shifting his jaw thoughtfully. "What about your sister?" His voice is low. His face is hard. He knows, somehow. Of course he does.

I take a fortifying breath.

"Don't," he says sharply. He leans across the table, looking panicked. "You don't need to tell me. Forget I asked."

I shake my head, picking up a breadstick and twirling the tip of it in marinara sauce. "No—it's okay. It's her birthday on the twelfth and I was going to tell you anyway. I'll be going home tomorrow... to visit her grave," I manage in a clear voice.

Despite that feat, I can't keep my eyes from springing leaks.

"Damn." I bring a napkin to my face to catch the stray tears, and then I hide behind it, because no amount of stern inner monologue will stop them.

In the silence, I notice the music—some Ke$ha song—and all the chatter of the place. It makes me irrationally angry, but I can tell the anger is really just a cover for the awful loss I feel—this week in particular.

A fresh slough of tears leaks out, and I swallow. I dab my eyes with the napkin and breathe deeply, and I feel something warm and hard settle against me.

Something heavy goes around my back, and before I have a second to get my bearings, Kellan pulls me up against his left side. I can feel his mouth against my hair as he says, "Fuck—I'm sorry."

I shake my head, reeling a little at his sudden appearance on my side of the booth. At how good his arm feels wrapped around me.

I force myself to pull the napkin down, despite being embarrassed. "It's not your fault." I take a deep, long breath, and let myself get lost in the blue of his eyes as I tell him the fact that is, for some reason, so painful.

"She would be sixteen this week." More tears make his solemn face shimmer. I dash them off. "I'm sorry." I dab the napkin to my eyes again and take a few deep breaths. "I didn't really plan to talk about it. Definitely not here."

I laugh a little, even though it isn't funny. Then our waitress is setting our drinks on the table. I look toward the wall, because I know how blotchy my face gets when I cry—and I'm embarrassed that I lost it out in public.

Kellan's hand is stroking my shoulder, and that makes me feel more embarrassed. That I took our business-sex relationship and made it awkward and heavy with this talk of Olive.

Even saying her name silently makes me need to take a few more deep breaths. Kellan just keeps rubbing my arm. Like he's my boyfriend.

Not your boyfriend, idiot!

I straighten up a little, offering him a chance to move his arm out from around me—in case he feels as awkward as I do. But he doesn't. When I get the nerve to look at him again, his eyes are gentle on my face.

"She was deaf just like my other sister. I guess I told you. That's the whole tattoo thing."

His hand, over my shoulder, clasps lightly. "So kind of like... be positive or something?"

"Or something. You know, like don't let negativity in, I guess. Olive was the most innocent person I've ever known, and not just because she died when she was five. She was just... so sweet and funny." I shake my head and draw another deep breath. "We should talk about something else."

"Only if you want to."

"Thank you." I shrink my shoulders in a little.

He pulls me closer to him, and I can feel his cheek against my hair. I feel his mouth move. "You embarrassed, Whatley?"

"Are you laughing at me?"

"Not laughing," he says. "Smiling. Wes Anderson-style."

I laugh. "You think my embarrassment is a racist, rich person movie about daddy issues?"

His eyes widen comically. "Touché, Cleo. Not an Anderson fan? That surprises me."

I roll my eyes. "I am a Wes Anderson fan. I'm offended that you felt so sure about it, but I am. I think his critics can go fuck a porcupine."

Kellan smirk-smiles.

"That's your thing," I say. "The patented Kellan Walsh smirk-smile. What's up with that?"

He traces a finger over my cheek. "What's up with this?"

"With what?" I feign surprise.

"You've got these little red splotches—"

"Shut the fuck up." I shove at him, but his arm tightens around me.

"It's cute."

"You think I'm cute?"

He rubs his face against my hair, but doesn't answer. And I wonder why. Does he think I'm ugly? I'm not ugly. No one thinks so. I'm not a model, but I'm cute at least.

I lean my head down, away from the warm cheek pressed against my hair, and turn to him so I can stick my tongue out. "I *am* cute. Everybody thinks so."

He pulls me back against the booth and presses his lips against my hair once more. "You are cute," he murmurs. "And your hair smells like flowers."

"I'm a fan of this gardenia-scented hair stuff."

And that's how dinner goes. Kellan leaves his arm around me until our pizza arrives. We both chow down on chicken pizza while we talk about a bunch of random things, like what was Sting thinking with the rhyming on the song "Walking on the Moon," and why killers whales have their name, and whether the animals at Sea World should be taking antidepressants anyway. And when I think we're leaving, Kellan orders cinnamon rolls.

While we wait for them, he slides his hand into my jeans, spreads a menu out in front of me, and rubs me off in the back booth of Mama McCalister's.

NINE

Cleo

AFTER I PROVE MY INABILITY to walk straight on my way out of the restaurant, Kellan scoops me up and carries me to his Escalade. He buckles me in, surprises me by leaning down to plant a quick kiss my nose, and shuts my door without a word. I'm still feeling all tingly and warm when he gets behind the wheel and gives me a long look.

"What?" I smile self-consciously—somewhat deliriously. This pizza outing has been kind of awesome.

He leans across the console between our seats, pressing his ribs against my arm rest to get close to me, and kisses my mouth so fast and hard it almost hurts. His hand wraps around my head, holding me upright as he devours my mouth.

His lips are soft but forceful, his tongue gliding against mine like hot velvet. I feel the firm warmth of his face on mine as we taste each other. I feel the puff of his breath on my cheeks and smell his cinnamon breath. Then he's got his arms around me; he's clutching my shoulders. He kisses my throat like a man starving. His hand runs down my ribs and lifts my shirt.

We're both panting when he pulls his mouth off mine.

All that warmth, and all that weight—gone in one heartbeat. And, shit, I'm lonely for him. I want more.

"Fuck," he pants. He throws the car in reverse, pulls out of the lot, and doesn't look at me again until we're out of the city, getting closer to his house.

"That was nice," he says. "The dinner." His voice is low, a little gruff.

I laugh, because honestly, I can't seem to stop the random laughing when I'm near him. "Yeah, it was."

"You like pecans?" he asks. The question is accompanied by an intense look that makes me laugh again.

"I love them." I tell him about how I used to pick them up with this handy dandy pecan-picker-upper and sell them for three dollars a gallon when I was younger and we needed money. He has a hearty laugh at the picture I paint, and then he quickly sobers. "I'm sorry that you... had to do that."

"Pssh. Don't be sorry. You can bet your ass I value them a lot more now."

"I want to make you something when we get home."

Mr. Perfect surprises me again when we get to his kitchen—by tugging my pants down, lifting me onto the granite island, and eating my pussy while I lie on my back, my fingers twined tightly in his.

After that, he binds my wrists with the ties of a black Dr. Who apron, lays me on my belly on the living room rug, and slides inside me from behind. He fucks me long and slow, wrapping a strand of my wavy hair around one of his hands and tugging gently as he pushes in and out.

Unlike other times, where there's usually a little dirty talk, he says almost nothing, except, once: "You're beautiful..."

When we're finished, he unties me and goes into the kitchen for a warm, damp towel. He helps me back into my pants—I remember he wanted to do this in the library that time—and then takes my hand and leads me to the bar stool where I had my breakfast.

He pours me a glass of water, plucks an uncut lemon from the refrigerator, and slices it into half-moon-shaped pieces, one of which he perches on the rim of my glass.

"Drink this," he tells me. "I'm going to make you cinnamon pecans."

Prickling warmth spreads through my chest, like I've swallowed sunshine, and I try to shake it off because it makes me feel uneasy. Why is Kellan Drake (Walsh), moody asshole and criminal SGA president, being nicer to me than most of my past boyfriends?

Is he starting to like me?

Should I even allow myself to entertain the thought?

I manage to loosen up enough to tease him about being a Southern boy at heart—what with the cooking and the hospitality, the button-up Polos and the sweet tea addiction—and he gives me a small smile that almost looks a self-conscious.

He leans against the granite countertop while I sit on my bar stool, and somehow he starts asking me questions about myself. At first, I don't realize there's intent behind it. It's easy to tell him about my pseudo-photograhic memory, about how well I do on standardized tests, about how I was good at math when I was little but fell miserably behind the year that Olive died; I never did recover. I blab about Mom and Grans' reaction when I got accepted to this little private college on a full academic scholarship.

Kellan is a perfect listener, crunching on raw pecans and sipping on his iced tea with one elbow propped on the counter. He looks relaxed and interested, as if my history is somehow meaningful to him.

He draws stories out of me like silk from a spider, soliciting details about my high-school parties, prom, graduation (I was salutatorian), the mundane tasks I had to do while getting 'rushed' (AKA hazed) for Tri Gam...

I tell him crazy things I never tell anyone, like how I've always wanted to ride a horse at the beach because of that movie *Wild Hearts Can't Be Broken*, and how, if my sister gets a partial scholarship to CC, I'll probably stick around in town for a few more years at least.

We discuss the merits of beets and the horror of goat milk in coffee, the necessity of quality in movies (we agree on a lot of the classics, like "The Godfather" and "Pulp Fiction"). I confess my desire for a slap-band watch and tell him about meeting Mark-

Paul Gosselaar at the mall in Atlanta when I was shopping for my prom dress.

I'm nearly sick from what seems like dozens of baked cinnamon pecans when I start to ramble on about how many kids I want.

"Two, at least, so they can be best friends. Four if they turn out to be easier than I think, but definitely two."

I can tell I'm losing him as I ramble about the virtues of young children, but when I ask how many siblings he has, I realize something else is going on.

He bites his cheek between his teeth, inhales so hard his nostrils flare, and says, "My parents had three kids."

And that is all.

It's plain to see this is a sore subject for my mysterious Mr. Drake.

I feel a pang of sympathy as he turns around and starts scrubbing the pan he used to bake the pecans.

I try to remember if I read anything about his parents or siblings in the brief news article about Kellan being suspended from the Trojans, but I don't think anything was mentioned.

I'm irrationally irritated at myself for saying something that has led to a rough spot in our smooth and easy night—a night in which I almost felt like we were on a fun first date.

A few minutes later, he turns back around, wipes his damp hands on his pants, and with an unreadable look aimed not quite at my face, says, "I'm going for a run."

I bite my lip, because it's what I do when I'm not sure what to do.

"You want to go?" he asks.

My eyebrows jut up. I can't help it. Sometimes they get away from me.

Kellan notices and smirk-smiles. "Not a runner?"

"No—I am a runner. Sometimes runner. I'm just... surprised you asked." And embarrassed for admitting my surprise. Way to be obvious, Cleo. "Do you run downstairs?"

He shakes his head.

"Outside?" I smile, because he looks a little spaced out. (Too many pecans?)

He nods a beat too late, then gestures toward the front hall. "Down the road."

Before I can give him an answer on whether I'd like to go, he looks in my direction—but not at me—nods a little, and says, looking at his cell phone, "I'll be down in ten or fifteen. Gotta go get dressed."

I wait a minute or two so I'm not climbing the stairs right on his heels. Then I go up to my windowed room, dig out a pair of hot pink running shorts, my white Under Armor running shirt, and my new-ish sneaks. I grab a rubber band and braid my hair in the bathroom.

I get down stairs after him, so I see him walk out a door beside the pantry pulling a gray t-shirt over his head. I smell a whiff of fabric softener, and then he walks around the island, and the sight of Kellan in his running gear takes my breath away.

My eyes cling to his incredible bare legs as he looks me up and down. "I like the hair."

I touch my hand to my French braid and try not to gawk at the muscles of his thighs in those navy running shorts. I think they're actually basketball shorts, because they're longer. Geez... that shirt, the way it outlines his pecs. He's just—*Shit*, have I said anything back to him? *Stupid Cleo.* I feel the heat in my cheeks. "Thanks."

He lifts his brows. "You ready?"

I nod. Truman shows up, flouncing happily beside us as we walk toward the front door. I follow Kellan onto the porch, where we stretch.

"Do you do this every night?" It's not lost on me that while I told him my whole life story, he told me exactly nothing.

"Almost. Especially if I don't do cardio downstairs."

"And how long do you say you do it for? The whole work out?"

"An hour and a half, two hours."

"Damn. Are you training for a marathon? Like, really?"

He smiles, just one corner of his mouth tugging up a little. "Something like that."

"Trying to keep your body lady-ready," I tease.

He laughs, which sounds like choking. "What?"

"You know—trying to be .gif-worthy Kellan baby."

I wiggle my brows, and he gives a low laugh. "You fucking know it." He rolls his shoulders. Jogs in place a little. "Ready?"

"As I'll be. You'll probably leave me in the dust."

And as it turns out, that's exactly what he does. I can see him trying to go slow for me, but we're unmatched. Kellan is a Spartan, and I'm a couch potato. He's also almost a foot taller than me, so his Spartan legs, in addition to being incredibly well-muscled, are a good bit longer.

I admire him from behind the entire time he runs. He even has good running form. He holds his shoulders square and straight without being too tense. Where I look like a Muppet let loose on the road, Kellan looks like the athlete he is.

I think, as we turn around by a row of mailboxes and point ourselves back toward his house, that today has been different than I thought it would be. What changed between yesterday and today? He took me out to eat. He put his arm around me. He roasted me pecans. He asked so many questions. And then he invited me to run with him. Am I crazy, or was the Kellan from yesterday mostly just an ass?

By the time we jog up onto his porch, I've got so many endorphins partying in my brain, I really don't care. I'm just slap-happy—and exhausted. So I'm taken off guard when we get into the foyer and Kellan yanks my running pants down.

"Kneel on the stairs and push your ass into the air," he orders.

I do, and he crouches behind me. I can feel his smooth pecs brush my backside as he parts my lips and starts to finger me.

He inhales deeply. "Fuck—you smell incredible."

Then he spanks me—hard.

"Ack! What the hell's that for?"

"One," he says, spanking me again, "for every—" *spank*—"word—" *spank*—"you—" *spank*—"just—" *spank*—"said."

Then he leans down, pushes his head between my legs, and eats my pussy from the back.

I'm so sweaty, so dirty, that at first I think I'm not going to enjoy it, but I'm surprised to find I come almost immediately. I come even harder the second time he pleasures me. Then he carries me up the front stairwell to the windowed room and lays me on my back atop the massive oak bed. He spreads my sore legs, pulls his pants off, and climbs atop me, revealing his long, stiff cock, and the nice, full balls hanging below.

He eases his head in, then pushes in so deep and hard, I gasp.

"I need to fuck this sweaty pussy."

He pushes my arms above my head, and I rebel and wrap my hands around his forearms. We fuck with him clutching my shoulders, and me clutching his arms.

Something about the angle is delicious. My clit throbs with every thrust. Inside, I feel so sensitive and full.

I peek my eyes open at Kellan and find his eyes closed in peaceful concentration. His brows draw together, his lips part a little every time he thrusts. His eyes peek open as he pulls out.

"So... damn good, that pussy."

My eyes drift shut as his thrusts grow harder. He moves one arm to the mattress to support the frenzied pace, while his other hand captures both my wrists. I relax and let him push my arms over my head and press them to the mattress.

I can feel his cock swell in me. His breathing has grown harder, faster. When he presses his face into the crook of my neck, I feel his cock pulse in me, and I come so hard my abs clench and I grunt.

"OH GOD!"

I watch his sweat-glossed back pump with his deep breaths as he hides his face in my neck. His hand around my wrist loosens just enough so I can free one arm and curl my hand around his warm, damp head.

"Kellan—that was so good," I whisper.

He lifts his head and gives me a dazed smile. "This will be better."

He looks exhausted, loose-limbed and satiated, but he moves quickly between my legs and drags his tongue between my swollen lips.

"Oh fuck!"

He blows his breath against my fevered skin. He traces the tip of his tongue around my clit, and I come off the bed.

"Kellan!" I grab his head. He licks me gently, so tenderly I'm almost sure I feel his tongue tremble. And then, when I'm thrusting against him, his tongue starts thrashing me. It's so intense it's almost painful. He shoves two fingers into me and I scream. "Ohhhh... ohh!" I suck back a huge breath as my orgasm steamrolls me.

I sag back to the mattress, and he draws his fingers out.

When I have the strength to open my eyes again, I find him standing by the bed, holding my robe.

"Come down."

He holds an arm out, and I use it for balance as I slide off the big bed.

He takes my hand and leads me into the bathroom. He runs some water into the sunken tub and when it's almost filled, he helps me in. I sink up to my neck in bubbles. The heat seeps into my bones, and I moan. Kellan climbs in after me.

He seats me between his legs, and with his huge erection pressed against my backside, he washes my hair.

"I like your wavy hair," he murmurs.

I stroke his thigh, tucked around mine. "Thanks."

I sit still and patient as he wraps my dark locks in a towel. Then he rubs some soap between his palms and kneads my shoulders.

"Ohhhh." I sag against him, giving in to bliss, but as soon as I do, I feel him twitch against me. I turn around and fold my hands around his cock.

"I want to suck it—please." I look into his eyes and smile. "May I?"

He drags his thumb over my cheek and then eases himself out of the water, so he's sitting on the tub's stone ledge. His cock juts up and out. Bubbles drip down it, collecting on his balls. I wipe the bubbles off and suck the head of him into my mouth, teasing him with my cheeks and tongue while my hands caress his shaft.

One hand wanders down to his balls. They're heavy and taut. I cup them and roll them gently, and take a little more of him into my throat: so deep now, I have to concentrate to breathe.

His hand rests gently on my hair. I look up and find his head is tilted back. His lips are slightly parted. His eyes are closed. I can feel the tension in his hips. The way his abs are clenched.

I suck my cheeks against him, and at the same time, I swallow him deeper into my throat.

He shifts his legs. His hand on my head curls into a fist.

I start to hum around him.

He groans. "Cleo... fuck."

I hum a little more, and his hand on my hair trembles. He makes a low sound in his throat and closes his eyes.

He's feeling good. I can tell because his dick swells in my mouth, and his balls, cradled in my palm, tighten a little more.

I brush the head of him against my throat and suck the rest of him tightly, with all the softest parts of my mouth. I tickle my fingertips gently over his balls, and then I tickle behind them, over the forbidden taint.

He jumps a little, and I suck him deeper.

"Christ. Oh shit..."

I bob my head a little faster. He pulls out a little. His breaths are coming louder, faster. His eyes are squeezed shut.

He strokes my cheek with his fingertips and pushes back in, moaning. His legs twitch. His balls draw up a little more.

I whirl my tongue around him.

"God you're... *fuck*. Keep going... Cleo, fuck don't stop."

I flick my tongue against the tiny slit at the head of him. He jumps. "FUCK," he groans.

He thrusts deeper down my throat, and his gusting breaths turn to tight moans. His fingers grasp the towel on my head. And then, just when I feel him start to really throb, just when every muscle in his body tenses and he breathes, "oh fuck," he pulls out. He strokes himself just once, and blows all over my shoulder.

I rest my hands on his calves while he sits there with his eyes shut, panting.

When he opens his eyes, he looks dazed. Dazed but happy. Satisfied, despite the way he pulled out of my mouth. "Fucking hell, Cleo. That's a gift."

I laugh. He wraps an arm around my head and pulls me in between his legs. I rest my cheek against his thigh.

"That felt so good," he says hoarsely.

"I'm glad." I kiss his inner thigh. Chills spread out from where my lips meet his warm skin. I smile up at him. "This has been a great night."

"You're what's good." His damp hand cups my cheek.

"I guess I kinda like being your slut."

Something about my comment makes his eyes look unhappy. As I'm wondering what bothered him, he climbs out of the tub and grabs hold of a towel rack.

"You okay?"

He laughs. "All the blood's gone down here," he says, nodding at his cock. It's still half-hard.

I watch him as he towels off. Once, as he turns, I think I see a small tat on his back, just over his left hip. I'm about to ask about it when he helps me from the tub, wraps me in a towel, and hugs me close while walking me toward the bed.

He settles me on it with my legs spread. "I need to eat you one more time before you to go sleep."

TEN

September 11, 2014

Cleo-

Fucking hell, I know it's wrong. It's dangerous—for you, for sure, but maybe me as well.

And yet...

The taste of your pussy is my drug. I wake up for the chance to be between your thighs. Your body feels so warm and soft when I hold you.

I'm surprised. My Sloth—I never would have known.

I need you now. Because of you? Because of me? I'm afraid I know the answer. I'm in a desperate state—that's true. But not just anyone would do. Maybe it had to be you.

I should send you home. I should push you far away before you learn more.

I can't. I can't!

My brother Lyon used to scold me for my lack of moral compass. I guess he was right. Don't worry, Cleo baby. I can keep my secret locked down. I won't break your heart. I fucking swear. I'll be sure you never, ever know.

I hope you're not too worried for your friend "R." Don't spend your time worrying for me.

Seventeen more days of you in my house. If I can hold out that long, I'm going to cherish all of them.

-R.

(It's his name. He was Robert Lyon. We both owe you.)

ELEVEN

Cleo

"CLEO?" SMOOTH FINGERS STROKE my face. His voice is soft and smoky in my ear. "Do you want to go with me? To the pick-up?"

I drag my heavy eyelids open. I blink at his handsome face. "What time is it?" I rasp.

"It's four-thirty."

I open my eyes wider and find Kellan standing over me, looking tired and distinctly soft around the edges. He's wearing a blue t-shirt that hugs his muscles, and...

"My God." I flex my legs. "Ohhhh."

"Sore?" He smirks.

"Oh... very. Ow." I sit up, groaning as I do.

Kellan helps me down from the big bed and I dress quickly in jeans and a black Tom Petty t-shirt, because I assume there's a certain time we have to be there.

As I sit in the wing-backed chair and tie my sneakers, looking out at the pitch black night through the window wall, he comes and crouches at my feet. He rests a hand on the shoe I've already laced and looks up into my eyes. "There's a risk here. I want to be sure you know that. Are you okay with that?"

"Yeah, sure." I finish tying my other shoe and straighten up. He takes my hand and rubs the top of it, so gentle that, for a second, my eyes drift shut again. I pull them open, finding him somber. "Isn't there a risk with dealing too?"

He nods, covering my hand fully with his. "But this is different. I'm not getting that much imported anymore, but this is a lot more than you've ever had on hand. I don't think anything will go wrong, but we could get busted. It's always a possibility."

I shrug. "Optimist, remember?" I push my hair back. Little strands of it have escaped my French braid and are hanging in my eyes, but I'm not going to take the time to re-braid it. Not here, anyway. Maybe in the car. "Hey, that reminds me. Where's that stray cat you were telling me about?"

He shrugs. "I haven't seen her lately." He stands up and pulls me with him. When I've gotten to my feet, he laces his fingers through mine, and as we walk through his room, I think how strange it is to just be holding hands. In a way it's even stranger than our casual-not-casual sex has been. He bends his wrist, bringing my arm a little closer to his body, and it feels so nice.

We walk downstairs that way, and I find he's already made us each a water bottle. There's a granola bar by mine. Kellan lets my hand go so he can grab both bottles. I grab my granola bar and Truman bounds over from some unknown Truman resting spot. The three of us clomp down the hall as if we're going to do something ordinary, like throw a Frisbee at the park, and I'm reminded of "Scooby Doo."

"Did you ever watch 'Scooby Doo?'" I ask Kellan as he locks the front door.

His mouth curves up in a lazy, sort-of smile. "Oh yeah. Did you?"

"Yep. I was always wanting to wear my Grans' old lady head scarves around my neck so I could look like Daphne."

Kellan laughs—a rich chuckle that makes my skin tingle—and steps in front of me to open my car door. I scramble into my seat, disappointed when I have to let his hand go. I beam at him as he closes the door behind me, then I smile out at the darkness through the windshield. I hear the door behind me open and close, and then Truman's head appears between the two front seats. I rub his ears as Kellan gets into the car.

I notice as he cranks it that the design on his worn blue t-shirt is a manatee. My eyes drift down to his thighs, which are clad in dark denim.

"You're such a California guy," I tease as he turns down the dirt driveway.

He tugs on his t-shirt and raises his brows.

"I love manatees."

"High school fundraiser," he says.

"I want to hear about your swanky high school."

Kellan reaches down by his door, pulling out a navy Braves cap that he presses onto his head. He adjusts the bill as he turns from his driveway onto the dirt road that will take us to the highway.

"Some other time," he says.

"Are you nervous?" I ask as we bump over the dirt road. Moonlight pearls on the hood of his car, so bright white it hurts my eyes.

He shakes his head, and I'm surprised to find that I'm a little disappointed by how focused he seems on the road, by how his free hand rests on his right knee instead of twined in mine. And realizing my feelings, I feel a trill of fear.

This isn't serious, I remind myself. But the words ring hollow in my head.

He looks somehow both younger and older in the ball cap. Like a high school baseball player—or a young dad. The light from the dash illuminates the planes of his face, and they look like *mine*. My heart says *MINE*. I squeeze my eyes shut.

"Who will we be seeing tonight?" I ask quietly.

"I get the imports from my Uncle Pace," Kellan says. "He's really a cousin, but he's kind of old, so we just always called him uncle."

"Oh. A family member."

He nods. "I used to get more shipments, but now I'm growing so much—so much good shit—that I only get a shipment once a month. It helps supplement in case something happens to my crop, and it gives us seeds to continue cross-breeding. The plants we're getting tonight are pretty young, so they're small. We're only getting twenty of them."

"Only!" I laugh.

As we start down the highway, headed for the east side of town, Kellan explains that he bought the abandoned toy factory at a bank auction; it has doors on the back that open like a garage. He tells me he's in the process of remodeling so he can sell it. Until then, it's used for deals like this.

The east side of Chattahoochee is the "bad" side of town. Even I, who rarely leave campus, know that. And tonight, the evidence is everywhere. Shadowed figures with bowed heads shuffle along the uneven sidewalk that runs alongside the street. Run-down cars idle in front of decrepit-looking buildings. We pass a violent jade Mercedes Benz with flashy rims, and my eyes slide to Kellan.

"Do other drug dealers know you?" I ask.

He smiles tightly. "I don't have any criminal enemies, Cleo. I'll open the warehouse doors with this—" he taps a flip-down compartment in the ceiling of the Escalade—"and we'll drive in. The doors will close right behind us. In the main garage area, there are no windows to the outside. No one will see a light in there and come to see what's up. There's an office attached, and all the lights will be off there too."

I chew my lip, and his hand spreads over my knee. "I've got a good security system, baby. Just because of the neighborhood it's in." He nods at the digital clock on the dash. "By the time we get there, Manning and Pace will already have things all settled. Only reason I go too is prudence."

"You mean you don't trust Manning?"

"Not at all," he says. He takes a left at a litter-strewn intersection and we drive slowly down a dark, one-way street. Kellan reaches up to touch the ceiling, hits the brakes, and a second later, we're driving into darkness. "I trust him," he says calmly as the dark garage looms around us. "But this is my thing. I'm the one in charge, so I should be here with him."

Just as my throat starts feeling uncomfortably tight, someone flicks the lights on, and I'm stunned to find we're in a large open space, almost like a skating rink, with creamy, sheetrock walls and a smooth, cement floor. About a dozen yards in front of us is a large white van, and by it, Manning's Harley.

"Lights flick off when we open the garage door, and flick back on once we're in," Kellan explains. He lifts his hand off my knee and tugs the bill of his cap in what seems like a nervous gesture.

Manning and a short, pot-bellied man walk out from behind a white van, and Kellan nods. "See the old guy?" I note the man's torn jeans and Pink Floyd t-shirt. "That's my Uncle Pace. I'll check things out, we'll do some back slapping, and then you and me are out. It should be simple." He winks, and I try to calm the riot rushing through my veins.

"I wanted you to see how easy this is," Kellan explains as he adjusts his cap again. "So if you ever had to do it, you'd know how."

"If I ever had to—"

Truman barks when he sees Manning, and I watch Kellan's face tighten as Pace raises his hand in a wave.

They both start toward the Escalade, and Kellan says, "Wait here. Manning is picking the stuff up. Don't know why he's on his bike."

My stomach twists as Kellan saunters over to them. I never noticed until now what a nice swagger he has. In a t-shirt and jeans, it's easy to admire.

I watch as Manning holds out a hand and Kellan clasps it in a friendly shake. It's weird, though, because as he does that, I see tension in his back and shoulders. Manning's face is serious. Kellan holds out one arm, and Pace holds out both hands.

I can't hear what's being said, but Manning's face tightens, and Pace looks unhappy. Kellan's arm slices the air. Manning touches his shoulder. Kellan takes a long step back.

Over the dull roar of the Escalade's AC, I hear someone shout.

Kellan? The low boom echoes through the empty warehouse. Pace gets right in front of Kellan, reaching for his shoulder. Kellan pushes him. My heart hammers as I crack my window.

Manning looks unhappy. Do I trust him? He seemed like a good ole boy.

Kellan grabs Pace's collar. "Don't you fucking mention Lyon! EVER! Goddamn fucking *Pace*!" I can't hear what Pace says back, but it doesn't go over well with Kellan. He shoves Pace's shoulders. Manning grabs Kellan's arm, and Kellan takes a swing at Manning.

"Get out of here." I think that's what he growls. Manning doesn't move—I think he's saying something I can't hear. Kellan scoffs. His face, which I can see from the side, looks as if he's laughing at Manning—but his shoulders are still heaving. Manning shrugs and gets on his bike. He looks pissed, but I hear him crank it, so that must mean he's leaving.

For the next minute, my attention is split between Manning riding slowly out the garage door, and Kellan as he and Uncle Pace begin to go at it again.

Shit!

Pace grabs Kellan's arm, and cold fear sweeps me. Kellan shoves his chest, and for the first time, Pace looks angry. Kellan gets up in his face, and after something else is said, he shoves Pace again.

My mind races. Is Pace a nice guy? Does he know I'm in the car? What if he hurts Kellan? I crack my door open, because I want to feel more mobile.

Kellan's voice booms through the warehouse. "I am!" Pace says something and he gets up in his face. "Oh no, you didn't think. Fuck you, Pace. Fuck you," he sneers.

I catch another low, pissed off voice, and possibly an "idiot" from Pace's mouth. Then Kellan leans closer, with his hand on Pace's shoulder. I think they might be making nice when Kellan hauls his arm back and smashes the shorter man in the jaw.

Truman barks—a low, intimidating sound that has me shrinking against the cracked door before I realize his tail is still thumping against the back seat. I put my hand on the door handle, clutching it as Pace shouts something.

He covers his face with one hand, and Kellan laughs—a bitter sound.

Pace says something loud and forceful. I see blood drip from his nose. Kellan shoves his shoulder, and he holds his hands out. I can't hear his words, but they are loud and they sound pissed off.

Shit, did someone sell him out? My pulse is so frantic, I can barely breathe.

I slide into the driver's seat and crack that window too.

"It's up to *me*. Not Robert—ME," he says, as Pace puts pressure on his bleeding nose. "You need to remember that shit."

Something else is said. Pace looks sad. Kellan seethes. Pace opens his mouth, and Kellan seems to take that as his cue to go.

He stalks back toward the car, his hands in fists, his long strides closing the distance between us quickly. He's within spitting range when Pace says something else. Kellan whirls around, stalks over to him, and slaps his shoulder.

"Fuck you then," I hear him say. He sounds resigned.

Seconds later, he is at the driver's door. When he sees me there, he walks around and gets into the passenger's seat.

"Drive," he snaps.

I do.

TWELVE

Kellan

I'M SO FURIOUS I CAN'T SPEAK. I can barely breathe as Cleo drives us back toward my house. I train my gaze on the night outside the windshield. Pace's words ping pong around my mind, and every echo brings on new fury. The rage I feel is thick enough to fill my chest, until I'm numb and heavy, curled around a fire deep in my gut.

After parking the car, Cleo shepherds Truman toward the porch, steers me up the stairs with her hand on my lower back, and uses my key to open the front door.

I feel ill as we walk toward the kitchen. All because of Pace—and Manning. Fucking Pace betrayed me. Fucking Manning. Clueless bastard. They took this shit I've been pushing out to sea and brought it crashing through me, crashing through my house. I can't be here. I stop before I reach the living room and look down the hall, at the front door. I could go. A part of me just wants to go.

Cleo's hand around my forearm brings me back. "Come on in here," her soft voice says. "Your hand is scraped. I can clean it up for you."

She leads me to the couch and I sit down, my eyes cast to my boots. I can't look at the TV. I don't want to see the sunset post cards on the end table. Even the sight of my own legs makes my throat tighten in impotent fury, but I can't escape myself. Not yet, anyway.

Cleo disappears. I feel a pang. When she returns, she's got my first aid kit. I don't move as she cleans my knuckles, smooths a Band-Aid over one of them. I rest my head against the back of the couch and let sleep tug at me.

I could go to sleep.

I can't go to sleep.

On every level possible, I have to rage against that bullshit Pace threw at me. I'm tired but I have to fight. I'm living on my own damn terms—but when I feel this desperate, I know of nothing that will help except to be between a woman's legs.

I fuck Cleo on the rug. I make a cage of my arms, my palms pressed to the rug on each side of her shoulders. With her hands unbound for once, she strokes me, her warm hands tracing up and down my hips, then up a little higher, where she cups my pecs and teases my nipples.

I hold nothing back. Three years ago, with Gillian, I fucked without a single rule, but even that was nothing like this time with Cleo. Every time I plunge inside her warm body, a ragged groan tears from my throat. Every time she sighs or gasps, I curl down closer over her, until I'm propped up on my elbows and my hands are holding her cheeks.

My mouth devours hers—punishing, then worshipping, teasing, raging, needing. I've never tasted anything like Cleo's breath as she moans between my lips. I come hard—so hard I nearly pass the fuck out with her ankles wrapped around my calves and her arms tucked over my shoulders. I fuck Cleo like a lover, and when I'm finished, I don't even have the wherewithal to clean her up.

Her soft hands urge me onto the couch, and then my head is in her lap. Her fingers in my hair. I'm lying on my back between her soft thighs. Cleo tightens them around my waist, and I feel... safe. So safe and so, so tired.

The demons in my mind are far away, and there is only her sweet voice, singing a song I've never heard...

We're playing checkers. The pieces are big, and they're all black. Lyon's hair is black, too. At least I think it's his hair.

I try to tickle him, under his ribs, so I can see him grin, but Lyon steps away. His face is solemn—more like mine.

"I didn't think I'd go before you," he says with his head down. "I didn't mean to, Kelly."

I look him over, head to foot. He's wearing his Trojan uniform, and it fits like it did when we both played. I stare for a long time at the crown of his dark head. I wonder why he's gone dark now. If it means... what I fear it means.

I grab his shoulder, squeezing hard enough to hurt—the way Robert taught us both. "I want to know where you went, Ly. This not knowing is killing me. I miss you." My throat aches. I pull him into my arms. "You're my older brother. You're my twin. I need to know."

"You know I can't tell you." He laughs. "If I told you, Kelly, I'd have to kill you."

My throat and stomach burn like someone dumped a vat of acid into me. Lyon is wrenched from me. I look around for him, but there is no sign he's ever even been here. The blue tiles are cold under my feet. Blue steam wafts through the air. I breathe it in, because along with poison, there is oxygen—and I haven't yet learned how to live without breathing.

"Fuck me." I clutch my throat. The shaking starts in my shoulders and spreads out, all through my aching body.

I never thought I'd feel this pain again...

I jerk out of sleep as if the hand of God has plucked me from the ether. Cleo's face is right in front of mine. I blink a few times before noticing that she looks scared shitless. Her hands squeeze my shoulders, and she's straddling my outstretched legs. "Kellan! Shit—you scared me."

"What?" I look around the living room, still stained with shadow but starting to glow from the rising sun. I look down at my busted hand. "What's going on?"

Her hand rises to cup my nape. "You feel asleep in my lap. You had a nightmare, I think." She puts her free hand on my chest, and I notice how fast I'm breathing.

I try to slow it down, but I keep feeling that ghost pain in my throat. "Water," I try. Cleo rushes to the kitchen. I can't breathe.

I stagger up and walk around the couch, into the kitchen, where I see her opening cabinets. I hang onto the granite countertop and try to focus on the cold beneath my hands.

I'm in my own house. I'm not going back there. I'm okay for now. I look down at my bandaged hand and want to scream. Why'd I do that? I'm so fucking stupid.

Cleo's hands are rubbing my back. I like that.

"I'm fine," I tell her. But I can't seem to slow my breathing.

I just stand there... flailing, while Cleo's hands stroke my fevered skin through my shirt, and my body echoes and my heart hangs from my chest in tattered shreds. I miss my brother so much, I can't breathe.

I try to ration my breaths, and Cleo keeps rubbing circles on my back. Like Lyon. He would rub my neck and shoulders—since when we were little kids.

My big brother... he knew what would make me better. *The one who didn't know was me...*

I lean over the counter and let my head rest on my arm. "Cleo?"

"What can I do?" she asks in a high voice.

I shake my head. I turn around and pull a cabinet open. I grab a pill bottle and shake a Xanax into my damp palm. It's been a long time since I took one, so they might be expired... A few fall to the floor, and Cleo rushes to gather them.

I hold one in my hand, thinking of cutting it in half. My fingers shake so much, I just put it in my mouth and chew.

She takes the bottle from me as I swallow bitter pieces.

I lean over the counter, too ashamed to look at her. "I'm sorry," I say as it starts to spread its numbing fingers through me. I pull my lead gaze up to hers. "I didn't mean to scare you."

"You were saying 'lie.'"

"Lyon." I let my eyelids slip shut. I feel her hand, a gentle pressure on my back.

"I heard you say it at the factory too," she whispers by my ear. "Did something happen, Kellan? I can tell you're really upset."

I open my eyes and find her worried face. I take her hand.

"Come here," I whisper.

I lead Cleo over to the couch and then I summon all my energy and walk to the DVD player.

I take the Trojans DVD's plastic case and turn the player on.

I sit beside her, feeling heavy.

"Look at this." My eyes shut as I pass her the leaflet from inside the case. "Find my name," I groan. I don't mean to, but I can't keep the pain out of my voice.

"I see you—right here. Kellan Drake."

"Now look below it," I rasp.

"Lyon Drake? I'm confused." Cleo pauses, and I hear the TV start to play. "Number thirty-three, the program says."

"His number?" I lift my head out of my hands as my eyelids try to shut. Yes, Lyon was thirty-three.

I nod, and she watches the screen. Lyon lines up in his tight-end position, and my chest fills up with nails.

"That's your brother?" she asks.

I nod.

"Is he younger or older than you?" she asks gently.

"Twins," I murmur. The word feels foreign on my tongue.

"Did something happen to him?"

I swallow, even though my throat is dry. I bury my head in both my hands. "He died."

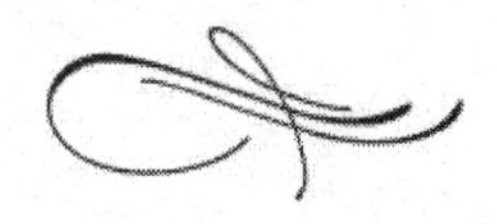

Cleo

I watch the phantom Kellan on the screen. It's strange because he has blond hair, like the Kellan sitting with me on the couch, so as he circles around my dark-haired Kellan with a giant cooler, my senses tell me that *he's* Kellan. He's got the same beautiful body, the same gorgeous blue eyes. But when he laughs, his face is different. He has dimples when he smiles, and Kellan only gets them when he frowns.

My dark Kellan darts away and starts to circle blond-haired Lyon. Lyon whirls around with him. When Kellan feints, his brother anticipates it in advance. He dumps the cooler full of ice in the exact right spot to drench Kellan.

Kellan jolts out from under the icy water and tackles his brother. Behind them, fans are filing out of the stadium. Other players join in, and as the brothers brawl on the football field, someone brings another cooler and dumps it on them both.

"Fuck you!" Kellan roars.

Lyon is laughing—laughing with his blond head thrown back. Laughing like a Kellan angel.

I can see where Kellan gets his darkness. It's the balance to his brother's light.

Someone starts to throw ice cubes, and the twins disappear into a mass of jerseys. I hear one final *whoot* from one of them, but it's impossible to discern which. My Kellan was younger, freer, despite his black hair. As if in answer, Lyon flits in front of the screen, smiling gloriously for the camera.

He shakes his wet head, sending drops of water flying at the lens.

"And that's all we have tonight, from Los Angeles Memorial Coliseum. Keep it cool, and we'll see you next week," the announcer says as the camera pans out.

I shift my gaze to Kellan. He's just staring. I can see no feeling on his face.

"When did it happen?" I whisper.

"September 18. 2011."

I nod slowly. "That date is coming up." I look at his hands, sitting listless in his lap, and I wonder about his fight at the bar. It was January 2011—just a few months after this game was filmed. Was his brother there that night? I didn't read anything about his brother in the papers. Was Lyon as talented as Kellan? Were they both untamed boys, privileged athletes living outside the lines? Were they using drugs?

"It must be on your mind."

I touch his thigh with just my fingertips, even though it makes me nervous—the act of reaching out and touching him when he's in so much pain. I don't want to hurt him more. Instead, he doesn't move at all. His body is like a statue. After a moment, he leans his head against the back of the couch.

He closes his eyes, and I stare down at my helpless hand on his jeans. My heart pounds with the need to comfort him somehow, but my mind is painfully blank. I feel a burst of panic as I watch the even rise-fall of his chest. I hope he didn't fall asleep. Not before I get a chance to comfort him.

"I'm sorry," he says raggedly. "I never take this shit."

"Please—don't be sorry." I have a memory of a letter I got from "R." once, where he replied to a note I'd sent about going to see Olive's grave. He told me I should take Xanax before bed after I went. Tomorrow—well, today—I'm going to Olive's grave again. Maybe I'll take a page from "R." and Kellan's book. "You should never feel bad about doing something that will ease your pain. Everyone deserves a break."

I raise my hand and ease it behind his head, dropping down to rub his nape gently. His skin is soft and very warm. His eyes lift up to mine.

"Can you not... rub like that?" He rasps. "I'm sorry." He drops his forehead into his hand.

"Of course. You want me to give you some space?" I start to move my arm, still hovering over his shoulders. He grabs my hand and tugs it down, settling my arm firmly around his back.

I scoot closer to him. My hip touches his as I tighten my grip on his back, hoping that the weight of it will make him feel less alone—the way he did for me at Mama McCalister's.

We sit like that a while, and I lean my head against his shoulder. A moment after I move, he does—raising his head to look at me with haunted eyes. "I need you again," he whispers. "Now, please."

I nod, and he lifts me in his arms. He cradles my body to his chest, my forehead on his shoulder as he slowly climbs the stairs. I'm expecting slow sex on the bed, so he shocks me by lowering me belly-first onto the hall runner, yanking off my pants, and coming down heavy over me. He fingers me until I'm gasping, then he fucks me without flair.

Just a pounding doggy style, until his warmth jets inside me and I clench around him. We groan in unison, splitting open the dark silence.

He braces himself there atop me for only a moment. Then he scoops me up, sets me on my feet, and smacks my ass so hard it echoes. I yelp and whirl around to face him. I find Kellan sharp-edged and somber.

"Go to your bedroom," he orders. "Lie on your back, in the middle of the mattress. Wait for me."

I nod quickly, and he walks through the door into his bedroom. He shuts it behind him. I can't quite say why, but I feel the urge to follow him inside. I count to thirty, then walk to his door on weak legs and turn the knob. I push the door open slowly, hoping he won't notice me peek in. When it's open just an inch, I align my right eye with the crack.

I find a large room stuffed with sleek, mahogany antiques, fluffy armchairs, a massive corner bookshelf, and—a wall rug? Yep, the right wall of the room is covered with what looks, to my untrained eyes, like a rug. And what's weird: it's swaying, as if Kellan smacked it as he walked by.

I have a flashback from a Nancy Drew I read when I was little, where there was a hidden trap door behind a wall-hanging. Obviously that's ridiculous, but even so, I can't contain my curiosity—and that part of me, deviant Cleo who likes her ass spanked till it burns, wants to see what punishment he'll inflict if he finds I followed him.

I slink into the room like a spider, one leg first, one arm, and then a full step brings me onto his soft, Oriental rug.

I stand there listening, and when I don't hear him, I walk past his bed and a cozy armchair, where a book rests. I put my hand against the rug hanging from a long rod up near the ceiling, and press down until I feel the firmness of the wall behind it.

I slide my hands down, holding my breath against the dust that is probably swimming all around my face. Then I commit to my insanity and lift it up so I can look behind it. I'm strangely unsurprised to see a door there. It's sleek wood—almost the same color of the mahogany bedroom set—and on its left side is a fancy, brass doorknob.

As I lower my cheek gently to the door, I already know that I will hear him on the other side—and so again, I'm not surprised. Kellan, breathing heavily. The cadence of his gasping is so fast, I have the sick fear that he's with another girl.

I don't dare move. When he roars his pain out, my heart forgets its rhythm. *Kellan...*

I stand there with my fist poised at the hard slab of the door, until I hear the sound of water running. Then I rush back to my windowed room.

I lie there in the morning sun for two hours before I close the curtains and the canopy and burrow into the duvet. I'll have to leave here in a few hours, and if I'm going to drive to Albany, I need to get some sleep.

THIRTEEN

Kellan

I HANG UP MY CELL PHONE just as Cleo steps into the kitchen. Her eyes are guarded: pleasantly neutral. It's the benign look on her face that gives her away. It's not a real expression, it's a dummy one. Probably because she's not sure where she stands with me—and with the dawning of her sister's birthday, she might be too tired to think it through.

Her gaze feels warm on my face, and I can feel the tug of her concern before she shifts her green eyes over to the island and the bar stool she's adopted as her own. I admire her getup as she hoists herself onto the stool. She's got her wavy hair tucked into a messy bun at the top of her head, and she's wearing magenta leggings and a flowing, tie-dyed shirt. I squint to make out her stud earrings, but I can't from where I'm standing, between the refrigerator and the sink.

I'm embarrassed, so it's tough to meet her eyes—but I can be tough when a situation calls for it.

I give her a small smile that seems to lift up only half of my mouth, and I nod at her. "I like your getup there."

I step over to the island she's sitting at and lean my elbows on the countertop beside the stove.

"Thank you," she says, twirling one earring. It's a tiny Hello Kitty.

"I thought I'd try to wear things she might like," she says in a voice that's slightly hoarse with pain, "if she was still here."

I don't even think about it first. I just stretch across the island and hold out my hands. My pulse hammers between my ears as she looks down at them. I'm not sure when's the last time

I left myself so open for another person. She gives me a small, sad smile and threads her fingers through mine.

I look her over more closely and—shit: her face is definitely sad.

My mind's hung up in a dark place too, so I feel like I'm right there with her. It seems almost like kismet—that I wrote out those instructions for visiting the cemetery, and she falls into my life a week before she treks to her hometown for that very reason.

I rub my thumbs over her small, cool hands and try to overcome the embarrassment I feel, being so close to her after last night. I don't even remember the ride home from the warehouse. I remember looking down as she rubbed something on my knuckles. How pain clenched in my chest, like a weed overtaking flowers, choking everything out of me but the agony of my losses.

I know I used Cleo for comfort. I remember how incredible it felt to get lost deep inside her. How smooth her palms were as they swept slowly up my chest. I remember her fingers in my hair, her legs around my waist as we curled together on the couch. And waking up... that way.

Like I'm so far from the living, nothing warm can touch me. Like there's a glacier shoved inside my ribs, and I'm not even breathing. No heart beating. Hollow and filled up with cold.

I know I lost my shit and let her see me looking wrecked and crazy.

... And I know she put her arm around me. Tried to rub my neck.

I remember all of that.

Afterward, upstairs... I went into the locked room because I had to. I didn't know what to do, and I didn't want to make any calls. I don't want to pull the trigger on my time with Cleo. I can't yet.

So I repaired things as much as I could, and by the time I was done, she was asleep—so I slid under the sheets beside her. Her body was so warm, and mine so cold. Even in her sleep, she reached for me. She cradled me. And for the first time in—*the first time ever*—I started to wonder what I need the most. And how, when I can't feed this growing hunger for her, I'll be able to do anything but die.

I look up at her now, at her sad face, and I feel the vestiges of my own pain fall away as I think of ways to ease hers.

"How'd you sleep?" I ask—because I want to know if she remembers being joined in bed by me.

"I slept okay." She rubs a finger over my scabbed knuckles and frowns down at them. "Did you hit something else?" She pulls her gaze up to my face and strokes her fingertip over my skin. "This little cut is still bleeding."

I shrug and draw my hands away. "I've got that punching bag..."

She reaches out for me. "You punched a punching bag? You shouldn't do that," she says. I lean back toward her and let her have my hands.

It feels so good to have her stroke my hand and wrists. I could shut my eyes and give in to her soothing touch. But today, the focus is on her.

"You want some breakfast?" I ask, gently withdrawing my hands from hers.

"I want you to let me put another bandage on your knuckles, especially that one that looks so puffy. I'm leaving to go home after that, so I'll probably just grab a Pop Tart on the road."

"Come here," I beckon with my hand.

She hesitates a moment, then comes around the counter, and I place a hand on her shoulder. I don't plan to, but I draw her closer, close enough so I could wrap my arms around her. And I want to. I want to so damn much. But I'm still feeling cold and dead inside, so I just stand there, breathing.

"Thank you for last night," I whisper. "You were very kind to me—with not much regard for you and very few questions answered." I release her shoulder and look at her pretty face. "Do you want to know what happened at the factory?"

She shrugs. "Only if you want to tell me. It's okay if you don't."

I owe her. I lean back against the counter and tap my fingers against the granite, trying to think of where to start. How much to say. And if it even matters. I'm surprised to find I want to tell her. When I meet her eyes again, they're warm; encouraging.

"Pace is a first cousin of my father, Robert. My father is... a powerful man—in many ways. Most people feel beholden to him. They do everything he asks. My father and I have been estranged for several years. Since Lyon's death," I manage in a steady voice. "But Robert can't accept that. Everything has to be... according to his wishes. So right now, he's trying to put pressure on me. He had Pace drive here—even though Pace is an employee of mine, he doesn't work for my father—He had Pace drive to Georgia with an empty van. To prove a point."

Her eyes widen. "He drove here from—where again?"

"From California," I tell her.

"He drove that far with nothing?"

I nod.

"Did Manning know about it?"

I'm surprised she was watching closely enough to see Manning was batting for Pace's team back at the warehouse.

"He didn't know, but Pace told Manning some bullshit, and the two of them tried to get me to... yield to my father's wishes. On something important. Something that's not their business, either one of them." I inhale; exhale. Robert is dead to me. I want to tell Cleo why. How I blame him for Lyon's death. But one look at her sympathetic face and I know this day should be all about her. Even mentioning this right now... it's selfish.

"I'm so sorry that happened," she says.

I nod. "I know you are." I let a breath out, releasing that subject, and look back up at her. "I appreciate it, Cleo. Now let's get some food and water packed."

"Um... what?"

"I'm driving you. Don't protest. I know it's hard to do this shit alone, and I want to go. Anyway, you don't have a car here."

"Oh, I guess I don't."

I start opening cabinets. "What do you want?"

I open the liquor cabinet, and her eyes widen. "Oh my God, is that Snow Queen vodka?"

I can't resist a smile. "It's my favorite. Have you had it?"

"I love it. This is really weird... but can we take some with us?"

I give her a gentle smirk. "Only if you tell me why."

She smiles a little, and I can't tell if it's sad. "My friend came up with some instructions for me once, for visiting the cemetery. One of the things was having some Snow Queen with me."

"You should," I say, trying to ignore the sharp twist in my gut. "Your friend sounds like a smart dude."

She frowns. "How did you know it's a dude?"

"You said 'he.'"

"Oh." She nods. "Yeah. I haven't heard from him in a while. I'm actually really worried about him."

All the air in my lungs dissipates, and I feel the color drain from my face. I draw a deep breath, taking care to look away from her. "What makes you worried?" I ask as I get the Snow Queen down and set it on the counter.

"He's got a weird situation. Kind of... risky." I wait for her to tell me what she means by that, but Cleo just runs her palm over her upswept hair. "I found out he has a P.O. box in a city like an hour from here, which is totally crazy. It's just across the Alabama line, in this little town called Eufaula. I was thinking of stopping by on my way back up to Chattahoochee, to see if anyone around has seen him." She rolls her eyes. "I have stalker tendencies—I know."

I smile a little at how ruffled she seems, even as I feel a yawning ache behind my sternum.

"We can do that. We can do anything you want," I lie. I keep my business P.O. box across state lines for security reasons, and there is no way we're going by there.

I stretch my arm out and rub my palm over the coil of her bun. Cleo stands perfectly still, her eyes level with my throat as I just... touch her. My hand lingers there, barely brushing the soft nest of her hair. Because I need to touch her. Because now that I know who she is, I feel a fucking tug toward her, as if a rope is tied around me and she's got the business end.

Cleo's hand touches my throat. "What's this?"

My muscles tighten. "What?" I trail my hand down by her ear, hoping to distract her—but she leans closer.

"You've got this little scar... right here." Her finger rubs gently over the base of my neck, just atop the thick throb of my jugular. "It looks exactly like a little white Sharpie line." She strokes me there again, and I suck in a deep breath.

"Oops, I'm sorry. Does that bother you?"

I shake my head. I guess I held my breath while she was touching me. I press my lips together for what I hope looks like a normal smirk. "You want to hear that story?"

She nods, eager.

I stroke her ivory white throat. "In the car," I lie again.

Cleo shakes her head and pulls her lips down. "It's not a car."

Goddamn, her mouth like that. It's fucking sexy, that little smirk. There's something feline about it—like a smug housecat pondering a bowl of milk. I want to kiss it off her lips.

"What is it then?" I ask, turning toward the refrigerator before she sees my boner. I grit my teeth and start to rearrange my canned nutrition shakes.

"It's a gas guzzler," she says, coming to stand on the other side of the refrigerator door. I train my eyes on the label of one of the shakes, because I can feel her eyes on me. She's so damn close, her gaze burns.

"Do you know the miles per gallon?" she asks.

I reach in and get two water bottles out, and I think of checkers. That's all it takes to kill my boner, so I'm safe to turn around. "You really wanna know?"

"I'm not sure. Do I not?"

I tug the sleeve of her shirt. "Are you a tree-hugger, Cleo baby?"

"Don't call me that." Pink spots bloom on her cheeks.

I grin. "What—Cleo baby?"

"Yes." She takes a step away from me. I step with her. She leans against the countertop, right in front of the sink. I come in close, so close our hips are almost touching.

I'm still grinning. "You don't like it?"

"It's... I don't know." She fusses with her hair. "It makes me feel like I'm... being teased."

I rub my thumb along her smooth jaw, smirking because I can't help myself. "Cleo baby?" I tilt my head at her. "That makes you feel teased?"

She leans back. "You *are* teasing me—right now. Don't act like you aren't," she says indignantly.

"You never answered me. About the trees."

She leans back toward me with reluctance on her face. I could step back to give her space, but where's the fun in that? I know my breath smells good because I chewed a bunch of Big Red after my run earlier this morning.

I rub my fingers over the hemline of her tie-dyed shirt. "You look cute in tie-dye, Cleo baby. Like you belong in California with me, hugging redwoods."

Her cheeks are even redder than before. I'm surprised, and irrationally charmed.

"I'm getting 'The Lorax' on my ankle next," she says, and then presses her lips tightly together to hide a smile she wants to beam at me.

That makes me laugh. I don't know why I find it so damn funny: that smug little smile she's trying to hide, and the thought of that damned mustached Lorax on Cleo's little ankle.

"Dr. Seuss." She shrugs, her eyes alight, as if my amusement has infected her. "I'm his number one fan girl."

I give her a grin, because fuck it, I can't help myself. I notice a glint of something silver at her throat and pull a necklace out of her shirt. I see a small sloth hanging from the chain and lose my grin.

I guess my face must show my feelings, because Cleo's eyes widen in response to what she thinks is disapproval. "Are you hating on my sloth necklace?"

"Hell no." I fake a quick smile for her. "I'm a lover of the sloth." I turn toward the pantry but I slide a glance her way. She's folded her arms and is leaning against the refrigerator, looking skeptical.

"Have you ever heard of Save the Sloths International?" I ask. She frowns as I step into the pantry, looking for some shit for us to eat. "I'm one of its biggest donors. Same money that bought the Escalade—" I stick my head out, giving Cleo my most earnest look—"I'll have you know, it saved three sloths."

She steps toward me. "What kind of sloths?"

"The slow, tree-dwelling kind."

"Sloths that live in... ?"

"Endangered locations," I tell her. "Much of South America is being pruned by... well, you know—Mr. O'Hare."

Her mouth drops open and her eyes widen. The shocked look quickly morphs into a smile. "You've read 'The Lorax?'"

"I helped write it," I tease.

"Kellan Walsh, you... sneaky trickster."

I laugh. Sneaky trickster—that's all she's got? I step out of the pantry with an armful of food and shrug. "I'm a closet whore for Dr. Seuss myself."

She shakes her head, still laughing, and then steps to take some of the food out of my arms. "Holy hell, Kellan. Do you think we have enough snacks?"

I lay out the array of food on the countertop, and Cleo starts to weed through it. "White powdered doughnuts—score!" She sets the two packs off to the side. "Twizzlers—these things are my super fave." She pushes them into the pile, and I smile at her enthusiasm. "Teddy Grahams—hell yes, childhood! Olive would love these." I watch as her smile falters, but she pastes it back on.

"KIND chocolate and peanut butter protein bar, yes, please. Hell yes, Nutella and these godly little dipping sticks. Kellan, you have great taste in junk food." I laugh, and Cleo wraps her arms around her food pile. "You're a shopping god." She moves a pack of candied peanuts, a bag of Nilla Wafers, and a small bag of Doritos into the stack, rejecting two bags of pork rinds and one bag of Fritos.

"No pork rinds?" I tease.

"Hell no. Those things are sick. Pigs are super smart, you know."

"But not when there's bacon around, huh?"

She hangs her head. "I know. I'm evil."

I laugh, and turn to get a grocery bag out of the pantry. "Manning left those here."

"Ewww. No thank you. Pork rinds are a Southern thing I've never gotten behind," she tells me.

I hold a plastic grocery bag open, and Cleo dumps her booty in. "This is going to be the yummiest sad day I've ever had."

That makes me smile. I take the bag from her and set it on the counter, then I grab a stick of beef jerky from the refrigerator and peel it open.

"You refrigerate your beef jerky?"

"It's the only way."

"How about just not eating it?"

I shake my head and rip a bite off. "Protein," I say between chewing.

"Eat an egg." She wrinkles her nose. "Eat chicken."

"I don't do leftovers, Cleo baby. And I'm not up for cooking right now. Unless you want something?"

She shakes her head.

I finish off the jerky in three more bites and toss the wrapper. Then I grab a TwoCal out of the refrigerator, peel the aluminum top off, and dump it into a glass.

"That looks disgusting," Cleo leans against the counter as I swallow the creamy liquid. Her eyes run over my navy blue Dr. Who t-shirt and my ragged ass jeans. "Is it for body building?"

I smirk. "You think I look like a body builder, Cleo baby?"

Her cheeks redden. "Stop calling me that."

I sweep my eyes down myself. I know I'm looking pretty cut right now. Since May, I've been working out like a fiend and piling on the muscle mass. My body fat has got to be low as shit, and yeah—before I started dropping weight these last two weeks or so, my shirts had gotten tight as fuck tight around the chest and arms.

I can't help a smug look. I toss back the TwoCal and set the glass in the sink, beside another empty one. Cleo peeks at them.

"You drank one of those earlier today, too? Like for breakfast?"

"You worrying over my diet, Cleo baby?"

She shoves me in the chest, and I wrap my hand around her thin, tanned wrist. I look down at her face—her teasing eyes, her playful smile—and all I want is to kiss those soft, full lips.

A heartbeat passes. Another as I try to bridle myself. Then I lean down, take her face in my hands, and kiss her like she's the last thing I'll ever taste. I kiss her with the power surging through my veins, with all the strength of my desire to protect her from this day. With all the want that's burning through me—want of more than just her body. Want of days and nights, forgotten things like the weight of a woman's body in my arms and the way the woods sound when the sun comes slanting through the trees like sheets of gold. Everything I long for, everything I can't have, I pour into her mouth—and Cleo responds beautifully.

Her arms twine around my waist, pressing her soft belly against my bulge. I'm so damn hard, I just want to push myself against her until she spreads her legs and lets me in. Instead I slide my tongue into the softness of her mouth. Cleo gasps. It makes me smile around her lips, knowing that I can make my dirty girl gasp with just a slip of my tongue.

I explore her slowly, wrapping an arm around her back and cradling her head, so when I thrust my tongue into the hot, slick sanctuary of her mouth, she doesn't have to work to stay upright.

I kiss her soft and slow, and longer, harder, until she's gasping and my hand is squeezing her breast. Her back is pressed against the refrigerator, and I'm thrusting against her.

She's rocking against me, too. She slides down the refrigerator door, and I take her in my arms and lay her on the floor. She's panting. I can see her nipples poke out through her colorful t-shirt.

I kneel over her. "Do you want to be fucked on my kitchen floor?"

She starts to nod, and I crouch over her, pressing my lips against her temple even as I straddle her and rub my bulge against her softness.

"Know what I think would be better?" She blinks up at me, her eyes liquid and dreamy as I shift myself against her. "We're going to do this sometime on the way there. I'm going to pick the spot."

She pushes her pussy against my dick. "But it's a—"

"A serious occasion?" I lift my hips off hers and work my hand into the elastic waistband of her leggings. "A sad one?" I ask, stroking her soft belly.

She nods. She looks down guiltily at my hand. My gaze rolls to her nipples, and when I don't see their outline against her shirt, I help her up and lean her against the counter.

"Here..." I twist the top off the Snow Queen. I get a shot glass from the cabinet and fill it to the brim, then hold it out to Cleo. "I don't think your sister would want you to have a shitty day. And you know what else I think?"

She takes the glass and shakes her head.

"I think you don't have to feel like shit to commemorate someone who's gone." I think of Ly and his khakis and his button-up Polos with the sleeves rolled up over his forearms.

"You know why I ran for SGA, Cleo?"

She brings the vodka to her lips and holds it there. "No," she whispers over the clear liquid.

"Because my brother loved rules and order. He was a dork who carried—" I swallow hard. "You know that calculator I had? That was his, and he loved that fucking thing. Our day school had a dress code, so we were all walking around like little CEOs but Lyon—he got off on that shit. He ironed his clothes and mine too, and Myra our housekeeper would always laugh at that. But he knew what he liked. He liked to feel like things were taken care of. He liked to be prepared. And when we started college he rushed, but he also went out for a spot on the USG Senate, because he loved that kind of shit. The boring shit? Lyon was all over that."

She slams the shot back, then gives me a wide-eyed look, her lips caught somewhere between a sad smile and a surprised oval. "So you don't like rules and order?"

I laugh. "Hell no, not those kinds of rules. I memorized *Robert's Rules of Order* and it damn near killed me. That's one of the things I did for Ly."

"You ran for SGA for him." Her lips tuck up, but it's not a smile. It's something more fragile.

I nod, and when I open my mouth to say something else, the words all lined up to come out are *I'm more of a wood-chopping guy*. Because—fuck me—I want her to fucking know.

For just this one dark moment in my spotless, stainless-and-granite kitchen, I want Cleo to know exactly who I am—and what my life is like. I want it so much I ache with it.

My jaw clamps shut, because I could never do that to her. I'll do everything I can to ensure Cleo stays out of my sick mess. No one really earns this kind of hell on earth, but least of all Cleo.

Least of all Lyon.

I have to turn toward the sink so I don't give myself away.

I suck a deep breath back and try to calm my racing pulse. Cleo must know because she doesn't make a move toward me. She lets me have my space to mourn my brother, even though what I'm really doing is mourning her.

FOURTEEN

Cleo

THE SECOND KELLAN AND I start down the stairs, a black cat streaks across the lawn, between the porch steps and Kellan's Escalade. My first instinct is to lunge after it, because that's the kind of spaz I am, but Kellan stops me with a squeeze of my fingers.

"Are you trying to catch her?" He grins.

"Possibly." I giggle.

"Wait here." He lets go of my hand and disappears into the house while I watch the yard for a black streak. I don't see one, so when Kellan re-appears with a bowl of diced chicken and sets it on the corner of the porch, I sink down onto the top stair and figure we're waiting for nothing.

That second, the cat pounces on my head.

I scream, tossing the cat off the porch, and Truman bounds out the front door and down the stairs.

"Shit." Kellan's hands rove over my face. "Are you okay?"

I laugh. "I think so."

"Okay—wait here."

He chases Truman down and hauls the dog back into the house. While the door is shut, the cat jumps back onto the porch beside the bowl of chicken and curls into a ball, blinking her green eyes at me.

"Helen—you pussy!" I smile at my own ridiculousness and crawl slowly over to her. She scoots back a little, but she's not going to leave the bowl of chicken. I watch her bend over to eat, taking note of how thin she is. But she doesn't look mangy.

I scoot a little closer to her, until I'm close enough to hold my hand over her back. She peeks over her shoulder at me, then keeps eating.

Kellan comes out the door. He slides a hand into his pocket and leans his shoulder against the door. God, he's hot. At a glance, he almost seems lanky, but his shoulders are so wide. And that face. He's giving me that gentle smile of his, the one that tilts up a little on one side and is always accompanied by a twinkle in his blue eyes. The world indulgent comes to mind. I look at the bowl of chicken and smile back at him. He is indulging me.

He indulges me for five or so more minutes, until Helen seems to've had her fill. She looks skeptically at me, and I just smile at her.

"Not going in for a rub?" Kellan teases.

I shake my head and hold my hand out. He pulls me to my feet, and I'm pleased to find the cat's still watching us from the corner of the porch.

"I don't want to scare her off. I'm playing the long game here."

He squeezes my hand. "Let's play it inside for a second."

"Mm, and why is that?"

He leads me through a formal dining room to the right of the stairs, and into a small half-bath, where he opens a cabinet and produces a bottle of soap.

"Antimicrobial. Aren't you special?" I tease. "Looks like you're a germophobe like me."

"Strays can carry diseases," he says, squirting soap into my palm.

"Helen doesn't."

Kellan gets a laugh out of her name, even though I've told him my intentions before, and I force him to spend the first thirty minutes of our car ride determining plans for Helen.

"If she's there when we get back, I want to take her to the vet tomorrow. I'll get her a purple collar, possibly purple with a leopard print pattern—" Kellan snorts at that—"and we can start litter box training."

Kellan just laughs at me, and after hearing all about my grand plans, he tells me he's allergic to cats.

"What a pussy," I joke, miming claws.

He does a hilariously realistic "meow," and I get a good laugh out of that.

The next twenty minutes are more subdued. We listen to a bunch of random stuff on Kellan's iPhone—none of it overly sentimental, thank God—and when he pulls over on a gravelly shoulder to let a police car fly past, he asks me to turn my back to him. He tucks a few stray strands of hair into my bun and plants a warm kiss on my nape, and after that, he takes my hand.

We talk about robots, and sex robots, and sex toys, and Kellan tells me I should get a job as a spokeswoman for LELO, which I tell him would be a dream come true. Driving through the miles of flat, hot farmland outside Albany makes it a little harder to keep things light, but Kellan starts quizzing me, asking me silly things like pie in the face or whipped cream up the ass.

We stop so I can use the restroom at the first gas station in town, and he has a shot of Snow Queen waiting for me when I climb back into my seat.

As it burns its way into my stomach, I feel an awful ache for "R."

I think the universe is trying to send me a sign, a show of solidarity or something... because we're driving past a bunch of businesses on the main drag when "Sea Ghost" by The Unicorns starts playing. My stomach does a back flip, the way it does when I'm riding a roller coaster with loops.

I can't look at Kellan. I just squeeze his hand and try not to cry, and of course I'm almost sure I will. I torture myself by imagining pretty, curly-haired Olive at school, talking with her friends, and Olive at the DMV getting her license.

Just as the first tear falls, Kellan pulls over at the mall in front of Books-A-Million, cuts the Escalade's ignition, and comes around to open my door.

"Where are we going?"

"You'll see."

And I do see. I see that he's a naughty, naughty boy. Instead of taking me into the store, he ushers me into the back of the Escalade, lets the seats down, and urges me onto my back. He pulls my shoes and leggings off and moves my limbs into a spread-eagle.

He teases my tears away by kissing up and down the inside of my thighs, and then he licks my slit so slowly, I wrap my leg around his shoulders and ram myself against his mouth.

He tenses his tongue so it's firmer than before and drags it through my swollen lips. Then he laps at my clit, so softly and slowly that my ass comes off the floor.

"Oh God!"

"I'm right here," he says in muffled tones. He drags his tongue from my clit down to the clenching, sopping core of me and, with no warning, he thrusts his tongue inside.

I lock my legs around his neck, tightening my thighs as I rub myself against his face.

"Oh God..." I shudder, and he twirls his tongue, stretching me gently.

"Kellan." I tug his hair, surprised to find, "I want you... inside."

He stops licking and smirks up at me. "What's the magic word, Cleo baby?"

"Please!"

He takes his t-shirt off and slides it under my hips. He tugs his jeans down, freeing his enormous cock. It's such a beautiful sight: a reminder of virility and life... I reach out and touch it, and he shuts his eyes.

He pushes two fingers into me, stroking his erection as he stretches me. I hear him rip a condom open—with his teeth—

and open my eyes to watch him roll it over himself. Then he slides his fingers out of me, rubs his plump head through my slickness, shuts his eyes, and pushes deep inside.

He fills me so thoroughly my legs fall open. I lift my hips on instinct but he's so deep, there's nowhere else for him to go. He shifts his hips and settles snugly into me. I let out a cry they probably hear inside the bookstore.

He leans over me and laces his fingers through mine. His hips pump, making me moan at the deliciousness of being filled.

"You like it when I fuck your pussy, don't you, Cleo baby?"

I nod, tightening my inner muscles around him. He grinds against me, burying himself deeper, so I gasp and arch up toward him.

"You like to have your nipples sucked," he says. I feel my nipple tighten, then his lips find it. His thumb comes over my clit, stroking gently, and my pussy pulses as I buck my hips.

"God—you're beautiful," he murmurs.

He suckles my breast, then kisses up my chest, toward my neck. I nuzzle his head and find his mouth with mine. I slide my tongue in, taking charge of this one thing, even as he dominates the rest of me.

I nip at him and lick his lips. He's so hungry, his kisses start to hurt. Our hips move in frenzied sync as he surges deeper. I tighten around him. I suck on his tongue and am rewarded with a sharp jerk of his hips. I feel his moan in my mouth... then inside me as he throbs with his release.

I tighten around him, coming in a violent rush. I'm still panting as he feathers kisses on my cheek. I peek up at him. His face is filled with soft intent; his big hand strokes my hair. And I feel cared for. Very cared for on this sad day.

"I think we might be soul mates," I tell him as we drive toward the cemetery. It's nestled in the middle of a well-off neighborhood, far from our family's house, which is closer to the Flynt River.

His hand is in mine, his thumb stroking my knuckles. It goes still at the comment.

"What makes you think so?" he asks in a voice that's too relaxed.

"Among other things, you just played a song I really like, one I usually play when I'm coming here. But other things too," I add.

"What things?"

"Like you how tucked my hair back up, and how you made me drink the Snow Queen. My friend used to always say to drink before I come here."

"Anything else?" He gives me a strange smile.

"I don't know. I just... feel weird about you. Good weird. Like I know you, even though I know I really don't."

"You know me better than most," he says. His fingers resume stroking mine.

"I have a feeling that's still not very well."

"Can't argue that," he says quietly. And that's the end of such talk.

I leave Olive a tube of my favorite lipstick and a shot glass full of Snow Queen. I ignore the bouquet of sixteen roses lying against her headstone, and I don't look at the card.

Kellan strokes his thumb over the seashells I left here several years ago. I look around the cemetery, searching for some sign, but there's nothing. The sun is shining, the sky is ordinary blue, the grass yields no secrets for me. It's neither dead nor particularly verdant. The trees sway in a breeze that's no different from any other day. The only thing significant about today is Olive's absence.

I don't stay too long before Kellan wraps his arm around me and guides me back to the Escalade.

The whole way home, I talk about an article I read in *TIME* Magazine about how, years from now, no one will die. I keep it technical, and again we talk of robots. When we get back to Kellan's house, Helen is waiting by the door.

FIFTEEN

Cleo

KELLAN CARRIES ME TO THE windowed room. I assume he plans to pull the covers back and peel my clothes off, but instead he tucks me into bed and disappears, returning a few minutes later with a mug in hand. Steam wafts off the top. He sets it on the nightstand and leans against the mattress.

"Sit up a little," he whispers, smiling softly down at me. I've got my head propped in my hand and I'm lying on my side, just looking out the windows and thinking. I drag my tired self up, and he plants a kiss on my forehead.

"Thanks." I wrap an arm around his back, and for a blissful moment, his forehead is against my neck—and I have him. The weight of him. The smell of him. All his wonderful intentions, and my fantasies, which have only just begun to simmer.

Then he leans back, hands me the mug, and winks. "Try that."

"What is it?"

"What does it smell like?" He smiles and tilts his head, watching as I take a tentative sip.

"Ahh, that's—whoa, that's really good. It's hot chocolate with..."

"Brandy and Frangelico."

"What's Frangelico?" I ask before taking another long, warm sip.

"Hazelnut liqueur. Italian."

"God." It pools in my belly, and with the next long sip, I feel a blanket of drowsiness cover me.

"You should get some sleep," he says. He walks to the head of the bed and I feel his hands on my hair—pulling the rubber band off the bottom of my braid, then separating the wavy locks.

I sigh. "That feels amazing."

"Good." He smooths my hair down my back and kisses my temple.

I blink at him. Is this the same guy who disarmed and cajoled me.... what? Mere days ago? I feel like I've known him my entire life.

"What will you do while I sleep?" I ask, folding my hands around the mug. As much as I'd love to go to sleep, I think I want him near me more.

"I've got a dealer meeting, then a thing with Manning."

"Oh, a thing?" I smile, teasing.

"We do it twice a week. I'll bring you to the next one." His mouth presses tight, then curves back up into a pensive half-smile. "It's for the charitable distribution."

"Oh, like for the ailing people?"

He nods.

"I'd love to go to one. I want to help."

"That's what I love about you," he says quietly. Without another word, he turns and goes.

I'm asleep in minutes, dreaming of his arms... his blue eyes, crinkled with his smile. Around the corner somewhere, Olive dances with my lipstick in her hand.

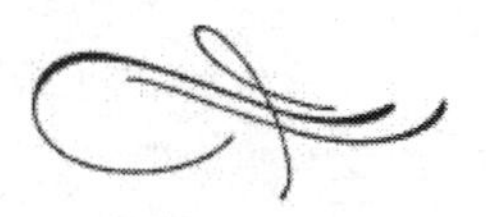

I don't know what time I wake up, roused by the strange and lovely sensation of something vibrating in my pussy. My legs are spread, my knees bent and the soles of my feet touching, drawn up under my bare ass. As the undulations grow stronger, I try to writhe toward the pleasure and I find I can't. I'm bound at the ankles.

I test my arms, both spread, and find they're tied as well.

I open my eyes and look around the room. The canopy is gone, so I can see the moonlight pouring through the wall of windows.

I see the shadows shift outside, and find Kellan outside on the balcony. He's leaning against the thick cement wearing nothing but an open robe, watching as I struggle with desire.

I roll my hips. I clench around the thing inside my cunt and feel my clit throb. *Oh*—I want to moan.

I tug against the binds around my wrists. I gasp as the vibrations change. Now the egg is throbbing, working itself deeper into me. So deep, I have to move my hips. I lift my backside off the bed and watch as Kellan glides across the balcony and pulls the door open.

The tempo of the throbbing increases. I pull against my binds because if I could just roll over, if I could get this egg thing closer to my clit, then maybe I could get off.

Kellan seems to drift onto the bed. In his black robe, he looks like the grim reaper as he leans his blond head down and licks my pussy. I'm reminded of a tiger's tongue—and then I only know the trembling of my fists, the fierce throb deep inside me. I'm already so aroused, it only takes a few soft, hot licks before I'm pulsing. I gasp his name and let my pleasure take me under.

When I open my eyes, I find Kellan sitting near my hips. He's cross-legged, his dark robe pooled in his lap.

I start to laugh at how hard I came, laugh out my embarrassment, when my gaze finds his face.

"... Kellan?"

His eyes are fixed somewhere out ahead of him, on the wall beside the door. He doesn't look down at me as I say his name, nor in the seconds after.

"Hey," I say more gently. "You okay?"

He blinks, and my gut clenches. There's something strange about his eyes. About his whole face.

My hand flinches in its knot. "Kell—can you untie me?"

He blinks.

"Please?"

I watch his Adam's apple bob as he swallows. Anxiety streaks through me. What's going on? I'm tied up—totally defenseless. How much do I trust him? Those are fear's questions.

Then I see his mouth move—just a tremble—and everything falls away except a thick swell of concern.

I try to turn my body toward him, try to reach him with my hand. I can't, of course.

"Kellan? Hey... what's wrong?"

His eyes shift to my body; not my face. He blinks again, doll-like. In a low voice, he says, "You should go."

"What?"

His eyes shut. As he opens them, he moves onto his knees and starts to untie me. I watch the gorgeous ripple of his shoulders, the column of his throat. His face is pained. His gaze is everywhere except my face.

As soon as I can sit up, I grab his arms and tug him toward me. "Kellan. Look at me."

He does, and I can see his eyes are red.

"Did you smoke?" Maybe that's it. I discard that almost as quickly as I think of it. He's not high. He's upset. Something. "What happened?" He rests his gaze on mine, then slowly tugs it away. He's looking over at my painting on the wall: *Thomas*.

I open my mouth to ask if I did something wrong, but I have a gut feeling it's not that.

I reach up and frame his face with my hands, tilting his head down gently. His eyes fall to my chin, to my throat. "Talk to me—please."

I watch his jaw clench. I watch his lips as they move uncertainly around whatever they will say.

I don't know what happened, but I can feel him wrestling with something.

I stroke up and down his back and press my cheek against his warm, hard chest. It rises with a long breath. His chin comes down atop my head, settling there slowly, like he isn't sure, he doesn't want to... but he does. He wraps his arms around me too and we are intertwined.

I can feel his heart beat—fast.

"There was a wreck... My Uncle Pace." He draws away from me, and finally, he gives me his gaze. I can see the pain in it. My throat knots.

"I've gotta go to Atlanta," he says thickly. "It's going to be a big thing... for my family."

Questions rise in me like bubbles, simmering and popping. I push them down and stroke his arm. "What happened? Is he going to be okay?"

"I don't know." He stares at something over my shoulder. He looks anesthetized.

"Are you okay?"

"I don't know." His voice sounds ragged. His skin is so, so pale.

I wrap my arms around him. "Kellan, I'm not going home. For one, I can't. Remember? I'm sort of banned from the Tri Gam house for now. I want to drive up with you. Please let me." I look up at him. "I'll do anything you ask."

His eyes find mine. "You can't. I can't..." He shakes his head. "My family."

"I'll wait in the car. I've got homework I can do. I just want to ride with you—so you don't have to be by yourself. Pretty please?"

He nods, the movement so subtle I almost miss it. "Okay." I stroke his hair. "It's okay," I whisper. "What can I do to help get ready?"

"Just get dressed," he says.

He's off the bed and out the door without another glance at me. I quickly check my phone: 3:38 AM.

I find him in the kitchen twenty minutes later, looking red-eyed, looking pale, and mostly looking lost.

I pack some food for us as he leans on the counter, hovering over his phone. I take his hand, and we walk to the door. When

Truman pitches a dog fit, I look at Kellan and he nods. "Whatever."

He lets go of my hand to lock the door, and after that, he props an arm against the outside wall.

"Are you okay?"

"Worried," he murmurs, tilting his head to the side so he can see me. His mouth is vulnerable and soft. I think of kissing it, but decide he may not want that, so I just take his hand in mine again.

He unlocks the Escalade and opens my door. After I've climbed into the passenger's seat, I look down at him and see his eyes are closed.

"What are you doing?" I whisper.

"Nothing." His eyes open to slits.

I slide down and take the keys from his pocket.

"Let me drive you, okay? You just ride." I open the back door. Truman bounds up. When I climb behind the wheel, I find Kellan is leaned back in his seat.

SIXTEEN

Cleo

HE SITS HIS CHAIR UP after a while and bends over his phone. He's got his shoulders hunched, his forearms drawn in close against his hips. His big hands curve around the phone. He looks ill—as if it was he who had the wreck.

I ask him where I'm going.

"Emory," he murmurs.

I drive for what feels like years, setting my attention on the traffic. When I look over at him, I find his eyes on me. His face is grim.

A few minutes later, he plugs his phone into the iPhone cord and the car fills with... The Beatles. "Helter Skelter."

I sneak a peek at Kellan and find him looking at the road. His lips are drawn into a line. His brows are tense. He doesn't move at all to the music. I don't even see him blink.

I weave in and out of traffic, which is starting to thicken with commuters, northbound toward Atlanta.

"Kell?"

He shifts his eyes to me. They're slightly wide in thought, but as soon as they touch mine, they turn wary. He looks down at his phone. A few seconds later, "Helter Skelter" stops abruptly, leaving only road noise in my ears.

I'm at a loss for what to say. I wish I could help him, but I don't know how. I don't want to pry, though at the same time, I want details. I force myself to swallow.

He shuts his eyes, even as I see his knee vibrate from the bouncing of his foot. He peeks down at his phone again. As I move from the left lane to the middle, a different tune fills the car. The music is redolent and rich, beautiful and simple. The lyrics swell in my throat.

As I try to decipher their meaning, Kellan says, "Can you drive faster?"

He clutches his phone and I glance down at the screen. I expect a text. Instead I see the song title. "Your Protector's Coming Home." I can't see who sings it, but I'm going to Google the lyrics while I wait for him.

Kellan

"Are you sure you don't want me to go in with you?"

I shake my head. My gaze is hung between my knees.

"I'll just park as close as I can, then," she says in her soothing voice. "I can call and tell you where. Or you can call me and I can pick you up at the entrance when you're done?"

I nod.

"Okay. Is here okay to drop you off?" I don't even look out the window, just nod and push my door open. I take a step and—"Fuck." I turn around—the parking lot careens around me—and grab onto the side of my car. It's still here. Because Cleo has the window down and is holding my phone out for me.

"Thanks," I murmur as I snatch it from her hand.

"Kellan—"

I turn and walk quickly toward the front of Emory University Hospital at Midtown, my eyes on the row of doors along the front of the tall, brick building. The morning light offers no warmth. I'm fucking freezing. I shove my hands into my pockets and fix my gaze on the grass under my feet. A few more steps, and I'm walking across a narrow throughway—the drop-off area for patients.

I shoulder through the door and stand in the lobby with my arms folded over my chest.

I watch a clock on the wall until fifteen long minutes have passed. Then I go back outside and start walking, across the throughway, across the small lawn, across a wider street and past the parking deck where Cleo will be, toward a smaller building as I murmur, "Glenn" repeatedly.

I reach the door and push it open with my forearm. As soon as I'm in the lobby, a pretty blonde woman appears at the mouth of a hall.

"Right this way, Mr. Walsh."

I follow her into a dimly lit room where piano music drifts through ceiling speakers. I'm offered a seat in a plush armchair, near an oversized house plant.

I give the woman a hard look. "How long should it be until Marlowe gives the okay to get things moving?"

"Ten or fifteen minutes," the blonde says, in a pleasant tone. "She's expecting you of course."

I'm there for almost five hours. The entire time, I wish I had sent Cleo home. Thinking she could comfort me was stupid. Wishful thinking of the worst kind.

I feel like shit when Pace texts me. 'I'm sorry, Kellan. Sorta stuck in the middle. Want a re-do of that shipment next week?'

I turn my phone off, feeling like the biggest asshole in Atlanta.

Cleo

"Cleo, damn girl. That is *cray.*"

"I know, right? I hate to talk to anyone about his personal issues, but I don't know what to do."

"It sounds like you're doing everything right to me. I mean, for one you're having awesome sex. He ties you up, that is so crazy kinky sexy. It's a once in a life time experience. And you guys are becoming close and stuff. I think it sounds like he likes you, girl. That hot chocolate thing? The vodka? I'm not surprised," Lora says. "You're easy to like, Cle. You're braver than I am, riding up there with him. I'd be too scared. Serious shit stresses me out. Sounds like he's being a little douchemonkey too."

"He's upset."

"An upset douchemonkey," Lora corrects. "But Cleo, what more can you do? There is literally no reason to worry, chica."

"Maybe I should have left his house when he asked."

I hear her chewing brownie. "Maybe," she says around the food. "But I wouldn'tof." She pauses. "Sorry." I hear a soft *glug*, like she's swallowing, then she enunciates her words. "I wouldn't have. You're trying to be nice. How much longer are you going to wait?"

"As long as I have to, I guess."

"I wouldn't sit there at all. Not in downtown Atlanta."

"It's daylight and stuff. I feel completely safe."

"If you don't, you should leave. Lover Boy can catch a cab."

We talk for a few more minutes, during which Lora reiterates the apology she gave me at the start of the conversation, and tells me she'll keep working on Milasy. Apparently Lora talked to her last night and told her she should let me come back to the house. She said Milasy clinked her—*my*—boots together and said "maybe," then smirked.

Another hour crawls by, during which rain starts to stream down from the upper level of the parking deck. I'm engrossed in homework when there's a knock on my window. I jump, and am surprised to see a girl wearing a pale blue rain coat. The first thing I notice is how pretty her face is. The second thing: her eyes. One is blue and one is hazel-green. She taps on my window.

Just as I'm about to roll the window down, my phone rings. *KELLAN*, the screen says. I hold up a finger at her and answer on the second ring.

"Hey, you."

"Cleo?" My stomach jumps at the sound of his voice, which sounds reassuringly casual. "You still around?"

"Of course I am, silly. Are you out?"

"I'm walking to the parking deck."

He definitely sounds better. Less... encumbered. More like regular Kellan. His uncle must be doing okay. I smile. "Cool. I'm on the first floor."

"See ya soon."

I belatedly turn down the Band of Horses song I'm listening to and roll the window down.

The girl leans slightly forward, then slightly back. "Is this Kellan's car?"

"Um... Who's asking?"

"Where is he?" the girl asks.

I feel my Spidey sense prickle. "Who are you?"

She looks around, as if she's worried someone might hear her. "Whitney," she says softly.

"Are you related to him?"

Truman leans up between the front seats, pressing his head against my arm, as if he wants to hear her answer, too.

She shakes her head, catching her lip between her teeth. But she must be with his family's entourage. "If you want to talk to him, he's almost back to the car. Should be here any second," I say.

She nods slowly. "What's your name?"

"I'm Cleo," I say, a little fiercer than I need to.

"Hi, Cleo. And thank you. I'll just... maybe I'll see him down in Chattahoochee soon. Could you do me a favor and please don't let him know you saw me?"

"Um, okay I guess."

Psyyyyyych. I'm telling Kellan I saw this bitch as soon as I get the chance.

She says, "thank you," tucks her chin, and wanders off into the sea of cars. I'm closing my books up, sliding them into my bag, when Kellan raps on my window. I push the door open.

"Get out," he says. He gives me a relaxed smile and closes his hand around my knee. I can tell immediately he's in better spirits, which makes me smile as well.

"Okay, Mr. Bossy."

He smirks. "I thought I was Mr. Perfect."

"What? Huh?"

He winks as I slide out of the car. "I saw a text from Lora. It was on your screen. Don't worry." He catches my forearm in his gentle fingers. "All I saw was her inquire about me, and you told her I was 'Mr. Perfect.'"

I scoff. "That's wasn't you I was talking about. Trust me, I refer to you as Mr. Bossy. Actually, just Bossy. Kind of like Big on *Sex and The City*." I smirk, and Kellan elbows me out of his way, as if he's going to climb into the driver's seat. Then he doubles back, catches my hand, and tugs me around the front of the Escalade. He gets my door for me and slaps my ass as I get in.

"You hungry?" he asks as he backs the car out.

"Starving. You?"

"I could eat something."

After evaluating the next few exits, we decide on Steak & Shake. I get a cheeseburger with light mayo only, and a small strawberry shake. Kellan gets a double cheeseburger but says he doesn't like to eat in the car.

"Why not?" I ask.

"I don't like being watched, I guess."

"No one is watching you."

He lifts his brows. "You are."

I smile and lean my cheek against his shoulder. "I am. I've been worried about you today. You seem a little better."

His blue eyes flick from the road to my face. "What do you mean?"

"A little less worried I guess. Just feeling better." I haven't wanted to broach the subject of his uncle, but I hesitantly do so now. "Is Pace okay? Stable and stuff?"

He nods.

I lean away from his shoulder so I can see his face. "I'm really glad."

He swallows and nods. I wait for more—a flicker of emotion on his face; details of what happened in the wreck—but Kellan just drives, perfectly still and quiet, as if he's alone in the car. I polish off my burger and relax in the silence, looking out the window at the swaying pines.

"What music do you want to hear?" he finally asks.

"Oooh, how about that song from earlier?"

"Which one?"

"The protector coming home."

He looks uncomfortable—irritated?—then says, "I don't know what list that one is on. Other requests?"

"Do you ever listen to Broken Bells?"

He nods. "Good stuff."

"Ooooh, no, I know what I want to hear! It's such a good song. If you don't think it's too cheesy, you'll like it. And you'll see why I like it. Total optimist song. Hmm, let me see if I can find it."

I pick up my phone, which is still plugged into Kellan's iPhone cord, and flip around until I find one of my favorite folksy bands, a Portland group called Blitzen Trapper. I start the song I have in mind—called "The Tree"—and adjust the volume.

It's a very uplifting song. Not blindly so, but with a kind of heaviness I appreciate. I'm disappointed to see Kellan looks more and more unhappy as it plays, until finally I turn it down.

"Not a fan?"

He shrugs. "It's nice."

"But you don't like it."

"I liked it."

"Not like 'Helter Skelter,'" I tease.

The corner of his mouth pulls up in a reluctant smile. "Can't knock The Beatles, Cleo. Not unless you want to hitchhike home."

"You wouldn't dare."

"Oh yes."

I thump his leg through the same worn jeans he had on yesterday, and think for a minute how weird it is to never see him in khakis anymore lately. The sun beams down in sheets of brilliant white as we near Chattahoochee.

"You can talk to me, you know," I tell him as he slows to exit. "About Pace, about whatever. I'm a good listener."

"Mm." His blue eyes meet mine, then return to the windshield. "Thanks," he says belatedly.

Whatever's going on inside his head goes on until we reach the dirt road to his house. Then I feel a shift in his energy. No longer distracted, he seems edgy. Restless.

I'm almost expecting to be hauled up to the bed when we reach his house, but it doesn't happen. Kellan dresses in khakis and a button-up, makes both of us a sandwich, and asks me if I want a ride to campus.

"You have a class?" I ask, leaning against the counter.

"Make-up lab," he says. I wonder when he missed it, but he still seems moody and I don't want to pry.

"Sure... I'll go with you. I've got a two o'clock I shouldn't miss. Stupid palliative counseling." I grab my bag as Kellan shakes his head. "Those dying bastards."

"Exactly." I smile.

He smiles. He takes my hand for the short walk to the front door, and I get that butterflies-in-my-stomach feeling I remember so well from middle school. I steal a glance at him and find him looking at me. One of the butterflies swoops. I laugh. We smile at each other like two idiots as we step onto the porch and Kellan locks the door. He opens my car door for me, gets settled behind the wheel, and cranks the car... and I can't hold it in any longer.

"I like you," I blurt.

Kellan's brows shoot up.

"Too much? Too soon?" I pucker my lips, caught between exuberance and embarrassment.

He surprises me by leaning in to kiss them. "Neither." As he steers toward campus, his eyes move over me. "Hey, Cleo?"

"Hey."

He brakes at a stop sign and looks full-on at me with those gorgeous blue eyes. "Thanks for going with me," he says softly.

"No prob, Bob." I squeeze his shoulder, but it's not enough. I nuzzle the softness of his shirt sleeve with my cheek.

I feel embarrassed as I pull away. Where did these tender feelings come from? I feel so... needy around him. Not just for sex.

This feeling is new to me. I think on it as he circles the psych building, and I decide it's a sensation of comfort—and affection. I'm comfortable around him—more so than I've ever been with any guy, come to think of it—and out of my comfort comes this... gladness. And appreciation. Gratefulness, I guess.

I think, as he edges nearer to the drop-off point and I begin to contemplate being in class—sitting at my desk; the teacher's caramel coffee; the dreadful small group study we always do—that maybe the worst thing about life is being "out and about" and having to just... be you. They say hell is other people. I believe that. But what I didn't know until now is so can heaven be.

Kellan brakes at the mouth of the walkway to the building, and I flash a silly smile at him. "You know, you're a kinky bastard."

"And?" His mouth quirks.

"I love it. That's all." His big hand comes over my head. I lean back. "You're messing up my hair."

He lunges for me with both hands outstretched.

"Eeeep!" I shrink against the window.

He surprises me by leaning over, framing me with his arms—his palms against the window—and leaning in to kiss me... on my nose.

"Kinky?" He wiggles his brows.

I reach out and ruffle his hair. He leans in and... closes his mouth over my boob? "Kellan!" His teeth clamp around my nipple and his warm tongue flattens over it. He nips a little, hard enough so I can feel it through my bra. I feel a shot of heat between my legs.

"People will seeeee!" I push against his blond head and he leans back, grinning.

I look down. "There's a wet spot!"

"More than one I'd bet."

I hmph. "You're evil."

He just lifts his brows and lays his hand between his legs. I feel another burst of warmth between my thighs as his fingers curve around a huge erection.

"God... that's hot. I'm not going to lie."

"Good." His voice is low; a purr.

He reaches for me again. I slap at his hand. "I've gotta go!" I giggle—not a sound my mouth is used to making.

Kellan's eyes are hooded. His smile back is dark. He pushes the base of his palm against his dick one more time, watching my face as I watch him.

"I'm putting you on Smuffins," I say. "It's decided. Secret footage... upload, BAM. Everyone gets to enjoy. Your dick is so big."

He strokes it and smirks. "What happened to 'I've gotta go?'"

"I do! Now leave!" I slide down from the Escalade and pull my shorts up—high. Then I bend down, pushing my ass into the triangle of space created by my open door.

I hear him groan as I straighten up and grin. "What? Just dropped my pencil."

I catch that dark look in his eyes again as I slam the door shut.

When I sit down in my desk in class, my phone's screen lights up with a text.

'Hope that ass is ready. Tonight... Pick u up at 5 after your art class?'

'Can't wait.'

I mean I can't wait to see him again, but I decide to let him think I'm clamoring to have his dick in my ass. If he wants to do it, I'll end up letting him, so might as well have the added satisfaction of seeing him all eager for it.

I sigh and clench my pussy. I'm so wet. I'm pulsing all through class.

Art instruction techniques, my next class, includes a lecture on sculpting. I can't quit picturing my hands over Kellan's naked body. God, he's hot. Soft, soft skin... The hardness underneath.

I can't believe things have taken a turn this way. Kellan the asshole, Kellan the kinky bastard, is someone I like. Like... really *like*.

I'm not sure I can sit through class, I want to see him so badly. I want to touch him. Want to suck his dick. I really do. I want to cup his balls and stroke my finger over his taint and feel his cock pulse in my mouth. I want to hear those hoarse sounds he makes.

I want to swallow. And then after he's satiated, when he's gone all sleepy and soft, I want to curl around him and whisper funny things into his ear.

It's strange to have these feelings. They're so big and... engulfing. But I feel happy to lay myself at his feet. Why? Because he's giving me something no one has in... ever, maybe. It's... this sense of peace. In my counseling classes, my professors go on and on about a happy place. It's like... this little mental cubby you create for yourself, a little bit of fantasy where you can just relax. It's a conceptual thing—something to tell clients in therapy; they think of something traumatic, you're supposed to steer them to a happy place when they're done—but with Kellan, *life* feels like that. Cozy.

I slip out of art class a few minutes early and go wait for him behind the building. Mmm. I'm going to stroke his dick while he drives us back to his house. When we get there... God, it's crazy to say, but I kind of hope he does put it inside me. Back there.

I smirk as I stand on the curb, watching the cars that flow in and out of the U-shaped lot.

I hope his uncle's still doing okay. I wonder if he'll talk about that sometime, and I hope he will. I think of how upset he was, and all I want is to make him feel good. The way he made me feel when we drove down to Albany.

I stand there for what seems like an entire day, feeling soft and raw and wanting and... exposed, in such a weird way. Like everyone who drives and walks by can see my longing for Kellan.

Maybe they can.

Geez, where is he? I check my phone, and find it's ten after five.

That's kind of strange. Maybe he got stuck in traffic. I don't know where he parked, after all.

By 5:20, I haven't seen him, and I can't get an answer on his phone. I'm stuck between annoyed and concerned—until I remember my car is here on campus.

I rush to his house and find him sleeping in the windowed room. His shirt is unbuttoned, and he's curled over with his palm pressed to his throat. I see a half a Xanax—it's got jagged edges, like he bit it—on the bedside table and feel a curl of sympathy. Concern.

Something's bugging him. My thoughts of sex fly out the window. *Later*, I think to myself.

I climb up behind him and wrap my arms around his waist. I press my cheek against the firm plane of his back. In his sleep, Kellan sighs gently.

SEVENTEEN

Kellan

WHEN YOU ADD IT ALL UP, it's never enough. It wasn't enough with any of the others, and it's fuck sure not with Cleo.

I watch her sleep. I stroke my dick and dream of sliding it inside her.

I'm not going to.

She doesn't know it, but our time is up.

Cleo

When I wake up in the canopied bed, I have no idea what time or even what day it is. Wasn't Kellan in here with me? He was... I remember, but he's not now. I'm alone. The window wall in front of me is dark, which makes it easy to see the flashing of my cell phone.

I hope for him until I see the number: (800) 627-7692.

Ugh. I quickly debate answering, and decide I will because I think it may be the Albany power company. One of the last times I went home, I dropped by the office and changed the phone number on my house's account from Grans' to mine. This way if they're late on the bill, I can pay off some of it, so when Grans or Mom gets the money to pay it, it's less than they expected.

I swallow, clearing the sleep from my throat. "Hello?"

"May I speak with Autumn Whatley?"

I slide off the bed, eager to go in search of Kellan. "This is Autumn—otherwise known as Cleo."

"Hi, my name is Cindy and I work with Be The Match."

My heart stops. At least, it feels that way. I urge my lungs to breathe again and lean against the bed. "Um... yeah?" The word cracks.

Fuck fuck fuck...

"I'm calling to request a preliminary evaluation. Our records indicate you might be a match for someone on our roster. Would you be willing to undergo basic testing in the next few days, understanding we may make additional requests pending results?"

I let my breath out. "That's why you called?"

"We're on an expedited timeline, so we're asking that you act on this as soon as possible."

I nod slowly, letting this sink in. It's been years since I heard from them. I never thought I would again. Not unless... I shake my head. "Sure... that's fine. No problem. If I am a match, I would... go through this again?" Would it be to the same person? My pulse races.

"If you are a match, you would be called upon again. I see here in your records that you've done this before." There's a brief pause, in which I try to breathe. Then she says, "Are there any other questions, Cleo? We're so glad that you're a part of Be The Match."

I inhale deeply. Exhale. Let my two-ton question tumble forth. "Can you tell me anything about Robert?"

"Robert?" she echoes.

"You don't know the name of my last match?" My tone is sharper than I intended, but I find I don't care.

I hear a brief pause, followed by loud typing. "What information are you requesting, Miss Whatley? I'm limited by—there are rules in place to—"

"How is he?" I whisper.

I hear a delicate clearing of her throat. "It looks like... mmhmm. I can see your chart is marked with blue—which means you've been flagged based on your file from last time."

My stomach hollows out. "Are you saying that I'm being called again as a match for R.—Robert, I mean? Could I be matched with him again?"

Silence fills the line. "What's the last report you received on Robert D., Miss Whatley?"

I clamp my teeth down on my tongue. "I haven't gotten one. Not since a while back. That's why I'm asking. It's been really bugging me, the silence from him."

A heavy sigh comes through my phone. My throat tightens. My stomach heaves, and I just *know*. I can feel the bad news coming like a train. "Cleo. I'm so sorry to inform you, your last match is listed as deceased."

"Deceased?" The word makes no sense. Less than no sense.

"I'm sorry that you didn't know. We don't want to discourage—"

Her voice sounds like it's underwater. I hang up the phone.

Eight forty-three PM, my phone says.

I sit down on the rug. I wait for tears, but they don't come. My face feels like a slab of wood. My heart thumps painfully.

I check Kellan's bedroom first, peeling the blanket away from the wall so I can examine the hidden door. As I dash downstairs, I wonder why I've never asked what's in there. I wonder why I didn't tell him about the girl I saw today.

But I already know the answer: because I didn't want to rock the boat. Despite the strong connection I feel to him—a connection that seems to grow stronger every minute—the boat with Kellan feels unsteady. Probably because he runs so hot and cold. My mom has always been that way: happy when she's on a two-day off shift from the factory; quiet and withdrawn on work days. I grew up trying to make her happy, trying to help keep our struggling household steady. It's why I got good grades. To avoid rocking the boat. I do the same thing now as I press my lips together to hold in a sob, despite the awful ripping sensation in my chest. I want to fall onto the floor and wail.

Instead, when I get downstairs, I stalk through the living room and kitchen, then the formal dining room, the half-bath, and the library, which I've only ever peeked at through a half-cracked door till now.

I can't find Kellan. I can't sit down. I swallow repeatedly as I get Helen more diced chicken, re-fill Truman's water bowl, and rearrange the pillows on the couch.

I pace the living room, peek out the back door, the house's front door, and then dash back upstairs. I give the rumpled bed a glance—I imagine Kellan and me, intertwined tightly enough to extinguish the awful ache behind my breastbone—before I change into a black cotton sundress, pull a gray sweater on over it, and slide my feet into black flip-flops. Then I step out onto the balcony.

The pine trees are a dark mass. I aim my gaze above them, looking frantically for Leo.

I drank a shot of Snow Queen for you 8/7 also. Maybe in an alternate reality, we were drinking them together.

Just as hot tears start to come, something pale near the ground attracts my gaze: a smoke cloud. I know without question that it's Kellan.

Why did he tell me he never smokes? What's the point in lying, I wonder as I trek down to the river. I want him to feel like he can tell the truth with me. So I can tell the truth with him. Raw pain slices my heart as I wonder if I'm being foolish, letting myself feel this way.

No choice.

I have no damn choice, I'm finding.

It feels dangerous. So dangerous, especially tonight.

Oh God...

I cross the lawn with long strides, my flip-flops sinking into warm, damp grass. *Please be okay*, I find myself chanting.

With this loss sitting heavy in me, the night air seems to vibrate. I can't see in the growing darkness. Unease is a small hand knocking on my chest.

I find Kellan leaning against one of the thicker pines, his bare feet planted in the muddy riverbank. The fingers of his right hand cradle a blunt. Truman sits beside him on his haunches, stiff-backed, as if he's trying to make his wayward owner more respectable.

I stand a few feet from them, waiting for Kellan to look over at me. When he doesn't, I press my trembling lips together and wait until I can't wait anymore. I murmur, "Hey."

His gaze glides to mine, and I feel cold in my soft dress and flip flops. The sweater I've got on doesn't shield me from the river breeze. The air slaps at me, seeping into my chest.

I fold my arms under my breasts and try to read his face. It's so... still. At the moment I need connection more than ever, Kellan gives me no clues to his mood. When he shifts his eyes back to the water, I look him over frantically.

The guy before me doesn't look a thing like the Kellan Walsh I met in the student center. He's wearing that same charcoal t-shirt from last night and what I think are black jeans. His soft blond hair is sticking up, like he's been running his hands through it. His handsome face, so kind at times, so open in quiet moments, has its doors closed.

I feel a sharp ache in my chest when I think of his arm around me at Olive's grave. The way he looked holding the mug of spiked hot chocolate... was that yesterday? God, I feel as if we're in some kind of time warp. Again, the sensation that I've known him for a long time. That I know him well. And now, the bitter truth that I need him.

I need something...

The sound of my exhale is louder than the rushing river, but he doesn't look at me. He doesn't want to look at me. I may not be a Kellan expert yet, but I can feel his withdrawal—his isolation.

It makes me desperate. I want to grab onto his shoulders and just... bite him. I could bite him hard enough to taste his blood. I want to throw him down and ride his cock. I want to sob into his chest.

I fold my wants away and level him with an impassive look. "I thought you didn't smoke," I say softly.

"I don't."

I wait a moment for his gaze to brush my face. I need the softness of his gaze, the touch of his interest. But his attention is mired in the river.

"Well you *do*," I say. I chew my lip.

"Sometimes..."

I want to grab his thick forearm and pull him close in that proprietary manner he uses with me. But the thought of it burns—because I don't feel like I can. Kellan calls the shots with us, and that's a shame, because he's stormy. Changeable. Sometimes I feel like I'm getting close, and then he flits away. Like now.

"When you go to sleep that night, be sure you've had some alcohol or even Xanax. If that's not your scene, fall asleep... I don't know. Reading. Or doing something else."

Kellan leans his head against the tree's trunk and slowly brings the blunt up to his lips. I watch the cherry flare as his chest expands; he holds the smoke in his lungs. A second later, his shoulders slacken, and a thick cloud pours out his mouth.

He takes another drag, then turns quickly to me.

He doesn't cup my mouth or take my shoulders in his hands. He wraps an arm around me, pressing my breasts against the hardness of his chest—and then his lips close over mine.

For a second I forget what I'm supposed to do. His mouth is closed so tightly over mine, I inhale instinctively, to ward off the sensation of being suffocated.

Stinging smoke fills my lungs, and Kellan's mouth lifts off mine. I gulp fresh, damp air. I brace myself for the removal of his arms, but instead, he holds me tight. He wraps an arm under my backside, so my feet come off the ground. He's holding me to his chest.

He leans his back against the tree. I feel a tremor flicker through him. Then he buries his face in the crook of my neck.

I tell myself it's just his high making him needy, but his grip on me is firm. His breath beneath my ear is warm and real. I can feel his heart pound.

He sets me down a moment later, and he doesn't look down at me.

Just when disappointment spreads through me, he shifts his night-gray eyes to mine. His lips curve up: a little smile; sad little smile.

"Let's go inside... so I can hold you for a while."

"That sounds good." I blink back tears.

Kellan takes my hand and shuts his eyes before we start to walk. I wonder why he seems so sad—if he can sense my loss. I worry that his uncle took a turn, or that the girl called him, but that doesn't seem likely—because his hand is threaded through mine. His fingers stroke mine, easing something taut inside me.

"Your hand is warm," I whisper as a lightning bug drifts over us. Beyond the blinking yellow light, I find the crouching lion, Leo.

"Your hand feels good." His voice is low and rough.

I run my eyes over Kellan's messy hair, his tired face... and this time he looks back at me. One corner of his mouth tucks up.

"You're good to me," he murmurs, heavy-lidded.

"You're good," I say back. *Oh, please be good...*

I want to throw my arms around his neck and cry. He seems to sense my building grief. His big hand squeezes mine at the moment my heart races, spurred by pain. It's perfection. I feel weak and warm. Strangely satiated, despite the darkness that hangs over us. I don't notice Kellan's stopped walking until I feel the tug of his hand. I look back and find his mouth stretched open.

I know what I'll see before I turn back toward the house. It's in the ether: hurt. Kellan's sweetness hid it from me, but it was always on its way.

"Why are you sad? I'm afraid I know the answer, and that brings me to my instructions."

It's her—the girl from the garage. Standing next to her on Kellan's back porch is his healthy-looking Uncle Pace.

I see the color drain from Kellan's cheeks even in the dark. In the faint moonlight, his skin looks alabaster.

His voice is static. "Go inside, Cleo."

My throat closes. I push against the pressure. "Why?"

"Trust me. I'll explain this later. I just need a few minutes."

"What?" I look from our joined hands to the duo on the porch. They look solemn. Maybe even angry. "You'll explain what later? Who's that girl?"

"She's no one." He shakes his head.

"No she isn't. She knocked on the car window. In Atlanta." I drop his hand as my pulse quickens. "Who is she? Just tell me now."

His eyes widen, and I know. I don't know exactly what this is, but I know enough to see that he's deceived me. His uncle isn't hurt. Why did we go to Atlanta in the middle of the night? To meet this girl? Who is she to him?

"Why are you lying to me?"

"Cleo—please." His tone sounds desperate. "You have to go inside. I need to talk to Pace alone." He actually pushes on my shoulder as the two of them descend the stairs, their eyes on Kellan.

The girl rushes forward to greet him, and I dart past his uncle, feeling sick. My heart is beating so hard, I can't even make it upstairs once I get inside. I stand at his sink, filled with those stupid shake-stained glasses, holding my stomach and looking at the dark window in front of it.

Through the glass panes, I hear low voices.

I wait to get my breath again. For the pressure on my chest to lessen. When I realize it's not going to, I run up the stairs and down the long hall to the windowed room, where I start frantically gathering my things. I hug my canvases to my chest, strap my bags on my shoulders, and step back into the hall.

If he wants to tell me the truth, he can call me. I'm not sticking around to hear that Kellan fucked me over. That I'm the only one who's fallen—into my emotions. I'm not sticking around to find out that girl is his ex or something. I can't handle that tonight. I can't.

That's when I notice his bedroom door open. I'm not sure what drives me to go in at this moment: curiosity that's been gnawing for too long and needs to be appeased, or some kind of masochistic urge to tempt his anger and up the ante of this shitty night. Either way, I step inside.

The room is just the same as last time I was in it. He's got a big, mahogany bed; a dresser; a recliner; and a trunk. The walls are pale green, bare except two charcoal sailboat sketches, both framed in dark wood. And then there's the wall to my right, covered mostly by his giant woven rug. I've never really looked at it before, except to note its dark colors, but now I spend a moment staring at it—this barrier between Kellan's bedroom and his secret door. Woven in gray, navy, and deep green, is a bear. It's on its hind legs. Behind it, at the top right corner of the rug, is a half-moon.

I walk slowly over to it and run my hands over the fabric. It's soft, more like a blanket than a rug. I take the fabric in between my fingers and realize it *is* a blanket.

I lift the left side of it almost reverently, and stare at the door. It's clearly meant to be hidden, because the bottom of it isn't flush with the floor. It can't be seen unless you know to move the blanket. What's it here for? To hide Kellan's stash: whatever amount of marijuana he keeps here at his house? That used to be my default guess, but suddenly I need to know for sure.

I try the doorknob, but it doesn't turn. I notice there's a keyhole to the right of it. A little, old-fashioned keyhole.

Of course.

I know I'll never find the key. I let the side of the blanket fall back down and step over to his bed. I lower my face to the duvet and inhale deeply.

I let out a long sigh. Tears brim in my eyes: for R. or Kellan? *Why*, I want to roar. *Why do things always go so wrong?* I can hear the R. voice in my head—a voice that sounds like Kellan, saying, "Get back to your life. Be glad you've got your thong, or your heart, or whatever."

I want to scream because it doesn't happen that way. I can get back to my life, but who's to say whether I've got anything at all? There are no guarantees. There is no fate. No kind or sensible undercurrent dragging us to where we're meant to be. Through the wall of windows, I hear voices, and I know—I can feel it in my bones—that something bad is going down.

Tears seep from my eyes. I blink, and there it is: a small gold key. It's lying on the duvet right in front of me.

My blood begins to hum. My heart quickens. I think I must be meant to see inside his hidden room. Why else would it be so easy? I dash my tears away and look up at the ceiling.

Thank you, R.

I scoop up the key and walk back to the blanket. My hand shakes as I pull it aside. I step fully behind it this time. It melds to my bare shoulders and a shiver skitters through me.

The key fits flawlessly into the lock, just like I knew it would. I turn the knob and push gently against the cool wood. The door swings open like a portal in a fairy tale. I inhale, step inside, and—*what?*

I look around the room: all five square feet of it. I look up and down, and left and right, almost expecting to see a lone toilet. It reminds me of a half-bath... except it's not. The wall to my right—no more than three feet wide—is a built-in bookshelf. Empty. The wall to my left—equally tiny—is dominated by cabinets and a sink, with a short swatch of black granite countertop.

I turn toward the cabinets and look them over, ceiling to floor. Clearly, they are the purpose of this small space.

My fingers flex. Which door do I open first? Should I open them at all?

I lean over the counter and close my hand around the knob on the right-side cabinet. I pull it open slowly, telling myself I'll find nothing but a bunch of marijuana.

I squeeze my eyes shut, and when I open them, my stomach hollows out.

Instead of seeds or marijuana baggies, I see bottles. Dozens and dozens of prescription bottles: orange, blue, green; tall, short. And scattered amongst them, glass vials; tinctures; gauze; gloves; tourniquets; syringes; filters. I grab a bottle. Oxycodone. Another one: Hydromorphone. I open the cabinet on my left and I feel sick as I behold more of the same.

This place is a miniature pharmacy, stocked with everything Kellan needs to numb himself to everything—including me.

I slip quietly out the back door while they talk on the front lawn. Kellan's back is to his big, brick house, his hands up in the air. Everyone looks sad-faced.

It's not hard to evade them. To stay behind the trees, inside the pool of shifting shadows on the lawn. I open my car's door and dump my things into the backseat. No one knows I'm here until I slam it shut.

As I sink into the driver's seat, I hear footfall. Voices lift in unison, tossed up toward the moon—and Leo. I don't give a fuck. I can't right now. I peel away so fast, I hit my head on the ceiling.

When I look in my rear view, I see Kellan's shadow—shoulders slumped, head down.

Guilty.

I don't let the first sob loose until I turn onto the highway.

PART III

"Unless you love someone, nothing else makes any sense."

-e.e. cummings

ONE

Kellan

November 13, 2010

WHEN LY AND I WERE little kids and Barrett was in junior high, our family lived in this cottage overlooking the cliffs near Malibu. My Mom would set her easel up on the porch, and Ly and I would ride our tricycles on the rough grass beside the house. We would dare each other to walk closer to the cliffs' edge, and Ly would always make up some excuse not to. I was always sticking one foot off. It drove Mom crazy. I guess it probably scared her.

There was so much wind there—all the time. I loved that wind. I loved the salty smell of it. I thought if I ever fell, I might just spread my arms and fly. I used to dream of it, at night when we would leave our windows open for the warm, wet air: flying over the water like an albatross.

I don't know why I remember that right now. Tonight. I guess because I'm standing at the front of Daniel Harmon's father's yacht, looking out over the choppy waters off the coast of Santa Monica.

Tonight was our last game of the season, so Daniel had almost the whole team here to celebrate. He's our captain, and he's generous as shit. I don't think he asked any of the guys to help with food or liquor, not to mention gas for this big bitch.

I know most guys couldn't shovel over the money. Lyon gave Dan a handful of Benjis yesterday, once Dan had gotten confirmation from his family's captain.

The two of them are pretty friendly: Ly and Dan. I heard them talking a couple weeks ago in the locker room, and I'm pretty sure it was about Ly becoming team captain in a few more years. Dan is a lineman, and Ly is a tight end—second string right now—and neither of them is consumed with playing, like I am.

Not that I would be team captain anyway. I'm not cut out for that shit. Lyon has always been. And that's a good thing, that one of us likes being the life of the party, because I'd rather take a knee to the nuts than spend a bunch of time with other people—most days, anyway.

Nights like tonight, it's cool. The bar is bleeding freely, there's a bunch of not-quite-strippers in the cinema room, and I heard Murray's making Mississippi hunch punch in the master bathroom.

I get a buzz on my phone and pull it out and yep, my boy Murray—our superstar wide receiver—is asking me do I know how to sink a honeydew melon. I laugh smoke into the humid air and turn around from my spot at the bow of the yacht. I flick my blunt over the rail and take the port side back toward the stern, to avoid where all the girls are, on the starboard deck. I'm kind of sick of Gillian and her mind games. If she wants me, she can come and find me inside.

I take my time going down the stairs and through the living area. It's big—way bigger than the one on Robert's yacht—and flashy as shit, with gold fixtures, a swank ass chandelier, and a bunch of leather furniture, all centered around the biggest flatscreen I've ever seen.

As I start down the rear hallway, I bump into McQueen and his girl, Fiona, with her hand in Mc's jeans. I give him a grin and he slaps my shoulder.

I pass a couple of staterooms before I get to a wide-ass door that's propped open with a fifth of tequila.

There's a party in the bedroom: a bunch of the D and a harem of girls who could either be strippers or their girlfriends. Since I'm not sure which, I don't say much either way.

I tip my chin at them, then bang on the bathroom door and yell, "It's Kellan, dumbass. Open up!"

Murray slaps the door open. I catch it right before it hits me in the face, then give his cheek a hard swipe. He steps back and shakes his head.

"Man, this shit looked easy when my older brother did it."

"Us little bros gotta stick together," I say. He laughs at that, because Murray is six-foot-five and three hundred pounds of lethal muscle—and some long, fast legs—so he doesn't seem like anybody's little anything. He told me once his brother, an accountant, is five-foot-eight with a fro and wire-rimmed glasses.

I follow him deeper into the bathroom, which has a flowery, funeral parlor smell, and Murray points to the melon floating in a giant Tupperware box in the shower. "I tried to cut that shit with this knife—" he passes me a fillet knife from one of the sinks—"but that motherfucker will not budge."

I laugh my way out of a smirk. "You know where the kitchen is, man?"

Murray nods.

"Go ask someone in there for a chopping block and a Kuhn Rikon melon knife, or something like that."

"Kuhn Rikon, you say?"

I nod. "Whoever's in there, they should know."

I think about telling him what to look for if the kitchen is unmanned, but no way it will be. Not with this many people on board.

Murray takes a fuck while to come back, so after I use the fillet knife to finish slicing the three watermelons he busted open on the counter's edge, I pour another bottle of Everclear into the box and stand at the door, listening to the boom of music from the bedroom.

I look around the bathroom.... at the giant whirlpool. Then I start the water, lock the door, pull my shoes and clothes off. Nothing like a good soak. I slide into the water with a bottle of Cristal.

I lean my head against one of the shell-shaped pillows on the tub's side and let my breath out. I'm pretty fucking tired from this morning's game, but very fucking happy. We went 7-3 this season, which is damn good for a team with me as quarterback.

I curl my right hand into a fist. Then I take a long pull of Cristal.

Now all I have to worry about is Gill. And Thanksgiving. My father will probably work the break away, and Barrett won't come home—he's down in Georgia, training with the Rangers—but even being in that fucking house makes it hard for me to breathe.

Dad's expectations stalk me through every echoing corridor, and my mom is still all over. The place is like a fucking shrine to her. Her art, her murals. Even a tapestry she wove. I guess I never noticed how much I hated it in high school. How I tried not to go downstairs for much, or even be home at all. Who can blame me? I don't think Dad has spent more than six or seven hours in a row at home since Mom's death. Sometimes I think he's trying to follow her, the way he always works and never sleeps. I know, I know—he re-wires tiny little baby hearts. Does things no one else knows how to do. But still...

I rub my forehead. My dad is a fucking prick.

The times we do see him, he makes Lyon get all stiff and quiet. Ly has got this low, serious voice he uses with Robert, like to show him he's a real man or some shit. It doesn't matter how much he trips over himself, trying to impress our father. Robert never bats an eye. He never has any praise to spare. At the end of every day we're there, Ly goes to his room and shuts the door. He doesn't even rant about what a dick Robert is—not anymore. He doesn't say a word to me about our bastard Dad. He hasn't in at least a year.

My strategy for being home is different. I get drunk, try to leave a bag of powder lying around, and see how rattled I can get him: dear old Dad—the esteemed pediatric cardiothoracic surgeon Dr. Robert Drake. He tells me what a prick I am, and I crack the knuckles on my right hand. I don't care what Robert thinks. Not anymore. My name's on TV every week. I've got my own damn fan page.

Maybe we should take Gillian and Whitney to Veil or someplace for TG. Whitney doesn't like Gill, but so the fuck what? I'll keep Gill in bed, stuffed full of my dick, and Ly and Whit can stroll the happy mountains holding hands like the old folks they are.

"Open up motherfucker!"

Murray knocks so hard the door vibrates. He yanks it open and steps in. I stand up and laugh as Murray whirls away from me.

"What the fuck are you doing, son? Damn!"

He tosses a towel over his shoulder, and I catch it before it hits the water.

"Put yo clothes on."

I towel off and reach for my boxers. "You get the knife?"

"I got somethin'." I laugh at Murray's Mississippi drawl.

We spend the next half hour finishing the punch, and then I hear Gill coming through the bedroom, making a big fuss as she tries to locate me.

I shut her up as fast as I can, bending her over the side of a chair in one of the lesser staterooms and fingering her tight hole while my other hand delves into her warm pussy. I wait until she's dripping wet and begging for it. Then I slide my dick inside her pussy for the moisture, draw out slowly, and take her asshole inch by blissful inch.

When we're finished, she's quiet for once.

I grin.

She huffs. "I don't know why you like my ass so much."

I shrug. "It's symbiotic, baby. That ass likes me just as much as I like it. Don't try to lie."

I step into the en suite and turn on the bath, then throw Gillian over my shoulder and lower her into the warm water.

"What is it with you and baths tonight?"

I shrug. "Cleanliness is Godliness or some shit. That's what Murray says."

Her lip curls. "Stupid Southerner."

"Portlander."

Gill makes a face at me.

My phone buzzes, and I step out without even checking who it is.

Murray. 'Get your ass in here. I got something for your bro Ly.'

I tell Gillian I'll be back in a few and elbow my way through the crowded hallway. I find Murray spooning hunch punch into some crystal we probably shouldn't be using. He hands me a glittering glass that's filled with red liquid and chunks of melon.

He grins. "Give this to Ly. I want to see him drunk off real hunch punch, the way we do it down in Jackson."

"You want to what?" The door cracks open, and my blond brother steps in. He looks from me to Murray and grins. "You making fun of me, Murray? That hurts." He puts a hand over his heart. "You think I can't handle some of your fruity punch?"

Lyon drains the glass in two long gulps and chews a chunk of melon. He smacks his lips together, then smiles his dimpled smile. A few minutes later, Whit pokes her head in.

"What up?"

Murray sends them off with two more glasses of the good stuff.

Lyon holds his glass up to me as the door shuts, asking me in twinspeak what the fuck is in it. I wink.

An hour later, when we're dicking around on the promenade deck and Lyon slips on some sea foam, I remember that moment. The way I winked and let my brother eat the fruit.

As Ly sails across the damp deck, Whitney grabs for him and so do I, because we both know Lyon is shit-faced. The two of us collide and send him sailing toward the guardrail, and at that moment, a big wave rocks the boat toward the starboard side. Lyon hits the railing with his middle, and flips over it like a gymnast on the bars.

My heart *stops.*

But he's got the rail. Holy fuck, he's got the rail! His hands are wrapped around the braided wire. His loafered foot is propped against the deck.

I lunge for him, grab his forearms. "Fuck!"

Whitney's shrieking draws a crowd, and seconds later, Lyon is hauled onto the deck by six strong hands—two of them my own.

He gives Whit a long, weird look before his eyes roll back into his head. He crumples to the slick deck like a blow-up doll deflating. When I drop down by him and shove my fingers to his neck, I find his pulse pounding too fast.

A second later, blood starts pouring from his nose.

My heart pounds too as Whitney screams again.

TWO

Cleo

September 18, 2014

HOW LONG AM I GOING TO SIT HERE? Like a lunatic. I've got my phone in my hand, and my car parked on top of the library parking deck. I've made myself a beacon for Kellan—and yet he hasn't sought me out. Not even a text to explain the lie about his uncle and the pretty girl with different colored eyes.

So I have nothing to assuage the awful feeling in my stomach. The one that tells me I messed up, wearing my heart outside myself. Letting him brush up against it. Letting him grab hold of it.

How many lies did he tell me?

He's an addict. Probably. I don't want him to be, but I'm not an idiot. Who has that many pill bottles and injection-type supplies for any other reason?

As I've sat here these last few hours, I've wondered if that's why his uncle and the girl were there: to stage an intervention or something. Was that what happened the other night, when Pace wouldn't deliver the plants? Manning was involved—as he would be if Kellan had a drug problem. And Kellan said something about how his dad was putting pressure on Pace. Wouldn't any father try to intervene if they knew their child had a problem?

Kellan.

Addict.

I saw that cabinet with my own two eyes, and still... I just can't picture it. He always seems so... capable.

And moody.

Okay, he is definitely moody.

Moody like an addict?

How the hell would I know?

He lied about the pot. I know that much for sure. Telling me he doesn't smoke, as if I'd even care, but then he smokes. He clearly does.

Maybe he lies instinctively. He would do it to protect himself. The longer I've known him, the more I've sensed something like that: an outer shell around the softer Kellan.

Maybe his entire life is a lie. Some people are like that. They can't commit to being just one person.

I think about how he joined SGA for his brother. How he doesn't even like it. And on top of that—the lie of posing as the type of person you aren't—he has an even more flamboyant double-life because he's an SGA president who deals.

So Kellan is a liar.

I don't care...

All I feel right now is desperate. Foolish. Why did I storm off like that? It was stupid to run off without talking to him. Especially after I saw his secret cabinet. Tears shimmer in my eyes.

R.

I couldn't help him! *Why not, God?*

I can't believe he's dead.

The more I think about my Kellan, swallowing a bunch of painkillers so he doesn't have to face whatever haunts him, the more restless—the more helpless—I feel. I want to go to his house, but I'm too scared. What if he hasn't texted me because he doesn't want me to come back?

He likes the affection—yeah. The holding hands, the non-stop touching. So he needs the contact to assuage some beast. But maybe I freaked him out when I told him I liked him. If he's an addict, he may think he needs to shut me out. Spare me some pain or some such martyr shit.

I feel the weight of his warm hand on my back as I stood by Olive's grave. I can see him, pale and stricken, in the passenger's seat, playing me that song.

Hey, wait... *The hospital!*

My hand drifts to my throat. Of *course.* I think back to the way he was on the drive to Emory—so listless. At one point, he was begging me to hurry. And before that, up in the windowed room at his house... I don't think we had sex. Wasn't that the time I woke up with that egg inside my pussy? And Kellan seemed so pale. So haunted. Was he going through withdrawal or something?

It would make sense. The way he seemed when we first met: a tiger, always on the prowl, demanding things. And how he seemed to grow more... quiet as the days passed. I wonder if the girl could be his AA partner. Or maybe he was going to—what's it called?—a Methadone clinic? And the girl knew the clinic hours, so she tried to intercept him there.

I get out of the car and start to pace. Back and forth, along the row where I'm parked. Moonlight glints off hoods and bumpers. A warm, magnolia-scented breeze tickles my skin. When headlights spill out of the lower level, signaling the arrival of another car, I step behind this big, green Ford F-250 and pray that it's an Escalade.

That's what I'm doing when my phone rings: hiding from the glow of unfamiliar headlights. I look for his name on the screen, but it's not Kellan. Not the 1-800 hundred number of Be The Match. This number is a local one that I don't know. *Of course.*

"Hello?" I say with trepidation.

"Cleo?"

My stomach somersaults. "Manning?"

"It's ole Manning."

I lean against the green truck's hood. "God, I'm glad you called. I was going to talk to you about something. Something with Kellan. I'm kind of worried about something with him."

"Why you worried?" he drawls.

"I... I'm sort of hesitant to say. But Manning, do you know what's going on right now? I was over at his house and his uncle and this girl showed up. He told me—"

"Cleo?" he says. "Why don't ya hold your horses for a second?"

"Why?"

"I need to tell you something. Kellan told me to..."

Fear scoops through me. "Okay, what?"

"He wanted you to know that you can get... that *thing* from Matt or me, at the prices y'all had talked about. You know that thing?"

"From *Matt or you*?" My heart is pounding, but my brain is running a step behind my body. I rub my head and frown. Is Kellan going—"

Manning cuts in on me, saying, "And he wanted me to tell you that I've got a check. I can bring it to you... whenever. Tomorrow. It's for twenty K. You know what I'm talking about?"

My blood pumps so hard I feel faint.

"Honey? Are ya there?"

I slide down the truck's grill, crouching on the cement deck. "So... ? He's..." My head throbs, referring pain behind my eyes, where tears are building.

"He's going back to California, with his uncle and that girl you saw. I'm real sorry, Cleo. That's his high school girlfriend. He was hoping to get back with her for the last couple of months. Since she got pregnant back in May."

THREE

Kellan

I BRING THE PHONE BACK to my ear and re-play Robert's message. It's so strange to hear his voice. So ridiculous to hear him making threats. What more could he take from me? There is nothing he can take. There is nothing I can give. I have no choices left.

I was going to go—to get out of here before my trouble pins me down. Go back to California, where I can settle everything the way I want—out on the water. But I couldn't bring myself to say goodbye to Cleo. Every day, I tell myself *just one more day*. Then Whitney and Pace showed up, with their pleas and their tears and their threats, and Cleo did it for me. She left *me*.

I tried to catch her as she got into her car, but...

But.

After she left, I sent Whit and Pace away. I stood by the door with Truman, slammed by the thought of never seeing Cleo again. God, it hurt. It hurt so much it made me shake. But... no choices.

Robert says he'll be here tomorrow morning. If I book a flight out of Atlanta, he'll know. He told me he's been monitoring my cards. It's how he knows what I have—or rather haven't—been doing. I can't book a plane ticket with cash, and I don't know if I could make the long drive home.

This is how terrible choices are made. It all comes down to lack of options. I should know that, shouldn't I? I should be an old pro at this. And yet... it doesn't get easier. It never gets easier. In fact, if time is any indicator, decisions like mine only get harder.

Because of Cleo... this is so much harder than it might have been.

I lean against the railing of the balcony and try to think. If I hadn't met her. If I only ever knew 'Sloth.' If I hadn't fucked her tight cunt. If I hadn't hidden my face in her soft hair. If I hadn't watched her leave that tube of lipstick on her sister's headstone. If I hadn't felt the warmth of her chest against my back, the firm squeeze of her arms around me.

"You seem sad. I like hugging you... I'm a hugger."

If I didn't know that, maybe this would seem more like the right choice. It's the only choice—but I don't crave it like I used to. Back when my need for control of my own fate outweighed fear or regret.

Now it's... different. Like I'm opening my mouth and swallowing water, when what I really need is air.

I walk downstairs. I get a postcard and my damaged fountain pen and press the card against my thigh. I close my eyes. Inhale. I open them and steady my hand.

September 18, 2014

Dear Sloth,

Long time, no write. I hope you're well. I'm sorry for the radio silence. The last thing I intended was to trouble you.

I moved to Okinawa, Japan in May as part of an exchange program. The first day I was there, I met a girl. She's

Canadian, and... yes, she calls me Lord.

I'm home for a week or so to take care of some family business, and then I'm flying back over. I wish I had the time to meet you. Maybe next time I'm stateside?

I still think of you often.

All the best, always.

"R."

I reach for the drawer where I keep my Post-It notes, then draw my hand back. I need to walk this to the mailbox myself; Manning might not send it, even if I leave it with a note. I get a stamp from one of the kitchen drawers, hold the front door open for Truman, and take my time trekking down my long, dirt drive.

I note the curve of the moon. I used to have a thing about the moon, when I was very young. I would ask Ly if it could see us. He would tell me "no" and I would argue for the moon's sentience. When Mom died, we decided one night that that's where she was. Up there, dancing in the glow.

I stop at the mailbox and look up and down the road in front of me. It should look different. *More.* The metal of the mailbox should feel colder on my hand. Truman flounces through the field in front of the house, chasing mice—like always.

My footsteps are the same as I turn back. My left knee still aches where I busted it up that first game of my junior year in high school. I feel the rise and fall of my chest. It's nothing special. I'm endowed with nothing but the weight of my own ego. Pretty soon, that will be gone.

I go inside and I stop looking for some fucking sign. I drift around the rooms upstairs, trying to smell Cleo in the air. I go into my little room and take a second patch out of the cabinet. Put it in the old spot, on the back of my shoulder. Right beside the one I put on when I woke up by Cleo earlier.

Then I step out onto the balcony and smoke a bowl of Silent Stalker. I try to calm myself. To focus on the dark treeline; the stars. Their brightness hurts.

I go downstairs and get the Snow Queen out and chug. A few more pulls—until I'm warmer and the hard edges are fuzzed.

Truman sniffs around my legs like he can smell it on me—dark intent. I laugh. Somewhere in me, there is an inferno—but I can't feel it anymore.

I tip my head back and drain the vodka bottle.

I blink a few times, slow and bleary, and there is Truman, sitting on the kitchen floor. So goddamned loyal.

I drape my hand over his head and step past him, into the pantry. "Here boy..." My voice sounds low, the rasped words barely there.

I shift my mind away from that and focus my clumsy hands and the peanut butter: twist the top off... set it on the floor. Truman's long ears perk in question.

"All yours." I blow my breath out. Wait—*no.* "Hell..." I scoop the peanut butter container up and get a spoon and dole some into his bowl. "The whole thing would make you sick," I whisper.

I blink a few more times and lean my head back. There now. I can see straight.

"Ummh..." I lick my numb lips. "Eat that," I murmur, setting Tru's bowl down.

I get another bowl—a big glass mixing bowl—and hold it under the faucet for what feels like several weeks. The water sloshes as I set the bowl down. "Now gotta... wash these dishes."

Truman doesn't eat his peanut butter. He leans against my legs while I load the dishwasher. I can feel the Fentanyl seeping through my skin, into my veins... Lifting me above the floor.

You'd think that it would help me forget, but I want her no less; *more.* I turn off the sink. Look at my hands. I know them. They are mine. I use them to pull my phone out of my pocket.

I can't call her.

"No you *can't,*" I whisper.

I set my phone down on the counter. Through the haze of Fent, I feel a sharp ache in my chest.

I walk into the living room and look at the stairs. I'm not going back up. Don't know if I could... walk up.

I strip off my shirt. Take my time pulling it over my head and sliding my arms out. It's weird to not be able to feel my skin. It feels good. I rub my hair. My face. Something to remember me by. I laugh.

I drift over to the TV. The DVDs... I never finished. It's okay. I feel like it's okay now.

Truman bounds over, moving faster than my dizzy eyes can follow. Then he's by me, warm and heavy. My throat is tight and sore as I rub his ears, then lean down and pull his body against mine.

"Thank you," I whisper hoarsely.

I kiss his head, and then again. I scoop my keys up and walk slowly down the hall.

I can't believe I'm really here now. Game over.

All I have left is my secret. And a flame of pride, because I never let her near it.

Cleo

I get into my car, and I start driving. I don't think of what I'll do or say. I don't think of anything but him.

I need to see him. Need to hear it from his mouth.

I'm speeding down a rural highway, en route to his house, when I have to dim my brights for an SUV.

It looks like Kellan's Escalade.

FOUR

Kellan

THE NEED FOR CLEO is an agony. I'm so numb, the only place I really feel it is my chest. It's like a fire in there. The deadened parts of me can sense the heat. My throat and face. My throat aches. My shoulders and my arms and everything feels... bad. My fingers rub the leather of the wheel. I have this urge to shift my legs, but I remember that I'm driving.

I fix my eyes on the dark road and I think desperately of where I'd find her. I want to see her one last time. I know I can't... but it's so fucking hard. Denying myself this.

As I drive, I think of what she'd say if she knew. What she might do.

I don't know. I *do* know.

She would hold me. It would feel good.

Today was bad.

I can't keep doing this.

My eyes blur.

Even through the haze drifting around me, I know what I have to do. Before he comes. Robert.

The car is bumping over the shoulder before I realize that my hands must have slipped. I hit the brakes. The Escalade fish-tails in the grass. Jolts to a stop.

I lean over the steering wheel.

Cleo. I can only whisper. I'm so tired.

I lift my head and try to will my brain to think. I can't pass out here. Need... to keep driving. But—no wrecks. I don't want a wreck that hurts someone.

I sift through the haze. Cleo. Not at the sorority house. My lips curve a little as I picture her sitting in her car atop the parking deck. She would wait for me there. It would be a fantasy.

The fire is back.

It wakes me up.

I look between the treetops and the moon.

Something... please.

I get out of the car. It's like my body... thinking on its own. I stumble in the grass and tip my head back.

There. The sky.

I don't want it. I would tell her I don't want to. I want her. I can't. I know. I have to hurry. Now I'm... just too tired.

I get into the car. I dream while I drive. Warm hands and her hugging arms. My mom's got cookies. Lyon with the football. Cleo on the bed.

She says, "You can talk to me, you know."

I start to whisper. I press a hand to my forehead... so I can think.

The bridge is near here... right? The rail is bent. The drop is steep.

I tell her all the things. The whole story. Flat green pastures gleam under the moon. I pass a cow beside his fence.

My speeding heart begins to slow, as if it knows the score. My mind clears like the sky as clouds shift, revealing a bright moon. Pale light winks over my hood.

Some ways ahead, the road bends left. I press the pedal: fifty-five... then sixty. I take the curve at seventy.

Cleo... Cleo.

The road runs straight. I can see the bright lines of the bridge's metal rails.

Cleo

It's definitely him. And I'm a stalker freak, because I'm tailing him. I wasn't going to. It started with an innocent U-turn. Why go to his house if he's not there? But then I saw his car pull over on the roadside. So I dimmed my lights and stopped a hundred yards or so behind him. When he got back in and turned onto another road, a more rural road, I just... kept following.

What do I want?

No idea.

Through the woods, I follow him. Along a winding road pinned in by fields. Beside the fence line, cows cluster. Moonlight stripes the long fields, casts crooked shadows through an orchard of pecan trees.

Pine-needles shimmer with moon dust. Kellan's inky car glints as he swerves a little to the right.

I picture her head between his thighs and press the brakes a little, halfway hoping that he'll see me in his rear-view mirror.

My eyes trace his silhouette. I can't see hers...

I picture her pink lips around his dick. The way his legs flex, right foot heavy on the pedal. The Escalade surges forward as if my narrative is true. I see a creek off to my left, glinting in between the trees. The road squiggles, and Kellan's Escalade dips into the left lane for half a heartbeat. I touch the brakes again, a mime of what I wish he'd do, but Kellan flies around the bend.

I punch the pedal. "Slow down, Kell..."

Next time I sight him, he is riding with the car's right side on the shoulder.

My head feels hot. My pulse picks up. I reach for the phone in my lap, to call who? The road curves sharply right and Kellan runs again into the left lane.

Fuck.

I top out at 75 mph and press the brakes out of sheer fear. But Kellan doesn't.

Kellan disappears around another wooded bend.

I come around it... see a bridge. The sheen of moonlight on its metal rails. The glow is blotted—for one second. *The rails are blotted by his car.* I hear the Escalade punch through the guardrail with an awful screech. I watch in horror as it tumbles toward the water.

FIVE

Cleo

September 19, 2014

I RUN DOWN THE SHOULDER, I slip, I tumble down the hill that skirts the murky swampland. I scramble up just feet from the dark water, which splays about as wide as a skating rink.

The Escalade is near the middle of the reed-laced marsh, nose-down in the water... pointed a little left, toward me. It's still moving, sinking ever so slowly into the muck. The waterline spills over the windshield. As I gape at it, the right side of the Escalade sinks down a few feet.

"Oh Jesus, God, fuck fuck!"

I jerk my shoes off, yank my pants off, and splash into the chilly sludge. I'm screaming, waving my arms above my head. I flop forward, belly-first, and try to freestyle, but the weeds are too thick. My arched feet fumble for the muddy bottom. I kick hard, but my feet touch nothing, so I'm swimming, gasping.

I hear a low glug-glug and see the car tilt even further downward on the front end. Fear cuts like a knife. Adrenaline makes my arms and legs move faster. My thigh bumps something hard. I shriek—fuck just a log. I'm almost there. Oh fuck, Kellan—what if he went through the windshield?

Treading water, I try to look around. The night bears down around me, dark and textured. I kick my feet and surge forward.

"Buckle up for safety, Cleo..."

Please be in there!

Oh God, I can barely see the driver's side door. The door behind it... I can open that. My throat constricts as I swim closer to the car: so large and dark. Over the stink of the water lapping at my nose, I smell burned rubber, maybe even smoke.

I shudder as I glide within reaching distance of the SUV. *Focus, don't be scared!* I kick a few times, hard, and keep on kicking as I try the back door handle with my wet, trembling hand. The car gurgles, bubbles rising around me.

"*Fuck!*" I pull the handle up and, while I grasp at the door with my left hand, sinking slightly I press my foot against the SUV's body. The Escalade lurches. I shriek. Fuck, it doesn't open!

I moan and pull the handle again, and the door opens fractionally. Water rushes into the Escalade. The door pulls shut again.

"FUCK!"

I pull the fucking handle one more time, and when the door cracks open, causing water to cascade into the car, I pull harder.

There is no doubt—no doubt in my mind that I will get to Kellan—so I pull the door open with all my might and dive into the gap between the door and door frame.

My forehead smacks something. I let out a sob and then I'm in the car! Water! It's up to my boobs, but in the front seat...

"Kellan," I sob. Fuck, the front is underwater. Is his face submerged? I feel the car tilt and realize water's pouring in through the cracked door. I yank the door shut. My breaths are shrieks, my limbs are clumsy as I splash between the front seats.

His face is not submerged, his head lolls leftward and there's blood…

"Wake up!" I grab his face before I realize *don't do that; the neck*, and "KELLAN.... please!" The car jolts leftward with my movements, water rising.

The seatbelt! Got to get the seatbelt! Don't look at his face! I reach into the tarry water and I feel and... *there*! My fingers press against it... tiny, cool, metallic. The belt comes undone. I'm panting as I work it off of him.

I try. It's hard. He's big. He isn't moving.

What if—

No.

I slap his cheek. His eyes open, blinking blood... His head is bleeding.

"Wake up! Damnit, fuckshit, wake the fuck up... Come on!" I grab his right arm, tugging violently. I jerk him toward the back of the car and realize when he doesn't move at all that he will have to move himself.

"Come on, you have to swim!" I shriek.

There's water to our necks now; Kellan's head is tilted back. "Kellan, please, please!" I sob.

He blinks twice, slow and dazed. His eyes roll... his eyes find mine.

"Come on, baby... Come on, we have to swim!"

I grab his arm, clawing his bicep as I tug him toward the back seat. "MOVE YOUR LEGS!"

He groans... His body twists. I hear a splash, and then he slams against me. We drift in a tangle to the back seat.

"Cleo..." He grabs me, looking confused. "What—"

"I'm opening the door now, kick against the seat and push yourself out of the car." The Escalade lurches leftward again. I hear water rushing.

"Right now, Kell! I'm opening the door now, come on! Get in front of me..." I push his broad back, ushering him in front of me, so I can push him from the cark. I reach around him to shove the door open. I can't push because he's in my way—but Kellan pushes. He pushes the door, and I push him, and together we get the thing open.

Water pours in so quickly I almost don't catch a last breath—but I do. I shove Kellan hard, and he disappears into the murk.

The second I swim out behind him is the longest of my life. When I break the surface I find him treading water, moaning with his head tipped back.

I nudge his shoulder. He fumbles and chokes. I push his chin up. "Swim!" Rich boy—can swim. "Toward the shore!" I hit him and he gasps.

"My shoulder..." He sounds hurt. Dark water laps around his head. His face is twisted. I grab a breath of air and sink and shove his lower back with both hands. Resurface.

"Fuck..." I give his back a shove, but I can't move him. He's too fucking heavy.

Fuck... That slimy—*duh, the ground!* That's the *ground* under my feet! "Kellan..."

I just barely get my arm around his neck before his eyes roll back into his head. My feet are mired in mud. I try to swim, to kick against the slimy ground. I cry as I struggle... then it's shallow. I can stand completely but I can't lift his limp body. I struggle to the shore with him, pulling his torso out onto the mud. He's bleeding... from his nose? His mouth?

I look around for help, but I don't have my phone. I start to cry. I touch his head, his bloody face.

"Oh God! What do I do?" I wrap my hand around his mouth, feeling for breath. There it is, a little bit...

I'm running toward my car when I hear sirens.

SIX

Cleo

"YES, I *REALIZE* NO VISITORS right now, but I just want an update." I smack my fist against the front of the looming counter in the Emory University Hospital ER and bite my tongue so I don't cuss this fucking woman out.

My hair is damp from sticking my head in the bathroom sink, the crevices of my fingernails are stained with Kellan's blood, I'm wearing scrubs and paper shoes and my head aches—and no one will tell me shit.

"I've called a doctor, and we're waiting on her, ma'am," bitchy receptionist explains. Bitchily.

I glare at the yellow smiley faces on her hot pink scrubs and whirl around to sit back down.

The ambulance ride was awful. I mean... I'm glad one came, of course. Apparently a fisherman heard the wreck and called 9-1-1, which is a good thing, but the ride itself? Traumatic.

The EMTs pulled two Fentanyl patches off Kellan's bare shoulder, which explained his blue lips, but after they got an oxygen mask on his busted face, they couldn't figure out why he was bleeding so much from his nose and mouth. They wrapped his left arm against his bruised chest and I held his right hand until someone stole it from me to stick an IV into him.

They kept talking about overdoses and something called "narcan," which I've since learned can help people who overdose on opiates. I said I was his girlfriend and they started asking me the basic questions like his age. I got his hand again, the fingers curled and cold, the wide, cool palm swathed in tape, an IV line curling around our joined hands, and as I stroked his fingers, I realized I know almost nothing about Kellan. I don't even know his real, true, legal last name.

I explained what I do know to the EMTs and told them that I thought he might use a doctor at Emory, and someone, somehow, sometime confirmed that we were headed here.

The ride was long. My eyes swept up and down him as I folded his big hand between my warmer palms. I could see the awful, awful bruising on the left side of his ribcage as they tucked his arm against it... strapped it down and then they covered up his pretty abs, his perfect arms and shoulders.

The blanket was gray, and underneath the plastic mask his face was gray. The female ENT kept pulling the mask off and wiping blood off his face with a white cloth. His nose and mouth just kept bleeding. The few times his eyes open, he looked hurt and scared. His eyes darted around until his gaze found me, and I would touch his hair and rub his shoulder as his body shook.

There was a neck brace on him, I noticed. When did that happen? His body was hidden under blankets but I watched his feet, stripped of their Keen sandals. His toes would curl as the EMTs shown light into his eyes and pulled the blanket back to stick a needle in... his thigh? He jerked. Their voices moved too loud and fast. The crackle of the radio... my mouth kissing his fingertips.

The male EMT prodded the inside of his left elbow and nodded at the female. "Lots of marks," he murmured, covering the arm again.

"Track marks?" I wailed.

The female EMT screwed up her face. The dude gave me a *no shit* look, and I started to cry. I never really stopped, just tried to keep it quiet as they labored over him, and Kellan's eyes opened and shut and I said sweet things to him.

By the time we reached the ER drop off, Kellan's face was snow white. The female EMTs told me to "stay put," he was in shock and needed blood. I had to let go of his poor, cold hand

and stop myself from running with them as they spirited his cot into the ER.

Someone brought me dry pants and these weird, papery shoes, and I cried some more, and talked to a cop who was nice and handed me a towel from his trunk.

Someone from the hospital—some sort of advocate woman—popped up and took her own notes as I answered questions for the accident report. And then the advocate told me she'd find out about Kellan, and she led me to a plastic chair.

That was coming up on three hours ago now. Physically, I might be the healthiest person in this room, but I can't breathe. I can't think straight. I feel like I'm being psychologically tortured.

Just when I think I'm going to end up wringing smiley-face receptionist's neck, a short-haired brunette in a white coat comes through the double doors. Her eyes dart around the room as she says, "Cleo Whatley?"

I rise and she blinks at me. She seems distracted, almost skittish. She tries to smile, stops half-way, and pushes a strand of short hair out of her brown eyes.

"Cleo." She waves me toward the mouth of the ER hallway. "Has anybody spoken with you yet?"

I shake my head. She ushers me down a short, white hall, into a small, white room with a brown table and three chairs. She sits on the side with only one chair and nods at the two in front of her, which makes me cry because if Kellan was with me there would be a chair for each of us…

The doctor plunks a tablet on the table and glances down into her lap, then up into my face.

"Hi there." Her face is stuck somewhere between kind and gravely serious. Which makes my stomach flip.

"Can you tell me how my boyfriend is?" I manage hoarsely.

My voice breaks on the word "boyfriend," as I remember that he's not. He's got a pregnant girlfriend. How fucked up is it that I still want him?

A box of Kleenex slides across the table toward me and I realize I'm crying again. I take two tissues and dab my cheeks.

"Is he okay?"

Her mouth flattens. Her face looks like *no.* "What do you know about Kellan's health, Cleo?"

I look worriedly into her wide brown eyes. To see where she is leading me, so I can shelter myself. But I can't tell. "I don't know," I whisper. "I... Does… He has a drug problem?"

She blinks, completely poker-faced. I watch her chest rise on an inhalation. "What makes you think that?"

My throat tightens—and I can tell I'm right. He *does* have a drug problem.

"I found a bunch of pills at his house... recently." I rub my finger over a ragged cuticle. "Also, in the ambulance. They said... I saw pain patches. On his back." My stomach twists so hard I have to swallow to be sure I don't throw up on the table. I look at her. "Is he okay? You're scaring me."

"Cleo..." The doctor leans toward me. Her eyes widen. "What do you know about Kellan's mental health?"

My throat tightens as if she's slung a noose around it. "Nothing." I bring a hand up to my chest. "Is there something I should know?" My voice wavers.

The doctor sits back in her chair. She looks almost relieved. "In June, he was admitted for an overdose attempt," she says, stroking her hair out of her eyes.

I gape. "He *was*?"

She nods. "He spent two nights in the psychiatric unit here, but he was discharged. I'm going to tell you about that," she says slowly, "but first you need to know he's being transferred to another hospital."

"He *is*? *Why*?"

"We're moving him to New York. It will be a plane transfer, and it will happen soon. There is an option for you to go along, if you want that."

I swallow. I blink, and tears fall down my cheeks again. "What's wrong with him? Why can't he stay here?"

She leans toward me, reaching across the table. Time slows as I watch her red lips move.

"Cleo—I'm sorry to have to share this news with you, but... Kellan is in the most advanced stage of leukemia."

SEVEN

Cleo

HAVE YOU EVER HAD YOUR whole life rearranged by something someone told you? It feels like surgery in a second. Like someone reaching in and moving things around so fast you're different before you even realize what they've done. Maybe they've removed a part, or maybe something's added. Maybe everything's the same, but shifted slightly leftward.

Surgery on the heart changes the way the blood is pumped to every other part.

It makes sense. I can't deny that much. It makes so much sense now that I know the truth.

Why he would pay me so much money to stay at his house—and for just three weeks. He mentioned teaching me more of his business, so I could maybe have a larger role, because he was "leaving."

From the second we first met, he was always holding my hand. Between the dirty talk and his pretty, perfect cock, he was always reaching for me. Needing to be near me, in me. Wrapping himself around me while he thought I was asleep.

How many sick people are getting marijuana at no cost because a bunch of college students pay for it?

Robin Hood.

I'm not even surprised he set up something like that.

And yet, I'm *so* surprised. I don't believe it—any of it. I can't fly to New York with him. When the doctor tells me what she tells me, I take a taxi back to Chattahoochee, to my car. I see the swamp, the puncture in the rail, the road muddied from where they hauled his car out, and it's meaningless to me. Like a scene from a film I watched while half asleep.

I drive straight to Kellan's house and find it unlocked. I go to the windowed room and go to sleep, and wake up in a ray of thick gold sunlight. Afternoon, it seems.

I reach the river as the sun sets, pinkening the sky over the pine trees. The black cat joins me. When I start to feel ill and I know I need to move, she follows me back to my car and twines her sleek body around my legs.

"And if we catch her and we have to put her down instead?" he asks.

"I don't know. I wish you wouldn't say that."

"It makes you sad to think about putting down a feral cat you've never even met?"

"I think pain should be reserved for something painful..."

I scoop Helen up and take her with me. I don't know where I'm going until I realize I'm in Lora's parking lot.

'I'm here. Coming up,' I text her as I look up at the third story.

I carry Helen up the stairs and knock and ring the bell. Lora's not home, but there's a spare key underneath the frog statue sitting by her mat. I take Helen straight to the kitchen, where I serve her water and a bowl of ham.

Then I pull a wicker chair out from the breakfast table and sit down.

Tired. I feel so—

Don't.

I pull my phone out of the pocket of the jeans I got from the overnight bag in my car, and turn the screen face down so I can't see the texts or missed calls.

Denial burns inside me, prickly, unsettling. I stand up and start to organize the counter. *Toothpicks, Lora? Three boxes of toothpicks?* I move two dirty plates, a vase of crumpled roses, and a sheer pink blouse, then spray the grimy counter down with a bleach-based cleaner.

The air in Lora's house is cinnamon-vanilla. It feels heavy, like the pressure of the water on a scuba dive, which I did once and hated.

I'm wiping the counter slowly, letting the bleach fill up my head, when my hand bumps into a stack of mail partially obscured by the toaster oven. The thing on top is from the power company. It's marked urgent.

"Lora, Lora…" I tear the bill open and mount it on the refrigerator with a magnet. I wipe the counter two more times and then thumb through the rest of Lora's mail. This girl makes me look organized. Probably because she has so much money. What's a late fee? I thumb through her other bills but don't see any that look urgent enough to justify my opening them. I'm setting the envelopes in a seashell-shaped pewter bowl beside her paper towel holder when a small, white square slips from the bottom of the stack. It flutters to my feet. I bend to scoop it up and...it's addressed to me?

I blink down at my dorm room address, and something starts to buzz inside my head.

I set the post card down. The post card with the campus scene. I turn around to face the throughway between living room and kitchen, leaning my back against the countertop. I touch my throat, which stings, as if I swallowed a chicken bone.

I turn back around, compelled, and as my hands grab for the post card—

Thwack!

I whirl toward the breakfast table. My phone has fallen to the floor. Vibrating. I step over to it. Face-down, so I can't see who's calling…

Dr. Marlowe's voice echoes. *"A relapse after three years… hasn't sought treatment… team waiting for him in New York…"*

I scoop the phone up, see the number, answer. "It's Cleo."

Desperate. Desperate. Desperately, I clutch the phone. I sink into a wicker chair. My mind cranks like an airplane: spinning slowly, faster faster…

Cindy. Be The Match. The international bone marrow registry.

My fingers tremble on my iPhone as she lets me know my blood arrived and has been tested. I am a match. She starts to tell me things I know from last time. I stand up. Circle the kitchen. I step over to the counter, frame the post card with my fingers.

I blink and stroke the glossy cover of my post card as she talks.

My brain…I must be tired. I feel wound up. Like things are connected when they aren't connected. Like I'm about to cry, or barf. I look over my shoulder. Where is Lora? Is it chapter night? What day is it?

I'm going to pass out.

Just turn the fucking post card over.

I feel strong resistance to the idea. Cindy's voice is driving me insane. She prattles on. My heart swells like a balloon behind my ribs. It takes up all the space. With a flick of my wrist, I turn the post card over. Read the time stamp: September 19, 2014. So…today.

I blink several times, and scan the text. It blurs as pressure builds behind my eyes.

"Cindy?"

She takes my interruption as a sign that she should wind things down. "So to proceed, we'll need a commitment. Verbal and—"

"Cindy?" A tear falls onto the card.

"Miss Whatley?"

I swallow, but my voice is still a rasp. "I have a question."

"Sure," she says indulgently.

My heart hammers. I swallow, but it doesn't help me breathe. Again, the chicken bone. "Can you tell me…when did R. die? What day?"

My chest is on fire. My head on fire. I lean against the table as my hand mangles the card.

"If you really want to know, I guess it couldn't hurt. Just one moment, Autumn, okay?" I can hear her fingers clicking on a keyboard.

"Cleo."

"Cleo? Okay, Cleo. I'll be back in just a moment."

My chest rises… My head spins.

"Sloth," he says. "Is that a nickname?"

"Chicken pizza? Are you kidding me?"

"What can I say?" He smiles. "Chicken? Pizza? It works. You agree?"

"I think we might be soul mates."

"What makes you think so?"

"You just played a song I really like, one I usually play when I'm coming here. But other things too," I add.

"What things?"

"Like how … you made me drink the Snow Queen. My friend used to always say to drink before I come here."

"Anything else?"

"I just…feel weird about you. Good weird. Like I know you, even though I know I really don't."

I hear a click. "Okay, Cleo." Cindy's voice is clear and crisp.

I close my eyes. I mouth the date. I mouth the words, because I know before she tells me. All this time I didn't know and I know now. I know.

"It was in September. September 18, 2011. That's the date, according to the charts."

I hold my breath as Lora's kitchen slowly tilts.

"I'm sorry, Cleo."

I jump up. *I'm* sorry. So fucking sorry. I look down at the crumpled post-card. Then I dash into the living room, where I hung my purse on the front door knob.

Cindy's voice pipes up: solemn, concerned. "I hope this doesn't make you feel…"

Her voice is static. I pull the check out of an inside pocket, fingers shaking.

No surprise. It's no surprise now. Now I know.

It's R.'s handwriting. Kellan's check.

R. and Kellan. Kellan, R.

Lyon. Robert. Robert Lyon?

Lyon is the real R., and Kellan was his stand-in. Writing after his brother was dead to thank me for giving bone marrow to Lyon.

I murmur a goodbye to Cindy. Then I dash to Lora's sink and vomit.

EIGHT

Cleo

September 20, 2014

I WALK THE HALLWAYS OF Memorial Sloan Kettering Cancer Center for hours, blank and brainless, carting all my bags. And I decide he didn't know. Kellan never sought me out at Chattahoochee College. He didn't know about our strange connection until I said "sloth" on the balcony that day.

This is the universe's setup. God's joke. It's so insane that, as I wash my hands outside his room on the bone marrow transplant floor, I question whether he'll really be in there.

This seems like a dream. One big, bad dream.

I keep seeing him on that pebble path behind Taylor Hall, walking with me in between the shrubs. The way his hair glowed in the sun that day. The way he smirked. I remember he was dressed up for a trustee meeting. I remember his wide shoulders, his muscular thighs…

"Why would you want to write and sell a book?"

"Maybe I was thinking of writing my memoir."

Kellan doesn't need a memoir. Nothing's wrong with him. I want to believe it so badly, I could almost convince myself. So I resent the nurse beside me, telling me about the unit's rules. Arethea, her name is, and she's pretty. She's got brown hair, brown eyes, and this soft voice, with a lovely accent I can't place.

So it's strange that I kind of want to throttle her. Doesn't she know all this is bullshit? I would never let Kellan have cancer. I wouldn't let him die. He's perfect Kellan. He's mine.

You know Manning texted me? That girl is not his fucking girlfriend. She was Lyon's girlfriend. Now she's in medical school at Emory, which explains why she popped up in the parking deck that day.

After she and Kellan's Uncle Pace showed up at Kellan's house—an intervention, where they begged him to seek treatment—Manning said Kellan was worried I'd find out. He wanted me to go away. He wanted to protect me. So he made up the bit about the pregnant girlfriend.

"Cleo? Your hands seem clean to me," Arethea says kindly. I look over my shoulder at her and find her face is tranquil. Kind and patient. Maybe even sympathetic. Something in me recoils.

"You want to go inside?" she asks, passing a paper towel. "I think he's sleeping."

It's horrible, the stepping through the door. With every cell I have, I protest. My stomach twists into a knot. My forehead sweats. My heart hammers so hard I barely notice my surroundings: teeny tiny hallway, widening into a larger room with blue walls.

He's not in here. He's not! I would believe that if I could. If I didn't want to see him so badly. But I do. I want it more intensely than I fear it.

I take soft steps down the tiny hall. I pause at the mouth of the room so I can listen to the beeping, breathe the strange, cool air. It smells like plastic, and some sort of cleaner.

"Why is Daddy in that bed? It has a rail like Olive's baby bed."

"He's sleeping, honey."

"Will he sleep forever?"

"I don't know."

Another long, slow step, and here I am. I blink at the wall of windows in front of me, then look left, at the TV mounted on the wall, beside an ocean print. Under the TV, there is a door. Maybe the bathroom. I suck a desperate breath back. I can feel gravity pulling harder on my body as I swing my gaze to the right.

Kellan's bed is empty. My throat tightens as I see the sheets tucked neatly, as if it's not been used.

He isn't here? I knew it! That's what my heart screams.

But I see an IV pole. With IV bags hanging from the top. I see a rolling table with a newspaper, a black thermos. Both things are right beside a recliner. The plastic-textured chair is angled toward the room's right wall. I can see the foot-rest part is out—and something wrapped in white on it.

I walk closer. Hard to breathe.

I don't know what I think I'll find, but as I come to stand in front of the recliner, I'm shocked and not surprised at all to find that the white bundle is Kellan's legs… My eyes race over him, and down and up again, taking it in. Kellan lying on his right side, bundled up in sheets. They sag down his left bicep, so I can see how bruised his shoulder is.

I blink a few times. Blurry. There are pillows propped behind his back and left side, cushioning him in this position, so all his weight is on the right side of his body. I can't see under the sheet, but his ribs are hurt just like his shoulder. I remember from the ambulance.

I rub my palm against my lips and blink, and his swollen shoulder blurs, as if the bruising is nothing but a watercolor. I could reach my fingers out and smudge it all away…

And still, it's easier to look there than at his face. Solemn face, closed eyes… His cheekbone and the skin around his left eye are bruised deep purple, almost black.

Anger bubbles up in me, even as I step around the chair and sink into a crouch beside the right arm. My face is level with his now. When he opens his eyes, he'll see me.

Breathe, Cleo.

The IV lines droop from the pole and trail beside me, disappearing into the sheets pulled up to Kellan's throat. I check him over from this angle. He's so still… His face so pale. Why is there a patch of gauze tapped at the base of his throat.

Fuck. I suck another breath in.

I watch his eyelids, watch his mouth. I can see his pulse throb over his brow.

Wake up, baby. Look at me…

My fingers flex. I need to touch him. Stroke his messy hair. He hasn't shaved. He looks swarthy, like a wounded pirate. Does that mean he's too hurt to get up? I blink quickly, and a tear drops down my cheek.

His mouth tautens. It's just a flicker of expression, there then gone, but it's enough to make my hand reach out and grip the chair's arm.

I lean closer to the chair and mouth his name. I don't mean to speak, but my throat is so tight, the sound comes out.

His eyes stay closed, but he shifts his shoulders, the tiny movement just enough to make the white sheet droop. I can see his chest now. Pretty throat, his collarbone, and…shit. The sheet falls lower still, and I can see his chest. The IV lines join up at a small, white tube that's punched into his chest, over his pec.

Fuck!

The IV tubes are threaded through his fingers, and his palm is pressed above his pec, as if he's holding himself together.

I tip my forehead toward the chair and sit there with my head bowed, hot tears dripping out my eyes.

I'm in a knot. I want to scream.

My palm trembles over his arm. I lean a little closer, till our faces are so close I feel his breath on my cheek.

Kellan

Cleo is here. I might be dreaming, but... I think I'm not.

I smell her tea perfume. I hear her voice. I try to.

I have a fever. I can't think because...the IV. If she's here, then she can see me. I float up from where I've been and I can hear the beeps of the pulse ox machine.

Pain flashes all through me. My face, my shoulder, ribs... My hips and back.

I feel Cleo's hand. I twitch, and I can feel the IV tubing tug. My chest is sore from where they put it in...

Regret and shame.

She *knows*.

I can feel her fingers in my hair. Her fingers... being nice. Making me tired. But if I fall asleep, I'll miss her. I peek and—fuck. Cleo—right here.

I can see her see me, see her face go soft and sad. She murmurs, "Sweetheart." Gentle fingers dance across my brow. "You're sleepy, huh? You've got the good drugs going. That's good." She strokes my temple. My chest goes heavy with pleasure.

"I wanted to tell you, Kell... I figured out about the letters. And R. I wanted to say...I understand. It's crazy... like, a big surprise. But I'm not upset with you or anything." Her cool fingers, sifting through my hair. "I talked to Manning just a little. It's amazing, what you guys are doing. You're amazing. I came to visit, but—" Her fingers dance like fog over my skin. I feel her face come up against mine, feel the warm rub of her cheek, and I'm surprised that she would…get so close. "I'm really here because...I think I'd like to stay with you. Umm...for a while."

I must be dreaming.

I think Cleo's crying, even as her soft hands stroke my hair. "I'm so sorry that I didn't know. About all this, and R. I'm sorry I'm crying. I'll be fine. I'm just..."

I shut my eyes. I try not to feel her hands, so I won't feel them when she goes.

I float a little. All the Dilaudid. I try to stay, though. To stay near her.

But I keep my eyes closed. I don't want to see...her look at me.

"Can you look at me, baby? I just want to see your eyes." Her voice cracks. "If I can help you over to the bed... I want to lie down with you. You seem sort of uncomfortable in the chair."

My eyes drift open—I see her, close but blurry—then they sink back shut...because Dilaudid. I want her. I want to lie with her. To have her touch me, but...I'm sweaty. So messed up. The last few days...have gotten bad. With pain.

She strokes my cheek, and my throat aches with want.

"I can help you get to the bed, or even call a nurse if you want. If you don't want to snuggle, I'll just leave you alone. Your shoulder, the left one... is it hurting? You keep moving it."

I do?

She kisses my hair. I feel a sob build in my throat. She's going to go soon. Godddamn.

I sit up, gritting my teeth against the pain of my cracked ribs. I forget to hold the IV lines. They pull from where they're threaded into my chest.

I curl over my lap, holding my throbbing head. My heart pounds hard.

"You...need to go." My eyes roll toward her, the words slurring.

I reach back for the IV pole, and miss it.

"Hey…hang on." She touches me. I shrink away. "Just let me put the leg-rest down, okay?"

I grit my teeth as she does, and my legs lower. My hips… I brace against the chair's arms, grunting as I stand. I shuffle as quickly as I can to the bed, but the rail is up. I have to move a lot to lay down. Ahh. It *hurts*…

I feel the cold linen under my fever-warm body and curl up, shivering. I put my hand up to my face. I tell myself that anyone would go. She came at least…

And then I feel the mattress indent. My eyes lift slowly open. Cleo's right in front of me. She melds herself around me, so my face is near her neck.

"It's okay," she murmurs, one arm wrapping lightly around my back. Her hand curves around the back of my head. "Just go to sleep. I'll be here when you wake up."

NINE

Cleo

IF YOU'VE NEVER BEEN HERE, you can't understand. How bad it hurts to watch someone you care for suffer so much.

That first day, we don't ever really talk. I hold Kellan, my arms encircling his shoulders, as the transplant team bustles around us, coming up with plans, adding and subtracting to and from his bloodstream via the three IV lumens that dangle from his chest. Arethea works around me when she checks his vitals and changes IV bags.

And Kellan sleeps.

I'm told they're giving him a strong painkiller called Dilaudid. It makes his breathing weird and unsteady. Sometimes his eyelids flutter and he blinks at me with glassy eyes.

Sometime later in the day, Arethea brings a wheelchair and I'm inducted into hospital hell when we take Kellan—and his IV bags—to a "procedure room" where he has to lie on his sore chest, his face in a pillow, his hands in mine, while a doctor does a bone marrow biopsy, digging into his back with this awful little metal rod until Kellan's body tightens and trembles.

He pushes his face into the white pillow and grips my hands. The doctor murmurs "almost there," and Kellan moans. I can see the doctor move the little rod. Kellan's hands around mine are tight enough to hurt.

I squeeze his hands and bow my body over his. It doesn't help. I can't protect him. His little moans into the pillow make me feel ill too.

When they help him off the awful little cot, his face is bone white, his hair is sweaty, and he's so sore, I think he almost cries moving back into the wheelchair.

Back up in his room, it takes both Arethea and me to help him up onto the bed. Right after I crawl up beside him and start tucking the blankets around him, a whole team of new faces comes into the room.

One of them, a tall, wide-shouldered man with salt and pepper hair and a blunt-featured face, is Dr. Willard, the leader of the transplant team, a native Texan who managed the pediatric ward when Kellan had his first bone marrow transplant here in 2011.

He prods Kellan's sore hips, eliciting a single, punchy sob from writhing Kellan.

"What the fuck?" I gape, then glare at him. The fucking bastard.

"Move over a little," Dr. Willard tells me in his slow, low, Texan drawl. I scoot down by Kellan's feet, sweating with rage.

But then I watch the doctor crouch beside the bed and talk softly to Kellan. Dr. Willard clasps his forehead with a gentle hand and urges him to try another transplant—and another chemo trial.

Kellan reaches for the doctor, and the doctor clasps his hand, and as they talk in murmurs, I realize how much I don't know. What happened here last time? Manning told me Lyon died here. He'd been discharged already, but Kellan was still sick, so Lyon dropped by for a visit, I gathered.

Why?

And how?

Why and how, any of this shit?

It's difficult to believe that the guy curled up in the bed is Kellan who disarmed me, strung me up from ropes, made me spiked hot chocolate.

How the hell did he do all that with cancer running rampant, and the awful weight of not planning to treat it?

What the fuck did he do? To deserve this?

I know him—he's strong and brave. He didn't want to come back here. Would rather die first.

I'm wondering what made him agree to fly to New York this time—if he even had a choice—when I hear the doctor talking about the different chemo drugs. Kellan asks something I can't hear, despite being right by him, and the doctor murmurs, "Two are different. One's Bleisic."

"Will it...be...like last time?" Kellan's words are hoarse and slightly slurred, just barely loud enough for me to hear.

"I don't know, but I'll send you on a good ole Dil vacation and this sweet girl—" the doctor nods at me— "will rub your back."

Kellan says something. The doctor looks around the room, at several younger doctors in white coats, and Arethea and a woman changing out the garbage can. "Everyone, we need a minute, just the two of us. And maybe her." Dr. Willard nods at me.

Kellan says something about, "hurt her," but I can't hear him as the room clears out.

"She came here on her own, right?" the doctor asks him. Willard's eyes flick to me, and Kellan nods once. "If she's half as tough as you, she'll do alright," the doctor tells him.

"You're late to the ballgame," Dr. Willard continues, "and I know you're in a lot of pain right now, but once I get you in remission, all the bone pain will be gone. If it goes real bad, I'll make sure you're comfortable—but I think we can do this."

A few soft words from Kellan, and the doctor presses Kellan's hand between his, arches his brows at me, and runs a finger over his wet eyes. And I know I should go.

I'm scared and I should go. Protect myself. But that's not what I do.

TEN

Cleo

THEY START CHEMO WHILE he sleeps that night. Arethea tells me he's getting a huge dose of steroids with it, and I should expect him to be restless. I guess restless for someone on a Morphine-like painkiller is occasional twitching and a few soft moans.

Sometime after Arethea's 2 AM vitals check, he stirs behind me. He runs his hands over my arm and sides, the motion light and reverent.

I'm breathless for a long moment as he settles around me. I think I understand. Why all great things are sad. Why silence aches. Why people lose their way. Why when I see a lone figure, I wonder who she's missing and not who she'll meet. Why babies die when they're not touched. Why young girls cradle letters from strange boys with nameless pain upon their hearts.

We're not meant to be alone. We're made with holes inside our souls. The only way to survive is to fill them. I think the catch is, you don't get to choose with what.

Kellan

I open my eyes. I think I opened my eyes... but I'm dreaming. Because I'm back at Sloan Kettering. I blink slowly in the dream and look around the room. The wrong room. The corner room. But dreams are like that.

I inhale. Shut my eyes. It smells like... antiseptic. And the sheets. Hospital sheets with their smell: the stale, papery smell. That fucking smell sends a jolt of terror through me.

Breathe.

I have these dreams sometimes. I have to close my eyes and breathe.

It's not real, Kelly. It's just a dream. My inner monologue is always Ly's voice. Thinking of him...that hurts, too.

I open my eyes. There's the wall, TV, rocking chair.

Cold fear sweeps me. My body tightens and...*my legs*. My hips and back... They hurt.

Fuck. Fuck me. All the sweat and... I'm wet. Water. I can see it spray over the windshield.

Cleo. Cleo... water.

I look down, but I know already what I'll see. It's not my old line. Not my old line in my chest. This central line is new.

I start to pant. I can feel the pain of each breath in my ribs. My sore cheek. I'm on my side. I'm in a bed. Hospital bed.

"Oh *God*." I think I'm going to be sick. I try to get up off the bed. I try to throw my legs over the side but something's—

"Kellan?"

Cleo.

Her hands cup my cheeks. My chest pumps, each deep breath a lance of pain. I look down at my panting chest.

Cleo's fingers skate over my sore jaw. Her eyes shine in the dark. "Are you okay?"

I inhale against her hair and pull her closer. I don't mean to, but I moan. "This room."

My fingers play with the silky fabric of my football jersey... I feel my brother climb into bed. His thin hands on my neck and shoulders. "The day before..." he died "he said he loved me." He was worried about me. Lyon was better. I was sick. That's why they came that day. To play checkers...

I look down at Cleo, pressed against my chest, and raise my knees around her, pinning her between my thighs so she won't go anywhere.

I don't know whose mouth finds whose...but our lips, our tongues are mingling. I stroke her velvet cheek and tangle with her tongue and clutch her head and pull her closer. I can smell her breath, it smells like peppermint. Her tiny fingers play at my nape. I deepen the kiss. I'm damp with sweat, my eyes are wet... I can't stop. Can't stop kissing her. She can't stop kissing me. I'm dizzy.

My mouth closes over hers. I breathe her breath. Warm breath until my head stops spinning.

Still spinning.

I let my breath out.

"Baby..." Tender fingers find my cheeks. Her eyes. I love her eyes. Her brows pull down, concerned. Her thumb traces under my eyes. "You had a bad dream?"

"Yeah." I lean my cheek against her hand.

I feel her hand behind my shoulder, rubbing my back. It makes me think of Lyon. I like the pain. Being here...I want to feel it.

I try to remember what she just asked, and what I said. The Dilaudid is making me fuzzy.

I lean away from her. Her face is blurry. I can only see her silhouette, a dark blot on the blue-tinged room. The blue is coming from the window. Curtain drawn. The city lights. I remember those cold lights.

I look down at my chest. Only one IV hooked up right now.

"Is there anything I can do?" she whispers.

"I've gotta get up."

She nods. "I brought you a bunch of lounge clothes but they're in the dryer right now. Our nurse is going to bring them. Until then, I got you this."

Our nurse...

She slides down off the bed and gets back up with something. I can't see it.

I blink. Something dark… A robe.

I push myself toward the bed's edge, using my right arm.

"Here—" She's standing by the bed. "Slide down and you can hold onto me."

I get down, and my legs and hips ache so much I feel tears burn my eyes. I can't believe I'm back here. My throat is so full, I can barely breathe. Cleo's arm comes around me.

She kisses me. She wraps her hand around the IV pole. She walks me to the bathroom, pointing out a giant, blow-up palm tree by the wall.

"There's more of that type stuff coming to decorate your room. Hope you don't mind." Her words are like another language. I can hear but I can't understand.

She pushes the bathroom door open. Light spills out. I look down at myself. These scrubs. They came untied... are sagging. Fuck.

She leaves me and I stare at the sink. The toilet. Blue tile.

Memories...

I piss, then stroke my cock. I think of Cleo and I get a halfie, even though I'm numb as hell. Okay.

I look in the mirror. Big mistake. My face is bruised and swollen. My lips are dry. My eyes look desperate and strung out.

I put on the robe. I don't know how it got in here. Did Cleo hand it to me? I'm shaking. The longer I stand up, the more things hurt.

I open the door, fast because I'm scared that she'll be gone. She's right there. We go to the bed. I lie down across it, on my side. My legs hang off. The robe is soft. It covers me.

Cleo climbs up on the mattress, leans over me. She holds up... some kind of towel? I watch a smile light up her face. Her hand is on my hair. "You can't get a bath yet, not for a little while longer, because they just put in the central line. But I don't think you've had one since the wreck. I thought it might feel good."

ELEVEN

Kellan

I BLINK, AND CLEO DRAGS a warm cloth over my calves. Oh God… It does feel good. I clench my fist, because I want to touch her.

Someone knocks, and Cleo leaves. Fuck. The water dries cool on my skin. My dick stirs.

She comes back into my plane of vision with an armful of clothes. "I bought some things before I left Atlanta, then I ordered some other stuff from a 24-hour delivery service." She's smiling. I think I should smile back, but I'm too tired.

She sets the clothes on the bed beside me and strokes my knee. Her fingers, soft and kind. It's too much. Fuck.

I scurry off the bed before I realize that's crazy. Then I look around, searching out an excuse for it. But I can't think straight. I turn back toward the bed and right my twisted IV line.

Damnit...

She acts like she doesn't notice I just freaked out. She lays a pair of boxer-briefs and long, dark gray pants over the bed's rail. I manage the underwear, but my hips hurt. I feel my heartbeat in the bones. My hands can't seem to hold onto the pants.

I get back on the bed and turn away from her. I cover my face with my arm. *Fuck.*

"I can help you get your pants on," she says in a voice that sounds like sunny clouds. "You helped me out of mine so many times, it's only fair, right?"

"I don't need them," I rasp.

"Okay then. No pants. I'm going to untie this robe if that's okay. Get your chest bare. If you don't mind?"

I grunt, because that towel's on my thigh—and I can feel my dick throb, somewhere...

She washes my hips and belly, gently. I can't feel myself like normal, but I can pay attention to the rhythm of her movement. And it's slow. I'm not embarrassed. I would be—if not for this.

My balls... They ache. I'm surprised to find I want to touch them. I want her to touch them.

Can I ask her? Would she jack me off like this? Or is it too fucked up?

She drags the towel over my sore ribs. It feels…kind of good.

Last time I was here, I tried so hard to forget my body. To pretend it wasn't really there, and neither was the pain. But this... good. Tears brim in my eyes as my dick stiffens. I love her. I just want to be inside her.

I would ask... I just...can't.

She's beside me now, leaned over me. Oh fuck. The line. She can see my central line up close. It's called a line, but it's a tube. A little tube that goes into my chest.

She won't want to touch me anymore. My dick forgets its gladness. I try to be still.

Cleo... steady. Soft. The cloth trails up my arms, my neck, my face. I want to cry. I want to ask her why she's doing this. There's... my robe off me. A towel. Then my hair is wet. She's stroking. I can hear the bubbles by my ears. So nice and cool.

She tucks a towel around my hair, and I look up into her eyes.

Her green gaze softens against mine. "Am I doing okay?" She strokes my forehead.

I inhale slowly through my nose. "Why...are you still here?" She's gonna go. Even my voice sounds…fucked up.

She sits down by me, takes my hand. "Because you're here."

"The water was cold." Did I say that out loud?

Cleo's breasts press against her shirt. She's talking. Emory. Her hand is on my shoulder. The hurt one. I don't know why...I feel my balls draw up.

Dilaudid. I'm fucking glowing. My dick's hard. I need to fuck her. She's talking about papers. Signing papers. Nurse. TBI. Something about consents.

She asks, "Is that okay?"

A nurse comes in. I think I get more Dilaudid, because Cleo goes away. I grab my cock. An anchor. It's the only thing I feel. My hand or her hands... ?

Cleo

His face is somber and his eyes are shut. I don't think he's touching himself the way I think he— *oh*. The blanket slips off him and I can see his hand stroking his cock.

It sends a bolt of lightning through me.

I watch his chest move up and down. The motion makes his face go tighter, even as he pumps his long, thick shaft. My hands yearn to join in his rebellion. Would he like that? Would he like my help? It might just be a comfort thing. Something he can do to distract from the pain.

The more I watch his fingers curve around his cock, the more I see the strength of his hand moving in its practiced rhythm—the more I understand why he needs this right now.

Heat begins to rise in my chest, gathering in a thick sting. I'm breathing deeply too, but he has no idea. I'm not sure he even knows I'm here. I watch his hand, the thickness of his shaft, the smoothness of that skin. His breaths come longer, louder and his balls draw up. And I can only stand here, feeling need unfurl between my legs.

Can I touch him? He would want it. I think he would.

I climb onto the bed. I trail my hand up his calf, then up his firm, hair-dusted thigh, so he can feel me coming. I hold my breath and touch my fingers to the taut sac of his balls. His hips jerk. He moans as I wrap my other hand around his hand, over his cock.

His eyelids lift. His eyes are glossy, but instead of vacancy, all I see are seas of need.

"Can I... ?" Shit. I can't even say it.

"Please. Cleo…" His eyes shut. I feel his thighs tense as my hand replaces his hand on his cock. I tighten my grip. I try to keep his rhythm.

"Oh God, Kellan." His legs spread. His ass lifts off the bed.

I move up and down his thick shaft, pumping his base and gliding all the way up to his swollen head, where I find a bead of slick pre-cum. Kellan's breaths are hoarse and shallow.

"It feels good?" I whisper.

He groans. I see the mottled bruising underneath his jaw as his head tips back, his blond hair pressed into the pillow.

"Good," he moans. "It's so good."

I bring my other hand under the blanket tossed over his thighs, cupping his warm balls. I knead them as I stroke him hard and fast, with steady, knowing strokes. Another groan rips from his throat. My hand slows, tugging his thick shaft toward me.

"Faster. Pull...harder." He reaches down toward me, his fingers spread, as if he wants to use his hand to guide me. He banks his palm over his lower abs. The fingers quiver, but he doesn't touch me.

I pick up the pace again. His cock is swollen, huge and hard and hot. He lifts his hips and groans, a ragged, mindless sound. I cup my palm around his head. He's slick there. I trace the rim of him with delicate precision.

"Squeeze," he growls. "My balls. Squeeze hard."

He thrusts his hips. "Harder," he begs. "Please... fuck, Cleo."

With one hand wrapped around his sac, I take his cock between the base of my thumb and the inside of forefinger. Then

I jack his rigid shaft. Up and down. I pump as my hand fists his balls with measured force.

He writhes. "Cleo—fuck... oh fucking shit." The words are low and hard. He thrusts his hips. "Oh God..."

I want to take him further. Take him away. I struggle with my idea for a moment, then decide to take a risk. I lean under the blanket and lick up and down his thigh, my hand still holding his firm sac, my fingers grasping the base of his cock.

I pick up the pumping on his dick and guide one swollen testicle into my mouth.

His hoarse voice fills my ears. "Oh fuck... Cleo... Ohhhh... I'm gonna blow... oh Jesus Christ..."

His legs tremble. I leave him like that, panting. I race over to my bag and grab a flavored condom I bought for this purpose.

I can't suck him bare; one of the rules. He twists his hips, moaning as I roll the condom on.

"Oh fuck... God. Cleo... please..."

I roll the condom down to his base and he thrusts against my jaw. I open up. He slams into my mouth, his hand grabbing my hair. I take him deeper than I ever have and roll his balls and lick the underside of him.

He bucks. "Ah—my *hips*." My heart hammers. Is he in pain? "That motherfucking mouth... motherfuck..." I squeeze his balls again, and suck his head. I twirl my tongue around him. His thighs grip my body.

"Squeeze my dick. Right now, squeeze hard." He's panting. "Harder. Press... down under. The underside... press. Aaaah..."

When my fingers press down underneath his cock, he moans and twists his hips. "Pull... on my balls. Harder..."

When I'm squeezing his sac so hard it has to hurt, his hand comes over mine, working from his head down to the base of him, smoothing like he's trying to keep his load inside. He growls. "Suck... me. My cock... in your mouth. Right... now."

I start to worry someone will come in—but I don't have much choice. He's got me by the hair. I feel his balls tighten, but then he stops me, urging me to rub my fingers down the underside of his cock and squeeze his balls again.

Each time he makes me do this, he seems lifted further from here. My mouth and hands make him forget the world and finally, the third time I drag my thumb along the underside of his thick cock, I realize: I'm prolonging this.

I do it one more time—until his monitors have started beeping and my heart is pounding hard, and then instead of stopping me, he plants his palms on each side of my head and fucks my mouth like it's a sport.

He comes with a sharp cry, his cock thumping hard before his cum fills the condom. By the time I pull it off, his eyes are closed.

I cover him back up and rush into the bathroom to take care of myself. As soon as I see the blue tiles and the rail by the toilet, I don't think I'll be able to do it... but I sit inside the shower, stuff two fingers inside myself, and focus on the memory of Kellan's hand around his cock.

TWELVE

Cleo

"If all else perished, and he remained, I should still continue to be; and if all else remained, and he were annihilated, the universe would turn into a mighty stranger."
–Catherine, from Wuthering Heights, *by Emily Bronte.*

I've taken to dramatic quotes. So sue me. When I placed an order at that 24-hour random shit delivery service, I came across an origami kit, and of course, I had to have it. I remember mentioning an origami sparrow in one of my first letters to R.

R.

Kellan.

I still can't wrap my head around it. Kellan Walsh—Drake, it legally is—is R. And he has cancer. My sweet, dirty lover, with the .gif body and non-stop boner, has leukemia. Not only that, he has relapsed AML that he was just... ignoring. What the actual fuck?

I want to ask about it. When it's dark and quiet in the room and he's curled on his side with IVs running into his chest, and I'm folded behind him with my cheek pressed against his back, I want to whisper, "Tell me why." I need a reason.

He overdosed this summer. Manning told me he cut up two Fentanyl patches, put them on his back, and took a hot bath. His friend Nessa found him. I asked about her—jealous, in a strange way—and Manning told me she's dead. Cancer. Cancer friend.

So from Manning, I know Kellan tried to take his life before the relapse could. God knows I can't judge. I haven't been there.

But I need to understand. I just need to hear about it from his mouth. Because I love him. I love him. And I need him to live.

I haven't asked about it, though.

Because Kellan isn't talking.

I fold the slip of paper with my Emily Bronte quote on it into a sparrow and then thread a string through one of the wings. I wrap the other end of the string around a piece of that special double-sided tape stuff, which pops off when you tug it for removal.

As I stand in a desk chair to press it to the ceiling, I look over at him, lying in the bed. I can tell he's awake because the gray box on the bed side table—the one with the red numbers showing his pulse and blood oxygen saturation—shows a pulse too high for him to be asleep.

But if I go over to him and try to talk, he won't move.

It's been that way for almost three whole days. He gets chemo 'round the clock, lots of IV fluids to flush out the chemo quickly, plus a ton of steroids, antibiotics, painkillers for the bone pain he still has, and a laundry list of random other drugs like Zofran, Ativan, etc. Yesterday and the day before, he got shots of chemo in his spine as well. Both times, I went with him to the procedure room, and both times I wrapped my arms around him as he curled over on his side.

He'll hold my hands and push his head against me. He might answer a question or two—as long as he's speaking with his eyes closed—but he won't really engage.

When we're in his room, he'll lie in bed and pretend to be asleep.

I've gotten good at gauging his pain level—the pulse number on the pulse-ox monitor can help me tell—so if he gets up to do something and I can tell he's hurting, I'll wrap my arm around him...and he'll lean on me.

But this is all—until night time.

Around nine or ten, I'll play a DVD—one of the episodes of *Walking Dead*, from the stack of DVDs Arethea pointed out when

I first got here. I'll slip into bed behind him, and I'll wrap an arm around his hard, lean waist. At night, Arethea only comes in every three hours, so I have time to really touch him.

I stroke his neck and shoulders...trail around his sides, down to the firm plane of his abs. And always, there's his dick, standing straight up. He will guide my hands to it, or sometimes urge me to come lie in front of him, so we can see each other. I'll pull his head against my chest so he can suck my nipples, and I'll stroke his cock until he comes in my hand.

Sometimes it takes a long time, and I know it's because of all the painkillers. But if I roll a condom on and suck him, play with his balls and tease the rim of his head, or drag my fingertip over his taint, I can make him come.

He lays his fingertips on my pussy...pushes inside. We both come, he falls asleep. He wakes again; I always wake to him. His hands grab me. His sleepy mouth strokes mine, his tongue delving inside. He says my name against my skin, and when I whisper his name, he moves against me.

Usually, after the second round, we're facing each other. I pull his head against my chest and wrap my arms around him. Once or twice, I think I feel him shake a little, feel some moisture on his cheeks, but I can never tell for sure.

As this third day of chemo wears on, I miss Kellan more than ever. I know that this is where I want to be—I withdrew from school this morning, via phone, from the shower in the bathroom—but it's lonely.

Dr. Willard explained that I have two choices: I can stay in Kellan's room and be part of his quarantine—a necessary thing while his immune system is so off—or I can come and go a little more, but when I'm in here with him, I would have to wear a mask and gloves. I've decided on the quarantine.

A few times a day, he has to get up to "stay moving." I lace my arm through his, but even then he hardly looks at me. This afternoon, he does PT and chokes down some chicken and rice. His eyes are tired. His face is pale. He falls asleep with the food tray in his lap. I tuck pillows around him. I hang more birds. No one stops me. By the time the sun starts going down, one-fourth of the room is filled with sparrows.

Kellan

I can't.

I think of it. I map whole conversations. Jokes. In my mind, I tell her that I love her. How soft she is, how good she smells. I tell her to stay in bed with me all day, to keep her hands around my dick all night, because I need that. I need her.

But that's a fantasy, a script. In the real world, I am silent. When she holds me in the daylight, I don't move. Poison drips into my veins. I tell myself if I don't speak, if I don't move my mouth, I won't get sick. I tell myself if I get sick, Cleo will leave. I can't be here without her. She is holding up the sky.

THIRTEEN

Cleo

September 24, 2014

"The heart of another is a dark forest, always, no matter how close it has been to one's own." –Willa Cather

Chemo day four, Kellan doesn't eat his breakfast of bacon, a biscuit, and a TwoCal. Dr. Willard comes in and asks him how he's feeling, and I'm shocked to hear him have a normal conversation with the doctor.

"My hips hurt some. Better, though..."

"We've dropped back on the Dil since that pain's lessened," the doctor tells him. "What about your stomach? Any nausea yet?"

He shrugs. "Sometimes. Not much."

"We can go up on the Zofran." Dr. Willard nods at the stationary bike and gives Kellan a teasing smile. "You been training on that thing?"

Kellan shakes his head, rubbing his forehead, like his head hurts. "I wish."

The doctor pats his arm. "Take this pretty girl and dance around the room. Just keep him up and down," the doctor tells me.

Kellan's eyes meet mine, and I feel warm all over. When did he stop looking at me?

When Dr. Willard goes, and Kellan lies back on his side, I perch on the foot of the bed. "You want to play a game or something? Maybe watch a show?"

He shakes his head. He's got his phone cradled in his hand, but I can't see what's on the screen.

"I think I'll take a nap." I swallow, because all of a sudden, my throat is aching. "Do you mind if I lie down beside you?"

"Sure," he says quietly.

I slip under the sheets, but when I go to spoon myself against him like normal, I find that I... just can't.

I lie there, staring at the small sky light above the bed. I feel him shift beside me. He turns on his back. I catch his eye and realize he looks more alert than yesterday. As I just saw, when he spoke with Dr. Willard.

I blink, making the ceiling blur.

Did I do something wrong? I thought he'd want me here, but... I cover my face with my hand.

"Cleo?"

I peek my eyes open and see him leaning over me. He grabs my hand and tugs it under the covers, where I find a rock-hard erection.

I stroke up and down his velvety length, slowly at first, because I'm not sure if I want to do this. But I find I do. I need him. I'll settle for anything I can get. I trace around his head and roll his balls in my warm palm. His chest rises with his heavy breaths.

"Yeah... oh... fuck... *Cleo.*"

I feel a pearl of moisture on the head of him. I feel wet too.

His thighs flex as he pushes himself into my hand. "Oh God... mm... underneath... my head again. Like that. Fuck."

I feel his hips tremble. I stroke his balls. I jack him a few times and return to his head, to the silken rim, where the barest stroke of my fingertips has him snarling in my ear and threatening to blow all over me.

I wrap both hands around his thick shaft. He thrusts as my hands pump, and when he comes he groans, "I love you."

"And if you are not a bird, beware of coming to rest above an abyss." –Nietzsche

My hands shake just a little as I fold the square of bright red origami paper into a sparrow. I kind of suck at origami. None of the sparrows look the same, but I don't care. I've got to stay busy...lest I go completely insane.

I'm sitting at the desk, over near the exercise bike, which is right by the room's big windows. Kellan's lying on his left side in the bed, eyes on his iPad.

He's lying on his left side. The side where he has two broken ribs and a fucked up shoulder. The side that puts him facing away from me.

I grab another square of yellow origami paper.

I love you, too. Asshole. -Sloth

I'm folding that into the shittiest-looking sparrow yet when he gets off the bed and pushes his IV pole slowly to the restroom. After a few minutes, he comes back out. From halfway across the room, I can't see him very well, but I'm pretty sure he's going out of his way to avoid looking at me.

This time, he lies down on his right side like a sane person, but he's quick to get the iPad back in front of his face.

Fury spreads its fingers through me. So he loves me, does he? Or maybe he just loves my hands around his dick. It feels wrong to be so pissed off at him, considering the situation, but I can't help it. I want to saunter over to the bed and let him have it, but that isn't fair. I tell myself that's why I take my own vacation to the bathroom.

For Kellan's sake.

Yeahhh.

I strip out of my clothes, pull a pair of loose gray sweats and a long-sleeved red t-shirt out of my bag, and seek refuge under the lukewarm stream of shower water. I don't know if cancer patients can't get over-hot or what, but this shower sucks.

Still, I stand there in the muggy, not-quite-steamy space a long time after I'm finished shaving and washing my hair.

Even if he really *does* love me, he'll never say it again. I bet he won't. I dry myself slowly and dress more slowly, then stash my bags back in the bathroom closet.

I hang my head upside down to dry my hair, so it's got a little more body than it has since I got here, and brush and floss my teeth before I brave the room again.

I'm surprised to find him on the stationary bike. His blue eyes flicker over me, then quickly come back to the bike's small, digital screen. I watch his legs pump for a minute. I can't help admiring the way his body moves, the way he looks, even with the IV lines in his chest. He's just...perfect.

I sigh. Fuck me. I thought this would be so different. I thought he'd be glad to have me here. I thought at the very least, he'd share his feelings. Fess up to liking me. Is that selfish? Maybe I'm not being understanding.

He has cancer, after all. The other day I came across the thick stack of consent forms—just for this one particular hospital stay—and learned more about what being here means for him. Trials usually don't promise specific survival statistics, but I've read the stats for repeat bone marrow transplants online...with a reduced intensity radiation regimen (as Kellan had—two sessions of radiation the day before I got here) and—*yeah*. They're not so fab. And by that, I mean like fifty percent, or even less.

God, I really *am* an asshole. Obviously, he's scared. Who wouldn't be? He's scared and feeling bad and I'm here, all up in his space, demanding things. Even if I don't say I am, I'm sure he can feel it. How I want him to talk to me.

I go to the recliner with my cross-stitching and watch him through the forest of my lashes.

A masochist. He must be. The IV pole stands beside him, and he's not wearing a shirt. The IV lines pump chemo into his chest. His eyes are sad and tired, his handsome face perpetually tight. I know it now: his look of pain.

I'm so fucking helpless, I can't stand it. I prick my finger with my cross-stitch needle just to do *something*. It stings more than I think it will.

I murmur, "Fuck."

His gaze tugs to my face. I roll my eyes. "Pricked my finger."

I'm surprised to see his legs slow their cycling. To see him move down off the bike, his motions slow and desperately careful. He walks to me in his lounge pants, pushing the IV pole. My heart beats like a drum the entire time. And then he's standing right in front of me. Just standing there.

I want to scream.

He stands there for the longest time. I don't look up. Not because I don't want to, but because I know I can't. All the desperation that's locked up in me would spill out, and he'd see it and know I care too much.

I care too much. Maybe I really do.

I sit there feeling nauseated. I just watch the needle and the thread, and make the "e" in 'bitterness.' Until he kneels in front of me.

His hand drapes over my knee, and I can feel his eyes on my face. "Cleo?"

God—I've really missed his normal voice. Not just his dirty whispers, but his real voice.

"Mmm?" I feel terrible for it, but I still can't look at him.

His hand squeezes my leg and tension builds between us. So much that I think I'll burst.

"I want to tell you something," he says quietly.

"That's new." I can't help it.

"I want you to go after your... after you donate." His voice is low and husky, making chills roll over my skin. "You're giving me enough. You've been here long enough... You have your own life to get back to. I know I...have to let you go." The words are thick and soft. I feel a shot of hope. My heart pit-patters as his blue eyes come to mine. "I'm being selfish," he confesses hoarsely. "It's my default with you."

I put my hoop on the table by the chair and reach for his handsome face. His eyes are full of pain. I want to kiss him, but at the last minute, I decide it feels better just to press my cheek against his.

"Kell..." My arm goes around his shoulders. "It's not like that with us. You know it's not."

He inhales, and I can tell it hurts his ribs because he also tenses. He presses his cheek against mine and wraps his right arm tight around my back.

"What is it like?" he whispers. "Tell me."

I curl my hand around his nape and kiss him near his ear. "It's like I really care about you. I love you... and I just want to be here with you. Close, so I can see you every day."

He pulls away. He looks anguished. "I feel like such a fucking bastard."

"No." I pull him back to me. "Why would you say that?"

I cup his head, and he lowers his forehead to my shoulder. His arm wraps back around me. I feel his fist clenched above my shoulder blade.

"Everything I do will hurt you." His voice breaks. "I make you go..." He shakes his head. "I love you, I'm a liability to you. I fucking hate myself."

"You are *not* a liability." He lifts his head at that, his blue eyes wide and pooling with emotion. Which gives me hope. He cares what I say here. I brush his lips with mine. "I love you and I want you any way you are."

His mouth tightens, as if my words hurt him. He hides his face in my hair again, and for a moment, I can feel him breathing hard.

"It's gonna get worse," he says in a broken voice. "You might... watch me die here. I don't want that for you. Goddamn, Cleo. I want you to *go*. Just get as far away as you can and don't look back. If I come through—" he shakes his head, his forehead rocking on my shoulder. "You're never gonna need this shit."

He lifts his head. His eyes are wide, intense. "Can you do that? Leave here after the donation?"

I smile sadly. "You know I can't." I drift my fingers along his collar bone on the side where he's still bruised from the wreck. "I've got a total Heathcliff thing going for you." I stroke his neck. "Now I know you know that. You're English and finance, aren't you? R. said he was an English major."

He shuts his eyes. "Cleo, you aren't Heathcliff. Don't be. Please?" He peeks his eyes open and pulls me close enough to kiss me. But he doesn't kiss me. His lips move against my chin, and I can smell the wintergreen mouth wash he's been using. "You be Cathy. You be rational… Be safe." His voice is soft and low. I love the sound of it. The feel of his words against my jaw.

"You know I'm the one who got your blow-up palm tree, right? And the bubbles for when the marijuana tincture gets here and you're high? I'm not logical. I don't want to be."

I squeeze him to me, nuzzling his scratchy cheek. He hasn't shaved in a few days, and he's looking rougeish. "Let's lay down, okay?"

His eyes slip closed just for a second, then he nods. He reaches around me for the chair, and I step out of his way.

"Can I—" help, I'm going to ask. But he pulls himself up, wraps his hand around the IV pole, and steps over to the bed. I hang back and let him get settled on his own. It's hard because I can tell he's sore, and I feel so bad that I let him kneel there for so long.

When he's lying on his not-sore side, I climb up behind him and snuggle up against his back.

Silence wraps its arms around us. I shut my eyes and focus on the heat of Kellan's body. I promise myself he'll be okay. All that stuff he said about me leaving... I tell myself it's not some prescient feeling he's having that things will go badly for him. He's just showing me he loves me.

I rub his back, so smooth and warm, still rippling with muscle, which feels more rigid than it ever has. "I'm really *not* leaving. I need you to believe that... and trust me." Tears make my throat feel thick. I swallow. "I don't want to be away from you."

I feel him stop breathing for a moment. "And if you stayed?" His voice sounds strong, more firm than what's normal in the last few days. "If you stayed and... things end badly?" he says, quieter now. "How do you think you'd feel about it then?"

All his muscles tense as he awaits my answer. I close my eyes and try to really go there. To imagine if he wasn't moving and his skin was cold, and this would be the last time I would be with him.

I swallow, because the first thing I think is, we would never get to be together in the long-term. Which makes it crystal clear what my heart wants. I press my forehead against his back. "It scares me... to keep saying this when I'm not sure how you feel. But I love you. I can't help it," I whisper. "I... need you. In this way that doesn't make sense, logically. But feels natural to me." My heart pounds, because it's terrifying, being so straightforward. "But if you died? I think I'd get comfort knowing I was here as long as I could be. Kinda saw you through... and didn't leave, you know?" Tears drip down my cheeks, trekking across my face toward the pillow. "I couldn't leave you. I just can't, so please don't make me."

I guess he hears the tears in my voice, because Kellan takes the IV lines in one hand and, with a wince, turns over to face me.

He frames my face with both his hands, even though I know it hurts to move the left one.

"I didn't think you'd come up here. I hoped you wouldn't find out Ly was your recipient. But now—" he looks into my eyes—"I know I fucked you over. I should never have let things keep on with you. Selfish."

The low beeping that I've almost tuned out picks up, and I realize his heart is beating fast.

"What were you really? You're not selfish. Were you curious? Once you found out I was 'sloth'... what was that like?" It's a question I've been longing to ask him.

He shuts his eyes and squeezes my hand. "I loved you too. Before we even spoke. Just watching you." His eyes open and focus on my face. "I didn't know it at the time, that that's what all the interest was. If you tripped on a fucking crack I wanted to go help you. You smiled at someone, I wanted that for me. I would watch your hair..." he works his fingers through it, "and I would want to touch it. See how soft it was. After a while, I realized I didn't like it, knowing I couldn't have you. Or anyone, because it wasn't fair. To let anyone get close to me..."

He leans his head down to my chest and hugs me carefully. "The whole thing... started getting to me. I told myself I was pissed off that you were threatening the business. All the charitable deliveries, they depend on the sales. I thought I just needed to get you under heel. But I think even then I knew it could go more places than that."

"I think we were meant to meet each other."

FOURTEEN

Cleo

HE LOOKS AWAY FROM ME, and I can sense a wave of pain come over him. I can tell because his body tenses, and after a few seconds, he draws a deep breath.

His eyes shut, and slowly open. "You know, to meet you I have to be sick."

"What do you mean by that?"

"Both times I met you, it was because of cancer." First because I donated to Lyon, the second time because Kellan was here getting diagnosed with his relapse when his dealers had a dry spell and noticed me.

He lays back against the pillows and pulls an arm over his eyes. "You know, sloth is a sin," he says softly.

"I prefer to think of it as an adorable animal."

He peeks at me from underneath his arm. His eyes are dark. "I knew in March."

"That you had relapsed?"

He blinks. "Not 'knew.' 'Thought.'"

"What did you do?"

"Nothing," he says bitterly. "I like numbers, remember?" He lets a sharp breath out. "I didn't like the odds."

I feel his jaw clench. "I drove off the bridge."

Tears drip down my cheeks. "That hurts a little, not gonna lie. It makes me sad that you felt so backed into a corner. I wish you had talked to me."

He gets off the bed. Starts pacing. "I didn't want you to be here. I didn't want this."

"You want me to go?" My heart pounds.

"Yes—of course I do."

"You didn't say that when I got here."

"A moment of weakness." His features tense, but that doesn't stop a single tear from falling down his cheek. "I hurt...worse than ever. The bone pain...the wreck. All I could think of was your hands. I couldn't live without your hands on me. I knew I couldn't."

FIFTEEN

Kellan

I STEP AWAY FROM CLEO. I can't think straight so close to her, so I grab a TwoCal Arethea left on the bedside table and walk around to the recliner, where I sit and take a long, disgusting swallow.

"Why'd you come here? Really?" My voice sounds hoarse. Because my throat is so tight.

Cleo's sitting cross-legged on the bed now. She lifts her eyes to me, then drops them back to her lap. She plucks at the blanket. "I guess…it felt like my place," she says. "Being here. I couldn't stand the idea of anybody else being near you when I wasn't." Her eyes flash in my direction. "You're mine. That's what—" She shakes her head. "It felt like I should be here taking care of you. Me and no one else. I can't explain. I…needed to in this weird way. I felt like that since we met. Like I didn't have a choice. I didn't even matter, though. I rolled with it. You're stuck with me." She smiles.

I swallow. Fuck, I love those words. I look down at my knees. What do I tell her? How hard should I try to drive her off?

Really hard, my conscience answers.

I take a breath and blow it out. "You know I'm going to get sick. Sicker than this. A lot sicker."

She nods slowly. "I don't want that, but if happens, I can handle it."

She doesn't know. She's only had a taste of this, a few days.

When I look up again, I find her looking curious. "Did Whitney stay here with your brother, just like this?"

I nod, trying not to let her see that it bothers me to talk about him. "She would hold his hands while someone pushed a catheter into his cock. She would let him vomit all over both of them. She's a freak, Whitney. Med student now."

"Maybe I'm a freak, too."

My stomach twists so tight I feel a wave of nausea. "I don't know why you would be," I rasp.

"Because I love you."

Cleo

"Cleo..." I watch his Adam's apple move along the column of his throat. He rubs a hand over his head, then folds his fingers over his eyes like a visor.

"It's a burden," he says quietly. "If you don't feel that way, you haven't been here long enough."

"God. That's what you really think? Who made you think like that?" I want to go and wrap my arms around him, but my chest hurts so much I can't breathe.

I'm filled with rage. "I really want to know who made you feel like that. Was it your dad? Where is your dad?"

He grits his teeth. "He came and left before you got here. It doesn't matter."

"Yes it does. Who else? Was it the last time? Who was here with you last time?"

"My college girlfriend came here once. She stayed for thirty minutes. And you know what?" He stands up. "She was shallow, nothing like you, but she wasn't a bitch. It's just too much. No one wants this. You'll see."

I slip down off the bed and step toward him, arms out. He doesn't lift his head. His mouth is tight and hurt. I twine my arms around his waist and lay my cheek against his chest.

"K... You're so wrong. *You'll* see." I nuzzle my head against his pec. "That girl was an idiot. I'm much better than her. I love you, and I *want* to help. It's not too much for me. I love being with you. I would never change my mind."

I rub his lower back, and he shakes his head. He clutches his forehead, fingertips digging into his hair. "You gave me love..." he rasps, "and all I can give you is pain."

"That's not true." I look up into his tortured eyes. "Every moment that I'm with you, I'm happy that I am. You're going to be okay—and in the meantime, all you have to do is talk to me and I'll be super happy. I want to know everything there is to know about you, Kell."

His mouth twitches. "I don't know why."

"Lie down with me…"

I take his hand, tugging him over to the bed, and hold his IV lines while he climbs up and settles on his side. I watch him shift his left shoulder a few times, then—when I think he seems comfortable—I climb up behind him.

"Lie on your back for a minute, so I can see you. 'Kay?"

He shifts onto his back, his eyes wary. I trail my fingertips over his forehead, just the way I know he likes, and he stares at the ceiling.

"Close your eyes, baby. Focus on my fingers." I kiss his chin, and keep on tracing the planes of his face. "Is your father your only living family?"

"No." He shifts his jaw. I feel his chest sink with a slow exhale. "I have a brother. Barrett. He's a Ranger, special forces. Just retired," he adds after a moment.

"You're not very close to your father, am I right? I remember that from R.'s letters. And at your house, I remember you said some things about your dad. Some conflict between the two of you."

His eyes open, blazing. "Lyon had a heart attack because the chemo was too harsh. He wanted to withdraw from the trial we did, but my dad pushed him to stay in. That's how he is. He wants me to be alive, I guess, but none of the details matter."

God. *None of the details…* Quality of life. How hard he has to fight for it.

"I'm so sorry." I wrap my arm over his chest and snuggle close to his side, my fingers still smoothing over his head. He shuts his eyes, but I can feel the tension in his body.

"The details do matter," I say softly.

I think about the burn of his forehead on my chest when he's fevered and I've got him pulled close to me. The way his hands crushed mine during the bone marrow biopsy.

"You've had so many hard details. Ones I can't even imagine." I press my face against his bicep, feathering my lips over his smooth skin. "I'm so glad you came back here. You're so fucking brave. Because I get it, why you wouldn't want to. I'm not sure if I could have."

My throat tightens when I think of Kellan coming here alone that day. How hurt he was, physically. How hard it must have been, coming to this place of nightmares. Tears fill my eyes as I meld myself around him.

I feel him shift a little. Feel him breathing. I want to see his face, but I don't lift my head from where it's pressed against his shoulder.

"When I first came to New York," his low voice rumbles, "I wasn't staying in the hospital. I was living out of this hotel, The Carlyle, and after hours I would go to bars, and drink and smoke. And fuck. I had a— I had been with someone, sort of."

"The girl you mentioned?" I ask softly.

"Yeah," he murmurs. His arm, around my back now, shifts a little as he strokes along my spine. "It was just an off-and-on thing. Back at school. But I was here and started...needing sex. I had a central line like this—" his right hand hovers above his chest—"so I would tie them up and…take them from behind.

Some of them knew me. From TV, you know? They would do whatever I wanted."

I bite the inside of my cheek and try to picture this—my Kellan with some New York girl. I feel a well of sadness where I had expected jealousy. "Had you ever tied anyone up before? Or was that the first time?"

His hand spreads out over my back, pressing me closer to him. The silence cradles us.

"It was the first time," he says finally.

I hug his chest tighter, taking care not to press myself too hard against his sore ribs.

"That must have been so hard," I whisper.

His forehead furrows.

"Clearly you were in denial, right? You were getting treatment and out partying?"

"It was definitely hard," he says dryly.

I tuck my leg over his and wait for him to speak. His fingers play along my spine, but he stays quiet. Waiting, I think. For my questions.

"Where was your brother during that time?" I ask.

"He was inpatient. He had a bad reaction to the chemo from day one. It made his heart fuck up."

I think on that. I try to picture Kellan Drake, star quarterback, at a bar, smoking and drinking and picking up women. Then going back to...what? Chemo pills? Covert hospital appointments? Did he wear a ball cap? Shades? Poor K. And worried about his twin the whole time.

I think of Kellan holding the counter in his kitchen, chewing a Xanax because he missed his brother so much. I meet his gaze. It seems to shove at me.

"I could have stayed with Ly." He grits his teeth. "I didn't. He was by himself. Whit had no idea. After the night on the yacht—after we found out he had AML—he broke things off with Whitney and he left the team. People found out he left the team and left town too, but no one knew what happened. Some fuckhead made a crack about him, how he wasn't good enough to hold his spot on the team, and I kicked his ass outside a bar one night. So when I got my diagnosis, my coach used me as an example." Kellan's teeth come down atop his lower lip. "It was different with me than with Ly. The whole thing became more of a secret."

"What do you mean?"

"I wanted football for a career. We thought I would do the treatment, then come back. Be fine. If no one knew, I'd still get scouted just the same. Now, they would find out—they look at your medical records—but I'd still be in the running. I could still move forward."

It didn't happen that way. I don't know the whole story—the story of the first bone marrow transplant, or why the cancer came back this year—but Kellan's chemo consent forms say that this is his seventh cycle. I nuzzle closer to him.

"Anyway, that didn't happen, did it?" he says. "I was fucking bitter after he died. I was here for a while, inpatient. I had left the hospital the day he died. Just took off, onto the subway and shit."

"Wow." That's a big no-no for a bone marrow transplant patient. We can't even leave this room. Something as minor as a cold could be serious for Kellan right now. Until he gets my marrow and his immune system re-starts.

"I got sick," he says. From going out on his excursion, he means. He goes on, "Not just from skipping out that day. Before then, too. Ly and I switched places after transplant, see. His took, and he was better fast. Angel marrow," he murmurs, nuzzling my head with his chin. "Mine wasn't such a good match, my donor. There was only one 10/10 match for us. Twins, right? And Ly was worse, so he got you."

I look up at him, bug-eyed. "What?"

"My donor was a German woman," he explains. "An 8/10 match. Still good, but not you." His hand comes into my hair. I shake it off.

"You're telling me I could have helped you last time?"

His lips twist up on one side, in a tired smile. "You mad now?"

"Hell yes. Why didn't—a"

His eyes shut. He interrupts, "It wouldn't work. We needed marrow at so close to the same time. The more the better, for each patient. Willard didn't think you'd have enough. And 8/10 isn't bad. Sometimes it's fine."

"But it wasn't," I fume.

He strokes my cheek with his thumb. "Yeah. I needed you."

"You don't look pissed off!"

"I'm not."

"So zen." I look at his face: pale and tired, like usual right now. So fucking hot, my guy. Why is he here?

Before I get a chance to get all philosophical, he rubs his foot against my leg and goes on. "Right about then is when I asked for your info. I was here, just me. Pissed off. And I was going to write you and say 'Guess what, it didn't matter, he died anyway,' but I don't know…" He shrugs. "I guess I couldn't."

I smile softly. "No. Of course you couldn't."

His eyes flare a little. "I wrote you more letters."

"What do you mean?"

He rubs his eyes, looks into mine. "I wrote to you all the time from my family's cabin. After I got discharged last time, I was so fucked up. My head was fucked. I was up there by myself, until they brought me Truman. I started telling you things, talking to you like you were all I had. I didn't send that shit. But you're how I ended up in Georgia. Figured at least one good person was there. Barrett's stationed there, Ft. Benning, but he's never stateside."

"Wow." My eyes sting as I prop my head in my hand and look up at him. "I didn't know that. I would never guess. Can I…sometime can I see the letters? The ones you didn't send me?"

"Yeah. I've got them."

"Here?"

He nods. "Manning sent them. I asked him to."

That really…makes me feel good. And more secure. As if he really does care for me.

I smile—almost grin. He liked me. Kellan liked me, way back when.

"I'm really glad," I say. "What are the odds, you know? It's almost unbelievable that we met at school. That we were both dealing. I'm sorry," I correct, smirking. "You were supplying and playing Robin Hood, and I was dealing like the bad bitch I am. It's like one of those cheesy local news stories."

He nods. "You being a dealer and at Chattahoochee College—that's some crazy shit. A hell of a coincidence."

"Because it's not…"

SIXTEEN

Cleo

September 25, 2014

"What makes the desert beautiful," said the Little Prince, "is that somewhere it hides a well..."

—Antoine de Saint-Exupéry, The Little Prince

Today is Kellan's last day of chemo. Yesterday after we talked, we had our best night here so far. Arethea gave us a chess board, and Kellan was a shark, acting like he felt shitty and then checkmating my sad self in no time flat.

We played three times before bed, and every time, he kicked my ass. And then the lights went out, and we had such a good time. So much better than I ever would have thought would be possible in a hospital.

It wasn't just what we did—although that was pretty damn good too—it was the time after. Kellan stretched out on his back and pulled me to his chest, and wrapped his arms and leg around me and played with my hair. And as we fell asleep, he made the ASL sign for "I love you" with his hand...and followed it with the sign for "I'm sorry."

"Kellan—no. You're not sorry. No sorry. I reject your 'sorry.'"

He sighed, but I got him to agree. We fell asleep with him more in my arms than me in his. Dr. Willard lowered the dose of steroids he got through the IV overnight, so he slept peacefully and woke up before mid-morning, for once.

He woke me up with a cinnamon roll he ordered for me from a nearby bakery. Unlike the oblivious days at his house, I noticed when he didn't have any breakfast besides a few sips of the TwoCal.

All morning, he talked to me and touched me and looked at the quotes I wrote inside another batch of origami sparrows. When the PT person came and made him do a shoulder workout, he didn't complain. When Dr. Willard came in with a bowl of rice and awful gravy (nothing like the South!), Kellan downed most of it—and then lounged on the bed with a can of Dr. Pepper.

We watched the first episode of *Orphan Black* sitting side by side, shoulder-to-shoulder, and then Kellan fell asleep leaning against me.

Nice, right?

But not nice. Because about this time, the room phone rings. The transplant unit's mail person tells me I have a package.

Gotta get it fast. It's marijuana tincture from Manning.

I slip my Ugg mocs on, strap on a face mask, shimmy my hands into gloves, and walk to the opposite end of the BMT ward. I get my package, and on my way back to the room, I notice a homey little sitting area, where I decide to stop off and call my mom.

She knows nothing about my situation. Just that I came to New York about a week ago. Now that Kellan and I have talked more, I'm feeling braver, so I drop into a leather wing-backed chair and dial her number.

And, surprisingly, I get her.

More surprisingly, instead of telling her a half truth, I tell her the whole damn story. It takes almost an hour and a half, and just as I get up to go—eager to see Kellan again—the phone rings. It's Cindy from Be The Match, telling me what I already know: my recipient is at Sloan-Kettering Memorial.

I guess some of the stress is definitely starting to ease up now that Kellan's talking to me some, because I chat with Cindy for a few minutes, telling her how he and I met each other. She says she wants to interview us both for Be The Match's e-newsletter.

"You have quite a story."

I agree.

I hustle down the hall, worried about how long I was away, but telling myself I should obviously chill out. The first few days were bad, yes—apparently Kellan had a strong dose of radiation before I arrived, and that made his bone pain much worse—but everything is so much better now.

So of course, as I open the door to our room, I can hear the awful sound of retching. I race to the blue-tiled bathroom and find Kellan curled up on his side between the shower and the toilet, unable to even lift his head as spasms wrack him.

"Kell... oh shit." I drop down and touch his sweaty back.

"Cleo!"

"Oh. Shhh, baby…" As his shoulders clench and harsh gags echo off the walls, I try to clasp his forehead so his face is off the floor. He pulls away.

"No, don't." I gather him against my knees me as he trembles and groans. "Oh baby—" God, I need to get a towel—a "It's okay…" He manages to stop the heaving, breathing hard and hoarsely. "Can you get up? Let's get you to the bed."

I try to help him off the floor and have to page Arethea because he's so heavy, so unsteady. The two of us get him up and moving toward the door, but after just one small step, he stops to curl over the sink.

The retching is relentless. There's nothing in his stomach now but bile, which burns his throat. Arethea starts another anti-nausea drug and gives more Zofran too, and brings wet rags and stickers we put on his wrists.

But nothing really helps. I find myself holding poor, exhausted Kellan by the shoulders, bracing his head against the bed rail as he gets sick so many times, he actually starts to drop off to sleep between dry-heaves.

I clean his face and throat, and wash hair. Arethea brings another bag of the offending chemo.

"The last one," she offers sadly.

Kellan rouses around midnight. When he tries to talk, his eyes spill tears.

"Damnit. I'm so sorry..."

I spoon a shard of ice into his mouth, then drop the spoon in my lap.

"Holy shit! I'm such an idiot."

The package I originally left the room to get is the marijuana tincture, one Manning told me Kellan made himself, for chemo patients.

I call Arethea in, propose a plan, and when she doesn't come back for an hour, I know I've been given my signal. She asked Dr. Willard, who felt no bad would come of it. It's permission, if not an actual endorsement.

I give Kellan two droppers full and after that, he sleeps.

He wakes up in the early afternoon on the official "rest day," and blinks at the ceiling. I can tell he's high, and not from Morphine or one of its icky derivatives, but from good ole fashioned reefer.

His face is looser. He's more apt to smile. Like when he sees the origami sparrows shivering over us.

"Birds," he whispers. "Lot of birds." He blinks at me, a little smirk on his face. "I want to... get up," he whispers.

I help him out of bed, and we walk to the window. I can feel him trembling.

"You want to try to get a shower? You sit down in there? I'll help you?" He nods, taking a handful of my hair and looking down at it.

I giggle. "High Kellan. Sit here in this desk chair first and let me change the sheets again."

I put on the Batman sheets I bought him, just for fun, and then we get into the shower. He holds onto my shoulder, and I bathe him carefully. By the time we're ready to get out, he's pressing his dick against my thigh. His eyes are dark with desire.

He takes my hand as we walk to the bed. He hands a condom to me—one of the flavored ones I bought—and I smile. "Yeah?"

He nods, and works his pants down chiseled hips.

"God, your dick is beautiful. If you want this, I can't wait to give it to you."

I roll the rubber over him and suck him into my mouth. After a few thrusts, a few sharp moans, he stops me.

"Not feeling well?"

He shakes his head and puts a hand on my arm. "I don't want to come," he whispers. "I don't want to fall asleep."

"Why don't you want to? Sleep is good."

He shakes his head and pulls me down beside him on the mattress. "I don't like it. I can't feel you there."

SEVENTEEN

Cleo

THE MARIJUANA TINCTURE IS A GAME-CHANGER. After a long night's sleep, Kellan wakes up feeling good. He seems so comfortable and happy when the doctors do their morning rounds, Willard decides to cut back sharply on the remaining IV painkillers. After a pancake breakfast he attacks with comical enthusiasm, Kellan nods off in the recliner, thumbing through *The Wall Street Journal.* I use the quiet time to sit on the love seat near the window and have a text with my sister.

Around lunch time, I move over to the bed and bring my laptop out. I'm combing through my list of favorite quotes when Kellan's eyes flip open.

"Cleo, fuck. My dick…" He blinks around the room, looking dizzy. His gaze smashes into mine. "Is this a wean?"

"A what?" I slide down off the bed and stand over his chair.

He reaches for my hand and brings it down to his cock, which even through the cotton of his pants, is so hard I can almost feel his pulse in it.

"Dilaudid," he rasps. "When they cut it back, I get these crazy fucking boners. I need to be inside you…now."

His eyes are dazed from all the tincture he's been taking. I grab a condom and urge him over to the bed, where he sprawls out on his back and draws his knees up. I can see his thick erection straining at his pants.

I rub my palm over the bulge and Kellan grabs my shoulders. "Fuck…please. Now."

I giggle, cupping his balls. Kellan squeezes me between his knees and thrusts toward my face.

I throw the sheet over us, and, crawling in between his legs, I press my breasts against his cock as I untie his pants and draw them slowly down his hips.

His cock pops out, pointing straight up. I feel a throb of warmth between my own legs as I notice the pre-cum pearled over his little slit.

I touch my tongue to it and work his pants a little farther down.

"Shit." He grips my shoulder, and I kiss his dick.

He groans. I plant my hand around his thick base, leaving his pants bunched underneath his heavy balls. I know I'm mean, but I love it. If he tries to writhe around, he'll be restrained a little.

I suck his head into my mouth and start to lick around the rim. He moans and rocks his hips, forcing his thick rod down my throat. His head and shaft are pulsing as I take him deeper…move back up.

"Fuckkkk..." Just two times deep-throating him, and his legs are trembling. One more and I can feel him swell and tighten in the condom.

"Mmmmm." I hum, and Kellan pants like he is running.

"Cleo…" I can feel how thick he is, how hard, how tight the rubber is under my tongue. He grabs my head and holds me down, filling my throat with so much dick, I'm gagging and my eyes sting.

"Jesus…Cleo… *Ahh*." He thrusts, his ass lifting off the bed. His thighs quiver… He's moaning like it hurts, except I know it doesn't.

Damn, his cock is sexy buried in my throat. I love the way his balls draw even tauter as I tickle them. I run my fingertip along the seam and Kellan barks. A little half thrust and he's gone, exploding in the rubber, pulling at my hair.

"Oh God…oh fuck!"

I run my tongue around him as he quakes beneath me.

"Fuck." He strokes my hair. He grabs my jaw. "Look up here."

I do, and find his eyes earnest. His cheeks are stained crimson. I stroke his thigh.

"You like that, baby?"

"Fuck yes." He tugs my shoulder. "Get up here. Come lie beside me. Spread those legs."

I do, and he fingers my pussy so expertly I'm biting at his chest to keep from screaming. With his fingers buried in me, Kellan starts to pant.

I reach for him and feel how hard his cock is. "Like a rock," I murmur. He thrusts into my hand.

I stroke him. He fills me with his fingers, swirls his thumb around my clit. I come stroking his hard, hot cock. As I pulse around his fingers, Kellan jets into my hand.

Afterward, he's still half hard. I laugh. "Are you serious with this?"

"I told you." His eyes are wide and brighter than I've seen them in days. "All day. Tomorrow too. Is tomorrow the rest day?"

"Tomorrow is your first day after transplant, K."

"Fuck. So that's today." He wraps a tissue around himself. I move his hand and clean his thighs.

"Too stoned to keep track of the days," I tease him. "It's okay. I've been taking my pre-donation meds, and I feel fine. I'm all ready. In fact, I think I'm supposed to get a shower."

He's quiet as we walk into the bathroom. I start the water, strip my clothes off, and pretend not to lust after his gorgeous man meat as he drops his pants. I catch his eyes flick to his reflection in the mirror before I help him remove his shirt, while being mindful of the IV lines. The left side of his chest is still bruised. Shoulder too.

He's leaner. Leaner in the legs and hips. He's still wide up top, but it's a different kind of top-heavy. His arms are more sinewy, his shoulders squarer.

"Mmm," I kiss his bicep, "that's a .gif right there."

He rocks himself against my leg and wraps his hand around my breast. "You're a .gif. I need a file for when you're not around."

"I'll always be around."

I strip out of my clothes. He whistles. I move the IV bag to its hook inside the shower and we step in, clutching each other.

I giggle at his dick.

He smiles a little, looking tired around the eyes.

"You feel okay?" I touch his forearm.

"I like being with you." An earnest answer. Thank you, marijuana. His hungry hands wash me. He fingers me again until I come under the shower spray. Then he strokes himself until his lids are low, his nipples taut.

"Why are you still here?" he asks as he works his cock.

I grab his balls and kiss his chest. "Because when we get out, I get to take this home." I grin. He smiles a little. "What a horny boy, and feeling so good too. Why don't you sit down on this bench?"

He does so without question. I climb up on his lap and sink down on his tortured cock. We come fast, both gasping. We step out onto the rug together, tangled in each other. I dry myself and then help him.

He leans down so I can dry his hair, and when I rub the towel over it, it comes away in patches.

He lets me shave his head with shears I ordered for this very day, and when I present him with the soft gray beanie hat I ordered on my second day here, he shuts his eyes and pulls me up against him. His lips move gently over my cheek.

He sits by the windows as the sun goes down. After a few minutes cleaning up the room and rearranging the pillows and covers, I join him on the little love seat, which we have pointed toward the window.

"So…no hair," he murmurs.

"No hair and a lovely boner."

There's nothing we can do but laugh.

EIGHTEEN

Kellan

"I UNDERSTAND SHE'S IN RECOVERY." I puff my breath out, wrap my hand around my iPhone. "What I'm asking is if you can have Arethea call me. Right away."

The nurse in outpatient surgery makes a growl-like sound. "I don't know this woman, Arethea," she snaps. "She may work at this hospital but she doesn't work in our department. I told you everything I can. Our system shows that Autumn Whatley is no longer in surgery, but is now in recovery. That's more than I should tell you, Mr. Whatley. You could be anybody. Especially since Mrs. Whatley did not check the 'married' box on any of her intake forms."

"We were separated. Back together now. It's not my fault you don't have current information."

"Congratulations, Mr. Whatley. Can I help you in any other way?"

I hang up the phone and walk from the window to the dresser. It's true, I swore I wouldn't leave the room, but Arethea swore she would fucking call me. If Cleo's been in recovery for more than an hour, something's wrong. I'm going down to find out what it is.

I have to hold onto the arm of a chair to get out of my black lounge pants and into a pair of jeans that Cleo bought me. I don't have time for underwear.

Even though I know I've lost some weight, I'm shocked by how easily I can wear the smaller size. When I button them, I've got about an inch of slack. Well, fuck. That's why I brought a belt, I guess.

Threading the belt through the loops is fucking hard as shit with my hands shaking like this. Drives me fucking crazy. Everything is so damn slow. And it's so cold in here. What the fuck is that thermostat set on? I pull on a button-up and look down at my chest as I button it. This is the real test of whether the weights I've got hidden under the desk have helped me maintain any muscle mass.

It's not snug like it was. But it's not that loose.

I hope tomorrow I can lift again. Maybe ride the stationary bike, or fuck Cleo from on top. Other than praying to the porcelain god right after Arethea came with a wheel chair for Cleo, this detox hasn't been so bad. I feel like shit, of course, but that's to be expected. Feeling lousy, jacking off all day.

The feeling shitty isn't new for me. I haven't felt great since January at least, when I noticed the first signs of the relapse. I'm actually better now that all the blasts in my blood have been killed off by the pre-transplant chemo.

My heart pounds as I think about the next few weeks. If I remember right from last time, that's when things get really bad. I hate it when my counts are this low. Always tired. All the fucking rashes and other stupid problems that go along with having no immune system.

I finish buttoning the shirt and look over in the corner where my shoes are. The door opens and I whip around, so fast I almost lose my balance. I see the front end of a bed wheeled in, and glee and anxiety hit me all at once.

I feel a deep trough of grief from out of fucking nowhere, that she had to go through this without me. Someone numbed her lower body and dug around her bones, and it wasn't my hands she was squeezing. I had Arethea give her a letter to read while they prepped her, but that's nothing. I should have been there. My presence at the surgery is one of many things I can't give her. I'm such a selfish fuck for what I'm doing.

Arethea smiles as she wheels the bed through my door. I stalk over, finding Cleo on her side, facing away from me. She's covered with these horrible white blankets that must be made in some third-world dungeon. I can see her hands clasped loosely out in front of her.

I'm too afraid to walk around the bed, so I flick my eyes to Arethea's brown ones. "Why is she on a bed?" I snap. "Is that a hep lock?" I ask, nodding at the IV in her hand. "I thought she would be discharged. What went wrong?" My heart pounds desperately as I walk around the bed and— Cleo's smiling.

"Hey you," she whispers.

My chest flares with heat. The room tilts. My cock throbs. Fucking withdrawal.

Arethea starts rolling the bed again, over toward a corner of the room where there's some empty space for a guest cot.

"Not there," I snap. She turns. I wave at my bed. "I don't want her in that crappy cot at all. It looks like shit. It's a fucking slab of metal with a lumpy mattress and four wheels. Put her in my bed."

Arethea smirks at me, and the smirk turns into a smile. "I see papa bear," she teases.

Cleo's eyes are on me. "I want to stay here for right now. It's okay. Just come and see me. I want to hold your hand."

I feel like an ass for not being by her side already, but I want this right. I move my bed over, so Arethea has room for Cleo's cot between my bed and the half-wall where the desk is, so if we're both lying down, Cleo is facing me.

I sigh, then run my hands over her hair. I lean over and kiss her forehead.

I give her the pink fleece blankets that I used to wrap the brick when I brought it to her at the Tri Gam house, and then her pillow, and then a stuffed sloth that makes her grin.

"I love him. And you."

"I love you too."

I wish I didn't. I wish more that she didn't. But who the fuck can change these things?

NINETEEN

Kellan

October 10, 2014

I JUST GOT THE NEWS THAT Cleo's angel marrow is engrafting. I kiss her head and pull her against me, even though she's sleeping. After the orgasms I gave her this morning, she was worn out. When she wakes up an hour later, I've got her chicken pizza waiting on the table.

She hangs another sparrow as she eats the pizza.

I watch from the love seat by the window. "What's that one say?"

"You might think it's cheesy." She smiles.

"Try me," I tell her.

"Okay." She wipes a strand of hair out of her green eyes. "It's by this author named Louise Erdrich. Honestly, I don't know her, but I saw this one on Tumblr, and I love it. Ready?" She holds up the unfolded paper. "It says, 'You have to love. You have to feel. It is the reason you are here on Earth. You are here to risk your heart.'"

I blink as heat fills my chest and throat. "Is that what you think?" I ask softly.

"Of course." She laughs, and steps over to rub her hand over my beanie.

I'm tired as fuck today, like every day lately, but I've got discipline left over from my football days. I drag myself over to the stationary bike, and ride until my ribs and shoulder ache. Cleo tries distracting me by reading dumb news from a celebrity gossip web site.

When I'm done, she helps me down and wipes my face with a cool towel. I fucking love this girl so much.

I tell her that.

She reaches up to touch my bald head, which for some reason, she's decided that she loves. We watch a *Game of Thrones* episode while I struggle with my dumbbells. I try not to feel like a loser when I don't finish the workout. Too tired.

I sleep so much the next few days.

One afternoon, after a nap that lasted all morning, I wake up with a temporary tattoo—a blue butterfly on the inside of my wrist—and Cleo blowing bubbles, cackling as she waves the bubble wand above me. "Are you high enough to appreciate them?"

I laugh. "Are you?"

I've been taking tincture every day. Willard knows and doesn't care. He says whatever works. And it does work. I'm weak regardless, but at least this way, I've been able to avoid the opiate painkillers. Either way, I won't remember most of this in a few months, but at least with the marijuana tincture, I'll be able to enjoy it as I live it.

Later, as we lie in bed watching HGTV, my mind cycles back around to that though. I realize why it stood out.

...in a few months.

I stroke Cleo's arm and offer her a glimmer of the hope I'm feeling right now.

"When we get out of here," I whisper to her hair, "I'll take you all over New York."

Cleo

It's the first comment he's made about us leaving here. I take it as a good sign, and I'm glad I do. We have a great night, wrapped up in each other's arms, sharing stories from our childhoods. It's perfect time—and so damn short.

The next day, Kellan gets the mouth sores I've heard so much about. His mouth and stomach hurt so much he's shaking in my arms as he tries not to swallow. Within a few hours, Willard brings the pain pump back.

But I know what to do for him this time. I know what comforts him. And I know how to wait.

I read *Gone Girl*, a few more things from the prolific J.S. Cooper, and a book called *Night Owl* by M. Pierce. I touch myself under the covers, rubbing the sole of my foot over Kellan's leg, as if that will make him more involved.

A whole week passes in this state: Kellan sleeping, giving me dazed, heavy-lidded looks, and leaning on me like a California redwood as he lurches to the restroom.

I get good at origami sparrows. After the aching quiet of his first few days asleep, I accept losing him to the Dilaudid again. Because I really think I'm going to get him back.

TWENTY

Cleo

October 12, 2014

FOR EIGHT DAYS, KELLAN SLEEPS. On the ninth day, his mouth and throat seem better, so Dr. Willard starts to wean the pain pump.

The following few days amaze me. Kellan's blood counts started rising—like they should—while he was on his Dilaudid vacation, but until Dr. Willard cut the dose, I didn't get a chance to see him doing better.

After a week spent mostly in bed, I thought he'd be too weak to even move—and he *is* weak. We walk down the hall the first night he's awake again, his arm intertwined with mine, and have to stop a lot of times for him to catch his breath.

We have to wear face masks when we leave the room, so I can't see his mouth, but I'm pretty sure he smiles almost the whole time. We make a big show of looking at the pictures on the wall when he's tired and needs to stop, and when we've walked enough to see them all, he stops and tucks my hair behind my ear as he catches his breath.

"You're pretty."

I tug his gray beanie down around his ears and kiss his chin. "You are."

His happy eyes look sleepy. We walk back to his room with our arms around each other, Kellan's free hand pushing the IV pole. Arethea whistles as we reach the door.

"The two love birds," she teases, in the soft Brazilian accent that I've come to love. She smiles at Kellan, then touches his cheek. "Up and moving. Onward, onward!"

She comes into the room with us, and when she leaves, we stretch out on the bed together. I tug Kellan's beanie off.

I swear, his lack of hair makes his eyes stand out more. All the weight he's lost hones his features in the best possible way—showing off his beautiful bone structure. No one has ever looked so perfect. Now that he's awake again and able to reciprocate, I can't keep my hands off him.

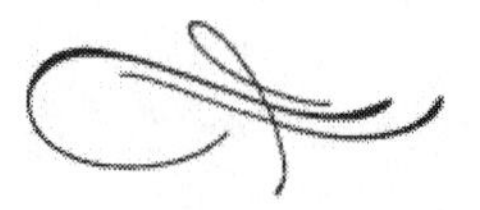

Our next endurance exercise is the following morning, when we go down the hall to the kitchen to cook eggs and toast.

Kellan insists on eating a few bites, even though all he's required to eat today is TwoCal and three cups of yogurt. We walk the halls for longer than I would have thought possible.

Kellan tells me where he grew up, in this cottage overlooking the Pacific Ocean. He tells me about a trip he took to Georgia with his family when he was little. About his first kiss—a girl named Molly, in the coat closet in his first grade class—and about his peewee, middle school, and high school football days.

He tells me about how his mother was an artist who got breast cancer. He says it "got her" fast. His dad was stunned.

"He felt like he failed her." It sounds like Robert Sr. withdrew from his kids emotionally, but he tried to watch over them anyway. A control thing, I guess. The result was he used a heavy hand and little of what felt like love—and things are still that way. Kellan tells me he came here late the first night Kellan was here.

"He just…stood by the bed. I was…wearing oxygen or whatever. Because I'd had so much Dilaudid, and I wasn't used to it yet." I nod as we look out the window of our room. Kellan's shoulders rise as he inhales. They sink as he exhales. I lean against him. "He did one thing. He messed with the oxygen tubing. Adjusted it or whatever. And then he left."

"He didn't say a word?"

I watch him swallow. Watch him struggle.

"It's okay." I take his hand. His longer, stronger fingers lace through mine. "It doesn't matter." I rub my lips over his knuckles. Then I press his hand against my cheek.

"He said you're an asshole," Kellan rasps. "And assholes win."

I blink back tears.

All morning, he tells me all about himself. How much he loves the ocean. How he wants to smell the salty air, and how he scuba dives. How he can cure my fear of deep water. How we can fly kites over the sand. We sit on the love seat, looking at the city, and I shift so my legs are wrapped around him, and he lies between my legs. He's looking at the ceiling and I'm stroking his shoulders when he talks about last time he was here. How Lyon's room was right by his, down on the pediatric transplant floor, and he could hear his brother and Whit laughing while he laid alone in his room.

"I didn't like the bed," he says, quiet. "That's why I didn't get in it at first."

I nod, pretending I'm not shredded, and blink back my tears. "You've got me now." I rub his neck. "The bed is the best place."

We move to it to watch a show, and even during that, he's open in a way he's never been before. He shares his thoughts and makes some jokes. He puts me in between his legs and folds himself around me from behind.

He falls asleep just after lunch and I tuck the fleece blankets around his shoulders, then curl up beside him. I've gotten used to napping, too.

I wake up to find him leaning his cheek in his palm, watching me. I lift my head and realize his other hand is stroking my hair.

I stick my tongue out, then grin, because I kind of love it—his attention. "You watched me while I was sleeping?"

"Only fair." He smiles.

I run a finger over his cheek, where the bruises from the wreck are almost gone. "I guess so. I could probably sculpt you now, as much as I've watched you. I drew you lots."

His eyebrows lift. "Is that right?"

I smile and nod. "You want to see? I'm not much of a sketch artist, but you might get a laugh."

"Yeah, let me see."

I go to the desk for my portfolio briefcase, and when I open it, I find three yellow legal pads. They're filled with Kellan's handwriting. I whip around toward him.

"What are these?"

I look back down and notice a sparrow tucked into the briefcase. It's folded badly. "You did this?" I flash a grin at him.

He just smiles, and I bring the things back to the bed. "Shall I unfold it? Did you write on the inside?"

His mouth twitches a little with his tired smile. "Look and see."

I unfold it to find a quote I wrote myself.

Followed by Kellan's familiar penmanship.

One night you fell asleep and you had written this but hadn't folded it. I crumpled it up and threw it under the bed. You didn't see it there for a day or two—or maybe one, or ten—but I found it again yesterday in the night stand drawer. I think I understand it now.

I understand, a little more, why this happened to me. Or if not that, I see the parts that are good. (Hint: The good part is all you).

The notebooks are from after last time, when I was at my family's cabin upstate. After you wrote me back the first time, I wrote you every day. At the time I thought it was because I was so lonely. I had a hard time after Lyon's death. I couldn't leave the cabin much. These notebooks got me through. But now I think I somehow knew you would be mine. Maybe I could sense the way things ended up. I find I kind of like to think that.

I love you, Cleo Baby. Thanks for making things make sense.

I lift the notebooks out. I was wrong at first glance; there are three of them, not two, and they are filled completely, back and front of every page. I blink against my tears. His tongue laps at them when they fall.

I cover my face. "Sorry, I'm being stupid."

His hand rubs over my hair as his voice rumbles near my ear. "Not stupid. Tell me why you're crying."

"It makes me sad that you were lonely."

He laughs, a rich chuckle. "Cleo baby... Don't do that. I'm trying to say it helped. Writing to you. Made me better. That's what you are. You're my medicine."

TWENTY-ONE

Cleo

October 15, 2014

"OH MY GOD, HOW DID YOU knoooow? Chocolate caramel sea salt cupcakes. Mmmmm." I swallow a bite of moist chocolate cake and luscious icing and flop back onto Kellan's lap. "Total mouth-gasm."

He arches a brow. "You want an orgasm in your mouth?"

I lean my head against his thigh. "Mmm. Maybe."

"I know what I want..." He trails a finger down my chest and grazes my nipple.

"Shower?" I grin.

He squeezes and I struggle not to shriek.

"We had one..." he twists; I pant..."this morning."

"But I'm dirty."

I can't resist delving between his crossed legs. He's wearing lounge pants, so I can feel every line of his perfect cock.

"Okay..." I sit up. "Shower it is."

We get off the bed, Kellan grabs a condom from their home in my purse, and he urges me toward the bathroom with his palm on my back.

I can't help thinking, as he strips off both our clothes, that just a few weeks ago I was undressing him and helping him wash. Starting when he woke up after his mouth sores healed, we had sex dozens of times with Kellan lying in the shower and me riding his dick. But things are better now. He's stronger. The last few days, I kneel on a folded towel while Kellan pushes into me from behind.

There are times now when the IVs aren't hooked up, so no more watching for the IV lines. If we time it right with nurses' shifts, we can have sex two times a day some days.

I turn around and run my eyes over his chest, down to his hips... then to his cock, which juts up to his abs.

I run my hands over his hard, lean sides... over his hips—such a perfect V—and take his dick in my hand.

"Mm." He reaches for my breasts, then leans down and bites my neck. He walks me backward into the shower, snatches a towel off the top of the shower wall, and tosses it onto the floor.

"Get down there. Put your fingers in your pussy. Spread it open for me."

He starts the water... kneels. I feel his hand brace on the shower seat and then he slams into me.

"You like that," he says, husky. "I can feel you get all tight... your pussy grabs me." He pushes deeper, and I slip down on my forearms.

"Bigger..." I groan. "Feels... nff. You... feel bigger."

Kellan chuckles. His arm wraps around my waist, his hand splayed over my wet hip.

I push against him with my muscles, welcoming as much of him as I can take, until I'm so full I'm moaning, heedless of who hears. His hand slides down my belly, fingers parting my lips... He lightly touches my clit, rolling his fingertip through my slit where I'm slick, then rolling back around my swollen bud, just grazing it...

I thrust back against him. "Ohhh.... that's good."

"You're so tight. Fucking... ahh. So—" he thrusts—"fucking tight and hot and wet for me... My little slut. Sticking things... into your pussy... while I slept. Sucking me off... Oh... couldn't stay away could you?"

His finger rolls over my clit, causing it to throb... My cunt tightens around him. Kellan moans.

"I made you come in the hallway, didn't I? Touching...your greedy little pussy...like right now. You're sopping wet. I feel those hips shaking...so full...full of cock... I've got you all filled up...all stretched and swollen. All except your asshole." His hand leaves my pulsing clit, grazing the base of his cock, stroking up...up toward my tight hole. His fingertip teases cruelly...applying pressure as my pussy clamps around his pounding cock.

"I think if I slide into you, your pussy would get real tight on my cock. Tight enough to hurt... Bear down baby." I do, and he shoves inside.

"Ahh!" It always stings a little at first. He holds still, letting me adjust, then pushes in until he's buried to the knuckle.

"Fuck," I grunt. His finger's wide.

I can feel him sagging over me. "So tight... oh God, I'm gonna come in you... I wanna fill you up..." I clench around his dick and push against him one more time, until his cock has split me open and his finger is deep in my ass. It feels so good. I quiver and keep thrusting my hips. His cock swells and hardens and I feel his finger curl.

"Fuck... fuck. Oh Cleo." He spasms, and then I'm filled with pulsing warmth.

"Ohhhh, yes." I sag. He holds me to him. "Ahhh." He draws gently out of me and leans against the wall. I rest my cheek against his heaving chest.

His hand trails over my hips, between my leg. He cups me. "I can feel it dripping out of you..." He parts me with his fingertip and eases just a little of it inside, where—he's right—I'm full and dripping.

"Mmm." Inside I'm full... it's warm... his fingertip feels good... the way they stretch me... "Kellan..." I giggle, pushing at, then pulling on his hand.

His mouth brushes my ear. He drags his finger up and down my slit. "What do you think? You want me to stop now?"

"No..."

His free hand cups my breast. His finger eases in... and then another one. I grunt. "You sure?"

I grip his forearm. "I want..." His fingers writhe. I clamp around him.

"Mmm... I could do this all day—and all night."

"Forever," I moan.

He kisses my neck, and fingers me until I scream. And helps me up, and wraps me in a towel. Then his robe.

We're back in bed in time to play some *Call of Duty* before Areteha starts the next round of IVs.

I lie on my side with Kellan's big, warm body tucked around mine. We both fall asleep, and when we wake up at half past nine, there's chicken pizza on the table.

Kellan yawns and shrugs. "I got a craving."

I drip ranch under the collar of his shirt and pull it up so I can lick it off his pec. We go to sleep like that, except I don't need as much sleep as he does, so I'm up at three a.m.—just me and the hospital room. I slip out of the bed and walk over to the windows. Look down at the busy streets.

I wonder what it's like, a night in New York? It's so weird that I've been here for almost a month and haven't even had a hot dog from a street cart.

I look over at the bed, where Kellan's sleeping on his side. The tiny, plastic IV tube stretches over the mattress, delivering... hmm? Steroids? Or that drug for GVHD, a post-transplant complication that's making his blood counts a little weird.

I walk slowly over to the bed and look down at him... really look at him. Now that he's getting fewer fevers, and we've got our pretzel sleeping position established, he never wears the beanie when he sleeps.

I let my eyes trace the curve of his head. Perfect. The other day, Lora asked me how I handle being here. All the unpleasantness... the hard days and the pain and sweat and blood and sometimes tears. I couldn't tell her. If you've never been here like I have, you wouldn't understand.

How every drop of sweat is precious. The overpowering evergreen mouthwash... the scentless lotion I would rub on him a few weeks back when his skin got ultra dry and kind of chapped (the GVHD again). I've held him while he cried dozens of times. I know that when he's done, he always hugs my neck and nuzzles up under my chin and strokes my cheek and often says, "sorry." And I never care, because every tear is precious too. If I could bottle them, I would. Wear them around my neck forever, like my origami sparrow.

I walk back across the room, to the little desk where I keep my portfolio. I sit down in the rolling chair and pull the yellow legal pads out of my folder. With my cell phone, I check each pad for dates.

I find the first one, then get up again to get my stuffed sloth from the foot of the bed. I curl my legs up in the chair and hug sloth while I read.

I read all night—and I realize, these aren't letters. This is Kellan's diary; it's just addressed to me. To Sloth.

I smile and laugh and cry onto the pages. It's not easy, reading all his pain. I can't go back in time. I can't even travel forward. I'm stuck here in this day. But in this day, I can do something. So I slip back into bed.

TWENTY-TWO

Cleo

October 20, 2014

FIRST THE DUMBBELLS. Then the stationary bike. I watch him work out while I cross-stitch in the recliner. And when he's done, we get a shower.

We dry each other, slip into our robes—he bought me one—and Kellan heads back for the bed, and *Game of Thrones.*

I head for the dresser drawers and thumb through his clothes until I find the ones I ordered just the other day. A pair of new jeans—32-32, rather than his previous 36-32s—and a soft, cream Irish Aran sweater. Wool socks, check. Ugg moccasins that look like bedroom slippers but have real soles, check.

I grab my own clothes, push a chair under the room's doorknob, and slip into my leggings and my own green sweater.

Kellan whistles.

"I might need a shower."

"Nope!" I drop his clothes at the foot of the bed, and he thumbs through the pile. "Going commando I see."

"Whoops. Forgot your underwear."

He laughs. "I'm wearing them, Cleo baby. Pulled them on before I got up on the bed. For Arethea. Keep her blood pressure down."

I roll my eyes and toss the jeans at him. "Get dressed then. Get."

His face goes serious and smooth, his eyebrows arching. When he speaks, his voice is soft. "Where am I going?"

"Not home yet. Which, duh. But... somewhere. I already got approval for us."

I let down the rail and tug his arm. He tugs back on me, pulling me atop his lap. "You need help dressing?" I tease him. He doesn't—anymore—but honestly, the idea of helping him now is kind of sexy. Kellan has the perfect legs, all sinewy and still remarkably muscular, probably from the obsessive working out he's been doing in the last week.

"To protect my heart," he always says.

I always wink and tell him, "I don't need protection." And then I try to forget what he really means by that: his twin had heart issues from chemo, and Kellan's had a lot of it at this point.

He kisses my jaw, my throat... I push at him. "C'moooon." I throw my arms around his shoulders. "This is gonna be amazing. For at least half of us. The other half that's holding us up right now gets the rubber chicken for dinner." I reach onto the bed side table and grab the actual rubber chicken I ordered a few days ago, as a representative of our favorite horrible hospital meal. Kellan squeezes its head, making it cluck.

"Okay." He drops it on the bed and sets me on the floor, then slides off the mattress. I touch his chest, parting the robe so I can see his lean, hard body. I stroke a finger down his ribcage, just over the broken ones, which are pretty close to being healed now. "I kind of want to dress you. Say yes?"

He smiles smugly, tugging on my tight sweater. "Wear this next shower, and yeah, you've got a deal."

"Kay."

I tug his boxer-briefs down, and Kellan's cock twitches. I pull them back up. "Okay... boxer-briefs, check."

Kellan chuckles as I pool the jeans at his feet, then stroke my palm up his calf. "Right foot first," I tell him, smiling sweetly. It's really weird, I know, but being down here at his feet, coaxing him into clothes, reminds me of how far he's come and makes me happy.

He complies, resting his hands lightly on my shoulders as he steps in. "I don't know these jeans. Are they new?"

"They're very funny. Great to have at parties. Nickname Blue." I run my fingers up his left thigh. "Left foot now."

When he's standing in the jeans, I pull them slowly up his thighs... With one hand gripping them on each side of his hips, I tug a little harder over his boxer-briefs. I catch his now-hard dick in the zipper area on purpose and then reach into the jeans. "Pshh. I'm so uncoordinated."

I fondle his balls, and Kellan hisses. "Damn, woman. You sure you want to leave the room?"

I push his dick down into the pants, then zip and button, giving his bulge a final pat before I grab the sweater. "Yep, I'm sure. And so do you."

I only fondle his chest for a minute before pulling the sweater onto him. When I'm finished, I present the moccasins and Kellan smirks at them. "I'm wearing these puppies outside?"

"They've got real soles."

"If you say so." He turns a slow circle, looking down at himself. "Not bad threads. Right size too."

"I know you inside out." I wiggle my brows. Then I push the gray beanie onto his head.

"You're gonna need this, baldie."

"You know you like this smooth head rubbing on you. When my hair grows back, you'll want it shaved."

I blush, because he's kind of right. It does feel good against my pussy.

We both mask and glove up. I take a moment just to look at his pretty blue eyes before we leave the room. We step into the hall and Kimmie, one of the nurses, grins at us. "You guys going somewhere?"

"Somewhere," I say. We pass Arethea at the nurse's desk and she presses a button behind the counter that opens the doors for us. Kellan's eyebrows shoot up to his hat.

"Well, fuck." It's murmured, husky. I take his hand, and we walk slowly out into the lobby just outside the locked unit. We both stop and look around. It's been weeks since either of us has left the locked unit. If I had left at any time, I'd have had to wear a gown, a mask, and gloves the whole time I was in his room. I couldn't do that—so I stayed.

The air out here feels cool. It smells... like food? Some kind of cleaner. Lemons.

We walk slowly over fresh-waxed tile and into a shining, narrow hall. Kellan stops and grips my shoulder with his gloved hand. "Cleo baby..." He blinks, heavy lidded, his face unreadable. Then he bends down, pulls his mask off, pulls mine down, and kisses my lips. It's gentle, sweet, and painfully brief.

Then we're walking hand and hand again, Hansel and Gretel following bread crumbs. To the elevator. We get in it and he pushes me against the wall. He leans against me, his face in my hair—and I remember. I remember what he told me about the day Lyon died: how he got in an elevator without shoes and fled the hospital.

I wrap my arms around his back and murmur sweetness in his ear. And then the doors tremble open. We shuffle out into a vast lobby.

Once we get a few feet from the elevator shaft, we stop and look around. It smells like car exhaust. People walk past us—real people in real people clothes. They look sad, tired, bored, irritable. They have long hair, no hair, dread locks. One pulls a wagon stacked with luggage. Another carries a small child.

My eyes travel up the columns, toward the glass ceiling several stories up. I look back down to find his blue eyes on me. They look wet maybe. I can't tell. I squeeze his hand.

"Want to keep going?" I whisper.

He nods, and we slowly walk toward the row of glass doors. I get all the doors for us, and when we get outside, I have to resist the urge to throw myself on him and shelter him from all the dangers here. Viruses... bacteria... fungi. For right now, he has no immune system and could catch anything.

For right now, he tips his head up to the sky. His eyes shut. I wrap arms around his waist and press my cheek against his sweater.

I feel him inhale. He murmurs, "Fuck."

When we look into each other's eyes again, I can see his are a little red. Mine probably are too.

I can him smile, despite the mask. "Where you wanna go?" his low voice asks.

I smile back. "The hot dog stand?"

His arm bumps mine, our hands still joined. "Gotta have a chili dog."

"Is that okay?" I feel a little bad, because he can't have one. Because of germs.

His fingers squeeze mine. "I'd say you earned a chili dog."

I giggle. "Maybe just a little."

"I've got one I know you'll like. Tastes best with a little soap and water." I look up, and find a dark spark of arousal in his eyes.

"I'll save room for seconds then."

We get my chili dog. I eat it from the little baggie it comes in, keeping my germy, gloved hands far from my mouth, and then we walk back inside the hospital. Kellan stops inside the doors and looks around.

"I guess you've seen this place a bunch of times."

"Not this last time," he says, almost absently.

"Where did you come in?"

"Around in back. The ambulance entrance."

"So it was plane, then ambulance?" I can't believe I've never asked.

He nods. "Want to see?"

I look up at his face and find it curiously soft. I nod and toss my chili dog trash and Kellan takes my hand.

We walk down a long, white and gray hall that seems to skirt the outside of the building, and Kellan's breathing is more audible. I stop us. I tug at his sweater.

"What are you doing?" he asks.

I smile up at him. "Just brushing off some white lint."

"Are you?" He smirks, because he knows I stopped us so he could catch his breath.

I wink. "Yep. We can resume now."

The walk is long, so I can tell he must really want to go here. And then we reach the "ambulatory transfer" area, and I blink. It looks a little like the warehouse where we met Pace and Manning that night. I see some nurses at a nurse's station, and a door to an ER, but otherwise it's empty.

"Nice place. Lively."

He smiles down at me. I wish I could see his mouth, because based on his eyes alone, the smile looks sad.

"It was lively that day. Lots of people." I can't help wrapping an arm around him. Standing extra close to him. I look up at his face. "People for you?"

He nods.

I squeeze my eyes shut, because I really don't want to make this about me and my guilt.

His gloved hand rubs my arm through my sweater. It's an absent gesture, showing how in tune we are with each other's unspoken thoughts; he doesn't know I feel sick with guilt, but he can tell I need his touch. I watch his eyes circle the room. And I realize with a jolt: I think he wants me to ask.

So I put on my big-girl panties. "What was it like?" I ask softly.

He pulls me under his arm, up against him, then he wraps an arm around my back.

"I don't remember that much," he says, looking thoughtful. "Lots of Dil." That's what the nurses call Dilaudid.

I don't mean to—not at all. But my eyes fill up with tears, and they spill down my cheeks. His eyes widen. He grabs my shoulders. "Hey—what's wrong?" His voice is low and hoarse, and warm... and loving. "Cleo baby..." His arm comes around me. "You want to go back upstairs?"

"No." I press my face into his sweater. I can feel him urge me down the hall. "I'm sorry, Cle. Those lights up on the ceiling? Flashing now. That means they're bringing someone in, in just a second." I open my eyes to see flashing lights over the hall.

"Oh shit. I'm sorry."

We move quickly down the hall, and then we spot an elevator. His hands touch my chest. "Cleo—look at me."

I do.

"Tell me you don't feel... sorry? That you didn't fly with me that day?"

Tears drip down my cheeks. "Of course I do. I hate it that I didn't come. I didn't know what to do, so I did the wrong thing," I whispered. "I took a taxi to my car. Rambled around and figured out the R. connection. And then I got here and…" I shake my head.

"That bad, was I?" I see his cheeks under the face mask. He's smiling. Trying to make me feel better.

"It was that bad. You didn't even look at me."

Kellan pulls me to him, wrapping me tight against his chest. He leans against the elevator's corner and tightens his grip on me, squeezing me so tight it almost hurts. His face presses into my hair. I feel his chest rise with a deep breath...

I hold onto him as we ride up up and then back down... and up again... and down. No one gets into the elevator, so we sink down to the floor and I sit tucked under his arm.

I can barely breathe. My heart is vibrating. My throat is so so full. I can feel it in him too. The things he wants to say are living in the air around us. Tap tap tapping. They are waiting to be heard.

So I'm surprised when he lifts his arm off me and pulls me to my feet. He tucks my hand in his, and we get off on our floor.

We walk to our room with no fanfare, and when we get there, Arethea connects two IV bags and Kellan lies on his side holding his phone, and I snuggle in behind him like I always do.

But when she leaves the room, he cuts the lights and turns toward me and grips my face so hard his fingers maybe bruise me and he whispers: "It was always you. That's what I think. Ask me when my mother died, Cleo."

"When did your mom die?" Chills sweep my skin.

"The day that Olive did."

Tears fill my eyes. I swallow, and they fall.

"Have you ever heard about string theory? Everything is tied together, works together, shrinks, expands, and breathes together. Maybe we're on the same string, baby. We're right beside each other. We're the same thing." His mouth takes mine. He pulls away. "My blood, your blood..." Another kiss... his voice hot on my cheek. "One day I tried to calculate the odds of how we met. The odds of February 14. There are no odds. For us, there are no odds because it isn't chance."

He's inside me mere seconds later. No one pushes the chair under the doorknob. There's no need to. Arethea skips the 2 AM IV—the only time she ever does.

When I wake up in the morning, I'm so hot. Like I'm living on the sun. I turn toward Kellan and my heart sinks.

TWENTY-THREE

THE HOUSE OF CARDS FALLS SO, so fast. I can tell by just one glance that something's very wrong. He's lying on his side, behind me, his right cheek against the pillow. His skin looks slightly gray, his lips a little pale—maybe a tinge of blue. His eyelids sag. His blue eyes almost seem to glow. I don't have to ask what's wrong because I feel him up against me.

He's hot. Really hot.

I turn around to face him. "Kellan?"

I'm so alarmed, I grasp his face. He winces, and I move my fingers off his bruised cheek.

"Shit, I'm sorry. What's the matter?" The fever isn't triggering alarm bells for me. It's the way his face looks. All his coloring is off.

He blinks at me, and his eyes have that glazed quality, which makes more bells peel for me.

He reaches for a strand of my hair. "Nothing," he says. "I'm fine."

But he sounds weird and raspy. Breathless.

My eyes fly to the little box that keeps track of his pulse and the amount of oxygen in his blood.

Pulse is 130, blood oxygen is 92 percent. I lay my hand on his jaw, just below the bruising. I stroke the stubble. "You're not fine. What do you think is really wrong?"

He reaches out for me and pulls me closer. "Just come here..." He tries to tuck me up against him.

"K.—we need to call someone."

His eyes squeeze shut. "Nothing…to…tell them."

"I can see the pulse ox and hear how breathless you are. Talk to me." I stroke his burning brow and feel a sheen of sweat. I look into his eyes in time to see them swim with tears.

"Oh... K. You feel really bad, huh? I'm sorry. Just let me call Arethea and we'll figure out what's up."

He shakes his head, and one tear spills down toward his nose.

I brush it off and lean to touch his temple with my lips. I smooth my palm over his hot forehead and Kellan grabs my forearm. "Cleo—please. Don't call... please. Not yet." He grasps at me. He wraps an arm around me, pulling me to him. Pushing my backside against his dick.

"I want to be inside you... need it. Cleo please." His voice cracks, and I know I have to call Arethea. "Kell, you can. I swear, I'll ride you just as soon as you have oxygen, okay? We have to call. We have to let them know something is wrong."

His hand comes up to his face, and my chest aches. "Kell... You're so strong. You're doing so well. I love you." I reach for the bed's remote, with the call button.

His hand grips my elbow. "Cleo—no." He pushes up, half sitting. He looks pale and dazed. "Don't call. Please. Hold me… I need you. Cleo, trust me—please."

I scoot back toward him, wrapping my arm around him even as I press the nurse call button.

"Yes?" It's Arethea's voice, thank God.

"Hey, could you come here please? Something's up—we need your help."

"Of course."

I look down at Kellan. He's wrapped both arms around me and his head is on my thigh. I'm sitting cross-legged but I shift us so we're lying face-to-face on our sides. I wrap an arm around him... kiss his fingers.

"You're okay. Don't be scared... I'm here. I'll be with you." I smooth my palm over his hair... behind his neck. Good God, he's warm. I feel his back shake on a sob and my heart stops.

"Baby... Hey..." I try to lift his face but he won't move. Arethea bursts in at that second and I'm so confused. She's flanked by several doctors from our team: the pulmonologist, the infectious disease expert, the trial coordinator, and finally, a few seconds later, Dr. Willard himself. Their faces are grim.

My eyes fly to Arethea's, questioning. Her face is careful. "Oxygen," I manage.

She nods, then looks at Willard.

"Kello, baby... It's okay." I kiss his forehead.

Dr. Willard steps to the bed as Kellan curls up to me.

"Cleo—I spoke with Kellan yesterday, while you were meeting with Arethea about the outing."

"What?"

"You ever heard of CMV pneumonia?" he drawls.

I look with wide eyes at the crew at the foot of our bed. "No... What is it?"

They explain: it's something a lot of people have been infected with at one point or another. In people with healthy immune systems, it doesn't cause any problems. He caught it from my blood. My blood was positive for CMV when he received the transplant.

"We've been monitoring him since then. It came up on his blood work recently, and now he's started showing symptoms. We'll need to do some imaging to really know but—"

"If it is, what will you do for it?"

"We've already started treating it with antivirals," Willard tells me. "It's a virus."

"And?"

"It all depends on Kellan." He looks over at Arethea, then at Kellan's pulse ox stats. His pulse is 112 and his blood oxygen level is 95 now.

"This is all the oxygen he can have," she says.

Fuck.

Dr. Willard looks into my eyes. "What he's got is serious. But I think he could beat it. Might have to spend some time on ventilation, but—"

That's all I hear.

A ventilator. Kellan on a ventilator.

Arethea rubs my shoulder as the doctor shakes his head. "I'll be honest, I'll be real surprised if we don't need to try the vent with him, we're on full-blast here and we can't pull a 97, 98... It's not what I'd prefer to see. But Kellan's strong. He can come through this."

I look down at him but I can't see his face. His arm clutches around my middle.

I take a few deep breaths and start my questions. Forty minutes later, all the doctors leave.

Kellan kisses me. "You said." His eyes are tired. "I want to be inside you."

"You've got a CT scan in thirty minutes."

He shakes his head, his grip on my shoulder surprisingly strong. "I need it. I need it."

I wrap my arms around him. "I'm sorry."

His hands rub mine. "I love you. You remember what I said last night?"

I shake my head.

"I love you more than anything."

I nod and cry and stroke his cheek.

He starts pumping his dick. I know what that means. He'll get himself close and then I'll ride him home. We did it more when he was sick.

A ventilator... fuck.

He nods, the signal for when, and I sink down on him, facing his feet. I bounce on him with practiced zeal, rolling his balls in my palm.

Kellan moans and bucks against me. Just when the monitors begin to peel, he spurts in me and grunts. My pussy quakes around him.

"Ahhh. Oh God," I whisper. We cling to each other.

"Cleo baby?"

"Yeah?"

"During the CT... go get me... I want another robe... one with an extra tie... in case... the ICU." His eyes roll slightly, and the pulse ox sounds its alarm.

Arethea comes running. They take him straight back to CT. I veer the other way, like Kellan said.

TWENTY-FOUR

Cleo

"I'M SORRY, MA'AM BUT you're not listed as a visitor."

I thrust my arm out across the desk. "I have an armband. I'm with Kellan Drake. He had a bone marrow transplant."

The woman scans the bar code on my arm band, and I hear a low, discordant thrum. "Your band expired, honey. If you want to get into the ward again, you'll need to have your relative notify us."

"I can't! He's going on a ventilator." I burst into tears. "Please let me in, I have to see him now. I don't have time to wait!"

"Sit down over there." I fidget in a plastic chair as the woman makes calls. Then she beckons me to the desk. "Someone's coming to talk to you."

A moment later, Arethea comes through the doors... pushing a cart. My belongings are heaped on it.

I clamp my hand over my mouth and have to struggle not to pass out.

"He's okay." She nods, and tears start dripping from her eyes.

"Arethea, what the fuck?" My heart is pounding wildly.

"He's okay. Come here..." She steers me around a corner to a more private nook, and sits beside me on a leather couch, wrapping an arm around my back.

"Cleo—" her eyes widen— "he doesn't want to let you back in."

"What?"

"He's worried about this. This ventilator," she explains.

"Are you kidding me?" I feel a swell of panic, followed by a sharp ache in my chest. "Can't you help me? Go get Willard!"

She shakes her head. "Yesterday, the going out. We all knew about the CMV. He planned this. I think he will change his mind. Kellan is strong. You might have to give him time."

"Just give him time?" I start to sob. "I want to talk to him. I need to see him, *please!*"

"I am so sorry."

"You can't do this! You can't just... throw me out!"

Arethea wraps her arms around me. I hop up and pace and try to reason with her. Cut a deal.

"He doesn't want you in there. Not right now," she says softly.

"Talk to Willard. He could let me in!"

She shakes her head. "Kellan is the patient. Cleo, we are with you...in spirit, but I can't let you in against his wishes. You want me to text you?"

"No!" I hold my head and sob so loudly, someone peeks into the little room to see what's going on.

Arethea sits with me until she's paged. She says she'll try to text me. I nod, even though inside I hate her. I hate all of them.

He's mine. Kellan is mine. I won't stop until I get back in.

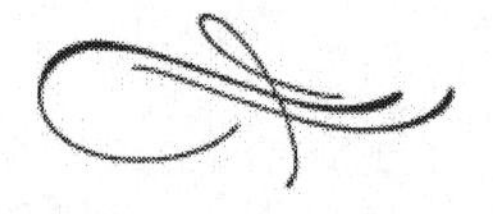

I don't leave the transplant unit's waiting room for three days. Arethea said she'd try to text, but I don't see a message from her. I play on my phone and do sit-ups and change my clothes in a nearby bathroom, never leaving the area outside the locked doors for too long, in case he calls for me.

As for me, I call the ward incessantly. I talk to every nurse I know and beg them all. When someone walks through my waiting room, I try to talk to them. I call Kellan's dad, his brother, leaving messages. I call Manning, Whitney. Nothing.

At the end of the third day, the woman at the desk appears in front of me with a short, red-haired woman, who explains that I can't live here, as they put it.

I give her the Carlyle Hotel's address, and before I leave, she passes me a big, tan envelope.

"Arethea left it for you that first day," she tells me, dashing all my hopes.

I rush to the Carlyle, get a room, and open the envelope in the privacy of my room: a new notebook from Kellan. When did he find the time to write in this? I flip through the pages. Love notes. Three's an envelope as well.

Afterward, it says. Fuck that.

I dress in something clean and go back to the hospital. I shower in the day and sleep in the main lobby at night.

The receptionist who sent me packing can't help noticing I'm back. I tell her our story. She seems sympathetic but she never gives me any news.

Five days pass. I forget to eat, forget to sleep. My mother calls. My phone rings and rings.

Six days.

A week. Unfathomable.

I go wandering the city blocks. I call his phone, and call and call. I buy myself a neck pillow so I can sleep out in the waiting room. The receptionist is my friend now. She says she is praying for me.

Manning shows up on the eighth day, and Whitney on the ninth. Something Whitney says turns my friend the receptionist against me. I'm asked to leave the waiting room and not come back.

I wander the hospital halls. I wonder if I do this long enough, if I can catch his cancer. They would let me in, then.

I ask every day about him. Sometimes janitors I recognize, a few times nurses. No one tells me he's dead. So I assume he is alive. I write him letters. I send them. I start a list of quotes I wrote on the sparrows and one day, in a fit of delirious exhaustion, I walk a few blocks down and get one tattooed on my ribs.

"Unless you love someone,
nothing else makes any sense."
–e.e. cummings

My clothes hang loose. I find a pair of Kellan's narrow-waisted lounge pants in my bag and vow to never take them off. One afternoon—day twelve, I think—I take the subway to the Carlyle and shave my head. My mother comes and tries to make me go. She threatens me, like Kellan's dad did him.

I call his dad's office. I call Manning, begging. Whitney comes again, this time with a plane ticket home. I refuse it. She claims she doesn't know how Kellan is. He made it through the first night on the ventilator, but no one is being updated.

He's on a ventilator. Kellan is.

"So he's in a coma?" My voice sounds dead and dry.

"Cleo... I don't know." She holds my hands. We're in my suite at the hotel. "You need to eat."

"I eat chili dogs. Did you know it's my blood?" Tears leak from my eyes. "I made Kellan sick."

"No you didn't. CMV is common. Very common. He got it at the most likely time for transplant patients to get it."

Whitney pulls me into her arms, and I sleep a little while. She takes me downstairs to the hotel restaurant. I push some eggs around and ask her to go with me to the hospital.

When we get there, she cries. "Cleo—I'm worried. You're so much like I was. After Ly."

"Is he dead? Are you telling me that Kellan's dead? I'm not like you! Lyon is *dead*!"

I run away and don't come back to Memorial Sloan-Kettering for two days. One of them, I drink in central park. I call Kellan's father's office. I call and leave another message for his brother, Barrett.

Manning calls me, asking how I am.

"How's Kellan?" I ask.

"I don't know."

"Liar. Fuck you, Manning. I want to see Truman."

Manning arrives with the dog the next day. Truman is wearing service dog clothes. "He's a PTSD dog. Kellan's service dog."

PTSD from what? But I know the answer: The first transplant. He was alone. I hug the dog. I fall asleep in the waiting room while Manning talks about...something.

I wake up in my hotel room. Manning wants me to eat soup.

I laugh. "I need a feeding tube, or TPN. An IV. I think I have cancer too."

Manning's freckled face goes serious and frowny. "Cleo, you have to stop. He wouldn't like this."

"Wouldn't? Or *doesn't*? Is he dead? Manning, tell me *please*." I start to sob. He shakes his head, like it's a shame, what's happened to me. I shove him. "Go away! If you know nothing, go away!"

That night, when Manning flies back home to man the grow house, I hatch a plan. I wait for my ex-friend the receptionist to leave her desk, and then I hit the "open" button on her desk and dash right through the doors barring the hall.

I run straight to Kellan's room—our room. I throw the door open and nearly pass out from the rush of seeing—

Nothing.

Holy fuck. Our room is fucking gone. The bed is stripped.

Kellan is dead.

I scream and wail. The noises are so strange. They don't sound like me. A second later, nurses burst into the room. I don't even look at them, just throw myself on our bed, clutching the railing as I curl into a ball. "I want to sleep here! One more night... *please, one more night!*"

TWENTY-FIVE

Cleo

"NO! NO, NO! CLEO! Look at Arethea!" Tight hands grab my wrists. "Kellan is not here."

"I know," I sob.

"No! He is discharged! He is discharged!"

"What?" I sit up slowly. My chest is heaving. "What did you say?"

"He is discharged," she says more quietly.

I note the nurses' faces. Sad and sympathetic. They file out. The room goes still. I'm tired, so I lie down on our bed. No more sheets. Arethea reads my mind. She grabs a blanket from the closet. She lies on the bed with me and holds me while I cry.

"He doesn't love me." I sob violently. "He didn't want me."

"It's not true. I held him while he cried for you. It happened many times."

Kellan

November 14, 2014

The apartment I'm renting is on the twenty-first floor of a new high-rise overlooking Central Park.

It's strangely designed, with just three rooms, all made of mostly glass. The bed is just your basic queen, pushed into the corner of two glass walls, at the corner of the corner unit on the twenty-first floor.

I sit on the bed and look out over the city. The park is a dark splotch, with gold freckles: twinkling lights. All around it, buildings gleam. Between sky-scrapers, the sun rises and falls, tossing streaks of color at my windows.

Tonight I watched the sunset sitting cross-legged on the bed, and since then, haven't really gotten up. I watch the world move out my window and am glad I'm up so high; no one can see me.

I found a shirt of Cleo's in my bags—a t-shirt that says GREEK SING—and I'm wearing it, even though it's a small and I've already gained enough weight back to need a medium.

The t-shirt pushes my central line against my chest, and that's uncomfortable. But I don't care. If I had her pants, I'd wear them too. As it is, I wear the pants she bought me. Lounge pants in green and black and blue. I never noticed what she did until I got packed up to leave the unit. How there are three pairs of each pant, two pairs of three waist sizes: 34, 32, and 30. I thought about why, and the only thing I could come up with was that she wanted it to be easy on me, wasting away. When I started dropping weight, she would just rotate the pants out and I wouldn't even notice when my clothes hung loose.

I drop my chin down to my chest and inhale. Do I smell her? She never wore her Green Tea perfume in the hospital, but she still had a scent. I tell myself I'm inhaling it right now. I rub my thumb and forefinger over the seam of my left sleeve and picture her arm in the shirt.

When I had Cleo removed from my visit list, I sent her stuffed sloth and most of the pink fleece blankets with her. I kept one, and Cleo's pillow. Selfish. No surprise there.

I sleep on the pillow every night, and wrap myself in pink blankets. The apartment has a living/area kitchen, too, as well as a large bathroom, but I mostly spend my time in bed. Maybe it's a side-effect of being confined to my hospital room for so many weeks.

I sigh. I stretch my legs beneath the covers, and in the process, I knock over a bowl half-filled with rice, ground beef, and gravy—all of which I made myself.

"Fuck."

I scoop the food into the bowl and set it on the night-stand. Then I hang my legs off the bed's side and take my breathing mask from atop another pillow. Twice a day I have to do this. Attach a cylinder of chemicals onto the bottom of the mask, strap the thing around my head, and breathe as deeply and as slowly as I can.

My lungs are still healing. Willard thinks they'll recover over time, but no one knows for sure.

I was intubated, on a ventilator, for six days, with only moderate sedation, meaning I remember every bit of how it felt to have the tube down in my throat. Sometimes at night, I wake up clutching my mouth, trying to pull it out. Funny, because my nightmares from the first transplant weren't very different really—focused on the mouth sores that, at that time, were the worst thing I'd endured. Before my relapse, I would often wake up with a phantom aching throat.

I chose the moderate sedation as opposed to deeper sleep because I could still move my arms and legs a little. Several times a day, a PT came and made me exercise, which cut down on the muscle loss. I dropped twenty-seven pounds my twelve days in the ICU, and since then, have tried hard to gain them back.

I do what I'm supposed to do, since I got discharged last week. Eat, sleep, lift weights, run on the treadmill in the living room. I have doctor's appointments almost every day. I have a personal shopper, because I can't really leave this space without risking an illness. Sometime in the next six months, that should get better.

After my breathing treatment, I lay down on my back and read a few unfolded sparrows. Even though they're worn and ragged now, I still think of the sheets of paper as sparrows.

I read through them all two times before I curl on my side and lift out the one I'm reading most often right now. It's a poem called "Longing" by Matthew Arnold. The words make tears fall from my eyes. It's nothing new. I cry a fucking lot since I moved out of the unit.

My "outpatient life" counselor keeps pushing me to do a screening for depression, but I know I don't need that shit. I don't need a pill, or some kind of therapy where I talk about my shit with someone who doesn't know shit about me or my life. It's fucking simple really. I like crying over Cleo.

No, it's nothing physiological. They all that shit, all the time. I'm healthy, in those ways at least. I'm A-okay. So what if I never use my dick? I still wake up with wood. My balls ache, telling me to let them blow sometimes, but I don't care. One time I ignored them for six days and woke up in a pool of my own cum.

Pathetic.

Just like last time after discharge, I avoid the mirror, though this time, the reasoning is different. My hair's growing back in—thick, soft gold—and I'm filling out from all the lifting, but I just... don't want to see my face. I think it will make me think of her face. Of her hands in my hair.

I scoot to the bed's edge and press my hand against the glass wall. The cool is soothing. I scoot closer and let my forehead touch as well. It almost feels like a cool hand. Her hand.

I look at the clock: 1:46 AM. I have a blood draw at 8 AM tomorrow morning. I need to go the fuck to sleep. I tug the blankets up to my neck and curl onto my side. Then I push a pillow behind me.

"Goodnight, Cleo. I love you."

Tonight, the darkness seems to leak into my heart. I ache for her. I hold her pillow to my chest and start to cry, so hard and fast it's sobbing.

She's not coming back.

I clench my hands and look at them, and see her hands around them. I need her. I can't fucking breathe without her.

Why am I here?

Without her... I pick up her stack of sparrows and I hug them to my chest. I get my breathing back under control. I swallow an Ativan. Maybe I'm wrong, about the crying feeling good. Right now, I just want to go to sleep.

I wake at 3:11 with a nightmare. I summon her voice. *"You're okay. Don't be scared... I'm here. I'll be with you."*

I'm lying on my side, holding my chest, when someone knocks on my door. Bangs. It sounds so frenzied, my heart starts to race.

Sometimes I think of fires…

I glance at my shirt as I stride into the living room. I look out all the windows, but I don't see flame or smoke. I am the end unit. Sometimes people get lost.

I look out the peep hole imagining her face—so when I see it, I blink once, twice, three times. Then my body goes white hot.

That is Cleo. Hairless Cleo, swaying on my mat. I'm so alarmed by how pale and thin and nearly bald she is, I jerk the door open without another thought.

The second that she sees my face, she starts to sob.

"Fuck…" I reach for her, heart beating so hard my head buzzes.

I'm surprised when her thin arms bat me away. "What did I do? You don't want me?" she shrieks.

"Cleo... Christ, what's wrong?" She sobs so hard she pretty much collapses. She's so fucking skinny I can pick her up. I haul her into my kitchen and sink down to the floor with her in my arms. "Cleo…are you sick?" My voice is shaky with a well of tears.

She folds her arms around herself and shakes her head. "You," she weeps. "You made me…and my heart sick." I smell a bite of alcohol and look down at her hands. They're marked with thick, black Xs.

I feel cold inside. Her hair…her face. Even her green eyes are duller. I swallow back my tears and open my mouth.

"What? Just say it!" she cries.

I heave a breath out. “Fuck. The ventilator is a sign. It predicts death. Read any research on transplants. Goddamnit, Cleo—I didn’t want you to see me die.”

“I died without you!” she roars. “I died for twenty-four days!” Rising to her knees, she shoves me hard.

I almost fall over, because I’m shaking. I feel sick with shame. Regret.

“Cleo...come here and let me touch you.” I hold my arms out. She backs away, and I reach my hand out to her. “Cleo… What happened? Are you sick?” She’s so fucking thin. She looks worse than I do.

“I’m not sick. My heart is sick!” She fumbles to her feet and grips the counter. “I kept giving blood for you, for your transfusions. We’re a match now, I thought…” She grabs hold of my refrigerator door and sobs. I scoop her up again. How good it feels. I bring her to my bed.

The room looks different. All the lights outside the windows…

Her blood buzzes in my veins.

TWENTY-SIX

Cleo

KELLAN. I HOLD HIM, CLAW AT HIM. Wrap myself around him. "I'm so sorry. I missed you. You smell good." I kiss him between his words. He kisses me. Our passion starts out slow but builds. I grope his cock, his rock-hard cock. His hand delves into my pants.

He shoves some papers off the bed. His fingers wriggle in my pussy. He's crawling down my legs and leaning down down to lick me... Tonguing me gently, then whipping me.

I come, and then he turns me over and pushes into me.

I'm so full. He's so thick. I'm wet. My clit throbs.

"Kellan!"

We come at the same time. He jets into me. He sags against me, and the weight of his body, his familiar feel and smell, make me feel like I'm about to cry again.

He eases me down on the bed, belly first, and gets up. He returns with a warm, wet towel. He cleans me tenderly. I sanitize my hands. He puts more in them and threads his fingers through mine.

After that we turn to face each other. Kellan pulls me into his arms. He pushes his face against my neck. I can feel him shaking, causing tenderness to roar through me. So many memories: us in bed.

I squeeze him gently. "You okay?"

"Yeah," he says. "I'm fucking good." I can hear the tears in his voice.

"Oh, my baby…" His body shakes. I hold him tightly in the dark, with the city winking all around us. I cry, too.

I can't stop running my hands over him. He can't stop doing the same. I run my hands all over his body. I even stroke the central line; it's so familiar, like a friend.

I kiss his throat. I taste his salty skin.

His lips are on my temple. His mouth by my ear. "I'm so sorry. I'm so fucking sorry, Cleo baby. I didn't know what to do..." His voice cracks. "I kept thinking of you there and me sedated, on the vent, if something happened… Whitney. On that day." I feel him shudder. "I thought you would go home. Why didn't you just go home?" His voice breaks. He draws me up against his chest.

"I told you I would never leave. I would sit there every day and watch for body bags going by. If I didn't see one, I had hope."

"Christ." Another shudder and some little moaning sound. "I'm so fucking sorry. So, so sorry." His lips are everywhere. My face and hair… He wraps me tight against him. "I did everything wrong."

"You did what you thought was best. I talked to Arethea the other day... she told me you were on the ventilator for six days and the first two were pretty touch and go. I'm sorry, baby." I stroke his face as hot tears spill down mine. "I'm sorry you were by yourself."

"It wasn't your fault."

"Arethea said Willard was bullshitting us that day you got the fever. She said you were lucky to pull through."

His forehead pushes against my fingers. "I kept seeing you. On the surface of the water. All your hair. I tried to swim to you."

I curl up against him.

We talk all night, and make love two more times. We fall asleep together, tangled and soul-weary.

The next morning I see all of him in the light. His hair. His pretty limbs. His chest and shoulders, and his perfect Kellan face. He's beautiful. So fucking perfect. And he's mine.

"How are you? How do you feel?" I kiss his abs.

He guides my hand between his legs.

"No…really," I press.

He pulls me against him, his chin rubbing my hair. "I have a lot of joint pain sometimes. My lungs aren't 100 percent. I have a hard time with weird shit, like Pig Latin. And remembering everything at the store without a list. Even the online store." He gives a little laugh. "But I still know my antiderivatives, and I know every origami sparrow you hung on the ceiling. I would make the ICU nurses read them to me."

"You missed me?" Tears shimmer in my eyes as I look at his face.

"I missed you every day, and every night. When I got moved back to our room... I had a bad time. I struggled about calling you, but I didn't think it was fair to jerk you around. I knew if I got close to death again, I would want you to go again. And then one time I thought I was... My heart did something. Sort of like a hiccup from the chemo. And I wanted you. Arethea climbed in bed with me. Hugged me. I would have been embarrassed as fuck if I wasn't so fucked up from missing you. But that was my last night inpatient. I came here, and I just…couldn't call. I didn't think you'd want me to."

I pinch his arm. "How could you say that, crazy?! You said you would take me all around New York. Kellan... I would take your call from anywhere. You know I can't leave again. I can't. I *won't*. If you want me gone, you have to tell me now." My voice cracks.

He lays his cheek against my cheek, kisses my temple. "It won't be normal—ever. I'm still taking sixteen pills a day. You can still trace both of my hip bones... I can't run for more than fifteen minutes. Still can't breathe enough."

"Kellan, please. I love you so much. I would want you with no legs and arms."

"Let's not wish for that." He strokes my cheek. "I love you too."

"Stay with me? Forever. You have to. You really have to."

He smiles a little, then it slips away. His face is gravely serious. Then he laughs.

"Cleo…"

TWENTY-SEVEN

Kellan

I TAKE HER HAND AND LEAD HER TO THE LIVING ROOM COUCH. She sits on the edge of it, and I struggle not to kneel in front of her. I laugh again.

"I've got something to show you." I sit beside her on the couch and pull her up against me. My hands stroke her belly through her shirt. "The only catch is," I whisper against her throat, "you read the instructions. And follow them."

She turns to look at me with wide eyes. "What is it?" She pets my short hair. I rub my palm over hers.

"Nice haircut by the way." I kiss her jaw. "Trendy."

"Kellan…" She pushes at me. "I don't like suspense. Or surprises. Remember?"

I get a good laugh out of that before I open the trunk-style coffee table just in front of us and close my hand around the sparrow.

I turn to her and open my palm. "I found this. Recently. I didn't unfold it because…" I inhale, and try to slow my racing pulse. "I didn't want to touch something you did." I grin, then laugh. *So* not fucking smooth. Cleo blinks. With her hair so short, her eyes look luminous.

I hold the sparrow out to her.

"Do you want to open it and read it to me?" I shift onto the floor, sitting cross-legged, so I am looking up at her.

She curls her fingers loosely around the sparrow, and I clench my jaw. I fake a smile. I can feel the blood drain from my face as she looks down at it. I wrap my arms around her legs and press my cheek against her shins.

I shut my eyes and wait for it to fall out in her hand…the ring. I can feel her muscles tighten when it does.

I'm not sure I can handle looking at her face, so I roll the words I wrote inside the sparrow back through my head. I read it many times before I folded it.

Dear Cleo,

It can be anything you want it to be. I would love to make you my wife—but I understand you may not want such a giant commitment so soon after all that's happened. No one would understand that feeling more than me. If that's the case, wear it on any finger. It was my mother's mother's wedding ring. It's not a blood diamond, so don't worry about that. It's two carats with one small imperfection near the top left prong, but I'm learning imperfections don't bother my selfless, strong, and loving friend, lover, and donor. You are everything to me. I love you with every cell I have, and I will always love you. Thank you. Thank you. Thank you for saving my life and my heart. Both are yours.

Kellan

She pounces on me and I feel her arms lock down around me. "Kellan!" Her fist hits my shoulder. "That's the worst proposal ever!" I open my eyes in time to see her thrust the ring at me. "What finger do you want to put it on, you lunatic?!"

She holds her hand out, all the fingers shaking.

I blink as my heart pounds. I look into her eyes, so she can see the feeling in mine. Because I mean it when I tell her, "Any finger."

She throws her arms around me, squealing as she bounces. "Please make me the crazy woman who waited in the hospital every day for almost a month for her *husband*!"

I smile down at her and blink fast as I take her left hand. My eyes meet hers again. "Any finger is okay," I rasp. "Would be an honor."

She lets out a sweet sob. "Kellan!"

I squeeze my eyes shut, then look into her face and slide the ring on the only finger she's got held out.

"Will you marry me?" My voice trembles.

She's already crying. "Yes! Oh, yes! I missed you so much…Kellan, I was going crazy. This is crazy…I know, but I don't care. I don't care…"

"No more going crazy." I scoop her up into my arms.

I carry her to the bedroom and make love to her as we look down over New York.

After that, we lie beside each other, face to face. Our hands roam each other. Cleo grins at her new ring.

"I'm hungry," she murmurs.

I stroke her neck. "You need to eat. What do you want? I'll go get you something."

"That's a risk. No germ risks. Let's order delivery."

I smile. "They don't deliver here. Restaurants stop at the fifteenth floor. Chinese? There's a place on the sixth floor. Manning liked it when he came."

"Mmmm. Chinese."

I kiss her hair. "I'll go." Her mouth opens. I kiss it shut. "No worrying. I have my own mask and gloves." I kiss her hair again. She smells so fucking good, I can't help it. "You want a bath while I'm gone? Get in there and relax?"

She shuts her eyes and pulls me to her. "Kellan—I love you. Thank you for the ring. I realized when I couldn't see you that I need you. To live life. And yes, I'd love a bath."

"I'd love to give you a bath. And help you live life. If you want that."

"I want that." She kisses me, and I go with it. I believe her. Cleo loves me. She wants me, and I want her.

I carry her into the bathroom and grin at the dance she does when she sees how huge the tub is here.

"I'm filling it up to my nose," she tells me.

I take her left hand. Kiss the ring. She sinks into the steaming water.

"I won't be long," I tell her. I slip into a CC t-shirt and then into my jeans.

"Mmm, mmm, those jeans are tight in all the right places. I might have to get out of this water and come check that out."

I wink. "I put a text order in for the food, so let me go get it and then…" I stretch my arms out. "All yours."

She sighs. "Always?"

"Always."

I leave Cleo beaming in the tub, moving her hand around so she can see the light glint on her ring.

TWENTY-EIGHT

Kellan

I RIDE THE ELEVATOR NEAREST to my flat—the one that gets the least traffic. With new gloves on my hands, I press the "6" button and lean my shoulder against the mirrored wall.

I can't help the little smile I give myself in the mirror. For just a second, I swear I see dimples.

Thank you, Ly.

I stand stone still, feeling…warm. Just really fucking warm and…glad. That things turned out this way. I inhale deeply. Fuck, I'm lucky. I love her so much. It was crazy, giving her that ring. I did it recklessly—because I love her. I can't believe she said "yes."

I step out of the elevator on the sixth floor still grinning like a fool and get a kick out of going into the restaurant. As always, people give me looks, but I don't give a shit. I've got my fucking woman in the bath tub with a diamond on her finger.

God, it's good. I close my eyes and fire a prayer off to somewhere. *Thank you.*

I get Cleo's little brown bag and hand my card to the woman at the counter. She hands me my receipt, which echoes my thoughts: THANK YOU. I walk to the elevator slowly, taking careful breaths because sometimes my lungs try to close up a little.

Right now, my chest feels tight. Excitement, I guess.

I press the "up" arrow and tap my foot as I hold the warm bag against my thigh. I can't fucking wait to get back up there to her.

I laugh. Did that really happen?

Yeah. It fucking happened.

I ball my hand into a fist and press it to my aching chest. I step into the elevator hearing birds caw…smelling salt water. I'll buy her a cottage by the sea. I want kids out there, playing on the sand. I think of Cleo at an easel, smiling as she paints. The feeling of my mother knots my chest up. My eyes blur a little.

I lean against the elevator wall and rub just under my throat. I grip the rail with my gloved hand.

The elevator lifts me. The door opens, and I walk out.

My chest feels…tight and heavy. Cleo. That's my first thought. Needing her. My cheeks and chest flush. My shoulder aches. I blink down at the hardwood, stunned by the crushing pressure on my chest. I dropped Cleo's food.

Fuck.

Can't breathe. I grasp at the hall wall. Can't see. I stagger toward my door.

Cleo!

My heart lights up like a fireball, spreading all through me.

I can't breathe without her.

Guess I really can't…

EPILOGUE

August 7, 2020

October 19, 2014

Dear Cleo,

The last six weeks have been the best ones of my life. Meeting you... Knowing you—it's the answer to the question "why," which I have asked so many times.

I flew from Emory to Memorial SK because of you. Just you. I never told you, because I didn't want you to feel burdened or obligated. Do you remember in the ambulance that night, the way you rubbed my hand? You kissed my neck and pulled my hair, you did everything you could to keep me awake, just like the EMTs wanted. I remember oniy pieces of this—individual frames in a longer, blurry film—but in one of them, I can hear you telling them, "You have to fix him. I love him."

I knew you really thought they could fix me, because you never said those words to me. You probably figured I was semi-conscious and I would remember. I think maybe you didn't want to burden or obligate me. You didn't know you had already. Meeting "Sloth" in person changed me before I even spoke to you. It was a lie: I watched you just for business. I watched you, stalked you, because my heart was sore and tired, and looking at you made me warm down to my soul.

So many times, you warmed me. What I wanted to say that night in the elevator was that when I got here in the ambulance, I had only one foot in. Despite the painkillers they had me on, I realized I was back at Memorial SK and I was fucking scared. I couldn't breathe. They gave me oxygen. Some Ativan. I started saying I wanted to be discharged. Arethea found me and she later said I cried for you. She told me she would try to find you.

I was so lost that night. You've been here now, you know why. I told myself if you reached out to me in any way—a text, a call, even a card—that I would do another transplant. I wanted you so much. There were no odds. Just you.

I don't know how to tell you... when you came. You showed up in my room. I remember you wanted me to get in bed with you. Cleo... you killed all my pain in just that moment. Every time I got scared that you would go, you showed me you were made of iron.

That's how I Knew, when Willard told me about the CMV, that if it gets bad, I will have to shelter you myself. If you're reading this, that's probably what happened. They say this shit is hard to beat. I hope you never see this letter. I'll try hard, I fucking swear.

But I want to Know—that if I have no choice—if I send you away so you don't have to watch me die and walk out of the ICU alone—I want to Know you have no doubts about my feelings.

I want to marry you. Do everything with you. Travel the world. Have children. Watch them grow. If I can, I will. I swear. (Unless you don't want that).

But if it doesn't go that way...

I wanted to leave instructions for you—wishes for the one I love.

Okay, Sloth. Here I go...

Don't guard your heart. I understand you'll want to. Keep it open. You're so strong. By far the strongest person I've ever known. Don't isolate yourself.

Actively seek love. Anyone could love you, Cleo baby. Go on lots of dates. Blind dates. Match.com dates. Please find someone to hold you while I'm gone. Nothing in this universe would please me more.

Have lots of children. (I know you want to). Millions of years of evolution compel me to offer you my banked sperm, but consider having children with someone you love, who's also living. If I have angel vision, I would love to see your pizza-loving Cleo spawn.

Please don't think of me too often. I know it will be hard at first, after what we've been through, so don't rush things.

Sometimes the pain will take you to your knees. I know that, baby. I've felt it, and I wish to hell you didn't have to. It never goes away, you know that already, but I know you can learn to live with it.

Have fun. Do what you love. I'm leaving you some money, baby. When they bring the check to you, take it without a fuss. For me. I still want to take care of you. It's important to me. You deserve the best.

Please don't regret a thing about the time we shared. Everything you did was good enough. Your marrow is a lovely thing. Do you know how much it pleases me to know we share your DNA? I'm going to leave this world perfect.

Don't worry with my resting place. I won't be there. Once a year, baby. That's all you need to do.

I want you to travel. See the world for me. Leave your angel DNA on every continent. Find someone to love, who loves you back, and take him (or her) with you. Share a cot in a hostel. Go to the beach a hundred times a year. Dancing in the rain is fucking cold and, in my opinion, unpleasant, but enjoy other spontaneous things, like extra nights on vacation, and a good fuck. Yeah—that's right. Don't forget to use that pretty pussy.

Also, keep painting. There's a grant waiting for you at my mother's foundation.

Don't hold onto bitterness and anger. I know it's easier said than done, but I want you to remember what, to me, is the most important fact of my life: I died knowing that you loved me.

Maybe I wasn't here for very long, but while I was, you gave me the greatest gift you could—your heart.

I don't know why I was here, or exactly how I got here, or even where I'm going, but I know the point of it was loving you. There is no doubt in my mind, Cleo. We love each other. I think that's the point, baby. I think that's why. We didn't need a lot of time. We took what we had.

Please keep Truman close to you. Don't walk down dark roads at night, baby, take a self-defense class. Be careful who you trust, or sensible. Cherish what I value most, okay?

When you meet your next love, kiss them as soon as you know. Put the poor bastard out of the misery of guessing.

Make sure he treats you like an angel. You are, and always will be, mine.

Your Kellan.

The bedroom door pops open before I have a chance to swallow back my wrenching sobs. I see Olive's small, blonde head, then Mary Claire's stunned face.

She scoops Olive up, stroking her hair. She reaches around Ol and, with her brows drawn tightly, MC signs, "Are you okay?" Her eyes widen, to emphasize surprise. "Do you need anything?"

I shake my head. "Go away," I sign back. My daughter's green eyes meet mine, and I give her an unsteady smile. "It's okay Ollie, Mommy's sad, but I'll feel better soon," I fudge. "Go play with Aunt MC."

My four-year-old nods knowingly. "I love you Mommy."

I feel a flash of mom guilt as MC carries Olive off, but it's lost quickly in the typhoon of grief roaring through my soul. I drop my head down to my pillow and give in to hysterics.

Outside my window, waves crawl up a long, deserted shore. The sky looms low over the sea. A bird caws, frantic—like I feel.

I hold my pounding head and squeeze my pillow close. I miss him. I miss Kellan so much. I picture his face and sob so long and hard my stomach starts to churn. I drag myself into the shower and sob as I wash. I pull a swimsuit on, then flop down on my king-sized bed. I need to get out of the house. Instead I grab the nearest framed snapshot off my nightstand and grip it to my chest, as if that can ease my pain.

I hear my daughter's gleeful scream echo down the hall. Poor Helen's sharp meow as Olive dashes after her. The sound of crashing waves floats in through the half-cracked balcony door. It's a perfect summer afternoon. I have to stop. No use in grieving all this now.

And yet, the more I tell myself to stop crying, the less I can. I curl over on my side, weeping helplessly…for how long?

I cry for both of us. For Kellan, mainly—all he went through, my poor K.—but for myself too. For all the pieces of my heart that cracked and fell away. The ones I never found again, and never will.

I used to think the pain of this would pass, but now I know it's a lie, what they say: that time heals all wounds. It doesn't. Time fades the scars a little, but like physical scars, soft spots on our hearts don't really mend. If you press hard enough on them, they ache. They even break wide open sometimes.

Like today. August 7. It's no wonder I'm a mess.

The door creaks, and I tense. I drag a deep breath into my lungs and brace myself for Helen's lithe body, or Olive's wide, green eyes.

Instead, I hear my husband's long, strong strides over the hardwood. I cover my puffy face with my arms and wait to feel his hands on me.

I feel him over me. Then his hands are on my back.

"Cleo?"

He clasps my shoulders, firm and gentle, then seems to decide against rolling me over onto my back, and takes my face between his hands instead.

His fingers brush the hair out of my eyes. He sees my blotchy face and murmurs, "Fuck."

I peek up at him. His blue eyes are wide and startled. His perfect face is twisted in alarm. "Did something happen? Lyon?" He bends down over me, kissing my cheek. "Don't leave me guessing, baby…"

"Not Lyon." I shake my head and wrap my arms around his shoulders. As I pull him down on me, he sees the letter. He hovers over me for a long moment, eyes locked on the yellow pages. Then he sinks down to the bed, pulls me to his chest, and tucks my head against his strong pec as he reaches for it. I can hear the papers crinkle as he holds them out in front of him.

"Cleo…why? After so long…" He sets the papers down and leans away from me, forcing me to lift my head off his chest so he can see my face. "Why right now, when things are so good, baby?"

My eyes fill with tears and tenderness gentles his face. He brushes his lips over mine, presses his cheek to mine. His skin is hot. He smells so good. Like…marijuana. And spices. Like Totally Baked, the marijuana bakery we started several years ago.

I inhale a long, slow, soothing breath. "I don't know," I murmur. Or rather, can't explain what made me open Kellan's goodbye letter this year, on this particular day.

I sink my hand into my husband's soft, gold hair. I can't help smiling at him. "You're home early. How did that happen?"

"Magic." He gives me a gentle smile. "I got something you might like." His eyes gleam. "From our old stomping grounds."

He reaches behind him, fingers delving into the back pocket of his jeans. He holds up a tiny swatch of pale grey fabric.

"Ohhh. A Chattahoochee College onesie." I take it from him, rubbing my thumb over the soft cotton.

"Got a shirt for Olive Arethea, too. I gave it to her." He grins. "She said, 'It's just like Mommy's!'"

I smooth the onesie over my pregnant belly.

"Looks good on you," he says softly. He reaches for my face, stroking his thumb over my jaw. Tears fill my eyes again. He wraps an arm around me and I turn to face him…my gravity. He smiles and draws me closer, sheltering my body with his larger one. His mouth brushes my eyes and nose and finally….so carefully…my mouth.

"You gotta tell me," he whispers. "What's with your timing, wife o' mine? Two days I'm down in Georgia with the franchise, you take a walk down memory lane?" He smooths my hair back off my forehead. "Lucky I got business taken care of fast and raced home to my woman, mmm?"

I wipe my eyes. "Not lucky! Unlucky. No more leaving till the baby's born. I mean it."

Kellan chuckles. "You would think I leave you all the time."

"You do." I wrap my arms around his broad, strong shoulders. My nipples harden as my breasts brush his chest. "That makes twice this pregnancy. No more. Please…say you won't."

His lips tug into a crooked smile. "I won't. On one condition." He reaches for the letter, and I watch him fold it. He smirks as his eyes flick up to mine. "You've gotta talk to me."

He slips the folded letter into his back pocket. Then his fingers tuck a strand of hair behind my ear. "You trying to feel sad? Get your pregnant woman emo thing on?" He's teasing, trying to make light of such an awful, painful subject. But the weight inside me can't be lightened.

I shut my eyes and rub my lips together. Tears drip from my eyes. "I want to be reminded of unhappy times. Because we're happy. That's why." I wipe at my eyes as my voice cracks. "We were them too, remember. *You* wrote that to me, Kell. Can you imagine? If I really had to read that?" Tears stream down my cheeks.

He strokes my hair over my shoulders. "No. I can't imagine. Never have and never will. We haven't had to." His blue eyes are deep as oceans. His big hand cradles my belly. "We are all four healthy. Here. Together. I'd say we're pretty fucking happy, no?"

I wipe my eyes. "We are."

"We earned it, yes? We waited for it. For a long time."

I nod, dabbing at my cheeks. After our engagement, we waited almost two years to get married. Kellan wanted to feel healthy, and that took some time. The day he passed out in the hall, I found him when the paramedics showed up, bustling and bumping the walls. They told me they thought he'd had a heart attack, and I was wailing when he started reaching for my hand.

The chemo *did* damage his heart. But it repaired itself.

Even now, with six years of remission under his belt, we still have our moments. But they're so many fewer. We forget for weeks and even months sometimes. Despite some aches and pains, expected side-effects from all his treatments, he's healthy and cancer-free. I know we're fortunate. I watch him smile again.

"Do you know what day it is?" he asks.

"Of course." I reach for his hand.

"Our anniversary." He kisses my knuckles. "I brought THC fudge from the café. In the fridge. But I really want to celebrate alone." His eyes darken. "What say you?"

He's already up, getting my soft, white cover up from the armchair and my favorite flip-fops from their spot beside the balcony door. I watch him move around our bedroom, gathering a blanket, a bottle of water, both pairs of sunglasses…even my favorite hair band.

He takes my hands and pulls me up from my beached whale position, smirking a little as I shift my hips to accommodate my belly. "Turn around. I'll get your hair."

I turn my head and feel his fingers sift through my locks.

I yawn. "Love it when you do that. Feels so good."

"That's what I'm good at. Making you feel good." He takes his time pulling his shirt over his head. Ensuring I'll relish the way his hard chest looks in motion. Like always, I feel warm between my legs. Like always, it's a struggle not to outright gawk at his bare body. I lick my lips as he kicks his shoes off, leans down to roll his pants up.

I love the way his shoulders ripple as he moves. I love everything about him. By the time he's got our beach bag slung over his arm, I'm smiling. He takes my hand and leads me out onto the porch…and down the sandy stairs, out toward a tiny wooden beach shack that is only ours.

We walk together on the hot sand, slowly first, and then with long, hungry strides. Kellan picks me up and twirls me, and the skirt around my bathing suit flips up.

I can't stop laughing. Then we reach the beach shack and I feel my pulse pound. He unlocks the door and I nip at his back.

He turns and sinks his teeth my neck. He pushes the door open, revealing just one room.

"Get in there…" He shoves me in front of him…but he can't keep his hands off me for long enough to let me "get." He scoops me up and lays me on the mattress. Parts my legs and crawls between them.

"For a woman who lives on the beach, I don't think you're wet enough, my dear..." He grins and slides a finger into me. He leans down, holding my gaze, and strokes my sweet spot with his tongue. "My wife..."

I grip his shoulders. "Husband."

"Always..."

THE END

AUTHOR'S NOTE

ON AUGUST 7, 2011, I GAVE BIRTH to my first child, a beautiful son with a myriad of rare health issues we had no idea about before his birth. I would say my worldview changed forever, but that doesn't even touch it. No words really can. During R.'s first year of life, doctors told me more than once that he might die. I signed consent forms agreeing to treatments that might hurt my baby even as they helped him. The stress and pain was unimaginable, as any mother of a very ill child knows. I struggled to find a foothold in the madness, but each time we would visit our state's children's hospital, my heartfelt more broken.

We befriended a family whose six-year-old daughter had nearly died dozens of times while waiting for a donor heart. Finally, the call came: a heart was on its way. The heart was perfect. Better than most donor hearts, even. But open heart surgery has many risks, and one of them is stroke. When I met this girl and her family, she was in a wheelchair, stricken with mental and physical challenges that to me seemed unspeakably unfair.

In our time at the hospital, we met many families with afflicted children—many struggling with congenital heart defects or cancer. Facebook is a game-changer for families of sick children, and through Facebook we connected with another Alabama family whose young daughter was fighting leukemia. Often, we brought R. to the children's hospital and left the same day, and I remember buckling him into his car seat dozens of times and thinking of the other family, locked up in the bone marrow transplant ward, unable to even leave their child's room many days.

There is no way to come to terms with these things. Eventually I realized that, and I stopped trying to make sense of it. My child was alive, and I was joyful. But as months and then years passed, I found myself drawn back to these children's Facebook pages. Even now, years later, I follow half a dozen children I met when R. was a baby. When possible, I enjoy donating to charities supporting children with congenital heart defects, but I've found myself especially drawn to pediatric cancer causes. Two wonderful blogs (and accompanying charities) are www.superty.org and www.rockstarronan.com.

How many of you will click those links? Probably only a few. And I understand that. No one likes to be sad. But people really hate to be sad over sick or dying children. The unfortunate result of this is that pediatric cancer research receives much less funding than breast, prostate, lung, and other cancers that afflict adults. Less funding means less effective—and less safe—treatments for kids with cancer.

In many cases, no one has even bothered to calibrate child-friendly dosages of radiation and chemotherapy, so children receive adult dosages by default, often with devastating consequences.

Lilianna, the girl with leukemia who was at the children's hospital when we were there so frequently, received a bone marrow donation from a woman in another country through an organization called Be The Match. (www.bethematch.org). I remember her mother's Facebook post explaining how incredible this was—that in all the world (at least as far as the bone marrow donors' registry knows), this woman was the only possible match for Lilianna. Quite literally her only hope.

The quote at the beginning of part three ("Unless you love someone, nothing else makes any sense." –e.e. cummings) is personal to me because it reflects the only conclusion I was able to reach with any peace.

When I learned about Be The Match from Lilianna's family, how easy it is to sign up for the registry (they mail you a q-tip, you swab your cheek and mail it back), and how unlikely it is that you will even be called to donate blood (only 1/500 get a call) before the cutoff donor age of 44, I started pushing my friends and family to sign up, too. This book is really just an extension of that effort.

I took some liberties in the hospital scenes—mostly to give Cleo and Kellan more…ahem, access to one another—and oversimplified other parts of Kellan's transplant to move the story along faster. But many of the details are correct, and I think it's safe to say that Kellan's experience is realistic.

(In a stroke of irony, I received an email from Be The Match a few months after I started working on Sloth, telling the story of identical twins who both needed transplants at the same time).

One of my main goals for Sloth was to be able to give a portion of my income from its sales to Be The Match, which offers the money to families of transplant patients who have financial needs. I can't announce this contest on my social media without revealing Kellan's secret, but…I'm giving away signed Sloth paperbacks to the first 20 people who sign up for the worldwide bone marrow donation registry via Be The Match, and the first 5 who donate $25 or more.

If you decide to do this, e-mail me at ella_f_james@ymail.com with proof, and I'll try to get a paperback out to you in the next few weeks.

Bone marrow transplants are often the last ditch option for children (and adults) with chemo-resistant leukemia. The idea is to use unusually harsh doses of drugs and radiation to kill the cancer cells (and, unfortunately, lots of healthy cells as well), completely demolishing the patient's immune system, to the extent that the patient will be unable to recover without the transplant, in which a donor's bone marrow (blood cells, etc.) "fills in the holes" and essentially re-maps the immune system. When successful, the donor's immune system is "engrafted" in the recipient's body, begins making healthy blood cells (on the basis of the healthy person's DNA), and saves the life of the recipient.

A large number of donors who do get a call from Be The Match are only asked to donate PBSCs (so, basically, donate blood). A smaller number are asked to donate bone marrow (like Cleo did), but the procedure is so minor many are back to work within a few days.

And…I think that's all I have to say about that. ;) You should probably get a prize for reading to the end of my little sermon.

I wrote Sloth during a tumultuous seven months—a long incubation time for an indie author. It was supposed to take no more than two or three months, and was formatted as a series of serials.

Sloth threw me lots of curve balls—in large part because of its inspiration (my son's issues) but also because of my personal experience with someone I loved who had leukemia, a more direct basis for this book. I missed Sloth's original late February release date, struggled my way through a serious depressive episode, and spent more than a month truly (and more than a little frantically) wondering if I could ever finish the book, and if I couldn't…what would I tell people? Writers write, right? What was wrong with me?

During this difficult time, I was supported by many friends. Without these people talking me off a ledge (sometimes tethering me to the cliffs or loaning hang-gliders, mostly at the worst possible times and oddest hours), I truly don't know where I would be. I talked to a number of readers online during the six or so weeks I was shying away from social media, and occasionally confided small details of my situation, which at the time felt shameful and humiliating. No one—no one—was ever anything but kind. If you were one of them, THANK YOU.

To Jamie, Rebecca, Kiezha, Leah, Sharon, Kim, Arethea, Ashley, and definitely at least one or two other people who won't be surprised to hear they slipped my mind: THANK YOU. I'm grateful to you for more than I could list here—and you each know why.

To the amazing women of Ella's Elite: Thank you for hanging in there with me. Your encouragement and enthusiasm means so much to me.

To my author friends, who offered kind advice (Roxy Sloane, M. Pierce) and technical assistance (Alexia Purdy), blurb assistance

(Roxy), web assistance (everyone), ARCs (K. Larsen, CD Reiss)…thank you. I appreciate each of you so much.

Thank you to the incredible bloggers who have supported Sloth, and me. So many of you sign up for every blitz and tour—and I know your names. It means so much to me. Thank you. Thanks especially to Rockstars of Romance, The Literary Gossip, and Give Me Books, for helping with Sloth promotion.

To Jessica and Beth, for dealing with Sloth in all its various incarnations, and waiting patiently for me at times and rushing at other times—thank you.

Milasy and Lisa, Rachel, thank you for being kind in February.

And to my family, for making many sacrifices in the name of Sloth. I love you.

The next book I'm releasing is called *The Boy Next Door* and is a contemporary romance—with some erotic content and also twists and secrets, of course!

You can add it to your Goodreads here:

https://www.goodreads.com/book/show/24488725-the-boy-next-door

The next sin I'm writing is *Covet*, and like *Sloth*, I promise it will be nothing like you think. It's set on a remote island inspired heavily by Tristan da Cunha, and I already love the characters so hard. You can add it to your Goodreads shelf here: https://www.goodreads.com/book/show/25867615-covet?from_search=true&search_version=service

If you want to keep track of my publication schedule, sign up for my newsletter, which honest to God, I almost never send: http://ellajamesbooks.us8.list-manage.com/subscribe?u=a22900f40502ee2fc5671a7bc&id=e7b30fab36

You can find me on Twitter (author_ellaj) and also Facebook (www.facebook.com/ellajamesauthorpage). My (rarely updated) website is www.ellajamesbooks.com.

Don't forget to join the Sloth Facebook Discussion Group: https://www.facebook.com/groups/1591666264454188/?__mref=message_bubble

57554587R00324

Made in the USA
Charleston, SC
16 June 2016